Jay Penner https://www.jaypenner.com

Printed in the United States of America

First Printing: Jan 2022

1.3 2022.10.16.07.41.52
Produced using publishquickly
https://publishquickly.com

## JAY PENNER

Join me @ https://jaypenner.com/join

Find all on: https://jaypenner.com or just Google search "Jay Penner books"

# SOLDIER

*The Spartacus Rebellion: BOOK I*

by Jay Penner

**Series**

Book I: *Soldier*

Book II: *Slave*

Book III: *Savior* (final)

https://jaypenner.com

*To the forgotten.*

WHISPERS OF ATLANTIS
THE ATLANTIS PAPYRUS
JAY PENNER

WHISPERS OF ATLANTIS
THE WRATH OF GOD
JAY PENNER

WHISPERS OF ATLANTIS
THE CURSE OF AMMON
JAY PENNER

WHISPERS OF ATLANTIS
SINISTER SANDS
JAY PENNER

WHISPERS OF ATLANTIS
DEATH PIT
JAY PENNER

JAY PENNER
THE LAST PHARAOH
REGENT CLEOPATRA

JAY PENNER
THE LAST PHARAOH
QUEEN CLEOPATRA

JAY PENNER
THE LAST PHARAOH
EMPRESS CLEOPATRA

THE LAST PHARAOH
A DANGEROUS DAUGHTER
JAY PENNER

THE SPARTACUS REBELLION
SOLDIER
JAY PENNER

THE SPARTACUS REBELLION
SLAVE
JAY PENNER

THE SPARTACUS REBELLION
SAVIOR
JAY PENNER

# ANACHRONISMS

———◇———

*an act of attributing customs, events, or objects to a period to which they do not belong*

Writing in the ancient past sometimes makes it difficult to explain everyday terms. Therefore, I have taken certain liberties so that the reader is not burdened by linguistic gymnastics or forced to do mental math (how far is 60 stadia again?). My usage is meant to convey the meaning behind the term, rather than strive for historical accuracy. I hope that you will come along for the ride, even as you notice that certain concepts may not have existed during the period of the book. For example:

*Directions*—North, South, East, West.

*Time*—Years, Minutes, Hours, Weeks, Months, Years.

*Distance*—Meters, Miles.

*Measures*—Gallons, Tons.

# DRAMATIS PERSONAE

**Spartacus**–Thracian from the Maedi tribe

**Gnaeus Scribonius Curio**–Roman commander, consul, proconsul

**Gnaeus Cornelius Lentulus Vatia**–businessman from Capua (*ancient historians may have mangled his name as Batiatus.*)

**Lucius Cornelius Sulla**–General and dictator of Rome

**Publius Vedius Porcina**–Senator of Rome and an estate owner

**Quintus Florus**–Centurion in Curio's legion

# TERMS

**Gladius**–a 1.5 to 2 ft. long sword, typically used by Roman legionaries

**Pilum**–a 4-ft tall spear pole with a 2-ft iron shank in the end. A standard issue for Roman legionaries

**Sica**–a curved sword used by Thracians

**Stola**–Garment worn by Roman women

# BEFORE YOU READ

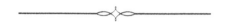

The events in this book take place in the years around 80 B.C.

Rome is a growing power, and its tentacles extend in all directions. Egypt is not yet in its control; a Ptolemy rules it, and it will be nearly another two decades before the famous Cleopatra is born. Gaul has not yet been conquered. The Romans have not yet set foot in Britain. It has been over a hundred years since Hannibal ravaged the Italian countryside, and the bitter memories of his devastating campaign are fading. But Rome is now engaged in a long-running war in the east against the formidable Pontic king, Mithridates. They have made inroads into modern Spain, Greece, Macedonia, Bulgaria, Turkey, and Syria. Italy is embroiled in its own troubles–the factions of two powerful statesmen and generals, Lucius Cornelius Sulla and Gaius Marius, are at war. There is much unrest and politicking in every corner.

Rome is still a functioning Republic. The two most powerful officials of the Republic, Consuls, are elected once every year. At the end of their term, they often take up lucrative governorships outside Italy or take command, or receive *imperium*, of Roman armies to conquer new lands. Men of the influential upper class are made Senators, and the office is for life.

The Roman military legions are a powerful force after the reforms enacted by Marius, and they are taking shape into a structure that will last for hundreds of years. The legions have found ways to incorporate non-citizens into their force. They call them auxiliaries, and these men—often in the cavalry, archery, and sometimes in the infantry—are offered regular salaries (lower than citizen legionaries) and the promise of Roman citizenship after a lengthy service. Most auxiliaries come from modern France, Belgium, Germany, Bulgaria, and surrounding regions. The great names of Rome—Gaius Julius Caesar, Marcus Licinius Crassus, Pompey Magnus—are in the picture and making names for themselves; Pompey is already venerated, Crassus is rich, but Caesar is just barely influential.

Slave trade is active and thriving—in fact, slavery is an integral part of life and woven into the fabric of Roman society. Almost one-third of Italy's populace will be slaves in just a few decades. The economic engine is irrevocably tied to the participation of a large-scale slave force. Slaves are supplied through Rome's thriving military adventures and sold for hefty profits. They come from regions that now constitute modern France, Germany, Spain, Bulgaria, Greece, and other eastern regions. Slaves are also inducted into the system through "slave-breeding"—the unfortunate children of slave mothers became slaves themselves. In fact, birth to a slave mother may have been the common source of slaves. Their conditions are exceptionally harsh; the laws that govern their lives are unforgiving and brutal. They are involved in a wide range of activities—artists, cattle grazers, hairdressers, tutors, herders, farmworkers, secretaries, singers, guards, maids, housekeepers, gladiators, prostitutes, and any number of other professions. They are considered property and have no rights. The laws that protect their well-being are few and rarely enforced—their lives are almost entirely at the mercy of their masters. For all the slaves do for them, the rulers see them with great suspicion—the memory of two slave rebellions, termed the first and second servile wars, still lingers in their minds.

Thrace, an important region for this story, is roughly modern Bulgaria. The Thracians belong to a branch of the Indo-Europeans. They are known to be brave and warrior-like but are divided by their many tribes. Not much is known about these people, and little about their languages and names remain. They are in the middle of two warring factions–the Romans and Mithridates. They do not know it yet, but their inability to unite under a single banner is about to put them in grave danger from the Roman legions crisscrossing their lands.

Dear reader, as we step into this tumultuous time and world, it is essential also to note that this is a *novel* and not an academic paper or a historical journal. I have strived to paint the picture of the time, and any errors, omissions, and dramatic license is entirely mine. At the end of the trilogy, you will find a notes section where I detail my portrayal of the key characters in this book and explain what is known from ancient writers like Sallust, Plutarch, and Appian.

And with that, let me lead you into the dark and murky waters of this long-gone world. And when you finish, I would greatly appreciate it if you could take a moment to leave a rating or a review.

Note: In the end, check out the link to a Google maps flyby–you can visit all the locations from the novel.

# UPPER SILARUS RIVER, 71 B.C.

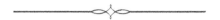

Marcus Licinius Crassus watched with some trepidation the large army encamped a few hundred feet beyond the ditch his men were digging. Six months of miserable pursuit through mountains and valleys, maneuvering, and the hour of a decisive outcome was near. What a travesty that he had to subdue and destroy the lowest scum that was destroying his land. What hubris! Men that arrogantly refused to accept their station had decided that they were greater than their destiny.

His legions were ready, but he knew their underlying worries. What if the bastard leader of this slave army once again managed to gain the upper hand? How long would this shame foisted on the Republic continue? But it was too late to contemplate. He was confident that the armies of the Republic could destroy the slaves, for Pompey was on the way, and so was Lucullus. There was no viable method for this rebel to fight *all* of them, no matter what barbarian gods showered him with benevolence.

The morning dew still lingered on the grass. The smell of freshly dug earth was inviting. The omens were favorable– the soothsayers said that two eagles had flown in their direction through this cloudless morning sky. The tinkle of the river was barely audible over the sounds of the many thousands gathered on either side of the battleground. His men toiled diligently, digging a trench six feet wide and four feet deep–not deep or wide enough stop an advancing army, but sufficient as an obstacle to slow it down. They had no time to do anything more ambitious, for the slave leader was dangerous and unpredictable. The wretched men were already throwing a ruckus, and some had begun to advance menacingly toward the ditch. But the enemy army had not pulled up in formation, and Crassus was not ready to offer battle yet.

What a contrast. These servile men, abandoned by their gods, dressed in rags and coming up against the mighty armies of Rome. He did not know whether to admire this astonishing enterprise or to spit in disdain at the humiliation they had brought upon the land.

Their leader was nowhere to be seen. But he was there—plotting, planning, watching.

Crassus removed his plumed and polished bronze helmet with its bright red plumes and general's insignia. He watched the horizon, busy with the immense slave army, and rubbed the smooth surface of his helmet absentmindedly.

How could a low soldier, who became a slave, build such a force and be seen as a savior?

# PART I

# CIRCA 80 B.C

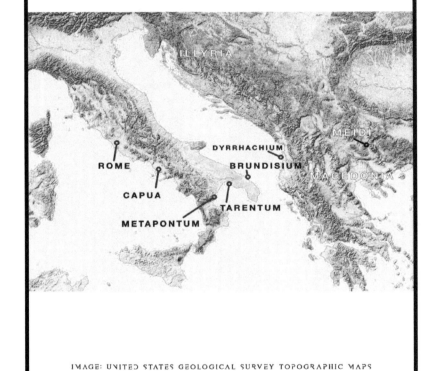

ILLYRIA

MEIDI

MACEDONIA

DYRRHACHIUM

BRUNDISIUM

ROME

CAPUA

TARENTUM

METAPONTUM

IMAGE: UNITED STATES GEOLOGICAL SURVEY TOPOGRAPHIC MAPS

# 1

## BESSI LANDS

———◇———

The nine men crouched and inched silently toward the small cluster of huts beyond the dense pine. Only a few fires burned, but the village was dark and quiet otherwise. No sentries were posted on the trees or the clearing outside the village. The village's northern border was the bank of a lake called the *Blade of Kotys*, a narrow, long, wedge-shaped, and spectacularly beautiful body of deep-green water, and the other three sides were dense forests and bushes.

"Be quiet," the leader cautioned them. He was a tall, powerfully built man, and those around him, even those who called him a friend, still listened to his every order as if he were their chieftain.

But then he *was* the son of the chieftain.

"Today is not to please *Kotys*. There will be no slaughter in her honor," he whispered. "We will only steal their ceremonial gold–"

"And carry away some of their girls. My loins–"

"Be quiet! The Bessi must learn that if they steal our sheep and burn our pasture, we take what belongs to their gods. *Zibelthiurdos* knows that we seek justice."

"And gold, of course," another man added helpfully, causing many to snigger.

"Do you want *Zibelthiurdos* to singe your balls with his thunderbolt?" someone else whispered.

"Does your father know we are here?" a voice asked the leader. "I did not know we were coming to raid the Bessi!"

Venturing into the Bessi lands was always a sensitive topic. That tribe was a violent bunch, and they responded to minor transgressions with murder. Most tribes hated the Bessi, and rightly so, for they were full of pride and cunning. The biggest problem was their numbers–they outnumbered everyone except the Odomanteans, but the Odomantean land was very far from Bessi lands, so there was rarely any conflict between them.

But *someone* had to humble the Bessi, or even confound them, from time to time.

"I am my father's son, and he did not rise in the tribe by waiting for orders," the leader said, slowly, in his measured manner of speaking, irritated at the question.

"I am sure his wife gave him permission," someone else sniggered.

*These insolent fools will get themselves killed!*

"I will beat you once we get home, Inthos, I will. Now everyone, listen carefully," he said to the cluster around him.

"Be quiet," the leader admonished them again. "We run along the periphery toward the temple, club the sentries if they are awake, grab everything from the temple, and we run. Is that clear? Do not wait and fight."

"The Bessi need a sound thrashing and a few lopped heads!"

"Not today. We are not sufficient in number, we are not well-armed, and they fight well. They are no trouser-wetting cowards like the Ordani. Today we are not here to die."

"Just to steal gold!"

"To claim justice," he corrected. "Are you all ready?"

A chorus of whispers and chants to *Kotys* and *Zibelthiurdos*, and they were ready.

With blood pumping through his veins and excitement coursing through his being, he sprinted, hidden behind thick bushes, toward a stone structure at the far end. The Bessi placed their sacred building to the eastern edge of the village, believing it allowed the sun to send in his rays without any obstruction. The soft mud below their feet made no sound. The few cracks of branches or crunching of gravel caused no alarm, for these dense woods were full of animals that made all manner of noise.

He felt the cool breeze on his face, and the moon hiding behind the clouds was a good omen. The gods were blessing his mission and providing cover! They halted behind a large bush cover facing the temple entrance.

*No guards.*

That was no surprise, for there were no rumors of anyone invading deep into Bessi territory. Even the Romans, whom he had heard of but never seen, had only skirted the Maedi territory some time ago and left for Macedonia and Asia.

The temple had no door, and a lone oil lamp burned inside.

*Bless us, Zibelthiurdos,* he prayed.

He waited for all their sounds to die down, leaving only the noises of the forest.

Once there was only stillness, he gestured two men to follow him and then ran into the temple. He covered the distance quickly and ran up the stone steps into the sanctum. The Bessi too worshipped *Zibelthiurdos*, only that he looked different in their statues. But they worshipped *Sabazios* more, always shown as sitting on his horse.

The sanctum was a small room constructed of stone walls placed close together and plastered. In the middle was a star-shaped stone dais on which stood a small gold statuette of *Sabazios,* his spear raised while seated on a horse. Several golden offering lamps were near the horse's feet, though only one was lit.

Next to the dais was a bronze jug and a golden staff.

*So much! Father will be livid but thrilled!*

He pulled out the linen bag tied to his belt and quickly removed all the gold objects–including that of *Sabazios*–he would ensure that the god received his prayers once back in their village. Surely *Sabazios* would understand why he had to be taken from the Bessi abode.

The two with him collected the bronze and copper.

*We thank you, Zib–*

A scream suddenly followed a loud thud, and then the unmistakable sounds of alarm rented the air.

*Pigfuckers!*

He rushed outside with the others while still holding the bag. Two men were running toward him and his companions, but his men charged from the bushes and clubbed them before they made contact. The village had woken up to the sounds of whistles, and many more emerged from the darkness.

Something had gone wrong.

But the rest were at a distance. He and his men had to escape while there was still confusion. The Bessi were known to inflict terrible torture on those who trespassed their property, and an invasion of their sacred ground would be treated even worse.

He shouted, "Let us go! run!"

And with that, they all turned and fled through a path they were familiar with. But this raid was a *success!* What a resounding success! He was filled with glee as it soon became clear that the Bessi had lost them. The trip back home would take three days, but in these mountains, forests, and narrow passes, it was exceedingly unlikely that anyone would find them, and no one would know who they were.

His father would send appropriate messages to the Bessi chieftain later. The Bessi would learn not to walk outside their territory and harass others. To many tribes, losing a god from his sanctuary was a bad omen.

With his heart ready to explode from the exertion, panting and tired, he gestured his men to stop so they could rest. He had arrived at a clearing on a mountain slope, and the space was surrounded by large rocks and bushes, affording good cover.

He waited as they arrived, one by one, emerging from the dense foliage, exhausted, bleeding, but gleeful.

He collapsed on the ground, his throat feeling like it was on fire. But there was a sense of accomplishment. For too long, he had been seen as the *big philosopher*, his ideas laughed at, and too many wondering if he would depart from his secondary missions with his father and do something truly bold and admirable on his own. Such qualities were prized in the Maedi, who prided themselves, like most Thracians, in their warrior-like life. He was no stranger to conflict, often defending his people from tribal warfare or fighting in skirmishes of their own making. Still, all that was under the organization of the town elders or his father. He was a good fighter, blessed by the gods for his physique and speed, but fighting was not what he loved. Taught by a Greek tutor since his childhood, he was perhaps one of the only two learned men in the village. But that was no cause for celebration.

It was time to show the village what he was capable of. Build his status. Show his *powers*. Let them see that he was not just a man of knowledge and philosophy and history. That his brave heart did justice to his impressive *size* and his father's station.

Even as he fantasized about the adulation, he realized more important things had to be dealt with now.

Once he caught his breath, he turned to one of the men. "Is everyone here?"

They perched themselves on their elbows and looked around. The stragglers were around them, lying down or kneeling.

"One, two, ...."

"Eight, including us," Inthos said.

The leader stood and walked around, counting again.

He cursed under his breath. Where was the ninth man?

And then he opened his bag to check whether all the valuables were present.

The golden objects shined under the moonlight that drenched them without the obstruction of a canopy. They were all there, except the golden idol of *Sabazios.*

The god had decided not to come with them.

Not only that, it seemed that the patron god of the Bessi had kept one of this raider's men back as a hostage.

There was punishment and celebration at home.

His father screamed damnation and condemned the men to twenty days of isolation from the rest of the tribe. But once that punishment was ordered, he held his hand and raised it in the air for many cheers, saying *see, he has the heart of a fighter, a true son of mine, blessed by Kotys!* In his father's eyes, there was pride that his son had finally broken his constraints and displayed an audacity so loved amongst his men.

The lost man's mother fell on her knees and despaired for his death or capture. She rented her clothes and shouted her son's name. She spat on his face, and then threw flowers for the bravery of the men. Her son's fate she saw as a matter of great glory, and the family would receive compensation by way of free grain and sheep, for death in conflict was the highest honor of all for the Maedi, like many other Thracians.

The elders lamented the loss of the Bessi god but placed the rest of the valuables in the Maedi temple.

A nightlong fire was lit in the middle of their village in honor of the raid and the missing man.

A loud revelry lasted all through the night, starting with the sacrifice and roasting of a lamb, a bath, wine-fueled dances to drumbeats, incantations to *Zibelthiurdos*, and then wanton sex by those carried away by the heady rituals, with offerings to Dionysus, the Greek god who had been inducted to the ways of the Maedi.

A priest poured the lamb's blood, collected in a silver vessel, into the fire as the first rays of sun painted the sky in the morning. Then the village priestess wiped her thumb along the inner surface of the cup and smudged his forehead in blessing.

"A fool or a warrior? Only the goddess *Kotys* knows!" his father finally said as he beat his son, laughing, and prepared to send him away to the "prison hut."

"A foolish warrior, perhaps," he said, with his typical modesty and light humor.

Many villagers screamed invectives and heaped abuses as a custom.

His wife made a dramatic and expected ritual of sorrow and pride by renting her clothes and ripping her hair bands. "How will you give me a son if you sleep alone?" she screamed.

The gods would be so proud, he thought as he walked away beaming, followed by his men.

*I am a Maedi. By stature, by action, and I have brought honor to myself.*

He had shown his father that he too could be bold, reckless, daring, and willing to go to extremes to hoist the pride of the tribe.

He had demonstrated that he could one day be *chief*.

# 2

## THRACIA

*Whack.*

*Sounds of running feet.*

*Sounds of a blade slicing into a chest. That wet sound. And that grind when the blade scrapes against a rib.*

*Loud screaming.*

*Smell of fire.*

He shot up from his hay cot in terror. It was dark, and the sounds and smells were not a dream.

The sounds of fighting were all around him. He dove into a corner and grabbed his sword, just as someone rushed into his hut.

It was the figure of someone determined to kill him. The intruder raised a *sica,* a short, curved sword favored by the Bessi.

*Were the Bessi here?*

He met the force of the downward swing with his sword. The impact exploded up his arms and shoulder. The attacker staggered, giving him the chance to roll on the rough mud floor and spring to his feet.

The attacker turned on him again.

He punched the man's belly with his left fist and then hacked his shoulder. The screams were lost in the battle cries and wailing all around him.

*Smoke!*

The thatched roof was on fire. He thrust his sword into the attacker's chest. The man yelped and collapsed.

He ran out.

The unmistakable signs of the Bessi raid on his tribe were everywhere. Corpses of his people–the Maedi–were strewn about. There were men, women, and children, all lying headless or with their bodies smashed by axes, their bodies reflecting the orange-yellow light of the flames of the huts on fire.

Men ran around, and groups clashed with each other.

His heart beating wildly, he ran to his father's house–a stone and brick structure in which his wife lived as well.

He decapitated a man who lunged at him.

It was mayhem!

Where were the guards?

His father's house was on the northern end of the town, which sat near the gorge's edge. The structure was engulfed in fire. Flames rose to the sky, and the still smoldering and headless bodies lay nearby. The size and shape of the dead left no doubt about who they were. In despair and refusing to believe what he had just witnessed, he ran around the hut, checking the ground nearby and calling for his father and wife. The heat of the fires prickled his skin.

"Get him!"

A group of mad Bessi was after him. He glanced to catch sight of several figures after him–and as good as a fighter he was, for he had killed men before, he knew that he was no match for several fighters attacking at the same time. None of his men were to be seen. Perhaps they were fighting other clusters or were dead.

He could not fight them all, but there would be another day. He turned and ran toward the sharp slopes to his left.

He knew the paths that led him down to the river that flowed on the bottom of the gorge. He knew every turn and every rock on that path, and even in this dim moonlight, he could make his way to the bottom.

The Bessi would die if they chased him.

"Tell Durnadisso we'll be back!" someone shouted. *Durnadisso*, the hated chief of a Bessi village, called himself a king. The Maedi hated the Bessi. They were madmen, driven by blood, even more than any other tribe.

It was Durnadisso's village that he had raided. But he had harmed *no one!*

As he balanced and made his way down the path, he sensed a pursuer scramble behind him.

"Where are you running, you bastard?" a receding voice taunted. "We'll find and gut you! Do you want to steal our god again?"

"Sabazios says fuck you!" someone else shouted, and a javelin *whooshed* past his head, missing the ear by a hair. "And Cleitus will never forget you!"

He ran, controlling his momentum to avoid losing balance and plunging to death.

Someone was catching up fast—the *crunch* of the gravel and sliding ground succeeded by a hard-breathing enemy charging at him.

But it was a fatal mistake in this terrain.

He stepped aside, suddenly grabbed the arm of the assailant, and flung him down to the side. The sounds of a shrieking body sliding down a gravelly slope and smashing against rocks stopped other adventurers from pursuing him.

The sound of the gently flowing river was getting closer.

His chest on fire, sweat pouring down his face even on this cool night, he managed to get to the bottom of the gorge.

He looked back to see if anyone was behind him—but all he heard was the distant sounds of whooping and the gentle yellow glow of the fires from his burning village on top of the gorge.

His mind was a conflagration of emotions.

His heart was full of shame, grief, and rage.

*I will come back. I will seek revenge!*

Violence was their way of life, and one that men had learned to leave behind and move on. Death and destruction were never too far away. And yet, even knowing the brutality of life, his heart ached bitterly for his father, wife, and others he loved. Who had escaped, and who had died, he had no way of knowing.

But he would get his revenge. For now, he would keep running.

# 3

## THRACIA

———◇———

Quintus Florus looked at the tall and muscular barbarian before him. "Name?"

"Sparatakos."

"Tribe?"

"Maedi," he said, haltingly, sounding unsure.

"Spartacus the Thracian, of the Maedi tribe, why do you want to join this auxiliary?"

The man looked at a companion beside him.

The companion addressed the centurion. "He does not understand Latin, sir. Knows a few words, that's all."

*Why am I in charge of recruiting the auxiliary when I know nothing of these barbarians' languages or customs?* the centurion wondered and muttered under his breath. He resented being appointed to lead the barbarians when he should have been leading a century of legionaries.

But this old man had brought good recruits for him before. If the auxiliaries proved their worth in the upcoming battles, he might regain the favor of the Legate and be re-assigned.

"You are his translator as usual?"

"Yes, sir."

"What languages does he speak?"

"The language of the Maedi and some Greek."

The centurion eyed the Thracian who called himself Spartacus. He looked like a hardy Thracian, much like his many war-like countrymen, with his dark, flowing beard and thick mustache, piercing black eyes, and bushy black hair with streaks of brown. This man–Spartacus–was also unusually tall and exceptionally built, like the trunk of a thick tree.

"Fine. Let us start from the beginning. Name and tribe?"

"Spartacus of the Maedi."

"Age?"

"He does not know, sir, maybe 27."

Florus looked up at the big man. *Looks older, but who knew with these bastards.*

"Does this Spartacus harbor any animosity toward us, knowing that Sulla ravaged his land last year?" The centurion had accompanied the Roman general's army when he had moved south toward Macedonia, leaving Legate Curio in this part of the world, as he waged war on the Pontic king Mithridates.

"He says that was the past and that no harm came upon their villages and that General Sulla walked the lands of the Sinti and not the Maedi, and that the Romans touched no hair on a Maedi and thus he holds no bitterness."

The centurion grunted. *Maedi, Sinti, Bessi, Odomanti, Bisaltai, Dardani, that and this. There were too many of these tribes to count.*

"Wife? Children?"

"All dead. No children."

He thought that was unusual, for these barbarian men often procured multiple wives and, like rats, produced many offspring.

"Is he a bandit? Why does he want to join the auxiliary?"

The two muttered something amongst themselves.

"He needs money. And he has scores to settle with the Bessi."

*Of course, he does. These barbarians always fight amongst themselves and kill each other, making it easier for Rome.*

"So, he knows we are planning a march on the Bessi lands?"

The old man grinned and nodded.

These men even sold off their children to slavery for want of coin. No doubt the Bessi had heaped some injustice on this man's tribe. *These people needed no reason to go to war,* the centurion mused, *perhaps the Bessi stole some cow shit.*

"Does he ride horses?" The centurion clenched his fists and made a galloping motion while looking at the Thracian, who nodded vigorously and said something to the old man.

"He says he is good with horses and has some practice. But he is very good on land, with javelins and swords."

"Is he a good slinger?"

"He says that is not his specialty."

*Is his specialty buggering sheep?*

"Has he fought in any auxiliary before?"

"No, sir."

The centurion summoned the old man closer to him and whispered. "Is he wanted by any Roman legion for desertion? I do not want troublemakers."

"No, no, sir. None. He has never fought against or for the legions. Theirs was a secluded village on the ridge. He has never even seen the Romans before, he swears."

Meanwhile, Spartacus stood quietly, his eyes scanning the camp entrance and beyond.

"What is his experience fighting? Our cohort is not equipped to train farmers and metalworkers. What does he mean he is good with the javelin and sword–who has he fought?"

"He has fought neighboring tribes many times, sir. He says that battle is familiar and that men have died by his hands."

*He knows to fight in that foolish method of theirs; not the way we fight,* thought the centurion.

He eyed Spartacus, who stood straight and barely moving.

There was a certain dignity to the man–unlike the boisterous, loud bandits he had previously recruited into the auxiliary. Those eyes showed not the wildness of some of these tribesmen.

"Does he know that he is being recruited into the auxiliary? He does not receive Roman citizenship until he serves 25 years."

"He acknowledges, sir."

"Handicaps? Injuries? Tell him to come closer and walk around."

Spartacus walked closer to the bench and did a short march to the left and right.

*A slight limp as he walks, scars on the forehead and back, sizeable visible mole below the left chest, otherwise very healthy,* the centurion noted into his recruitment record.

"Why is he limping?"

"He says the gods granted him a leg that is slightly impaired compared to the other and that it is neither a mark of injury nor a cause for impediment."

"Can he run or charge without problems?"

The old man said something to Spartacus, who smiled. He then bowed to the centurion and gestured as if to say *shall I show you how I can run?*

Florus flicked his finger as if to indicate *fine.*

And then Spartacus took off with impressive speed-he ran a distance, pivoted, and then returned. The limp was no concern.

"Tell him he will be expected to undergo a medical examination before his recruitment is confirmed," he said, no doubt these concepts were alien to these barbarians.

"Yes, sir."

"And now I will cover training and discipline because it is no secret that you Thracian tribes lack discipline and know nothing about military regulations," he said sternly. The old man translated it, and Spartacus nodded his acceptance.

Florus addressed him directly. "You will be under my command. I am a centurion, and my name is Florus. My commander is the legate, honorable Gaius Scribonius Curio. You will abide by *our* military rules. Do you understand?"

*"Yes, sir,"* he conveyed his answer through the translator.

"There will be no dissent, and this is not a tribe. If you fail to follow orders, you may be flogged or executed, even crucified, depending on the crime. Desertion is a crime punishable by death. Do you understand?"

*"Yes, sir,"*

"Your family, or whatever is left of it, may not travel with you. If you take a wife or your many wives between campaigns, they cannot travel with you unless specifically authorized by the Prefect or the Legate. Do you understand?"

*" I have no wife, sir. Yes, I understand."*

"You will perform a variety of non-military duties during your service. You will dig ditches and trenches, you will fix roads, you will build ramparts, you will clean horses, you will build tents and bridges, and you will do all that is asked of you. Do you understand?"

"Yes, sir."

"Now I will talk about pay," the centurion said, turning to the old man again. "Make sure you explain this to him slowly and clearly. I have had to deal with greedy pigs who think they will be paid more than the Tribunes."

"Yes, sir," said the old man.

"His pay will be one-hundred-forty denarii per annum, paid in installments every ninety days. He will get rations, camp quarters to stay, a *scutum*, a gladius, a javelin, and footwear. Anything else for protection he must buy himself. Auxiliaries receive no uniform. If he loses his equipment, he pays for replacements. If he wants additional rations, it will be held from pay. Ask him if he understands."

After what appeared to be an energetic discussion, Spartacus nodded.

"And if his service is valiant, the legate or general may announce booty and bonus, but none of that is guaranteed. Does he understand?"

"He understands and agrees to the terms, sir."

"He will be pressed to service very soon as we move to the Bessi territory. Is he ready to begin?"

"He is ready to start now, sir."

"Fine. I will have him sent to the auxiliary unit for orientation. He will have to learn Latin if he wants to survive and succeed. Tell him that."

Spartacus nodded to the translator's comment. "Yes, sir," he said, in his thick, guttural voice.

Florus completed his enrollment records and waved to a legionary. "Take him to the auxiliary and have him inducted."

The legionary signaled Spartacus to follow him. The Thracian bid goodbye to his acquaintance, paid him something from a leather bag hanging from his belted skirt, bowed to the centurion, and then walked behind the legionary.

"He looks like a good fighter," Florus told the old man. "Here's your fee."

"Thank you, sir."

"You have a nice scam going, old man. You find men aggrieved by the acts of your tribe, and then you make money by recruiting them here to fight your own. We pay you. He pays you. It's quite the racket with you barbarians."

The old man grinned and bared his yellow-stained, broken teeth.

# 4

## THRACIA

———◇———

Spartacus was made to wait in a holding area outside the camp gates, along with many other recruits, until a legionary arrived to escort them inside. The camp was impressive, and a twelve-foot wood-log rampart protected its perimeter. Guard towers rose at regular intervals. It was clear that all the recruits were men of local lands, and they stood quietly without speaking to each other after being yelled at by a legionary.

Two men who began complaining loudly about not being selected were beaten with a stick and ran out. The legionary who escorted Spartacus and the others to the camp spoke little, for it was apparent the man, who looked Roman, disdained them all as barbarians and knew little of their language.

The camp was neatly arranged with rows of tents on either side of a grid of narrow mud roads, with what appeared to be a commander's tent in the middle. The site had been constructed in a narrow valley, and mountains, whose tops were hidden in wisps of clouds, loomed on either side.

The old man had explained some of the Roman army's characteristics as he had enticed Spartacus to join the auxiliary. *You will make money and learn to fight; what can be better for a Maedi? They will allow you to loot the conquered as well!*

The wooden-log rear wall of the camp was ahead, and a dense cluster of tents was on either side of it. The legionary pointed to the left side and grunted. He then handed small bronze tokens with holes to each of the thirteen men and said, "go."

Spartacus walked with the others toward a group of men standing by a large tent. He then lifted the bronze token and showed it to them, and the others followed. One of the men nodded and went inside the tent to call someone as Spartacus waited. The humid morning was causing his skin to stick, and flies buzzed around several cooking pots outside the tents. Some of the others had begun to chatter amongst themselves.

A tall, bearded man wearing a Roman tunic, leather corset, belt, and a poorly fashioned cloak came out and walked toward them. Unsure of how to greet him, not knowing who he was, Spartacus bowed slightly in his customary fashion and touched his chest with an open palm. Others made their manner of greetings.

"All of you. Stand in a line! This isn't your father's village. Now!" He spoke an accented version of Greek–possibly an Odomantean variant. He made gestures pointing at the ground and drawing a line, causing the men to scramble and position themselves.

*We stood in a line in my father's village too.*

"Which tribes?" the man asked. Most regional tribes shared a common language separated by dialects and accents, and all generally understood simple sentences.

A chorus of names sprang from those who understood the man's words, and then the others joined.

"Maedi!"

"Sinti!"

"Pieres!"

"Odomanti!"

He eyed them all.

"Latin? Greek?"

The answers were varied, but only one man knew Latin.

"Greek!"

"Some Greek. Very little Latin," Spartacus said.

A few had learned to say *No* in Latin and said so very vigorously.

"Find somebody who speaks your tongue. And then you will learn Latin if you want to be in the good graces of the officers! My name is Erducos, and you will address me as *sir*."

*Sir Erducos. Fancies himself a Roman, it seems...*

Spartacus was one of the two physically most imposing of the men. Erducos walked toward him. "I can speak Maedi," he said. "My wife is one. I purchased her years ago."

Spartacus smiled. "You are of the Odomanteans?"

"Yes. You have an ear for our accent," Erducos said, then stepped back to address the group again. "Group. I am responsible for your assignment and conduct. My officer is Florus, the centurion who sent you here."

Erducos spent the next hour familiarizing the recruits with the camp, explaining the arrangement as they walked together. It was clear that Erducos was well respected, for the men stood when he walked by or acknowledged his presence with nods or salutes. However, all the men were clearly of Thracian stock–for none seemed from the Italian lands. There were no Celts or Germans, and no Persians or Greeks. It seemed strange that the tribes that fought each other all the time were now under the same roof, fighting for the Romans. A few times, men yelled in their tongues to the recruits and made small chatter with familiar words, causing Erducos to scold them.

"Either centurion Florus or I will assign your duties starting tomorrow. There is trench work to be done, or you might need to go out with foraging parties."

The men nodded.

"Why are we here in this corner and not in the other more spacious tents?" Spartacus asked.

"We are auxiliary. All those are legionaries, and they are Roman citizens. You can become one too after twenty-five years of service. We get paid a little less, and we do not receive their uniforms. We all train the same and perform similar duties. In battle, we are usually positioned in the front."

"What is a cohort?" another man asked.

Erducos nodded. "The Roman army is made of Legions–about five thousand men in each legion. And each legion has ten cohorts. Each cohort is six centuries led by a prefect. Each century is eighty men. The legion commander is called a legate, and our legate is Gaius Scribonius Curio. He commands one legion in Thracia, half of it is here, and the other is further south. The legions are mostly legionaries and a few auxiliary centuries. We are one of the two auxiliary infantry."

There were a few murmurs and some vigorous nodding.

"I doubt any of you understood all that," Erducos said, grinning. "But you will learn that during training that starts tomorrow. I know most of you are lawless bastards who listen to no one, but we'll make obedient dogs out of you."

"Hur, hur, hur," he laughed.

Erducos looked at him. "Is that how you laugh? You sound like a grumpy pig."

Spartacus patted his mouth in embarrassment.

"An ass is more like it. Even his eyes squint when he laughs," someone else added helpfully to sniggers.

*You sound like my mother.*

Spartacus grinned. People mocking his unique laughter was nothing new.

"Anyway, what was I saying?" Erducos said, "Yes. About making obedient dogs of you."

Spartacus knew that Erducos spoke the truth. The tribes had no concept of military training. They were loud, boisterous, disobedient, and itched for reasons to fight and quarrel. They were brave, bold, withstood much hardship, and were loyal to their kind to a fault, but discipline was always a subject for mockery. He wondered how different the Roman camp would be.

*Are you a Roman's obedient dog?* Spartacus wanted to ask but realized that he too was here to be under Roman command. Perhaps if the tribes of the land stopped fighting with each other, they too could be as strong as the Romans. Or even stronger.

"You will train for a few days, and those still standing after that will receive orders. The Legate wishes to move north toward the territory of the Bessi–"

"I desire to fuck the Bessi so hard that they will never get up again," someone yelled for a chorus of hoots. The auxiliary had none from that tribe, either by design or choice.

*And I want their blood in barrels.*

Erducos ignored the retort. "Remember that your success in battle and in making money is dependent on following orders. If the Legate orders a battle, we fight. If he orders negotiation and true, we obey."

"Fuck truce! Fuck it like taking their whore mothers! I didn't join this huxoliry, whatever, to itch my balls and kiss the Bessi," one of them yelled.

*Wild as always.*

"Auxiliary."

"Whatever."

Erducos ignored it and let the sniggers subside. They spent the rest of the day settling, receiving their weapons and shoes, instructions for camp rules and assembly the next day, getting introduced to men in the century, and learning how to address the superior officers from the army. During this time, Erducos struck a casual conversation with Spartacus, saying that he saw potential in him by his physical appearance and ability to shut up and listen.

"So, no wife or children, and you have an ax to grind with the Bessi."

*We all do. Retribution must be just and proportional, and the Bessi have never honored that.*

"I do not care about them. But Durnadisso must pay."

"Chief of that tribe?"

"Or some part of it. The one that came to my village."

"Tell me your name again."

"Spartacus."

"Why that name? Are you a Lacedaemonian?"

Spartacus laughed. "My father said our ancestors came from Laconia. That we were long ago a ruling class, the Spartans. But then, my father had a fascination for all things Greek. My grandfather knew not a word of that language. He was a butcher with not a hint of nobility in his actions or words."

Erducos chuckled. "You are well-spoken, Spartacus, are you learned?"

*Everyone asks me that.*

"My father was chief, and he had a Greek tutor teach us their language."

"You can read?"

"Yes. Not very well, but I can read signage and read pages given enough time. I have read about Greek and Rome."

"Have you been to Athens or Rome?"

Spartacus laughed again. "I have not seen a tree beyond our lands."

"And perhaps a few incursions here and there," Erducos winked. "Very few of the men from our lands can read. It seems all we do is fight."

Spartacus kept his thoughts to himself.

"You will be a valuable fighter for the unit, Spartacus. I hope you know how to obey orders and train."

*It is not I that you should worry about, Erducos. My thoughts are higher than most of the men around me.*

Spartacus nodded. "I need the money, and I want Durnadisso's head."

"Well, let us hope that this Durnadisso is one of the men we will fight," Erducos said as he slapped Spartacus on his shoulder.

But as he was about to move, Erducos turned to Spartacus again. "Fight well, Spartacus. You will either have glory in death or money in life."

Spartacus grunted in agreement.

Sleeping in the cramped quarter, on a rough hay mattress hastily constructed on the dirty floor, pushed against other men, was uncomfortable after years of sleeping in the open air or the comfort of his own house. But none of that mattered, for the shame of having run from the village on the night of attack still burned in Spartacus' heart.

The training was intense, the duties backbreaking, and the discipline was harsh. He learned to thrust the *gladius* and not swing it like a sword. He learned to wait for command and not rush without direction.

He learned to space himself from those next to him. And he learned the right way to hold the *scutum*, the shield, and protect himself from missiles.

The men trained until the sun crossed their heads, ate gruel, and then dug trenches around the camp or built ramparts. He saw men tied to poles and flogged for infarctions. While the treatment of auxiliaries was harsh, it was not much worse than what the officers subjected the legionaries to. A sentry who fell asleep on night duty was executed in full view of the cohorts as an example for breaking discipline. Two auxiliaries had the skin of their backs ripped off through whipping for breaking command rules. Spartacus himself was caned more than once for poor posture, not tying his footwear correctly, or stepping forward before a march was called. His arrogance that he was above others had slowly crumbled, for he was no different, toiling under the regimen and gasping for breath.

But through it all, he watched and learned how the army functioned–which was massively different from the rambunctious gang warfare of the tribes. He had heard that the Bessi knew how to fight Romans, but it was yet to be seen.

He had also seen the Legate Curio only once during an inspection. The centurion, Florus, was heavily involved in the training. Florus was a talented man, but he was alternatively cruel or lazy. Whether that was intentional or simply his nature, Spartacus did not know, for he had not served under a different man yet.

Curio's particular punishment was starving insubordinate men and forcing them to dig sections of the trench and carry the mud until they collapsed. Then they would have to endure a beating before they received a meal. But the Thracians joked that having lived a harsh life already, these were minor annoyances, and the hardest thing to endure was following orders.

Fights often broke out in the camp at night, requiring intervention or more beatings. The land was known for its fine wine, and if there was one thing that united the men, it was drinking and arguing until someone took it too far.

And in this environment, Spartacus grew accustomed to his new "home." After twenty-six days, they received an order to assemble.

The Legion would march toward the land of the Bessi the next day.

# 5

## SOUTHERN GREECE

Lucius Cornelius Sulla was in deep thought. The war with Mithridates was settled for now. Sulla's campaigns in Asia, Macedonia, and Greece had ended, but the Marian faction and their insidious forces were arraigned against him in Rome. They had sent no messages of reconciliation.

His magnificent achievement, putting to end a war that had vexed Rome for years, gave him no benefit by those opposed to him.

Their demands that he answer for his many imagined crimes and lay down his arms was preposterous. Not one to surrender easily, Sulla would now take his war to the gates of Rome.

His legions were now marching south toward the port of Dyrrhachium. They would consolidate a great many warships so that he may sail to Brundisium and bring violence to the Marian doorstep.

Sitting in his tent, Sulla took stock of his forces. What he had now was insufficient to take on the Marians entrenched in Italy. Sulla only had three legions with him, supremely qualified yet inadequate to destroy the enemies. He had sent missives to those he believed may align with him—Marcus Crassus, Pompey Magnus, and Marcus Aemilius Lepidus, and hoped they would meet him with their armies once he landed in Tarentum in Italy.

He summoned one of his Legates and asked, "where is Curio? Is he still in the Thracian lands?"

"Yes, General, he has not been summoned yet."

Sulla shook his head. The theater of war was large with many campaigns and designates, and he had forgotten to send word to Curio. Or perhaps he had intended for the talented Legate to stay there. He could no longer remember; he smiled inwardly.

"There is no need for Curio to spend time warring with the tribes. Send orders to summon him; he must march at haste and come to Dyrrhachium."

"Yes, General."

"And send an advance guard to Dyrrhachium and have the shipbuilders begin their work. Ask our allies to muster as many boats as they can immediately."

The man who had subdued and forced the troublesome Mithridates was determined to cross the sea into Italy and destroy the Marian faction.

# 6

## BESSI LANDS

———◇◆◇———

The six-day march was swift and impressive. The auxiliary infantry was positioned at the train's rear or around the baggage carts during long walks in constrained spaces or split to the flanks in open spaces. Spartacus learned how the army operated daily. The Legate Gaius Scribonius Curio was a hard taskmaster, making the cohorts wake before sunrise, begin marching before the first sliver of the golden sun, and continue till it was time to lunch and rest. But the rest was brief. They marched again until sunset before establishing temporary camps and a security perimeter.

*It is true,* he thought, *these Romans are as disciplined as rumors suggested.*

Commands were almost unquestionably followed.

The centurions were harsh but put in hard work themselves. Quintus Florus, Spartacus' commander, was prone to yelling at them at every chance he got and demanding perfection. Some said that the scrawny loudmouth aimed to become the *primus pilus* someday, a distinguished title accorded to the senior centurion of the first cohort that was usually twice the size of a typical cohort. His aim, it seemed, was to do everything to please the Prefect. But tongues wagged as to how a citizen had become a centurion to the auxiliary, surely a demotion or punishment.

The Legate, Curio, was no slouch–for he was often seen urging the men on the march, always inspecting the work, issuing orders, riding back and forth along the lines, and even going on sentry rounds in the night. Spartacus, used to the rowdy, disheveled, trouser-wearing warlords of his tribes, found the impeccably attired commander with his plumed helmet, red cloak, fresh tunic, and polished bronze cuirass both amusing and admirable.

The scouts had spotted Bessi scouts on mountain ridges as the army moved deeper into the territory, but unusually so far, there had been no contact.

"How many battles have you fought for the Romans?" Spartacus asked Erducos during a march. Erducos, while nominated as a supervisor for the unit, had no special rank when it came to the army hierarchy. He marched with everyone else, with Florus leading them.

Erducos chuckled. "Seven, excluding some skirmishes."

"Have you always been stationed here?"

"No. Spent some time in Macedonia. Then Greece. What do you know about Mithridates?"

Spartacus had heard about the conflict between Rome and the Pontic king, but primarily he and his tribe had managed to escape being involved in the war. But all that was changing with Roman armies marauding through Thracia, Greece, and Macedonia.

"Very little. The Romans never came to my village though they came to conflict two years ago."

"Yes. Sulla. He is the general to whom Curio reports. There are rumors that Sulla will summon Curio to join him soon."

"And go where?"

"Who knows?" Erducos said. "Maybe Asia. Maybe Rome. We are not privy to those decisions. I just learn what I can when Florus mutters and curses."

Spartacus laughed.

Erducos turned to him. "Do you always laugh like that?"

"Like what?"

Erducos mimicked Spartacus. He closed his eyes to a sharp squint and shook his shoulders up and down, shaking his beard. He grunted like a donkey intentionally. "Like this."

"What's wrong with that?"

"It's comical for a man of your size. Did your mother never teach you to laugh like a man?"

"And how do men laugh? I'm more man than most men here. Are you blind?"

"They laugh in a dignified way. Like this," he said, as he puffed up his chest and made a serious *ha, ha* sound.

"Fuck you and your grandmother, Erducos. You're all jealous of my mirth."

"Oh, look, the philosopher *swears*. My grandmother is dead, by the way, and she bore fourteen children. You would feel like you're entering a cave—"

"Have you no respect for your elders?"

They both ribbed each other and laughed. Erducos often teased Spartacus for his gentle demeanor and light humor. Spartacus' father always told him that *gravitas* came from a measured countenance and not a mouth that spews vitriol and vile curses at every opportunity. But he had to admit that sometimes it was nice to scream invectives, but only when it truly warranted.

A respectful friendship had developed between the two men since Spartacus' joining, and Erducos had helped Spartacus stay clear of Florus' ire.

Spartacus had learned meanwhile that Erducos had been captured during a Roman raid, volunteered to join the auxiliary, and had served ever since. He said he had a wife and four children but did not know their fates. Sometimes Romans sold captives to slavery, and Erducos had not heard from them. Spartacus wondered how Erducos could work for the men who sold his family, but sometimes the gods forced a man to walk a thorny path. He sensed Erducos' shame, and Spartacus had his own, so he was no greater man.

*You have abandoned your family, and so have I. And that shame burns deep, and it will continue until it is extinguished by Durnadisso's blood.*

Spartacus had told his story to Erducos. After running from the attack, he lived as a bandit for a few months, hidden, roaming the hills, and stealing the occasional sheep. He then approached a neighboring Maedi village to exhort them to combine arms with others to make an armed, planned attack on Bessi lands. But the Maedi elders would not forgive his shame of having left his village and not dying defending it. They would not listen to his thinking: no good came of everyone dying, no matter how lauded the courage. It was better to survive and attack instead. Like many tribes, the Maedi code was built on their fierce reputation and unblinking courage. Spartacus now saw that as a strength and weakness, for blind courage collapsed in the face of structure and training. After failing to get any support and at risk of punishment, he was back roaming again, his mind hungry for revenge, his stomach tired of hunting for food until approached by the old man who recruited him for the Romans.

"Ah, that man. He's a clever recruiter. He finds the disaffected and entices them with promises of food, clothes, money, and revenge. It works," Erducos had laughed.

The Bessi land was a mountainous region with narrow valleys between green forested hills capped by snow in the winter. The ground was rich with grass, rivers flowed, and access to water was not a challenge.

The Romans had a peculiar penchant for bathing–all the officers, and even most legionaries, never missed an opportunity to bathe in the rivers, and they did it every day! The men also had incredible skills to build bridges, ramparts, and even bathhouses quickly, often within hours. Florus also commanded the auxiliaries to perform ablution at least once in two days. Spartacus, used to bathing once in five to seven days, realized he immensely enjoyed it.

*When I am home someday, and am made chief, I shall teach the Maedi to build beautiful bathhouses that draw water from the abundant streams and make everyone partake in the activity every day,* he thought, and amused himself with the scenes of Maedi outrage.

The sun inched higher on the sky, now directly above the head. The air was stifling due to the lack of wind. The hills were silent as the column, now just four men wide with each century in twenty rows, entered a deep valley with sharp cliffs rising from either side. A stream of water flowed to the right of the column, and the gravel and stone slowed the baggage trains with stubborn mules refusing to move quickly. Twice Florus ran back to scream at the handlers to keep the carts moving and avoid being separated from the main lines.

Spartacus watched the ridge. *I know this place,* he thought to himself, for he had been part of loot raids into Bessi territory in his younger days. Stealing their sheep or wine was a pastime, knowing that those who caught would find themselves hung upside down and eviscerated.

*A glint!*

He looked around. *Had anyone else seen it?* The column was arching ever so slightly as the path turned into a section with enormous rocky outcrops on either side.

He stared at a section below the ridge. Many rocks were jutting out, and Spartacus knew that the tribesmen often used such spots to descend from cliff faces using vines and hide behind the stones. From there, they could rush down at a terrific speed, launching into attacks.

A perfect place for an ambush.

He looked to his left and was sure he spotted movement behind bushes high up.

"Centurion! Centurion!"

But Florus could not hear him, marching far ahead. *Why hadn't the scouts noticed? Did this army not have experience in this landscape?*

A cavalryman came charging from the front, blaring a trumpet. Then, for the first time, Spartacus saw how the army swiftly oriented itself with soldiers splitting right in the middle, back-to-back, and taking defensive positions. They *had* noticed.

"Hold positions! Hold!" Florus screamed. "Gladius out, scutum in front!"

He crouched with the rest, the shield, *scutum*, held in front with his left hand as he held the gladius in the right. He had spent many hours during training on how to push and thrust.

Then came the *thud, thud, thud* of the stone projectiles. Spartacus knew the Bessi slingshots, they were experts at it, and exposed heads would explode like melons if a stone found its mark.

"Hold! Hold positions!" came the order.

*Where could they go?* Spartacus wondered even as his chest thudded with anxiety as the stones smashed on the shield, causing his entire body to shake. Behind him was the stream, and in front was a steep rocky incline. There was nowhere to go! But he knew what was coming next.

A chorus of screams rose from around them, and through the narrow opening between his scutum and the man next to him, he saw the almost-naked Bessi warriors rush down from behind the rocky outcrops. *Like rats emerging from a hole on fire.*

Spartacus' first battle violence began when a Bessi man ran headlong onto his scutum, screaming expletives and trying to open his skull with a stone ax.

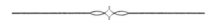

The power of closely held lines, javelins, gladius thrusts, and rigid discipline were apparent once the fight was over. The Bessi had barely made a dent in the cohorts, and scores of the tribe lay dead. The trumpets sounded the end of the fight, and the chaotic lines reorganized into clean, straight columns. Spartacus had killed two men but had never even seen their faces. One man from his century had been severely wounded, and Spartacus knew the practice that if the man were beyond saving, they would give him a merciful death. If he were a Maedi, someone from the tribe would render prayers. Those lightly wounded received linen bandages and were expected to hobble along.

The dead legionaries received a hastily constructed mass funeral pyre. The army was ordered to march on until they found a safer, more expansive space where they could protect their sides.

In no more than a day, they would be near the great lake of the land of the Bessi, dotted with villages of the tribe.

Including Durnadisso's.

A great excitement spread over the auxiliary unit when they were rushed to assemble.

Across the broad valley, on the gentle slope, stood thousands of Bessi, clustered in many groups and making a great noise. They had cavalry, too, with perhaps fifty horses on one side.

The Legate had called order to battle, advancing his cohorts in three lines, with Spartacus' auxiliary positioned in an angle in front of the left flank between the infantry and the cavalry, which was made up entirely of Romans.

The formal lineup was mesmerizing. With him being taller than most others, Spartacus had a full view of the breadth of the cohorts, with the centurions dotting in front of every century and standing beside the standard-bearers. The auxiliary had no standard-bearer, and Florus stood alone. The bronze helmets of the legionaries reflected light, and the wall of red, due to the Scutum's held close, created an intimidating effect.

It was the first time he had seen the army in battle formation after spending days in narrow columns.

*How does it look to the Bessi?* he wondered. *Had they ever faced an army like this before?*

Over the days, he had learned that the Legate was a talented commander who had previously run campaigns for General Sulla. How much of Sulla's greatness was a myth and how much actual was murky, but if this Sulla was half as good as the men portrayed him to be, then Curio would be highly competent as well.

The Bessi were making a tremendous ruckus—banging on heavy bronze plates, ringing bells, playing their trumpets, and waving their arms. Many of the warriors in the front were heavily tattooed, with dark and colorful imagery of goddesses, lions, wolves, or demons covering most of their bodies. The men fought almost naked, with little protection, and Spartacus wondered why the tribes, including his own, had ignored this essential precaution. Their women lined the horizon, screaming, shouting, encouraging their men. The spirit of violence was deep within them as well, and Spartacus knew that they would not hesitate to join the battle if needed.

But a strange uneasiness and fear washed over him. Sweat formed on his eyebrows, and his heart quickened. Until now, all the bravado of attacking the Bessi, slaughtering them like animals, being victorious like conquering warriors, all sounded wonderful in the company of his men and the ruckus of the tents. But Spartacus had only killed a few men in his life, and that as a defensive measure during tribal attacks—never as part of any large army or systematic invasion.

This was different.

They were now up against the Bessi for nothing that tribe had done to Romans. He had no quarrel with many of the wild-haired yellers in the front. And yet there he was, with his men, baying for their blood. It all seemed surreal.

But his musings came to an abrupt and unkind end when the first slingshot from a Bessi slinger whistled through the air and smashed into his scutum, causing him to flinch and drop all pretense of going soft.

The Bessi slingers' projectiles were deflected by the shields or fell short of the lines, and after some time, they tired of the futility and stopped.

The Romans had archers. Where were they?

As much noise as the Bessi made, the Legate gave no order to advance or launch missiles, preferring to watch and wait. *Could it be because of the incline?* Spartacus wondered. *Would Curio wait for the Bessi to tire and make a mistake?*

The sun inched up the sky, and water-bearers went around with leather bags giving thirsty soldiers sips. Even as the Bessi ran around shouting and tiring, the cohorts stood quietly.

Spartacus was itching to move.

*What were they waiting for?* His heart thudded with anticipation of the conflict—the chance to gut these animals for what they did to his people. *Kotys* demanded this revenge!

And then, without warning, the trumpets sounded loud and clear, and the signifier, with his eagle, began to walk forward. On either side, the cavalry charged ahead, kicking up mud from the grey-green grassy ground, and the cohorts started to march.

All the training would come to this, and Spartacus was about to learn how to function as an auxiliary. The Bessi roared in unison, and they came rushing down the gentle slope, their thick hair flying in the wind, their axes, spears, and swords held high, their plate-bangers running down with the fighters, unafraid and with manic glee. They did not stop even when a volley of legionaries' javelins, *pilums*, punched through their bodies and killed scores even before they impacted the advancing infantry. And their women, hair disheveled, shouted encouragement for their men and let loose volleys of curses on the enemy.

And when the wide-eyed, shouting first row of Bessi smashed into their lines, the first to take impact was the auxiliary that had been positioned slightly ahead of the legionaries.

Spartacus' world collapsed into a narrow space of mayhem and violence.

It took no more than an hour before the battle was called to halt. Whistles filled the air, and a large gathering of the Bessi who had turned and ran further up the slope were waving surrender flags. An exhausted and bloodied Spartacus, along with many men in his unit, collapsed to the ground to regain their breath as a Roman cavalry surrounded the surrendering tribesmen. A few changed their mind and tried to run, only to be cut down swiftly by the riders.

It took some more time before the order was settled, and Spartacus understood the outcome. Messengers conveyed the startling result to each unit. They said over seven hundred Bessi were dead but only seventy legionaries and thirty auxiliaries. The auxiliaries had borne the brunt of the proportion of casualties, and Spartacus knew why–they were comparatively poorly equipped, the men had only a fraction of the experience of the legionaries, and their forward position meant they took the worst of the initial hit.

"You did well," Erducos said, "You fought like a beast. I saw you kill three men and save two of ours."

Two men beside Erducos joined the praise, and Spartacus beamed.

"*Kotys* watched over me," Spartacus said. "She desired for me drive my sword through the bellies of the bastards."

"You fight with the vigor of youth, but you are still clumsy with your gladius. Your advance-and-retreat footsteps need practice," Erducos opined.

"I am sure we will get plenty of practice," Spartacus grinned.

The Legate came to address them for the first time since Spartacus had joined.

"You have fought well," Curio said, in Greek, his piercing eyes scanning over the men who stood in attention. "And the many brave Thracian tribes do not see eye-to-eye, I know that."

He paced in front of the men with his red cloak trailing him. "You are required to fight under my command, with unity amongst yourselves, no matter what tribe a man belongs to. Do you agree?"

A translator repeated the words in two dialects. Many murmurs rose from the crowd.

The Legate took deliberate steps to stand close to one of the auxiliaries, making the man fidget. "I am told you speak Greek."

"Yes, sir."

"Does any man disagree with what I said?"

"No, sir."

*Why is he haranguing us about unity when we just fought for him, and some even lost their lives?* Spartacus wondered.

Curio stepped back, smoothed his polished cuirass, and fiddled with the cloak pin. "You may be wondering why I speak of harmony."

The men watched in puzzlement, unsure of what the Legate was hinting at. Had someone spread rumors of discontent? Was someone about to be punished?

"Very well," Curio said and gestured to an officer standing further away. And then, from beyond the mound, soldiers appeared, surrounding a large group of unshackled prisoners who were marching toward the auxiliaries.

*No.*

# 7

## BESSI LANDS

———⬦———

Spartacus watched as a stocky man walked in front of his men with pride and a glint in his eye. As was customary, in view of the Roman forces, the Bessi chieftain made a great show of surrender, falling to his knees before Curio, raising his arms, and loudly proclaiming his desire to cooperate. And behind their chief, hundreds more supplicated and waited for Curio's decision.

What was conferred was beyond their earshot, but Curio said many words, and the Bessi chief assented vigorously. Spartacus watched as Bessi messengers made haste toward the Bessi village, accompanied by Roman cavalry.

"He will seek hostages," Erducos whispered. "The Romans will demand that their important men surrender their wives or children to the Romans until as when release is determined. If he refuses, they—women and children included— will be sold to slavery."

Spartacus had heard of this custom but, having never seen it, was curious as to how this worked. How long would the hostages be kept? How would they be treated? It was not uncommon for the tribes to conduct conflict by such means, though an exchange of hostages in many cases also led to marriages as a condition for peace.

It did not take long for Spartacus to find out who Durnadisso was. And it was the Bessi chief. The most distressing aspect was the prospect of Durnadisso being allowed to get away and live in peace, back in his village, plotting against others, and escaping justice by Spartacus' hands. He had humbled the Bessi fighters, but all this was to waste if he could get to Durnadisso.

Was his whole plan just foolish?

How did he expect to find that man and kill him in a battle?

Spartacus chastised himself for the blind anger and terrible plan.

There was no news for three days as the army camped and fortified. There was no mischief by any tribe, the wounded were tended to, and the dead received burials and pyres as the custom may be. The army conducted its foraging raids and received tributes from surrounding villages. Curio suspended training, giving men the time to rest and recuperate.

But on the fourth day, as the sun vanished from the sky and the camp prepared to settle for the night, Curio summoned all his cohorts. Men were ushered out of their tents and asked to assemble, yet the orders indicated no conflict. The Legate made his announcements, and Florus and his translator conveyed the messages.

"General Sulla, whom I call commander, has new orders for me. I am sure you are well-rested, your bellies full, and your spirits light with victory and peace."

*We march elsewhere,* Spartacus thought.

"After another day's pause, we march south toward Dyrrhachium. We shall move without rest, and we will seek no conflict. Messengers have traveled to the many tribes that dot this land and cautioned them against mischief, and we are assured of safe passage."

The Legate, dressed in his commander's attire, his cuirass glinting under the night flames, adjusted his brooch and shook his shoulders–a habit Spartacus had noticed.

"But our journey does not end in Dyrrhachium. These cohorts, including the auxiliaries, will join the general's legion for a greater cause. Men! Many of you will cover yourself in glory in your land. We return to Italy and march on Rome!"

It took a few moments for the message to percolate. While Spartacus and the auxiliaries processed this with no fond emotion for Italy and Rome were far from home, the legionaries exploded in celebration. They hailed their commander and made a great noise.

Spartacus wondered if he would ever see his house, or what was left of it, again.

The next day, Florus appointed Spartacus to lead the training regimen for the unit, replacing Erducos, who had been complaining of severe pain in his knees on account of his age and the exertion of the march and the battle.

But as if the gods were laughing at his consternation, and that his boldness to dare take *Sabazios* from his abode was a crime still not entirely settled, a new group of auxiliaries was inducted to Spartacus' unit that night, with strict orders for them to lock arms with the men whose people they had just slain.

And a new man, his lips curled up in a cruel smile, his back supported by over eighty Bessi men, was nominated by Curio as the new camp supervisor of the auxiliaries.

Durnadisso.

# 8

## THRACIA

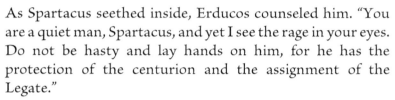

As Spartacus seethed inside, Erducos counseled him. "You are a quiet man, Spartacus, and yet I see the rage in your eyes. Do not be hasty and lay hands on him, for he has the protection of the centurion and the assignment of the Legate."

"How could they induct the Bessi to our unit knowing the conflict they have caused? We just killed scores of their men!" Spartacus said, his words tight with anger, reflecting the sentiment of the many Maedi and Sinti, who had many grievances against the Bessi. But now the men knew why the Bessi had been inducted. The order from General Sulla came with an additional note to increase the strength of the Auxiliary. The Legate had decided that the fastest way to do that was to show clemency to the Bessi and have their man lead the Auxiliary as a compromise and a sweetener to ensure that the battle-hungry tribe remained invested in the Roman cause. There may have been other enticements, but no one knew what it could be–but one thing was clear; Durnadisso could not be touched, for he had the direct patronage of the Prefect himself.

His vengeance had to wait, for he had no desire to kill the man and die himself. He would not give Durnadisso that satisfaction if he looked down upon him from the afterlife.

"The problem, Erducos, is you know that this will cause stress within the unit. You know how difficult keeping peace amongst the tribes is–we have lived centuries fighting and killing each other, and the Bessi have been most egregious in their behavior. Why do you think the Macedonians and Greeks made such inroads into our lands? Because we kept fighting amongst ourselves. And now, when there is finally harmony among other tribes, we have the Bessi poison poured into our cups."

"I can–"

Spartacus' temple throbbed. "You cannot control them," he hissed. "You watch as they assert themselves due to their patronage. Watch as Durnadisso curries favor and his men bring ugliness."

He watched with anger as the Bessi contingent strutted about. He would have to bide his time.

Since the induction, the Bessi had become insufferable, with Durnadisso favoring his men over others, passing judgment and unkind remarks on the other tribes, threatening them of retribution, and heaping all manner of abuses when away from Florus' attention. Spartacus had twice locked his eyes on Durnadisso, and the chieftain had no recognition of who Spartacus may be, for the theory was that the man left behind had been caught, tortured, and had given up the mission and the source of mischief. Whether Spartacus had been described and implicated was unknown, but Durnadisso had shown no special disfavor to Spartacus, for he treated them all with equal disdain. Durnadisso's right-hand man was a mousy character named Cleitus, whose favorite pastime was to needle other tribes, eavesdrop, gossip, and annoy everyone about how good a hunter and scout he was.

"Do the Romans not see this? Is Florus ignorant of the discord?" Spartacus asked, exasperated, after a scuffle with Cleitus over camp cleaning duties. Spartacus' skills as a trainer and his boldness in standing up to the Bessi had gained favor amongst other men.

"That is the Roman way, Spartacus, and the troubles between the tribes are of no concern to them. You are expected to leave your past conflicts aside," Erducos counseled.

Spartacus shook his head. "He does not yet know who I am, and perhaps this is *Kotys'* way to give me justice."

Erducos gripped Spartacus' arm. "If you cause harm, they might crucify you. There will be no justice for you in that. You must learn to control your emotion."

Spartacus breathed hard. *Control!* That was something he had to do a lot more than ever, now under a rigid discipline. He saw the benefits, yet he missed the unfettered sensation of decisions made of his own will. But he was a man who was respected but mocked in his tribe as the *wise sage*—the one who spoke words of wisdom and was not given to rash acts. *If a man rushes into Spartacus' hut to defile his wife, he will invite the man to a debate,* his men had often mocked in jest. And yet, when once Spartacus had decided to show his bold spark by raiding the Bessi temple, the consequences had been severe.

There was virtue in patience. In planning. And now, marching for the Romans, he had seen how that discipline and patience worked.

He breathed deeply. Erducos was right. The Bessi had already suffered. They had given hostages. Their men had died, and they had lost a lot more than the Maedi. And to be hasty would lead to no favorable conclusion–and Spartacus knew that his nature to think logically than by heart was how the gods intended it to be.

The march from the Bessi lands toward Dyrrhachium would take more than twenty days, even on the rapid march. There was excitement in the air about besieging Rome, and even Spartacus was carried away by the thought of arriving by the gates of the city he had heard so much and returning with great loot and perhaps even a slave or a servant. With that money and prestige, he could afford a new wife and one of great beauty. And then he would buy cattle to live off a farm; the salary was more than adequate–though there was one disconcerting matter–they had not been paid now even well after fifty days since joining. The excuse was that they would have to reach Dyrrhachium to have access to coin, and the Legate had assured them all that no man would go unpaid. The rumors were that the legionaries had been paid, but the auxiliaries, as usual, received the worst treatment.

But the relations between the Bessi and other tribes only worsened, with Durnadisso, as overseer and supervisor of the auxiliary unit, increasingly testing their resolve. Regular taunts of *dogs, sons of whores, cockless effeminates*, escalated into abuses on family and gods, incorrect disbursal of rations, mysteriously vanishing footwear, and relentless haranguing. Florus slept separate from the Auxiliary tents, and most of the shenanigans happened at night. No man wished to break protocol and go to the centurion, lest that lead to more trouble than justice. Spartacus had become the leader of the Maedi and other smaller Thracian tribes on account of not only his demonstration during the battle but by his words, status in his tribe, and his education. And this Durnadisso noticed.

Men coming to blows was no rarity, but Erducos was respected enough that he could often quell the quarrels, bring peace, keep the conflict away from Florus and prevent punishment. *Let the matter of the tribes be within tribes*, he would say, and for that, the men saw him as a chief. But now, his words had little sway without the formal power, and Durnadisso always found means to insult or ignore anything he said.

"Spartacus, I heard you once had a wife," Cleitus said, chewing on a leaf and scratching his ears. "Did she leave you before you couldn't get it up?"

"Leave him be," Erducos warned. This was not the first time Cleitus had come to frustrate Spartacus.

"Walk away, little mouse," Spartacus said, flicking his fingers like a rat scurrying.

"It's true, isn't it? She didn't leave, and she didn't die. She probably moaned under a Bessi cock as we ravaged her. That's it," Cleitus said, thrusting his hips.

*What a stupid man. Why all this pettiness? It made no sense.*

Spartacus was confused as to why Cleitus was unnecessarily provoking him. To what end? It was simply not in the tribe's blood to take insults and be quiet. He would have paid with his life if this was their land. Spartacus clenched his fist and tried to ignore the insults. But he knew that standing back and letting his family be dragged through the mud impacted his standing.

"Oh! Oh! I bet that's what she said before we slit her throat. Maybe that's what happened to the whore!"

Spartacus, close enough within striking distance, slapped Cleitus so hard that the Bessi man smashed into a wooden post behind him and fell. Men howled and laughed, and a few of Erducos' men restrained Spartacus from kicking the man to death.

"You dishonor my family again, and it will be far worse," Spartacus yelled at Cleitus, who wobbled back to his feet.

Cleitus' eyes were ablaze, but his lips turned up to a grin. "You will pay, Spartacus. Everyone sees you have no control. Why are you the trainer? You should be a cleaner!"

Spartacus took two steps at him. He turned and fled from the camp.

Two days later, centurion Florus walked into Spartacus' tent. "Come out," he ordered, and Spartacus walked as others looked on curiously. Getting summoned by the centurion at this time was not something to look forward to.

Once outside, three legionaries surrounded him. Florus stood before Spartacus, who maintained a soldier's stance before his officer. Durnadisso stood next to Florus. A translator stood on the side.

"Spartacus, the unit supervisor levies on you charges of insubordination and fomenting drunken violence. How do you respond?" the centurion asked.

Spartacus was confused but maintained his composure. Insubordination came with severe consequences, including death, but *Zibelthiurdos* did not intend for him to go this way, for no great cause, and with no bloodshed!

"I request the specifications of the charges, sir," Spartacus said.

"The dog needs *specifications*! What are you, the prince of Maedi?" Durnadisso, bold and insolent besides Florus, taunted. Cleitus stood behind Durnadisso and sniggered.

Florus turned to Durnadisso. "Quiet! Leave it to my determination."

He then turned to Spartacus again. "So, you say you know nothing of the matter?"

"I do not, sir."

Florus sighed. "Durnadisso here says the Maedi have ganged up and been intimidating the new Bessi auxiliaries and you that you have recently beaten a Bessi man. You are aware that the Legate expects absolute discipline and harmony? You are a good fighter, Spartacus, but there are many more like you."

Durnadisso grinned—he was behind Florus. The centurion could not see the games played, or perhaps he did not care.

"The Bessi man heaped many curses on our women and gods—"

"He does not refute the charges! And he takes it upon himself to dispense violence, contrary to your orders!"

Florus turned to Durnadisso. "Do not test my patience, Durnadisso."

That shut the Bessi chief.

"Speak," the centurion said to Spartacus.

"The Bessi, on account of their loss by our hands, and now drunk with power by Durnadisso's appointment as supervisor. They have been conducting themselves without honor, centurion. My act of violence on the Bessi man came only at the end of many taunts and insults and after threats to our safety."

"And why did you not, then, report to me?"

Spartacus knew he had no answer. He lowered his head and answered. "And for that, I accept responsibility, but know that–"

"I need know nothing, auxiliary. Punishment is necessary. You men test my patience. Do not think that misbehavior within your barracks goes unnoticed, even if I have taken residence elsewhere. Legionary! Prepare for a flogging!"

Durnadisso's glee was evident in the upturned crease of his mouth and the dancing of his bushy eyebrows.

Spartacus felt panic rise in his throat. A flogging could be severe, depending on the centurion's mood or how this bastard had turned his mind. But it was not the pain Spartacus was worried about–sometimes flogging left the skin ripped and opened the muscle. If the gods were angry, there might be significant inflammation and suppuration of the wounds, causing fever and delirium. The army might discharge him from duty and leave him here in Macedonia. Such a situation might mean death or capture by those not inclined toward him. What good would it do to him to lose his money, and then his life, over a trivial matter and without even the revenge of the man who had caused the death of his family?

"Before the lashes descend upon me, centurion," said Spartacus with as much dignity he could muster, "may I beseech you to ask Erducos once so that you may know if my reaction was warranted and deserving of mercy?"

Florus paused. So far, the centurion had shown no great affection for his unit, on his account of feeling unfairly assigned, but had not done anything that one might consider as fundamentally unfair.

"Call Erducos," he said, and a legionary went seeking the Odomantean. Erducos appeared soon after and presented himself to Florus. The murmur was that while Erducos and Florus had a cordial relation on account of Erducos' lengthy service, some of that affection had recently been lost due to pay disputes, the nature of which had not been divulged by Erducos, not even to Spartacus. But it appeared his words still carried some weight.

Florus turned to Erducos, briefly summarized the situation, and then asked, "What say you, Erducos, why might Spartacus not warrant a flogging?"

"Spartacus has proved to be amongst the most valiant of fighters, centurion," Erducos said, "and given the passion between tribes, he has also demonstrated remarkable restraint in the face of mockery and invitations for violence."

"But that gives him no right to strike another man and cause discontent in the unit. Those are the rules."

"As they are, sir. But he is new. His talent brings notice to your unit, and to you! He is a Maedi, and it is no surprise that men of these tribes come to blows over trivial matters, so in that respect, he has demonstrated remarkable discipline to warrant your mercy."

"These dogs always find excuses, centurion! They–"

"Did I ask your opinion?" Florus addressed Durnadisso coldly, cutting him off. Spartacus had the urge to grab the shorter man by his neck and break it like a twig.

The centurion turned to him. "Very well. A flogging, as deserved at it may be by army regulation, may put you out of commission. You have served the unit–so a caning it will be, just to remind you that my patience is limited. The Legate has no tolerance for insubordination. Remember that."

They all knew better than to argue.

Spartacus was tied to a pole, and a legionary began to cane his back and buttocks sufficiently hard enough to cause stinging pains but not hard enough to leave serious injuries. But with each strike, Spartacus' rage grew.

*Thwack!*

Of being at the receiving end of deception.

*Thwack!*

Of being under the rules of men not of his land.

*Thwack!*

Of being subjected to this pain and humiliation by the man responsible for his family's death.

*Thwack!*

He closed his eyes and suffered through seven lashes, refusing to look at Durnadisso or Cleitus and giving them no pleasure by screaming.

# 9

## LUCANIA

———◇———

Felix stood in a corner as the slave overseer, Mellius, harangued him. The fever in Felix's body had not left him—his forehead was hot, his limbs felt weak, and chills still racked his body even in the warm and humid air.

"You little rats always have an excuse!" Mellius shouted. "The master isn't feeding you to laze around and rub your cock, and your little drama doesn't convince anyone. One more complaint and I'll have you tied to the overhang bar and left that way for two days!"

*No! No! Not that!* It was horrible, and he had seen another slave left in that terrible way, unable to sit or sleep, with the hands pulled high and tied, crying, pleading, pissing all over his leg, losing control. By the time the master ordered him freed, the man had become delirious and come close to death.

Mellius, who managed the slave barracks, was a sadistic brute. Yet, his ways had favor with the master who, beyond ensuring sufficient food and clothing to the slaves, did little to control the injustices under his authority. Sometimes, the master Publius and his wife joined the show of boys being beaten by Mellius or his men for minor transgressions. They laughed when the boys cried, so what justice could Felix expect from a master whom himself had no decency? Besides, Felix had heard that his master, *dominus*, was called a Senator–which meant that the whispers in the barracks about complaining of their treatment to a magistrate were just that, whispers, for there was no one to complain to.

Desperate to escape punishment, Felix implored Mellius not to chain him after promising that he would report to work as always and prevail over his condition. Anything to avoid being tied and left alone.

Mellius' red eyes stared at him, and Felix looked down, afraid and defeated. *Perhaps a day will arrive when the master would grow kinder,* he thought.

"Now get out, join the master herder, and do not come back until the grazing is complete."

"Yes, Mellius."

Feeling tired and weak but having no choice in the matter, Felix picked up his grazing stick and walked out to the hot sun. His skin felt strange–at once hot and cold, and he controlled himself from swooning and falling. Some in his barracks said he was now fourteen years old, though he had no idea of his age and that he was becoming a man and much more was expected.

Nigrumus, *the black one,* master herder, was letting out the cattle from the pen and gestured at Felix as he neared. "You do not look too well, boy; the affliction still troubles you?"

"Yes. But Mellius has ordered me to join you."

"He is an evil one. He thinks his station is beyond what he is because he is now an overseer. The master will have him beaten to death with no remorse if the situation demands."

*I hope he does.*

"Come, come. Today we see new routes. We will have two more boys with us. We must be wary of bandits, so carry a robust cane."

They were disallowed from carrying any weapons–knives, axes, swords–nothing. Magisterial orders were exceedingly strict–any slaves caught with weapons could be crucified, that awful, *awful* punishment reserved for slaves. And that meant herders and other slaves out in the open land had to fend for themselves with canes and sticks. If it rained, they had to build makeshift shelters. They sometimes had to even find food themselves. The estate was growing, and Nigrumus was the master herder who led the boys and others for grazing duties. Nigrumus often complained that because the master would not pay enough, they did not have sturdy men who were most suited for shepherding and cattle grazing–leaving much of the stress on the aging man and his young acolytes.

Nigrumus continued. "You cannot run behind the cattle in your state, so stay hidden in the bushes and warn us."

Felix nodded. Nigrumus was like a father. His skin shined like a black rock. He was a kind man, and they said he came from lands very far away, a place called Aethiopia. But his mother–

"Boy!" Nigrumus yelled. "Walk with me!"

Felix took slow steps with Nigrumus as the cows trotted ahead of them, corralled by two other slave boys in the household of Publius. The master owned a large estate near the mountains that loomed far to their left, and the sea was only a few days of marching from here, they said, though Felix had never seen it. And his master was one of the significant estate holders in Lucania, even if lacking sufficient manpower. They said that the master was not making enough money to hire more men for the many duties required to run a large estate.

He tried to distract himself from the exertion. *What does the sea look like? Is it as big as it is? Lucia is so pretty. Does she like me? Will the master keep her in the household and not force her to marry someone?*

First, they came upon a familiar area with plenty of grass, but they always had to contend with competition from a neighboring estate that also sent its herds for grazing. Today it all seemed quiet.

As Nigrumus and the two others managed the grazing, Felix found higher ground to watch. His heart thumped like a hammer, and he felt weak. But it was a long way for a meal, and the stomach ached for a piece of the *durum* bread.

He wiped some sweat and surveyed the area around the grazing area.

*Boys!*

"Nigrumus!" he shouted hoarsely. But Nigrumus was far away, and the wind blew opposite his voice. The cowbells added to the noise of rustling trees, so Nigrumus paid no heed.

Felix scrambled to his feet and ran down the slope, his legs wobbling and lungs already feeling like they were on fire.

But the boys, very likely pig fuckers from a neighboring competing estate, ran up and chased Felix, having seen him. A feverish Felix, sweat running down his forehead and his neck feeling cold, tried to outpace them but failed. "Nigrumus, Nigrumus!" He shouted but could not make out if the master herder heard him, hidden behind clusters of bushes.

He turned to face his pursuers. Two boys, no older than himself or perhaps even younger, still in loincloths, had long sticks in their hands and rushed him.

"Stop, stop–"

One boy swung the cane at Felix, striking his shoulder. And the other ran to the side.

*Trying to come behind me!*

"Nigrumus!"

Felix used all his strength to strike the younger boy in front of him, and he yelped in pain as the stick found its target on the torso. But before he could turn and face the other boy, on whose snarling lips the slightest of hair had begun to sprout, the boy swung his thicker cane and struck Felix on the forehead.

And his already swimming head barely registered the pain as everything went dark.

# 10

## TO DYRRHACHIUM

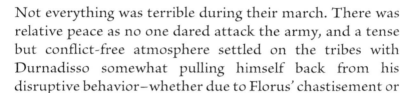

Not everything was terrible during their march. There was relative peace as no one dared attack the army, and a tense but conflict-free atmosphere settled on the tribes with Durnadisso somewhat pulling himself back from his disruptive behavior–whether due to Florus' chastisement or something else was unclear.

Spartacus thoroughly enjoyed training his Century of eighty men, and he knew them all by name. There were thirty-two Maedi, including himself, eighteen Sinti, thirteen Bessi, seven Odomanti, three Bisaltai, five Dobere, and two from the Odrysian kingdom to the east. These men he forged into fighting machines each morning during the rest periods during the march. For all the burning hate he had for the Bessi, the men conducted themselves with respect and obeyed his orders. Their fears and aspirations were no different from his, and from the many conversations, he also realized that a good number had no hand in the attack on his village.

For all his failings and his lack of interest in developing his unit, Florus was a highly experienced centurion. Spartacus knew that men did not attain that position without valor and skill, all which Florus had surely demonstrated before he fell out of favor for reasons unknown. But when Florus did his duty, teaching or lecturing Spartacus on maneuvers and battle strategy, so that he could then put it to practice with the unit, Spartacus learned greedily and listened with rapt attention. And Florus enjoyed reminiscing his glory days or showing off his broad knowledge of Roman tactics and history, though he never forgot to sprinkle his lectures with *why am I wasting my time talking about this with uneducated barbarians?*

And in this way, Spartacus taught his men the finer points of the crouch-defend-and-thrust maneuver, how to stab from over the shield, how to swing the shield horizontally to strike at the face of the enemy, how to relieve men in the front in a smoothly executed line rotation, how to regroup and align when a line breaks, the right angles at which to launch the *pilums*, javelins, and how to parry Cavalry attacks. He was untiring in his efforts to encourage, harangue, push, and even occasionally deliver an excellent beating to shape the fighting skills of his men. However, unlike him, they had little interest in strategy or larger discussions of politics. And when he tried to engage them on such topics during their meals or before sleep, they gave him a nickname as the *limpy lord*. "Our trainer is a poet with a limp, oh what a disgrace!" they said.

Erducos was his companion, and in rare situations, even Florus, to satiate his hunger for an exchange on those matters. And one such discussion around the fire, about a general named Hannibal, greatly fascinated him—he had not heard of this man before. Alexander was known by association with the Macedonians, but he was long ago during his forefather's time. Hannibal had hailed from Carthage, far away by Libya, and led his armies into Italy. Florus laced his description of the Carthaginian general and his "barbarian" armies with invectives and pejoratives. Still, it was evident that the centurion was in awe of what Hannibal had accomplished. He had destroyed Rome's armies multiple times and camped in Italy for nearly fifteen years. A Roman general named Scipio had finally vanquished Hannibal. As he heard these stories, Spartacus often fantasized about himself at the head of an army, leading a powerful Thracian force and taking on even Rome and other kingdoms. It was Florus' descriptions of battle strategy, about how large troops moved, how they were supplied, how they divided and flanked, how they sieged the enemy, how they recruited and disbanded, that excited Spartacus most. He understood the power of planning and cunning and why bravery alone guaranteed little against well-trained forces.

"Spartacus wishes to be the king of the Thracians, eh?" Erducos often teased. "Perhaps one day you will depose the Odrysian king and become one yourself!"

"Maybe I will become king of Rome," Spartacus retorted. "Why settle for Thracia alone?"

Erducos looked at him thoughtfully. "Perhaps one day you will, son of Maedi."

*Perhaps I will. From the son of a chief, to a chief, to a king, to an emperor. Why not?*

The salty air, the pungent smell of seaweed, and the numerous fish sellers on the road heralded the nearness of Dyrrhachium, from where they would cross the sea to Italy.

# 11

## DYRRHACHIUM

————◇————

The swinging boat made him sick and vomitous but having never seen the vast sea or been in a boat, it was a remarkable experience. On arrival at Dyrrhachium, the men had only a few days of rest before they were ordered to embark to the city of Brundisium in Italy, from where Sulla's legions would march on Rome.

The scale of the entire operation had stunned Spartacus. There were five whole legions here already, further enhanced by Curios. It was said that there were one-thousand-two-hundred ships ready to ferry them. The Roman camp at the port was massive, though there was no rampart or ditches, unlike in their previous camps. It seems the general was confident in his strength and alliances and that no one would dare launch an attack on this gathering.

Everything was ordered, and there were many rules to follow. And yet, even with thousands of men, there was a discipline and method, and few dared to misbehave now under the eyes of the general and senior commanders. As a body, the entire army was now on the way. He had never gotten a chance to see the Roman general or his Legates—men who commanded the legions. The incredible display this army projected had strangely excited Spartacus, as if he were now a part of something greater, something powerful. However, relations among men had soured again due to Durnadisso's behavior, but they all tried to ignore him the best they could, hoping that things might improve once they reached Italy and were on the march with the general.

"You will see them all when we are arranged in battle," Erducos had said. "You think you've seen much in our skirmishes? It's nothing. This will be a sight to behold!"

But now, clutching his stomach and hunching down controlling his urge to vomit, Spartacus thought of something else. He was part of a great legion, fighting for marvelous men, in a marvelous war for a marvelous city, and all for marvelous money–and yet the men were not of his, the land was not his, the cause was not his, and the spoils would not belong to his tribe. What wonderful thing it might be, he thought, if he were commanding legions that fought for the Maedi, to create an empire of his own and to whom the others bowed. Including the Bessi–who had made his life miserable. Durnadisso's further attempts to draw him into violence had failed, and yet the need to listen to the man felt like fire below his feet. But he had what Durnadisso and Cleitus did not–his men's respect. The Bessi chief's abrasive behavior had alienated many of his men.

Spartacus stood to relieve the unpleasant sensations and breathed the salty air. There was no land as far as he could see. They said that Italy appeared beyond the line where the water ended, and it seemed like the water would never end. The waves crested and fell, and soon the seagulls that caused much noise slowly fell behind and vanished from view.

It was nothing but water, and Spartacus, having never been on a body of water so large and so endless, felt anxious and uneasy. What if the boat capsized? What if demonic creatures from the deep rose and toppled the vessel? Seafarers shared many terrible storied in the barracks, and whether it was to tease those who had never experienced the sea or if they spoke the truth was never clear. The boat creaked and made all manner of distressing sounds as if it would break in two and drown. It was crowded, with men packed like fish on the upper deck and the rowing section below, and thankfully no senior officers were in view haranguing them. It was said that expert boat builders from Cilicia and Levant had built these boats, and nothing would cause them to sink–Spartacus hoped all that was true.

"The Maedi dog sees the water and controls its urge to piss into it," Durnadisso said, smirking, and some of his men laughed. The auxiliary supervisor, the man who had ordered the destruction of his village and thereby causing the death of his family, was now back to what he enjoyed doing– needling others, not of his kind.

"Shut up, Bessi bitch," someone near Spartacus retorted.

"Leave them be," Spartacus said, staring at Durnadisso. "They are like cockroaches which are always scurrying about."

Durnadisso, shorter than Spartacus and stocky, leaned on the balustrade of the swaying ship, his hair flying in the wind. The men had all been forced to shave, and the transformation had elicited much mirth and laughter. *Look at Spartacus, the Greek philosopher from the Maedi tribe!* his men had teased him. But they were allowed to leave their hair so long as they tied it before the battle. *What a pretty man!* Durnadisso had hollered. *Many Roman Senators will want you for their bed!*

No one had ever called Spartacus pretty. His thick nose, broad lips, and narrow eyes belied his thoughtful manner and careful words. His mother would tease him: *If you weren't built like the gods wanted you, I would let a wolf take you away and eat you, because what woman would want you and give me grandchildren?*

The ample hair on his head and face hid some of his features, and now his face was visible for all the world to see, much to his discomfort. For what amusement had Zibelthiurdos created him this way, with the ever-so-slight but noticeable limp, a thick torso and bulging thighs, and a face no woman would call handsome. But his wife, well, his now-dead wife–he sometimes thought of her–adored him. Perhaps it was not always about a man's face.

Spartacus turned to Durnadisso. "We are here to enrich ourselves and return home. Why sow discord among our men and put us all at risk?"

"Big words! You speak like you are the leader here, Maedi. But I know why you joined the Romans–you wanted to end us. And now you want us to return home happy and content?"

"That was not what I said, Durnadisso. What bad water flowed between the tribes means little when we must fight as one in the Auxiliary and protect each other. The more you force a division, the harder it will be for all of us."

*I will deal with you privately later.*

"See, the Bessi stand proud and fight. Gods most favor our priests. If we were not backstabbed by all you weaklings, we would be standing tall in Thracia."

"You sent murderous raids against those who were of a lesser number. It was a sign of cowardice, not bravery. And yet when you were cowed by Roman superiority, you lament that the tribes betrayed you. You were never with the tribes, you never cared for any, and you sought no peace among us."

Durnadisso scoffed. "You speak like a chief. The men say you are a dramatist. You are deliberate with words. You pretend to be a scholar. A noble. But beneath that veneer, do not forget you're just a brute. A lowly auxiliary. A soldier whom the Romans will forget in a ditch."

"As you say," Spartacus said, tiring of this. What was Durnadisso getting at?

"So, tell me, Spartacus. Where did you get this air of Hellenic superiority? Where did you learn to pretend to be Greek?"

*Was it that obvious?*

Spartacus was surprised. "I pretend nothing. I had a Greek tutor named Hermos and he taught me to read and write, and he told me many things about their world."

Durnadisso threw his head back and laughed. "It seems this Hermos was quite influential because you picked up his tricks like a dog. Just because you speak Greek and know a thing or two about their ways of life or their grand books does not make you an aristocrat."

*What do you know about culture or philosophy or history, brutish fool?*

"I never pretended to be an aristocrat, unlike you, still pretending to be chief after kneeling before a Roman."

That slight seemed to have annoyed Durnadisso somewhat.

"I thought you were a dandy in the king's court," he said, referring to the so-called king who lived in his little capital and never really ventured out.

"You can think what you want. I give little credence to Bessi that live and behave like animals."

Tired of needling Spartacus and not getting much in return, Durnadisso inched closer. "When I was sleeping last night, a little demon appeared out of the darkness and whispered something in my ears."

Spartacus ignored him.

"The demon said *have you looked closely at Spartacus, the Maedi rat? What does his description remind you of?*"

Spartacus turned to him but said nothing.

Durnadisso's lips parted in a snarl. The face of ill-natured taunting had vanished, and there was a wicked purpose in its place. "And I listened to the demon, and I began to think…"

*That's a surprise that you can think, Bessi ape.*

"…and a picture formed in my head. *Sabazios* seemed to be telling me, *it's him, the Maedi mongrel who came to steal me from my abode.* It's just that your man, when he howled in agony when we broke his bones one by one and gouged his eyes, used your pet name and not your real one, so it took me a while."

Spartacus stiffened. Cleitus, Durnadisso's toady, a habitual tormentor, and annoyance, had surreptitiously made his way behind Durnadisso. Centurion Florus was somewhere below deck, probably drunk. The winds whipped through the sail, and cold water sprayed on them. Spartacus wiped his face and then moved his hand to the scabbard and watched as Durnadisso's eyes traced his hand.

"It was you, wasn't it, pig's son? You dared to come from the Maedi land to our sacred abode to steal our god because you think it's the same as raiding another village and stealing girls to rape."

Cleitus, who stood nearby, added. "Do not think we wouldn't figure it out, mongrel. When your man screamed, he said the leader was a chief's son. With your big words and pretend greatness, I wonder who that is."

Spartacus controlled his breath. This was deliberate incitement. Perhaps Durnadisso was just throwing a guess to force a reaction, and then Florus would be unmerciful this time.

"I know nothing about what you say," he said. "And your gods laugh at your juvenile attempts at forcing conflict. Not now, Durnadisso."

But Durnadisso did not budge. "What a weakling you are, Maedi monkey. Is there no fire in your belly now? Where has your boldness vanished? Is that piss I see on your legs?"

Cleitus laughed. "Not just piss."

Spartacus' eyes darted to understand the situation. The ship was crowded, but other men were oblivious to this dialog. Conflict amongst them had become so common that most simply ignored raised voices and taunts. Durnadisso and Cleitus had become thorns in his back.

*When Durnadisso isn't polishing Florus' shoes, Cleitus is pouring poison in the centurion's ears.*

Erducos was nowhere to be seen; he was perhaps among the cluster of men at the far side. It was just Durnadisso and his two.

"Leave it be," Spartacus growled. "Make your money and go home."

Durnadisso inched closer. Spartacus could feel his breath and see the vessels in his yellowed eyes. Cleitus shifted slightly, and his hand went to the concealed knife in the folds of his tunic.

"Who will go home is you, Spartacus, and that home is not on this earth," Durnadisso whispered as his hand inched toward his belt.

*This is it.*

All the pent-up rage exploded from deep within. Spartacus swung his fist and struck Durnadisso's throat. The Bessi chief croaked, and his eyes opened wide in terror. But even before the two men behind him could react, Spartacus removed the gladius from his scabbard in lightning speed and drove it between the Chief's ribcage and twisted it, and at the same time grabbed the hair of one of his men and smashed his head against the railing. Hugging an instantly dead Durnadisso close and drenched in his blood,

Spartacus reached down to the Bessi chief's scabbard and removed his gladius. Cleitus, big in his mouth, but small in stature, stood in shock. and Spartacus hissed at him. "Be quiet and do not try anything."

Spartacus sliced his own shoulder quickly—a shallow wound that would require nothing more than a bandage. By then, men had surrounded them, and thankfully most were Sinti or Maedi. Recognizing the situation for what it was, two men quickly restrained Cleitus. At the same time, Spartacus lifted the unconscious man and threw him into the water. The news would travel to the holding below, so Spartacus had his audience agree to the simple story: Durnadisso had accused Spartacus of raiding his village and attacking him, and Spartacus had killed him in self-defense.

That was it and nothing more to it.

*But what of Cleitus who had witnessed it all?*

They had to do what had to be done, so they dragged a howling Cleitus to the edge and threatened him—one word to anyone, and they would finish him. There was no fight left in the man, who begged to be let off, and that he was under Durnadisso's fear and without the chief, his life would be better. He scrambled to his tribe, and Spartacus knew that to kill Cleitus would simply create a lot more suspicion. They would have to deal with the implications later. Cleitus was a dangerous man, not by the skill of the blade, but by his cunning and opportunistic nature. Spartacus would have to keep an eye on him.

His temple throbbed from the rush, and he let his wildly beating heart calm down. This was sudden and unexpected, and he thanked *Kotys* and *Zibelthiurdos* for the opportunity and for giving him the courage to act. He felt a sense of satisfaction for the revenge he had extracted, by killing the man responsible for the death of his loved ones and had been sowing discord amongst his people.

Now he would wait for Florus to come screaming.

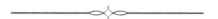

Florus looked unconvinced at the story but seemed disinterested in investigating it further. Perhaps he had tired of Durnadisso's behavior himself and was secretly relieved that the Bessi chief was dead. Curio was busy and would care not a whit and probably never even learn of this incident. Cleitus, usually obsequious in Florus' presence, kept his mouth shut and promptly blamed Durnadisso for the situation. The Maedi and Sinti repeated their stories that they saw very little for it all happened too fast and that they had heard Durnadisso threatening Spartacus.

From his side, Spartacus mostly spoke the truth—how Durnadisso had pointed the finger at him and threatened his life, leaving him with no choice to defend himself when the Bessi lunged.

The matter settled, Florus half-heartedly issued threats of flogging, crucifixion, and so on, and then left telling them to be prepared to impress the Legates or he would have their hides. When it came to Spartacus, he was more concerned about his ability to fight rather than whatever he had done to Durnadisso—but his examination of the light wound gave him some relief that Spartacus could fight and train the men without a problem.

But there was one more thing. "Well, now with Durnadisso dead and Erducos complaining that he is no longer fit to oversee the auxiliaries, I suppose you have the most credible following," Florus said. "You are now the new leader. Keep the peace."

Spartacus saluted the centurion. This role came with some minor perks. More than anything, it was a recognition.

It often gave him a better vantage to the management of men and organization than being only an auxiliary soldier. But quickly, it also dawned upon him that Florus had not done this from the goodness of his heart, but because he would be reprimanded if the Auxiliaries did not put up a good fight and displayed discipline. Under the circumstances, Spartacus was the best man.

Spartacus hoped he could inspire his men and unite them, unlike Durnadisso. Little was said after the centurion left, and the swift violence had somewhat quelled the unease in Spartacus' stomach. Erducos was shocked, and he privately chastised Spartacus for the risk but commended him for the boldness. "You are destined for greater things. But pay heed to the circumstances around you."

A physician on the boat tended to Spartacus' wound– applying a healing salve to prevent it from festering and then tying a bandage to help heal the superficial wound.

Hours later, someone shouted, "Land!"

And there, far ahead, rising like a magical structure, was the hazy outline of land.

Italy.

Almost no one, including Erducos, had been to Italy. Florus was the only one, and he was no cheerful storyteller. Stories were abundant, but all from secondary sources, which meant one could not distinguish truth from exaggeration.

*Rome is so significant is extends from the west to Brundisium!*

*What if we are being tricked and are taken are slaves?*

*They say parts of Italy are just like Thracia, but the women more aloof and less beautiful.*

*Full of stiff Romans and their rules.*

*They say there is a mountain somewhere that spews fire and smoke, and the gods of Italy dwell there.*

*It seems Romans are mainly in Rome, and the Southern side of Italy has many Greek cities, and they speak different languages!*

*If I die here, tell my father I died bravely.*

*If you die here, I will make sure to visit your wife.*

*If you visit my wife, you will come back with something missing between your legs.*

*He has something to go missing?*

*One more word, and I swear I'll beat you to death.*

*Come, come, let's see!*

"Stop! Stop! You idiots!"

And so it went until the men heard the whistles and trumpets to assemble on deck and prepare for disembarkation.

And finally, as the orange sun slowly set far ahead of them, Spartacus set his foot on Italy.

# 12

## LUCANIA

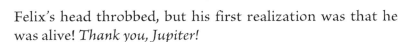

Felix's head throbbed, but his first realization was that he was alive! *Thank you, Jupiter!*

"It seems you will not die easily," Nigrumus was saying as he grinned, displaying all his brilliant teeth.

Felix groaned. All he remembered was the two boys cornering him, and then the light had turned dark. "What happened?" he asked.

"I gave those two little runts a sound thrashing. But I had to carry you on my back; you're not a skinny lad anymore."

Felix was groggy, but he balanced himself on his elbows as he straightened his back and leaned against the mud wall. He was back in his barracks, but his left leg was shackled already. The overseer usually chained them all in the night, including Nigrumus, for that was the master's order so that no slave might get adventurous. The only ones allowed to be free, with oversight, were men who would sleep with one of the young slave women so that they would produce babies. If the woman had three children, she was free of hard work, and if she had five or more, she became a freedwoman and was allowed to leave, but with the condition that her children remain as slaves until they were twenty.

And that was how Felix's mother had left him when he was still only five–and since then, he had only seen the barracks and the master's fields.

It was not yet dark, and Mellius was not here to scream and yell. The fever had not broken yet–his skin was still clammy, and he was starving. "Do you have some corn or bread?"

Nigrumus shook his head. "I might need to finagle some from the kitchen. You wait here."

When Mellius was not around, the slaves used cooperation to get some extra food and delicacies here and there—and perhaps the master knew but chose not to act on it, for it kept the slaves feeling like they had some freedom.

Nigrumus groaned as he got to his feet. "Carrying you broke my back, lad!" he grumbled.

Felix smiled at the good-natured scolding. What would he ever do if Nigrumus was not here?

"But I know whom to send here with some bread," Nigrumus said, with a knowing smile, causing Felix's heart to flutter.

Lucia walked into the dim barracks holding a large piece of hard bread and a cup of water. Felix watched as she demurely came before him and knelt. *How pretty she was!* A word barely squeaked out of his throat as he accepted the bread and the cup of water. "Thank you," he finally managed.

"Nigrumus said the boys from the neighboring estate beat you," she said softly. He could not see her face correctly, with the evening light from the door open behind her. Felix felt ashamed that he could not tell her that he had beaten them valiantly.

"I was outnumbered. Otherwise, I would have thrashed them," he said, deepening his voice and trying to sound bold.

He could make out that she was smiling. He had known her for many years now—she had arrived with her mother and was inducted into the household. Her mother still worked in the estate, but in service of the lady, the *domina*, and specialized in hair, makeup, and serving guests. Perhaps her mother's looks had something to do with it.

Lucia was a younger version of her beautiful mother. And her mother's position gave Lucia a chance to be away from back-breaking farm work many other girls and women were engaged in–planting seeds, tending to crops and olive trees, pressing, peeling, watering, washing, and so on. Lucia mostly stayed in the kitchen and host service. But there were times when their paths crossed, and over time, a friendship had developed, and for Felix, an infatuation as time progressed. Lucia was at least a year or two older than him, and he felt she had more experience in matters of the world and that his affection for her was a lost cause. But that did not stop him from desiring to see her or have her near him. And if that meant taking bread from her after having a fever, being beaten, fainting, and then being carried back home, so be it!

"Nigrumus said you were brave and fought them well," she said softly, in that mellifluous accent. He beamed at that affirmation. Lucia had told him that she was an *Aquitani* from a region far to the north of where they now lived and belonging to a tribe of warriors that the Romans called Gauls. They had been sold as slaves due to something her father did, had been transported to Italy, sold once more in a northern town, and then finally to the master.

And it was known that Mellius had his eyes on her, among others, and her honor had not been invaded only due to her mother's influence. But of course, if the master himself had designs for Lucia, nothing could be done, for she was his property to do as he pleased. But so far, even if in the flimsiest of possibilities, Lucia was somehow *his* for she brought bread for no one else in the barracks.

Suddenly Lucia reached out and held Felix's hand, and it was as if a lightning bolt had struck him. "You should be careful. Do not get killed! I must go before Mellius sees!"

With that, she got up hurriedly and dashed out. Nigrumus walked in shortly after, grinning. "Well, I hope the beating was worth it," he said, squatting beside Felix.

Heat rose Felix's cheeks, and his embarrassing erection died quickly once Nigrumus pointed to his raised tunic and laughed some more. *I hope Lucia did not see it! Or maybe that's why she ran away so quickly!* He was mortified. But that moment of joy and shame ended when Mellius barged in.

"Why was she here? She is not supposed to be in these barracks. Did you send her here, Nigrumus?" he demanded.

"Do you want one of your best shepherds to starve to death by negligence?" Nigrumus asked. "Go easy on the boy. You know that the master has struggled to keep good slaves who can graze the cattle and sheep."

Mellius glared at Nigrumus. "Do not take me for granted since I have not laid my hands on you, Nigrumus, and that you are older and therefore assume you are wiser. I know better what the master wants, and this thin little stain putting his cock in her is not what he wants."

Felix controlled his urge to shout at Mellius, knowing enough of the repercussions for such behavior. He could be reassigned permanently to be outside the estate, she could be put in danger due to his incessant scheming—or worse, he could be beaten to death and written off as an accident.

"Mellius, the boy barely has hair on his lips. His limbs are lithe and like a girl's. What he does best is run and herd. What makes you think Lucia has eyes for him? She will fetch a handsome price for the master should he decide to sell her, not to mention every handsome man wanting her."

The words cut deep into Felix–but he knew that Nigrumus had to say these things to push Mellius away.

The overseer sneered at him and made a sign of cutting with scissors." Stay away from her, little dog. Do your work and come back and sleep. But maybe he is right–why would she want you?"

Then he turned to Nigrumus to assign tasks for the next day and issue master's new orders, none which had any import to a humiliated Felix. By the time Mellius left, he was seething with anger.

He nursed his head with his thin hand and cursed his mother for leaving him.

But there was a new resolve.

He would make Lucia his. He would tell her how he felt. He would kiss her. He would *kill* Mellius if he tried anything.

And then he would run away with her.

# 13

## ITALY

On landing in Brundisium, a busy city with a magnificent harbor unlike anything Spartacus had seen, every unit was made to take an oath: that they would not run from the army, damage property or lay waste to the Italian countryside, and hold steadfast in their loyalty to the general. There was some rumor that many legions had even offered to surrender part of their pay to the general, for he was of want of coin to recruit more forces to take on the immense forces they were arrayed against. Spartacus had also warned many of the Maedi to be careful of Cleitus, who was now trying desperately to be in Florus' good books and may have been the cause of many leaks from the tents. No doubt that the Bessi was currying favor acting like a spy within the Auxiliary tents.

On the third day after landing, it was finally payment day. The auxiliaries had not received their pay on schedule, and it was more than forty days due. The excuse was that the men would be paid in due time for large campaigns needed time to shore coin and arrange salaries. It was only the promise and the fact that the men received their rations on time, and no man lost his mind due to hunger, that there was no rioting or mutiny. The day was warm and humid, and everywhere they looked, it was a beehive of activity as Sulla's legions prepared for the march ahead. Florus had arranged a table and had his accounting record books next to him. A representative of the treasury sat next to him. As a supervisor for the Auxiliaries, Spartacus would receive the salary first for his Century.

The arrangement was that part of the payment would be paid in sesterces, the remaining due would go into the record books for payment at specific intervals. There was merit to this, Erducos had explained, for sometimes men stole from others, and if what they carried in person was lost, the rest was at least safe with the records. Not only that, but many men were also lacking in discipline with their money–they squandered their salary on wine, women, and other vices, and then they quarreled and stole. The salary schedule inculcated some discipline. The Romans were usually very diligent in their bookkeeping and following the forms. It was an unheard-of arrangement for the tribes valued the weight of a man's word above all others.

But just before he appeared before Florus, Erducos had simply said, cryptically, "Make sure you count. Do it slowly. Do not get into a fight. We'll talk later."

Spartacus came before Florus and shielded his eyes from the sun.

"Here you go," Florus said casually, as he handed a pouch and then pointed to a row on the record books. In the days since joining the Auxiliaries, Spartacus had spent significant time with Erducos to learn the basics of Latin, including their numbering system and methods of addition and subtraction. He could understand simple phrases and respond as well.

Spartacus counted his *denarii* and then looked at the number on the record book.

*Spartacus the Maedi* and numbers next to it.

But the sum of both added to less than what he was owed–, almost a fifth less, as he counted in his head.

"What are you thinking, Spartacus? Move! I can't sit here all day and pay others," Florus said impatiently.

"Sir. This is less than what I am owed."

Florus looked irritated. Spartacus caught the expression exchanged between the centurion and the treasurer. "Well, looks like the barbarian can add. Yes, this is your real pay."

"It is a fifth less, sir," he said, keeping his voice friendly. "Will that go into another record as arrears?"

The treasurer scoffed, and Florus looked annoyed. "No, Spartacus, the rest is a fee. It is owed to the Legate. Every new auxiliary and legionary recruit pays it. You will get your full pay after a few cycles."

Spartacus had heard of these cuts before. Officers skimmed new auxiliary pay, knowing that most had little power to protest and that their loss would not lead to mutiny. It was a clever scheme.

He controlled his rising anger, knowing Erducos' warning.

"Sir, when will we–"

"Do you want me to put you on a boat and send you back, Spartacus? Or would you like me to put you up on a marketplace and sell you?" Florus said, his voice having an edge.

Cleitus, who stood like an obedient dog nearby, joined. "Others are waiting. Stop bothering the centurion!"

But with no means to complain and worried about risks of taking on the centurion, Spartacus seethed but held his tongue. His men would be unhappy, and many would not even know that they had been swindled. How many had accepted this as a fact of their life, that they were under the will and whims of Romans?

But Spartacus had to make his protest heard, for he knew that the centurion could not simply take and sell him, not here under the standards of the whole army. "I protest, centurion, and I hope you will hold to your word that our full payment will be reinstated soon."

Florus stood from his chair and leaned forward. His eyes were hard and jaws tight. "Do not think you are something great, Spartacus. Obey like a mongrel, and you will prosper, or I will make life hell for you." His breath stank of wine, but Spartacus knew not to press Florus anymore. Whether under military regulations or not, centurions still had enormous power. They could do many things that would render a soldier unfit to serve or be placed in harm's way and certain death.

"I apologize, sir. My first pay," Spartacus said, his eyes on the ground.

Florus grumbled something under his breath and gestured Spartacus to leave the line for the next man. And now, as supervisor of his Century, he would have to handle any other man who might come to him with complaints or questions or quell dissent before it spread. And that evening, three "complainers" surrounded Spartacus, accompanied by several others.

"How can they do that? I noticed that my pay was less than what was promised, but I did not want to ask," one of them said. "Should we make noise?"

Spartacus asked them to follow him. "I am aware. But this is not the time, men. We must be patient, for not all of us have been subjected to this, but only a few who are new. This ensures no one else follows us, and it will be easy for Florus to subject us to further evil if he senses discord."

"But Spartacus–"

"Listen to me! We are no longer in our tribes where our words were honored or where a few blows could settle disputes. These men do not care for us, and they are the majority. We are now in their land and under their authority. All we will receive is retribution if we seek justice when there is no desire to dispense it. Leave it to me to find the right time, for we do not know if this is Florus' scam or if his commanders are in it as well."

Another man scratched his chin. "True. If we petition the Legate and he is the one behind this, imagine what good that would do to us. I wish he were a Bessi—we could have tied him to a tree and lit him up."

"What we wish is not what it is. Realize that we have a roof on our head, no one is trying to murder us every night, we are fed and clothed. We will find ways to redress this once we make a name for our valor and strength," he said slowly, with a strong voice laden with conviction.

He did not entirely believe it. It was no secret that not many valued the auxiliaries' services, and their deaths were mourned little. But for now, their unit had to be seen as solid and dependable and get no attention from the superiors. The inability to speak their mind as they did back home was stifling. But the gods knew it was they who had resigned themselves to this fate and had no one else to blame. After all, as Florus said, they could get on a boat and leave.

But Spartacus did something they did not expect. He offered to share a portion of his pay to those who had theirs skimmed. Surprised and encouraged by this magnanimous proclamation, many others contributed to do the same, leading to most of the Century, barring a few, agreeing to spread their salaries such that all men were paid equally. What each man would lose was very little, but the act made most men loudly proclaim loyalty to Spartacus.

After convincing the men, Spartacus made his way to Florus. He had to douse any fires that may be burning in that man's mind–at least until Spartacus had a chance to address the situation in his favor at the right opportunity. Florus was preparing for the next day's plan and looked irritated. "What is it?"

Spartacus lowered his voice. "I have extinguished any questions on the pay, centurion. We understand and are ready for the march. You will hear nothing more of it from us."

Florus stared at him. "Good. You should know what is good for you, Spartacus. Keep them on a leash, fight well, and better things will happen. And Cleitus, treat him better."

Spartacus said nothing in response. He hated Florus. This weasel, a coward who did so little to inspire his Century, skimmed the men's earnings, and talked to them as if they were dogs. Auxiliaries or not, after all, did they not fight like the rest? Did they not bleed like the rest? No wonder the Legate had shifted him from the legionaries to the auxiliaries. Even during the fight with the Bessi and other skirmishes, Florus never really charged ahead. Instead, he let the men fight around him. That was not supposed to be the quality of a centurion. *Coward.*

"Yes, sir."

"General Sulla has issued orders. We march tomorrow. Now go."

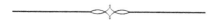

In the morning, to the sounds of trumpets and organization whistles, to the colorful cloaks of senior officers charging up and down the lines on their horses, the army assembled in a long column, four men to a row, nearly four miles long. The general had other auxiliaries in the force, and they had been placed at certain strategic positions: some surrounding the large baggage train, some guarding the rear, and some in the front. There was auxiliary cavalry too, and men from many lands augmented the army, the Celts, Germans, Thracians, Macedonians, Greeks, Syrians, Dacians, all in their colorful attires, trousers, pointed caps, and all manner of tattoos. Spartacus continued to be impressed by the Roman organization.

News trickled in that General Sulla was not in Brundisium, but instead, with two legions, had landed in a town called Tarentum, and the armies would march for a day and join about midway. He had split the force in Dyrrhachium as a precautionary measure. Purpose was in the air; an expectation of significant conflict and loot, and an unstated thrill of taking Rome.

But they had received no specific details on where they were headed next or whom they would face in battle.

Centurions ordered and exhorted their men, and Florus recited the orders drily with his raspy and weak voice devoid of much excitement. They were told these words were straight from Sulla himself. Florus spoke in Latin, and Spartacus, with Erducos' help, would try to translate the best they could at the end of the speech.

In the end, Spartacus delivered the speech in the Maedi dialect that most in his Century could understand, aware that he may have heartily butchered whatever the original message was, which he understood only in parts. "Auxiliaries! Your services will be richly rewarded. Today we march on Rome. We face fifteen hostile commanders and more than four hundred cohorts. But the gods are with us, and the omens tell us that we will be victorious! Fight with purpose, for divinity is behind us. Capture is not an option! If we must succeed, there must be minimal harm to the people and farms in Italy but know that there will be bountiful opportunity to loot!"

The promise of *loot* was his invention, knowing that it greatly excited the men. There was much cheer, and Florus looked at them quizzically. And finally, with their standard-bearer and centurion in the front, Spartacus' Century, placed near the rear, began its march toward the rendezvous with the general's army.

There was not much of a road to speak of; the rough and muddy but well-trodden path was good enough, and they learned that they would be on the main road to Rome in a few days after the army became one.

"This land, unlike home, is so dreary and drab," he said.

"I know. Dull green bushes everywhere. Nothing like the beauty of those green lofty mountains, tall forests, those sparkling streams....," Erducos concurred.

"I used to spend all my time by the river near my village. Hated swimming but washing cows and throwing rocks into the river was such fun," Spartacus reminisced.

"We have a little lake near mine with plenty of giant boulders. Some of those rocks still have imprints of my bum as I had my way with some pretty women."

"Yes, Erducos. The god of Greeks and the king of all Odomantean lovers."

They laughed together as the feet kicked up dust.

"Look at them gawking at us like we are monkeys," Erducos said, pointing to people lined up far away and staring at them. "But it must be interesting to watch an army on the move."

Nothing here was particularly inspiring, and the onlookers looked... normal. Spartacus mused how he once wondered what they might look like.

The pace of the march was relentless, and finally, late into the evening, messengers conveyed that the general's army was only a few miles away and that this division would unite with his in the morning. They rested for the night, and there was not much chatter this time, for there was certain anticipation and apprehension on what was ahead; this was no longer the realm of skirmishes and fighting untrained tribes. By now, news had spread on whom Sulla was fighting against. They would face other talented Roman commanders with formidable armies of their own.

*They mock our tribes for fighting each other, and yet they kill their own at greater numbers,* he thought.

In the morning, with a grand celebration, troops stood in attention to welcome General Sulla. The general, wearing a bright purple cloak, a gold-and-bronze corset, his plumed helmet high and proud, led his horse and accepted the salutations of every cohort. A loud trumpet, harp, and drum band accompanied the general.

When Sulla passed Spartacus' Auxiliaries, he raised the staff in his hand to acknowledge them, giving much cheer to the men. Behind Sulla was his senior officer, Quintus Caecilius Metellus, commander of the Legions, and then behind him, Legates who commanded individual Legions, including Curio, and then, behind them, Cohort Prefects. It was pomp and show, unlike anything Spartacus had seen, and conducted in a way to ensure the men were awed and stayed by his side. Spartacus was beginning to see the power of the symbolism, the flags, the standards, the eagles, the attire—all made to project an unyielding strength and unrelenting superiority.

Once the ceremonies were over, messengers arrived at each cohort to convey the general's orders. The brightly attired man with a booming voice stood on a stool and addressed them.

" You will march forthwith toward the city of Capua on the western side of Italy, capture the town, and then move north toward Rome!"

The men listened with rapt attention.

"You will have stops for restocking baggage carts, conduct discreet forage missions, and always be prepared for conflict. The great and honorable commanders Marcus Licinius Crassus and Pompeius Magnus are now aligned with General Sulla, and the gods are with us!"

Spartacus did not know who they were, but it was never a bad thing that more commanders were coming to Sulla's aid.

"The general asks for your loyalty and promises you riches! Now, prepare to march!"

While the march toward Capua was generally uneventful, Florus' distrust of and his conduct toward Spartacus had worsened. He berated Spartacus for minor transgressions and imposed pay penalties for perceived insubordination, such as *not standing in time for the centurion's presence or not using the correct titles for the senior officers* and so on for matters that were quickly addressed only by a few words. But Spartacus hoped that the impending battle might change the equations and perhaps give them a new commander.

Keeping the men's bellies full was done admirably. Rations, by way of wheat or barley, vinegar, olive, coarse bread, were dispensed once a day. The remarkable salt was available in limited quantity for purchase, and since they all loved it in their meals, the units pooled their money to obtain it in small amounts for special occasions. Individual cooking units, usually made of seven to nine men, decided how to cook their meals. But the men were so far not wanting for portions, and while minor scuffles broke out for what to prepare and how much to use what, there was good camaraderie within the century. Spartacus' stature grew with each passing day that was peaceful. His job was to divide the century into working units, manage breaks and operational duties, settle minor disputes, and ensure that the centurion was only called in for matters that required officer intervention, which usually went poorly for the recipient. His only challenge within the century was the discord sowed by Cleitus and his gang of men favored by Florus.

*This is not a terrible life,* Spartacus sometimes thought. Perhaps he had made the proper judgment to join this army and why men of all nations fought for the Romans. They were well taken care of so long as they fell in line with the orders.

On the sixth day, somewhere around noon, the army merged into the main road to Capua. This wider path was along the river Volturnus which meandered from somewhere further north. The road was deserted with no onlookers or merchants, indicating impending conflict. Further ahead, the road entered a valley with a mountain to the left, which messengers called the Tifata, and the river and other mountains to the right. The army had to cluster and increase in density as it came to the narrow section between the mountains, hemmed on one side by Tifata and the river on the other. At that time, scouts came charging down the line, "Prepare! Prepare for orders!"

Suddenly there was much clamor–an impending conflict? Whistles, telling the men to stop immediately, rented the air. Then came the loud trumpets and runners conveying battle orders. "The army of Consul Norbanus is moving to block the road to Capua! Prepare to assemble in battle order when issued!"

Spartacus' heartbeat quickened. *Finally!* He had become bored of camping and marches and setting up tents and pulling apart quarreling men. His gods had sent him to this world to be a warrior, to show his skill on the ground, against bold men, and to bring glory to his kind. And now, he would do it in a spectacular battle. He had often heard that there were often *days* of preparation for large battles. Setting up camp near the battle position, sometimes waiting for hours in a line only for the fight to be called off, and finally, the eventful day. And yet here, with almost no warning, they were being called to order.

"Everyone, move faster! Run! Assemble into lines now!" an officer on the cavalry screamed. Like a frenetic snake, the entire army switched to a trot until it passed the two hills on either side and came to an open field. He could not see much ahead of him except the heads and implements of the men, but things became more apparent once the legions began to spread.

"Auxiliary infantry, move! Run ahead to left flank!"

With his entire body suddenly energized, Spartacus ran just behind Florus as his Century split to the left and rushed to the front. Here, the river fell away from them, curving to the right, leaving a broader open space with the mountain Tifata behind them. In the wide area ahead was the Consul's army, their red-painted *scutum* all lined up, bronze helmets glinting in the sunlight, and cavalry waiting on either flank. It was a "true" battle formation as Spartacus had learned.

There was barely any time as the Legions poured from behind, squeezed into the land not wide enough for the traditional three-line formation. General Sulla passed orders for an overlapping stack. Auxiliaries on each end, along with a few cohorts, overlapped with the cohorts lined up behind. Spartacus was focused on the front, with his Century positioned to be among the first to clash with the enemy once they charged. There was palpable nervousness in the air. Even without the messengers conveying the size of the enemy, it was evident that Norbanus' army was much larger, perhaps as much as three Legions advantage over Sulla's. Would the gifted general find ways to defeat Norbanus? They would know very soon.

Even in this heat, a different kind of warmth enveloped him.

How would this all—

Loud cavalry whistles filled the air.

*Begin!*

His breath quickened as the cavalry on either end charged. There was barely any time for the men to settle and ready the stance, and then there it was—the battle trumpet! That loud, ear-splitting, but hair-raising sound calling for blood.

*Pooommmmmm. Pom. Pom. Pom.*

The standard-bearers began to trot. The centurions raised their gladius, blew their whistles loudly, and shouted, "March!"

With his shield in the front, *pilum* in hand, and his gladius firmly attached to his belt, Spartacus exhorted his men in Maedi. "Show the Romans what you are made of! Draw their blood for *Zibelthiurdos* and for the pleasure of the goddess *Kotys!*"

The men all bayed and shouted but knew better than to break into a wild tribal charge knowing the stringent discipline required in a Century march. Spartacus was proud of how far they had come to inculcate military discipline. The far ends of the army were now clouded in dust from the cavalry charge. Still, Spartacus, who was positioned such that he had a clear view of Sulla's army moving to his right, just behind, had to admit that the sight was thrilling—the flags, the legion standards, the eagles, the beautiful uniforms of senior officers and centurions, all added to a heady sensation of glory.

*Trot! Trot! Trot!*

The enemy was now more apparent, and their formation was remarkably similar. *The Romans have turned this into a method,* Spartacus thought. *Perhaps that is what makes them so successful against others.*

As the enemy came closer, Spartacus knew from the speeches what would come next. An increase in pace as the lines neared, a volley of *pilums* at the enemy even as they protected themselves as best they could from the return, and then it would be *scutum* vs. *scutum, gladius* vs *gladius,* push-and-shove, thrust-stab-and-maneuver until somebody's line broke, or the flank crashed.

It could take hours.

*Phreeeeee! Phreeee!* Whistles!

*Run! Attack!*

His muscles tightening, heart-pounding, and his vision now narrowed as they hunched and readied to throw the javelins while under the protection of their *scutum,* Spartacus knew that this one would be bloody when the Auxiliary came face-to-face with the enemy Legionary Century, a better trained, better equipped, and better rested enemy.

Everything was a swirl of cacophony and exhaustion. Even as he thrust, hacked, beat, pummeled, and evaded, Spartacus shouted and encouraged his men.

"Bunch closer! Fight!"

"Come back! do not go too deep!"

"Around the centurion, men!"

But Florus was barely to be seen. He was *supposed* to fight from the front! Lead them! And yet, Florus, once again, had slunk away somewhere behind them, within the protection of multiple units. The fight had gone out of the man, and all he cared about was skimming Auxiliary pay and relaxing in his tent as his men died. The bastard. But who cared?

"Lie there! Someone will take you to safety. May Kotys watch over you," he said to a badly wounded man who lay groaning on the muddy ground, half his arm hacked away and dangling uselessly, and a deep gash on his side. He would not live.

Twice Spartacus escaped narrow death as a blade sliced his thigh, and one missed his belly. He had learned quickly in battle how to hold the *scutum* effectively and not raise it too high, exposing his legs for a thrust or too low, leaving his face open for a stab. His shoulders, chest, neck, knees all hurt from the running, turning, crouching, even as the two armies pushed, shoved, and fought. It seemed it would go on forever, with no whistles or retreat or victory, no commands asking them to change maneuver, and it was all just screams, moans, strange sounds of thudding, blood pumping out of severed heads and hands, men wailing or shouting, all of it blinding the senses. Besides, similar uniforms made it harder and harder to distinguish friend from foe. While Sulla's legions had a distinct ribbon on their hands, many had lost it, or it was coated in blood and body matter, and thus they had to resort to the watchword while worrying if they would be murdered.

Spartacus learned that the legionary was a remarkably dangerous foe, and his skill almost ended Spartacus' life more than once. Only the Thracian's larger size, greater strength, and mindful application of his training techniques saved him. He killed four legionaries and wounded a few others. But how long could this last? His chest burned, his arms became weaker, and it felt like the dense enemy lines were not breaking. Many of his men were dead, having been the first to be exposed to attacks and lacking experience in this kind of battle.

As dust rose all around them and the metallic clash became overwhelming, there was the loud sound of hoofs and then ear-piercing whistles and trumpets that cut through the medley.

*Pfffommmmmmm. Pommmmmmmmm! Pommmmmmmm!"*

*Victory trumpets!*

Out of nowhere, a senior officer charged through the lines shouting, "Stand your ground! Norbanus is retreating!"

And just as suddenly, the tide turned, for the enemy stopped pushing forward and instead turned and began to run. Some pursued them, but the whistles and cavalry commanders forced the infantry to halt the advance.

"Everyone, stop! Do not pursue!" The orders came loud and clear through a multitude of methods, and the tired men, close to collapsing, were all too glad as most of them dropped their weapons and fell to the ground in relief.

Spartacus cared not a bit for dust settling on his face or that a head, its severed neck still wet from the blood that had drained out, was near his shoulder as he tried to let his thundering heart slow down. His tongue was dry and sticking to his throat, but he hoped the water carriers would be around soon.

*How many of his men were dead?*

The clearing of battlegrounds took hours–and once again, the men were expected to get up and conduct labor.

Heaping the dead for funerals.

Taking injured men to physicians who would decide whether to administer a merciful death, treatment, or discharge.

Stripping the dead was another task–every gladius, knife, corset, scutum, cloak, shoe, intact *pilum*, was valuable. They had to remove the items, take them to holding stations, wait for accountants to inventory them, and find more. Men casually pilfered as much as they could, but no one chastised them for it, for it was a tacit agreement that keeping some of the loot was a means of reward. Spartacus kept two gladii', a golden brooch, two gold rings, a silver pendant, and a delicate bronze corset. He was pleased with his haul.

Once the chaos settled, news finally trickled in. Norbanus' much larger force had buckled under the cavalry attack, and two of Sulla's legions had punched through the center. Even the Auxiliaries had done an exemplary job holding their ground and had sustained considerable losses. Norbanus had lost over seven thousand men, and Sulla, they said, less than a few hundred. But lies were the norm, and Spartacus knew that the truth lay somewhere between. The enemy's loss was always exaggerated, and one's own consistently underestimated. The Maedi did it fighting the other tribes and the Romans did it fighting their battles.

It was unclear why the general had not turned the enemy's rout into a massacre, but those were considerations far beyond Spartacus' understanding. Perhaps the general despaired of killing many his countrymen or feared the exhaustion of his smaller force in pursuit, only to run into another army and be slaughtered. What if Norbanus had large reserves or any other legions were on the way?

The army settled in for the night, and Spartacus, nursing his various bruises and cuts to ensure they did not flare into something worse, received an order to present himself to Florus. As he limped across the nightly landscape now lit in various spots by funeral pyres of men dead and soon to be forgotten, he wondered what the centurion wanted. The Auxiliaries had been hit hard–his Century had lost thirty-five of the eighty men, an exceedingly high proportion compared to many other units. First to clash, poorly protected, they knew that they were expendable and often used to dull the impact on the legionaries.

But they had fought hard and well. Would there be a commendation? It was not uncommon for senior officers to hand out various recognition and rewards after a victorious battle. This was spectacular by all accounts, beating the larger "home" army.

Florus sat on a worn-out little cloth cushion inside his hastily constructed tent. Two soldiers from a different unit waited nearby.

This was no commendation welcome.

"You asked for me, sir?"

Florus looked tired, but his face curled up in a snarl. "It appears the barbarian supervisor of my Century lacks the discipline to fight in a real Roman battle but enjoys stealing afterward."

# 14

## LUCANIA

———◇———

Felix sat on a grassy mound overlooking the estate's olive grove. This was one of his duties, to keep an eye out for wolves or foxes invading the estate and injuring the women who toiled by the rows of trees. He preferred this to the back-breaking work involving digging trenches or the danger and misery of taking livestock for forage.

He could sit and dream.

His fever had long gone, and he had regained his strength. He also checked his lip several times a day to see if there was sufficient hair there, stung by Nigrumus comments weeks ago. Did Lucia like a man without a mustache or beard?

Mellius' threats had only made Felix bolder. Who did that miserable son of a whore think he was? Lucia's standing in the household made it harder for Mellius to touch her, and if Felix managed to create a stronger bond with the girl, that might afford him some safety too. Lucia was not only whom he desired, but her position also had many other benefits.

But he was not interested in the paltry benefits of living this hell. Chained like a dog every night, afraid of painful punishments for minor mistakes, the constant stress of the overseer or the master, the pervasive threat of being murdered by bandits and estate gangs, this was no way to live. The freedmen in the estate and the master and his wife all lived in so much comfort! They slept in their room. They ate all sorts of food. They went wherever they wanted. They were not shackled when they were not working.

He had heard that there were big towns where most people were free!

So why could he not be like that?

Why not run with the girl who filled his dreams? No one would find them in these forests and ravines. Maybe when they get to the sea, they could build a boat and sail away to some beautiful lands with no masters, where fruits and sheep were plentiful. He could feed her and himself with ease. She knew how to cook and serve. They could live without fear. Felix wondered what life was *without* fear, for he had never known a day without it.

Maybe *he* could be the *Dominus* and she the *Domina*, but they would be kind to *their* slaves! They would not shackle them at night and beat them only with sound reason!

Could it even be possible that there was a place without slaves? That seemed extraordinary–no impossible–for he was always told, and believed so, that the way the world is that some are masters, and some are slaves. That was ordained, and it was up to the men in these stations to move up from that of wretched servitude to something higher, and if not, they *deserved* their life. Such was the order the gods imposed on people. But gods never said anything about slaves having to always be slaves.

At some point, Lucia came out from the large, red-roofed house and walked toward a group of women. His heart quickened.

He waited for her to finish whatever she was speaking with the women. She radiated in her simple stola designed for modesty, and her station in the household even afforded her a little ornament on an ear.

*I hope she sees me!*

And she did.

Her face lit up with a smile.

A smile so beautiful!

He grinned ear-to-ear as she gave the smallest of waves.

Felix decided right then that he would seek counsel from Nigrumus, a wise man who knew much about the world here in Italy and outside. After all, Nigrumus came from a very faraway land, traveled through many countries, spent time as a free man before being made a slave, had seen other masters–Nigrumus could impart him much knowledge in support of his plan.

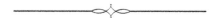

"So, there are lands where Romans do not have authority?"

Nigrumus smiled. "Yes, I have heard of them. Lands south of where I came from have no Romans. Egypt has slaves, but they live much better lives. Parthia, the land I told you of, has slaves, but they are better treated than here. And then, far away, there is a land called India, and we know nothing if they have slaves or how they are treated. Many other great nations have been free, but perhaps now they are under Roman dominion. But one must go far to escape Romans. Why do you ask? You have never been all that interested."

Felix pretended to be nonchalant. "As I grow older, I am more curious. All I see is this estate and lands nearby. I want to know how the world is, far beyond."

"It is a beautiful world but very dangerous too. The sea is magnificent–you cannot see land in any direction for days! But it is very frightening... the storms create waves," Nigrumus said, standing and raising his hand, "this high. And then there are a great many beasts beneath the water that can consume entire boats!"

Felix was astonished. "Can one not jump and wade in the water or swim away?"

Nigrumus laughed. "Oh, you innocent boy. The sea is so deep that a thousand men can stand on each other's shoulders, and they would still sink. Gods and demons dwell in those deep dark waters, for it is beyond a man's realm. And it is so vast that you will tire and sink well before you even make a few strides."

Felix's hopes of building a boat and crossing the sea were somewhat dampened.

"Then there are places called deserts. There is no water. Only dust and sand, for as far as you can see, but magnificent in their hostile beauty."

Felix was enjoying this conversation. He was such a fool never to have engaged with Nigrumus like this before. The old black rock knew so much!

"What about where I came from, Nigrumus? What do you know? Surely my mother said something?"

Nigrumus walked behind a large cow and vigorously slapped its hindquarters, yelling *pflap*, *hop*, forcing it to move to a new pasture. Felix kept pace, avoiding thorns and sharp stones on the ground, for his footwear had long shredded, and Mellius was unwilling to ask the master for replacements. Nigrumus had procured a few cloth strips that Felix tied around his foot as protection.

"She came from somewhere east, but one must either cross the seas and travel north on the sight of land or take a much longer and dangerous route through the north of Italy. They say the land is full of fierce warriors and tribes, always warring with each other. There are many lands to the north and east, Gaul, Germania, Thracia, Dacia, Macedonia, Greece; all these names I have heard over the years."

"So I have the heart of a warrior!"

Nigrumus laughed. "You are a resourceful, stubborn boy. Whether you have the heart of a warrior is yet to be tested. The slim legs and feet do not show a warrior yet!"

"I will beat you," he said, and Nigrumus chuckled.

"What about my mother's land? Is it like Italy?"

"I have not seen it, boy. But your mother said it was full of mountains, forests, and lakes."

"Certainly more beautiful than here," Felix offered as he winced from a thorny bush brushing to his ankle. He wiped the tiny sliver of blood and thanked himself that this was not another type of bush with white sap. If that fluid touched broken skin, it caused much itching and pain, and eventually, small boils with pus appeared, causing much misery.

"Why do slaves not dare to run away, Nigrumus?" he finally asked, feeling bold, with no one near earshot.

Nigrumus turned to him. But his eyes were hard this time, and there was no smile. "Think carefully what you are thinking, boy."

Felix was surprised that Nigrumus guessed his intentions so easily. "I am only asking."

The older slave stopped and walked toward Felix. "I hope you are only quenching your thirst for information so that I will indulge you. Slaves do not run away because most do not know where to go. They are usually easily caught if they get out, for they have no money. Their attire and manner give them away, and most, like me, are branded on their forehead, ankle, or back and easily identified. When caught, they are returned to their master to endure worse punishment."

"What if—"

"Let me finish, boy. Most slaves have a roof over their head, are fed daily, clothed in most cases, and are allowed to have wives, husbands, and children, and not every master is cruel. So why would a slave run away, only to lose it all, still get caught, and then have the skin thrashed off their back? And even if they escaped, most would only go back to their miserable lives, begging on streets and nowhere to sleep."

The reality was settling in. And yet he had heard that some *had* done it successfully—those with hearts of *warriors*.

Nigrumus gripped Felix's arm. The older man had the strength of a bull. "And do not ask me if some slaves kill their masters. There are murmurs that a new law requires that if a slave murders their master, then *all* slaves in the household will be crucified. Did you hear that, boy, everyone will be crucified–have you ever seen one on a cross?"

Felix felt a chill up his spine as Nigrumus coal-eyes bore into him. "I never asked that, Nigrumus, and I never thought of it!"

"Good. I just wanted to make sure. What are you thinking, you fool, that you would run away with Lucia to a bountiful land?"

*How did he guess?*

Felix put a hand around a cow's neck and gently pulled it away from where it was headed. The cow *mooed* once, swatted him with its tail, and then continued to graze happily.

"I think I must run before Mellius kills me. You know that he will do it, sometime or the other," he said, with finality in his voice. Did Nigrumus not see the situation for what it was?

Nigrumus said nothing. He rubbed his head and then patted Felix with his calloused hand.

"Why am I—we— treated so harshly? Look at the herder boy from the green roof estate. He looks healthy with scarcely a scar on his back. I spoke to him some time ago, and he says his master feeds him well and the overseer is kind."

"Those are rare, boy. Rare," Nigrumus said. It was true that some masters realized that it took little to keep the slaves comfortable but yielded much in loyalty and quality of work, but the cruel nature of some men—including their master—overruled all that.

Over the next few days, Felix incessantly questioned Nigrumus on all things unrelated to their life on the estate. His questions inevitably ended with ideas on how they might run away and live comfortably, no matter how much Nigrumus discouraged the thought—but then Nigrumus would grudgingly admit that Mellius' cruelty combined with their interest in Lucia unquestionably put Felix at risk. The boy might be in grave danger sooner or later.

And so, on another hot day, after another tiring grazing session, Felix returned to his favorite topic. "You know that Mellius will kill me. And our master is a bastard who wishes to see us suffer and does little to improve our lot. It surely looks like some of those boys from Licinius' estate are well fed. They do not even have scars on their back! I wish we could kill the master, and then Mellius would have no power! But of course, I do not want us all to be crucified."

Nigrumus shook his head and looked out to the distant hills. He sighed loudly and scratched his chin. With his curled hair, thick nose, white-speckled beard, Nigrumus looked like a basalt Zeus, the god of the Greeks. He was such a wonderful man, so kind, and yet the gods had delivered him to the Romans as a slave. Sometimes the wishes of gods made little sense.

"I said nothing about anyone getting crucified if a slave overseer gets killed," he finally said.

# 15

## CAPUA

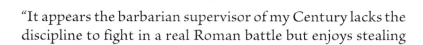

"It appears the barbarian supervisor of my Century lacks the discipline to fight in a real Roman battle but enjoys stealing afterward."

*What?*

Spartacus was dumbfounded.

"Our unit has fought ferociously and honorably, at the front, centurion!"

Florus stood up slowly. "That is not what I saw. I saw many wild-haired barbarians flailing about instead of standing low and pushing the enemy line. I saw men with no discipline and no sense—"

"We stood and pushed before—"

"Be quiet! Keep your mouth shut when your commanding officer speaks to you, dirty scoundrel. What you saw as bravery, we laugh at. What use is bravery if it is not applied with intelligence? But then you are no better than monkeys, and it is my misfortune that I must report high losses of useless men dead because you do not know how to control them!"

Spartacus knew that the Auxiliaries had fought hard and well and that the deaths were a result of their exposure and lack of armor. Florus was doing this out of spite due to their conflict over salaries and other perceived grievances about insubordination. What was he trying to do?

"I disagree with great respect, sir. Our losses are because we bore the brunt of the first attack, and as you know, we are not protected as well as the legionaries."

"That is because you are auxiliaries and not Romans! It is your responsibility to buy for your protection!"

Spartacus gritted his teeth and clenched his fist. "But we were never paid until recently, and then we were underpaid, sir," he said, his jaw tight, controlling his mounting anger.

Florus glared at him. "You bring up pay again. I will have you taken out and whipped to death. You stole from the dead, I know. I saw you barbarians making off like thieves. That is why I called you. Collect all items not accounted for and have them reported to me. We will then take them to the accountant and surrender them. We need auxiliaries, not thieves."

"We are allowed some loot like everyone else, sir, regulations!" Spartacus bristled, keeping his voice under control but knowing what Florus was doing—punishing them all unfairly. But more importantly, Florus hoped to take a share of their spoils but was angry that Spartacus showed no inclination to play the same dirty game.

The centurion had to balance his career and the requirement that his unit demonstrates its worth, requiring a strong leader who could manage men of a different type. Then he would have to find ways to enrich himself. Spartacus had delivered on the first but had made the second one difficult.

"The loot is for legionaries, not for auxiliaries. You dogs should go last when others have finished. This is my order, Spartacus. Surrender the items or have you and two others tied to a pole and enjoy as your muscles are ripped off your bodies. Do you understand?"

Tears of rage sprung in Spartacus' eyes. His temple pounded, and his chest beat like a drum. The utter *unfairness* of the man after his Century had fought so hard and long, without giving ground to better armed and protected enemy, and taking what belonged to them. And yet the hopelessness of fighting this injustice, with no one to go to!

What could he say to his men? How would he keep his honor and face if he had to tell them that they not only had to put up with pay losses but that they could not keep the loot either?

"Now, now, Florus, do not be so harsh on them," came a voice suddenly from behind.

"Sir!" Florus scrambled to attention, and Spartacus turned to see the Legate Curio, still in his uniform.

"Sir!" He saluted.

Curio nodded and walked into the tent. "I overheard some of it, Florus. You are an experienced centurion, but your men are new to this. Your bar is high. Give it some time!"

"Sir!"

"The auxiliaries fought well. I even saw you," he said, turning toward Spartacus, "shouting encouragement to your tired men. Your centurion is a harsh man, but it is he who has forged you."

*He forged nothing. The coward hid among the men, sir.*

"I only wish to keep them alive and disciplined, sir. Perhaps my threats were a little harsh," Florus said, and Spartacus knew the dripping dishonesty in that humility.

"Of course. Of course. Anyway, I was making rounds to make sure my cohorts were battle-ready, for we have many more ahead of us before we are at Rome. Is everything else well? Are the men getting paid?"

"They are, sir. Everything is as planned."

The Legate turned to Spartacus. "Surely I have heard your name before. Marcus?"

"Spartacus, sir."

"Ah, yes. Spartacus the Thracian. I have heard about your skills as a trainer. Keep up the good work."

"Yes, sir!"

Spartacus wondered if he could request a hearing, as the Legate seemed like a reasonable man. But one never knew with Romans.

"We siege Capua next," Curio continued. "And then we march on Rome. I want every alive man under you fit to fight. Do not thrash anyone to death yet. We need them all."

"Yes, sir."

"And let them keep the loot. I'm sure these rewards will keep the men enthusiastic. Surely you were only threatening them," he said, laughing.

Florus forced a smile. "Of course, sir! The men get to keep what they find, otherwise who would keep fighting! I just had to remind them to stay disciplined and obey orders."

"Indeed. Well, Florus, I must meet others now. Spartacus, tell your men their bravery is recognized. And follow Florus' commands to avoid questions on insubordination. The general is demanding and quite unforgiving of troublemakers."

"Yes, sir!" Spartacus saluted the commander, who nodded and then walked out to the darkness.

*Who was the troublemaker?*

Florus waited until Curio was out of earshot. And then, when he turned to Spartacus, his voice was cold. "Well, it seems you gained some reprieve. Do not think this is over."

"No, Florus, it is not," Spartacus said, boldly, knowing now that Florus, in his delicate situation still being assigned to the Auxiliary, could not afford to do anything that would damage the fight-worthiness of the unit and bring his reputation into question.

Florus glared. "Your insolence will find its way to your end, Spartacus. It's just a matter of time."

He did not answer the man for no good came of a continued argument. Instead, he saluted and turned, ignoring Florus' curses.

# 16

## LUCANIA

———◇———

"I said nothing about anyone getting crucified if a slave overseer gets killed," Nigrumus finally said. Felix's heart skipped several beats.

"Are you saying we will kill Mellius?" He whispered as if he were afraid the wind would carry these dangerous words and convey them to the Estate.

Nigrumus did not look at him. But the wizened man sighed. "I have lived a slave so long, boy, that I have forgotten what it means to dream of freedom. I have forgotten what it means to have a woman's touch. I have forgotten what it means to live as one's own and not under another man's foot. And my name. I have even forgotten my name! It was certainly not the *black one* as the master called me, for my mother surely sang to me by something else."

Felix walked beside the man he almost treated as a father and gently held his arm. The cows furiously twirled their tails to drive away from the pervasive flies.

"Athena, this side! Athena," Felix yelled at one of his favorite cows. Athena was a feisty beast who did what she wanted because she produced more milk than anyone else. And it was Felix's duty to ensure she was well fed, cared for, washed, protected. He slapped her back and caressed her neck. *Pffap, hopppp, bappp*, he enticed her to return.

She complied without much protest and went back to her favorite pastime–grazing.

He always thought that the animals in the master's stable had more rights and better care than the slaves. Felix returned to Nigrumus once the cattle were where they needed to be.

Nigrumus, who was watching and waiting, continued. "Mellius has been speaking of you in increasingly harsh tones. It has gotten into his head that you will defile Lucia, thereby getting the master to cast aspersions on his control or be upset that the girl could not be used for his pleasures, which it appears he has not taken so far."

Felix could barely *hear* those words without feeling despondent and upset. There was nothing anyone could do should the master decide to have her, for she was his property. But for Felix? She was his life. How he longed to see her, how much he enjoyed the eye contact, the smiles, and the electrifying sensation of even a tiny touch and gesture and small talk when they crossed paths. He was sure she liked him, though many other young slaves coveted her. The stifling atmosphere made it impossible to further their "relation."

"He will injure me grievously or kill me," he said fearfully. Already, a few days ago, Mellius had stripped him naked and whipped him with his dreaded shredded-leather strip for coming back to the estate too late, berating him for the indiscipline, and accusing him of trying to run away. And he did that deliberately in front of the estate's female slaves. The welts on his back had burned and taken days to heal, but the humiliation burned greater.

"Maybe it is time."

"How should we kill him? Should we make him come with us, making up some story, and then throw him in the ravine?"

Nigrumus ruffled his hair. "Oh, boy. If only it were that simple. Even the hint of our involvement is enough to put us in severe trouble, and besides, Mellius is clever enough to walk with his two attendants."

The overseer's henchmen conveyed and enforced orders given to many slaves in the household. And knowing his reputation, Mellius always suspected foul play and rarely went around alone.

"Can we convince his attendants?"

"You are full of dreams and yet naive. No, imagine the risk of them even getting a hint. It must be the right time and place. I will finally put that diseased dog to the ground."

"We will, together!" Felix declared.

"No," Nigrumus said with a definite tone. "Unless something goes wrong and we both die. You have lit a fire within me, boy. I see your dreams in my eyes—it is as if I live my younger days through you. This is for me to do, and only I shall do it."

"But—"

"No. If you need my help, you shall speak no more of this. Once Mellius is out of the way, let us see if the master makes me the overseer or someone else kinder, and then we shall find ways for you to find your destiny."

Felix was ecstatic. "Thank you, Nigrumus! The gods certainly smile upon you!"

"You are a fool, boy, but perhaps better to live and die a fool than a slave."

Felix grinned. His mind was conjuring various possibilities already, confidently ignoring all the dangers and risks and uncertainties of such an undertaking. "I will help you in any way I can!"

Nigrumus gripped his arm so powerfully that Felix winced. "No! We shall no longer speak of this. Be quiet, say nothing to anyone."

"Will you come with us? All three of us can run away!"

Nigrumus laughed. "Look at me, boy. How far do you think I can travel without being apprehended? See this," he said, showing the distinct brand on his back, burned by slave traders, "The first thing anyone will ask is for my master's permission or freedman declaration."

Felix knew that Nigrumus had little realistic chance of getting anywhere. But when the time arrived, surely they would find a way to take him with them.

"What if Lucia has no desire for you, boy?" Nigrumus asked. Strangely, he had never asked this before, and Felix had dreaded this question. His flights of fantasy were based on nothing overt from her. Perhaps her heart was already given to someone else, or the master had already lined up a suitor for her, which was very likely. Slaves could not legally marry, but the masters found companions for them so they could breed and produce children who could be slaves. There were many young men in the household, including some who did many duties inside the estate. Even better for the master if she produced many children, some like her, whom he could employ or sell when they came of age. He was despondent at the thought.

But he knew what he wanted to do. "Then I shall go myself, Nigrumus. And take you with me if you are willing."

Finally, Nigrumus warned him to be quiet again and wait until something happened. Felix knew that the wise black rock would be able to do what he resolved to. Many slaves in the barracks loved Nigrumus, and surely they would protect him.

And then Felix returned to the content Athena, caressing her forehead, and scratching it. He kissed her fat jowl and imagined a life where he and Lucia owned a farm, many beautiful cows, some sheep, a few olive trees, a few slaves whom they would be kind to. On his way back to the Estate, there was a spring in his step, dreaming of all the beautiful possibilities of life.

# 17

## TOWARDS ROME

—◇—

Spartacus' journey north toward Rome was both terrifying and thrilling. While he never always learned what was happening, the tidbit of information that came to him was always interesting. It appears that the omens always favored the general. Soon after the siege of Capua, a busy town that was mainly left unmolested after Sulla's victory, the army headed north. Spartacus noticed how the general kept the populace subdued yet sympathetic to his side–for the soldiers were under strict and unforgiving orders not to harm civilians or destroy property. But these orders had come after much harm had been inflicted upon numerous smaller towns and cities on the way to Capua, causing much grievance and opposition to Sulla's cause. Sometime later, at Fidentia, one of Sulla's commanders, Marcus Lucullus, confronted a much larger enemy force. And when they wondered whether to give battle, it seems a gentle breeze from the plains of a meadow showered flowers on the army, thus emboldening them with this favorable omen. And then, Lucullus attacked and defeated the enemy, slaying more than eighteen thousand men. Such stories further imbued strength and solidarity to Sulla's forces, including Spartacus' auxiliary, which now took much pride in being part of the general's army.

But the journey to Rome was fraught with danger and conflict, but the general was a sly fox and a lion. First, Sulla pretended to negotiate with Scipio, the new Consul but enticed twenty of Scipio's cohorts to defect by enticement, bribery, and coercion. And with this defection also came several auxiliaries. However, they were not assigned to the Thracian units because they were rambunctious Gauls and Germans who spoke none of the Thracian languages and tended to conflict and quarrel. Through activities like this and more, commanders saw the wisdom on the side of being on the general's side, and his army grew, now, to about nine legions even after the losses during the march.

Then, Marius the Younger, the son of a powerful man named Marius, once Consul and a talented general himself, confronted Sulla's army near a town called Signia, a place on the hilly ground surrounded by low mountains. It was said that Marius, with his eighty-five cohorts, challenged Sulla with his eighty. The most exhausting and terrible battle of all that Spartacus had fought was enormously complicated by the incessant rains. The soldiers' feet slid in the mud, their eyes clouded by the torrent, the hands slippery and slick with water, all significantly adding to the misery. Water streamed down the upper slopes of the mountains nearby and caused them to fall often and bruise themselves on the stone-filled muddy earth.

After two hours of this, the army became so weary that groups of soldiers simply receded and lay down, wet in the mud, with no danger of the enemy coming upon them, for they too took respite. And when whistles rented the air suggesting the two armies rest, perhaps on account of entreaties to the generals, and the men stopped, Marius attacked again after making a pretense of receding. This enraged Sulla's soldiers, who took great offense to the betrayal of honor, and Spartacus, himself having killed seven men by then, renewed his effort with great vigor and demonstrated valor to all his men. "No rain or mud stops a Thracian, men! What little drops are these compared to the stones back home? What mud is this compared to the thick soup we waded as children?" he shouted, causing much cheer to his weary men. Florus was missing in the front, as usual.

"Get behind me! Men!"

"No, there, Stamos, here! May Zibelthiurdos infuse you with rage!"

"Group, men! Together! Together! Idiot, put your shield up, now, now, now!"

"May the blade of Kotys descend upon them like a bolt from the heavens!"

*Fight, men, fight! Let glory coat your skin more than this rain can ever drench you. Come!*

*I hate this sticky mud.*

His voice was hoarse, and his shoulders burned. But he led them, cajoled them, exhorted, and threatened them, all while Florus used the mayhem and the showers to hide somewhere else. Finally, by the time a sliver of light broke through the clouds, bleeding from his arms and a cut on his back, Spartacus collapsed as the trumpets of victory sounded. Letting the drizzle cool his heaving body as he lay on the mud, Spartacus thanked Zibelthiurdos and Kotys for another victory and now firmly believed that the gods were sitting on the shoulders of General Sulla, for what man could overcome so many adversities and still win against such odds? It also said something to Spartacus, who previously believed that numerical superiority was always the determining factor—yet here, often outnumbered and in hostile situations, the genius of Sulla and the fierce loyalty of his men had snatched victory from the grip of defeat.

But how many more battles would he have to fight?

*When will this end?*

He closed his eyes to the soothing chatter of the light rain, now picking up again. The calm wind blew from the higher ground caressing his face like the whispery touch of a beautiful woman. He fell asleep, only to be woken up by yelling officers telling them to report to camp building duty. They would now dig trenches in this muddy mess, build a hasty rampart, and set up tents for the night.

The following day, his bones hurting and flesh still raw from the blows and travails of the previous night, the auxiliaries were put to the task, amongst others, to collect the dead still lying in the mud; their blood has drained out.

The earth and everything around was wet and cold, and the clouds threatened another storm, so a traditional funeral and pyre were impractical. And thus, Sulla ordered that the men be heaped along the road, their own and foe as well, and priests would make prayers on their behalf. Messengers conveyed that Marius had lost twenty thousand men and Sulla two hundred, but Spartacus knew that to be nonsense, for he had seen so many of their own army dead. The grim task would take hours as the dead piles lined the road as far as one could see, left there, stripped of their belongings, and forgotten. They would soon rot, and dogs and animals would feast on the dead flesh and bones. Some bodies, having their guts ripped out by the opponent's blades or javelins or by roaming dogs, had already begun to smell, and the stench pervaded the air.

Spartacus led a gang of twenty auxiliaries and his task was to clear a section of the bodies and pile them to the side. Spartacus resented this work. As much as he had lived the life of an auxiliary under Roman command, there were some activities that he found it exceedingly difficult to accept as appropriate for his station.

"You and you, pull those here and pile up," he ordered the men, as he stood back and avoided dragging the dead.

"Will you not lend a hand, Spartacus?" one of the men asked.

"Shut up and follow the orders. I am your supervisor and did not grow to be a corpse-puller," he shouted at him. And then he raised his hand on another who looked to him to help drag a large, bloated body.

"Move, men! Clear the space!"

He pushed them hard, and at one point Erducos came to say something, but he sent him away, saying now was not the time. The grim task took hours as he directed the gang close to exhaustion and collapse, but they finally had their piles.

This time, when Spartacus pulled rings off swelling fingers and kept a couple for himself, Florus made no mention of it, for the man was nowhere to be seen. Spartacus' men, now dwindling in numbers on account of the battle, were themselves pleased with their loot, which the general himself sanctioned. There was also news that Sulla had captured eight thousand soldiers, who, no doubt, would readily join the general's forces. Most of the legionaries cared little whom they fought for, as long as that leader would be the winner and bring them riches.

The army needed to move camp before the corpses rotted, for they all knew that sickness followed putrid, noisome, and bloated bodies, knowing that the evil in men was released on their deaths, bubbling through the swellings, and then entered others. Tired and close to collapse, Spartacus and his men were finally allowed to rest after the army moved a few miles north from the road of the dead.

He and Erducos sat on a flat rock. "I hate this! I am the son of a chief. Blessed by Zibelthiurdos. And here I am, piling up the dead. Who likes touching cold corpses whose lifeless eyes look at the ghosts beyond? Why do they make us, even auxiliary supervisors, do this work when they can put to work the men beneath us?"

Erducos smiled. "None of it matters, Spartacus. Sulla does not care if you are the son of a chief, or the chief, or the king of the Maedi, or the king of Thracia. You are a barbarian in the auxiliary, and you will do as you are told."

"But still–" he whined, and then regretted his tone.

*Doesn't Erducos get it?*

His friend and mentor placed a hand on Spartacus' shoulder. "May I say something, big man?"

Spartacus was surprised, for Erducos never asked permission to say something. "What might you say that could offend me so much?" he said, smiling.

Erducos gently slapped Spartacus' shoulder. "You have grown before my eyes. I never once doubted who you might be from the first day, for your words are measured, and your strength and skill are unparalleled."

*Bless my father who has instilled these within me. And glory to Zibelthiurdos who has brought me to this world this way.*

"But…" Erducos' voice trailed.

"But what?"

"There is an arrogance in you, Spartacus. An *expectation* that because of who you were, you *deserve* a certain thing. An entitlement–"

"Ha, ha," Spartacus said, brushing it away. *What was Erducos talking about? He had led his men from the front, fought valiantly, protected their interests, and shielded them from Florus.*

"I mean these words," Erducos said gently.

Spartacus threw up his hands in exasperation. After a long, miserable day, he was in no mood for a lecture—and that too from a friend who was no longer the supervisor! "What do you–"

Erducos furrowed his brows and put his palm up. "Be quiet and listen! You have most qualities of a man destined for greater things, but to earn the genuine love of your men, you must be greater still! Your snide remarks and comments about things *beneath* you, and how you deserve *greater* things do not go unnoticed, Maedi! Your valor and compassion and care for your men get covered in the mud of your arrogance and diminish your value. Just look at what you did while piling the dead–you made your men do it, while you should have been the one among them."

Spartacus felt deflated. No words bubbled up. His friends' words were harsh and yet they had unquestionable truth in them. He kept his head low and rubbed the wet rock. Then he shook the cold water off and wiped his palms on his aching thigh.

"Why do you think Curio is respected? Just because the man is a Roman aristocrat? Have you seen how he works?"

*Not as much as you have, my rude friend.*

Erducos was in his lecturing spirit. He continued. "Curio may be in a big tent with men saluting him all day. He could, like our fine centurion, shrink from his work. But Curio wakes up before we do, and then he sleeps after us. He spends countless hours discussing strategy with the centurions, inspecting the lines, dealing with requests and orders from the general, handling disputes, settling squabbles, and then he leads from the front and charges into battle. And yet when he addresses his men or deals with them, he *never* speaks of his greatness or what he *deserves* because of *who he is.* And that is why his legion marches with him, no matter the hardship, no matter the pain, because they *feel* that he *feels* their effort. And that is what you must become, Spartacus, *one with the men,* and not *one above them forced to be with them."*

Erducos' words were like lashes. But he was not done. "The men's tongues wag. They say you fight from the front and that your skills are like a god on earth, and yet you see them as lesser, like how the Romans do. And if you do not watch your words, you will find their admiration recede. Lead them, fight for them, and fight as if you are one of them."

He brought up his aging arms and held Spartacus' shoulders firmly and looked into his eyes. A rare gesture of affection.

Spartacus nodded. His face was hot even in the cold air, for no such words, raw and powerful, had been spoken to him. Perhaps no one dared to.

Erducos' features softened. His voice dropped. "But it is in our nature to feel a certain way. You will not change today, not in a year, for sometimes passions and inclinations rise within us uncontrolled. But try, Spartacus, because if you try, you will succeed."

*Big lectures from a man who— Stop it! His words are true. Painful but true! Want to punch him. No. Stop it. His words are true. Scalding but plain. Be the leader.*

He turned to Erducos and nodded. "I never knew," he finally said, slowly, as it dawned upon him those men listening to him or looking up to him did not mean they loved him as their leader. Maybe that was why many spoke little to him even if they listened to his words or followed his orders.

Erducos smiled. "May glory be to you and the gods bless you eternally. You were part of this victory and will be for many more."

But what did this victory mean? How close were they to Rome? There was no question that the fighting would get more complicated and vicious as they neared the great city.

But Spartacus was tiring. This was not what he dreamt of. The illusions of glory and battle had all long vanished. Perhaps such aspirations were suited for greater men who rarely lost their lives, did not have to dig trenches, or carry rotting corpses and worry about the next meal or escaping the next punishment. Those men had the luxury of dreaming of greatness, and luxury men like Spartacus would never have. The poor men, farmers, cattle herders, blacksmiths, and fish-sellers either made some riches or died and vanished under the mud.

He would ask for a discharge from duty after the capture of Rome, take his pay, and find work in an estate, for he had seen so many wealthy ones and knew that it would give him a comfortable living. He could find a wife, and then, when sufficient coin was gathered, he would make his way back home, hopefully with a family. He had never had children; the two that his previous wife carried had never come to life.

That night, under the flickering torch light, Spartacus went to sit among his men. To apologize would be weakness, so instead he enquired after their well-being, listened to their complaints, teased a few, prayed for the dead, and waited to be the last one to sleep.

As a new dawn arrived, he marched on, as the general prod them ever closer to Rome.

# 18

## LUCANIA

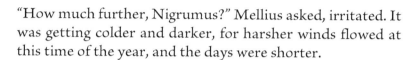

"How much further, Nigrumus?" Mellius asked, irritated. It was getting colder and darker, for harsher winds flowed at this time of the year, and the days were shorter.

"Be patient, Mellius. Only a little more time, near the foothills of the great hands," he said, referring to the large mountain near the estate.

His chest hammered relentlessly.

It had taken a while for today to happen, and yet here was Mellius, the estate tyrant, walking with him, unsuspecting. No one else knew that Mellius was accompanying him, for he had enticed the overseer with news of hidden coin, perhaps left behind by someone fleeing their pursuers. *I need your counsel to decide what to do, Mellius,* Nigrumus had asked the overseer. *Surely there is some way to be rewarded?*

A greedy Mellius had readily agreed to keep the secret to himself and promised that the master was kind to anyone that enriched him in unexpected ways. *A slave has no use for gold, for what can he do with it except to hide it?* Mellius had agreed, *But better rations, clothes, more specific duties, the chance to fuck some pretty women? Worth more than the gold!*

The trail got more challenging as they neared the foothills. The bushes were thicker and thornier, and it was well off the beaten path where few ventured. Few knew of the caves that Nigrumus had talked about–and even fewer came here for recreation. Mellius had no idea where these caves were, for the man rarely ventured outside the estate.

A dead man would never be easily found here.

Mellius was a bigger, younger man. Nigrumus, whose advancing age, now nearly forty, gave him no chance in open combat. The overseer was a man of hardy stock from the north. In his younger days, no doubt Nigrumus could overpower Mellius through his skill and dexterity, but years of hard toil had made his bones brittle.

"If you've made me walk all this way for nothing, old man, I will have your rations taken away for two days."

"Why would I risk that, Mellius? You are the overseer," he said politely, "And what would I gain from angering you?"

"Who knows. You are always finding ways to anger me by your laziness and your protection of lazy and disobedient younger slaves."

Nigrumus parted a thorny bush with his herding pole and stepped gingerly over sharp stones littering the narrow path that went deeper into the forest. Trees surrounded them, and he shivered in the cold wind.

"Remember your own younger days, Mellius. Did you not wish to have a kinder overseer?"

Mellius scoffed. "I was a good slave when I started. I knew how to survive well. Look at me now!"

Nigrumus did not turn to look at the fool. *You are still a slave, Mellius.*

"How much farther?"

The man was like a petulant child. He was complaining incessantly and berating everyone all the time. No one would miss this bastard.

"Lucia is getting prettier by the day. The master will have her sooner or later," he said.

Nigrumus knew that Mellius would bring up the topic. Needling slaves was one of his favorite pastimes.

"As the master has the right," Nigrumus said flatly.

"Well, surely your son *Publipor* does not think so."

*Publipor*, "Publius' boy," was how Felix was often called. Many male slaves did not even have a name; they were simply called the master's boy, like Publipor or Marcipor, Marcus' boy.

"Why does it matter to you what that boy thinks? Pick someone your size, Mellius–there are many others."

Mellius laughed. "I do not need your suggestions on whom to pick, you old fool. Those two are talking more frequently these days, I've noticed," he said, referring to Lucia and Felix.

"Part of his duty, which *you* assigned, is to watch out for foxes and dogs coming into the olive groves. And she comes there to give orders to the slave women. They talk, just like how many others talk."

Mellius slapped Nigrumus back hard enough for him to wince. "Well, well, you are really like his father. Or his pimp. Who knows?"

Nigrumus controlled his temper. The cave was nearby. He had prepared the location well—first, he had dug a spot to make it look like a hiding act. Then, he had filled it in with some abandoned, torn linen bags to make it look suspicious. And nearby, he had placed some heavy, ball-sized rocks good enough to smash his skull.

"Did you know that many weeks ago, a general landed at Tarentum and led his army toward Rome? We're lucky to have escaped a raid. The master was quite anxious and went to supplicate before the general."

"What concern is all that to us? We're always someone's slaves anyway. And our master is a Senator–so surely this general had business to do."

Mellius grunted and mumbled. "I can tell you that the master was not happy."

Finally, when the entrance appeared, Nigrumus turned to Mellius. "I told you. Here."

The overseer kept his pace behind Mellius. Dark shadows fell on the path, and the trees rustled under the strong cold wind. They had to climb a few slippery boulders to get to the entrance, and Mellius cursed him some more.

There were finally there.

The cave itself was about two men's height and not very deep. Whatever deeper passage there was to the mountain had been blocked by rocks. But it was getting dark, and difficult to see much inside.

"There," Nigrumus said. "I just dug it, checked, and then returned. Who knows if someone else was watching it?"

Mellius' excited voice neared him now. The greedy overseer's pace had quickened. "And you found it by just strolling here?"

"We spend hours grazing cattle, Mellius. We find many places and explore them to escape boredom. I just got lucky!"

*Come forward, Mellius. Look.* If Mellius never gave him a chance to attack, he could always make an excuse that someone else had beaten them to it.

But Mellius did not come forward. Instead, his cold voice came loud and clear, just as Nigrumus realized that other footsteps were entering the cave.

"Not so lucky, you old pig-fucker. Thought you'd kill me so easily? See, there are dangers of running errands for boys who can't keep their mouth shut and cock hidden."

# 19

## ROME

---◇---

The march toward Rome paused after a few more battles once the weather cooled and the frost made fighting risky. The quiet months during the winter quarters and the arrival of a new year helped Spartacus learn a lot more about Roman rule and society, its leaders, the functioning, and politics of the Senate. He was also much more versatile with Latin, now conversing in simple sentences and understanding normal dialog. The conversations with Florus had switched from using translators to now between themselves, and the centurion had still not gained enough grace to be transferred. But Curio, it seems, was pleased with Spartacus' leadership that he had reinforced Spartacus' century with some men from the Gaelic and German cohorts, restoring the Century in total, and promised Florus a transfer after the "final battle." And this created a tense but mutually acceptable relationship between the men–the last few salaries had been paid in full for him. However, many in the unit continued to be skimmed, and Spartacus had to maintain peace by the power of his stature and the promise of loot and restoration. All this also helped Spartacus understand how the Germans and the Gauls functioned, and he learned various Gaelic and Germanic curses that all involved fornication with multiple animals.

The winter quarters also helped Spartacus regain his strength and resolve. He was still of the mind to request a discharge, for it was not all too uncommon for generals to disband their armies after great missions and allow men to return to their lives until they were recalled for a new ambition. And at this new year, news arrived that Carbo had been elected Consul again, along with Marius the Younger, and it would be these men they would fight. There was also news that a battle-hardy people called the Samnites and Lucanites, with their experienced armies, might make a march toward Rome and bring the battle to Sulla. News and rumors swirled in the cold morning mist, the warm fires of the evening, and during the endless watches and exercises.

Once the weather began to warm, the army was moving again. There were more skirmishes and battles in which the general remained undefeated. They learned of various factions fighting for or against Sulla. Soon, as the colder months progressed to the heat of the Italian lands and then again to the cooler days, the names and politics became too numerous to remember. Skirmishes and deaths became routine, and Spartacus persevered through it all. His senses for a fellow man's death or misery dulled, but his skills sharpened.

It was finally the Kalends of November when Sulla's army encamped closer to Rome. Spartacus had little information on what was going on or what they were expected to do until a horseback messenger galloped through the camps ushering the men to ready for a final rapid march toward Rome.

The whistles and trumpets, the harps and drumbeats, all generated sufficient excitement to the men who had tired of forages, trench digging, rampart building, and the various mind-numbing camp duties. This would not be a skirmish march–this was a real camp closure and permanent move, with the baggage train in tow and men fully armored and suited. By then, Spartacus had looted and made enough to equip himself and his men, who were finally pleased with the spoils of war. He now had a fantastic fitting leather belt, a thick hide-and-bronze corset, a finely polished helmet, two recently forged, sharp gladiuses, a knife, knee guards, and suitable thick footwear. His attire received much ribbing from the Maedi who called him the *bandaged son of the chief*, the Germans who called him a *dolled-up whore*, and some Gauls who just spit on the ground when he walked to tease them. But over time, they had quietly realized the importance of valor with protection and had all either paid for or looted armor for themselves. Even Florus had to grudgingly admit that his Auxiliaries looked rather formidable.

The journey toward Rome was unrelenting. The general gave little rest, and the news was that the Samnite army was fast at march toward Rome and that another Marian army was on the way. It seems the Sulla had sent a seven-hundred horse cavalry to impede the Samnites while he exhorted his fast-moving army to proceed to Rome. On the final day, the march began well before the sun rose and when their eyes were bleary, and a wave of anticipation passed through the men who were told that they would be within sight of the northern walls of Rome, near one of the gates called the Colline gate.

It was already noon by the time the army halted. They were exhausted from the punishing progress, and there was not much of a thrill when the walls of Rome finally appeared to their left. Far to their right, the Samnite army had already assembled but were scrambling to come to order. It soon became apparent that they were not ready to give battle. The Marian forces were there too, and some manned the walls, harassing the army already. The formidable gates at the Colline gate were shut. The general asked the army to rest in the broad field as the two armies eyed each other to avoid being attacked from behind. It was a fabulous afternoon, and they hoped to relax for the day and prepare for battle in the coming days.

"Let us stretch our legs and rest our backs. I want a deep sleep tonight, by the walls of Rome. And then we will see what this magical city has!" Erducos said. The strain of the march had worn the Odomantean–and he seemed far older than when Spartacus had met him more than a year ago.

"The wall is formidable. I can see the terraces of some buildings from here!" Spartacus said, still quite excited to be here. *This* was the city that spawned men who conquered kingdoms, led mighty armies, and built great structures. He wanted the chance to stroll through its streets and experience what being in the greatest city in the world felt like. He wondered if even being a slave in Rome would be better than a free man elsewhere–surely their lives were well taken care of by the rich.

He got up and ordered the eight-member groups to bring out their pots and prepare their afternoon meals. With the campaigns of the past several months, they could even afford more salt that made the coarse bread and mild, mild grain soup more palatable. The vast camp was tranquil, no doubt the hungry and recovering men wanted to do nothing but satiate their hunger, and even their less-than-inspiring meals tasted heavenly. Spartacus had forgotten what meat even tasted like. While not abundant, it was still routine during feasts back home, yet it was unheard of in military rations. It seems only the richest could afford meat.

"When do you think General Sulla will ask us to attack?" Spartacus asked Florus, who strolled nearby, in his full military gear, including the centurion's red cross-hat plumes. The man wore a uniform which he no longer made proud.

"When he decides," Florus said dismissively and walked on.

Spartacus ignored the usual slight and turned to Erducos, who lay on the grass and supported his weight on his elbows. "It would help the men if we had a day or two rest before this. Do you think once we take Rome, there will be a respite for a while?"

"Yes, I sure hope so. But remember, the general is unlikely to let the army inside the gates. We will either be camped outside, or we will have to disarm."

Spartacus knew of these customs. He cared little for all that–he looked forward to being disbanded and allowed inside.

"Maybe get yourself a Roman wife?" Erducos said. "You, the big, hairy, powerful Thracian, I am sure they will come running."

Spartacus scoffed as he watched the bustle around General Sulla's tent not too far from where he was but at lower ground on the gentle slope. Did the general not rest? Why not take a nap?

"They look down upon us. Is that not obvious?"

"Not when she looks down your tunic," Erducos said, and they laughed. Spartacus felt a sense of peace before the impending terror.

This would be it. The final battle in a while and a new life for him. A more peaceful one. The mostly-full belly and the cool air began to lull him into a nap. Thankfully there were no camp duties–this was a rest stop before the next battle order.

"You dream of a joyful life," Erducos said, yawning. "You watch your back, Spartacus. Keep an eye on Florus and Cleitus."

Cleitus had somehow survived the battles, and the man was no coward either. But he had ingratiated himself to Florus and was always in his ear, causing Spartacus to be exceedingly careful in what he said and to whom. The slap a long time ago still haunted Cleitus, and he had never forgotten the insult. Durnadisso's death and the threats had made him even more resentful.

But for now, he felt at peace. "I will, Erducos, I will," he said as he yawned loudly. He placed his scutum beneath his head, moved to an area with soft, thicker grass, adjusted his belt and corset, put his new helmet on his face, and closed his eyes.

"May we emerge victorious, Erducos. May Zibelthiurdos look after you," he said, yawning again. Sweet merciful sleep was upon him, embracing his being like a loving mother.

"And you too, Spartacus of the Maedi, may Sabazios lift your spirit and bring you home with all your limbs intact! Even your cock!"

Spartacus looked at his friend and mentor, saluted him in jest, and closed his eyes. He then cupped his testicles and said, "My cock says he will be fine."

The cool November wind was soothing. And soon, the afternoon dimmed into nothing.

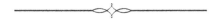

*His legs are buried up to his knees in the wet mud. There is no one around him except heaps of rotting corpses, their sockets empty and mouths wide open as rain falls into them. Even though it is a storm, he does not feel wet–it's a pleasant sensation. But behind him in the Bessi chief, Durnadisso. With a whistle in his mouth, the mad man is chasing Spartacus. His hair is wet with blood, and his torso has a deep gash inflicted by Spartacus. "Rome! Rome!" Durnadisso shouts, taking the whistle out of this mouth, and then places it back again, causing*

*a shrill ear-splitting sound. Spartacus turns to the man to strike him. Why is he back from the dead? Why is he– Then suddenly, there's a large trumpet in Durnadisso's mouth. What? Durnadisso blows it hard like a maniac, but Spartacus' shoulder feels the sharp pain of a whip. What?*

"Get up! Up! Line up! Battle orders!" Someone was screaming and whipping him.

His eyes opened with a jerk, and he scrambled to his feet, disoriented. Officers were running around, waking up groggy men. The sun was inching closer to the horizon, and at a distance, the legions were already lining up. The twelve-foot stone wall of Rome was behind them, and the enemy was scrambling to order, as was evident from the busy activity and rising dust at a distance.

Florus, red-faced, came running. "Left flank! Report to the left flank! Run! Get your men ready, you lazy sleeping bastard! Now!"

Spartacus ran around waking his men–kicking them in the ribs, yanking hairs, shouting orders. Many woke up grumbling, coming from their deep slumbers into the shock of a surprise battle order.

*Why now? Late into the evening even before the men sufficiently rested?*

His Century rose and quickly assembled behind Florus and their standard-bearer, *Aquilifer*, and began to trot toward the assembly area. The arrangement this time was a classical triple-line, and the Thracian auxiliaries had been ordered to the left flank, which meant they had to run nearly a mile to get to their location. The sky was partially cloudy, with raucous crows. *What did that mean? Were the omens favorable?*

He could see occasional toppled crosses on the battlefield, and some vertical beams still stood straight. There was no one hanging on them, yet the sight of these terrible instruments stirred bad feelings in him. He had heard that Romans often crucified some criminals and other miscreants outside the city walls, with the space near Colline gate being one of them.

Florus passed on some details as they made their way. "The general is center-left; we are at the left flank, facing the Samnites. They are good fighters," he wheezed, "And our right flank is a new commander named Marcus Licinius Crassus, a very wealthy man. Mostly Marians against him."

Spartacus had heard of Crassus and other men like Dolabella, Marius, and Damasippus, but there were simply too many names. He hoped that this Crassus was an able commander. There was news that another famous general named Pompeius was on the way to rendezvous with Sulla, but he had not yet arrived.

"Why now, centurion? The men are not rested, and it's about to become dark!"

Florus did not turn. "Have you not learned yet? We do not question!"

Spartacus wondered how Florus would save his hide this time. Where would he slink away like a rat?

"Faster! Faster!" officers were screaming.

More on cavalry charged between the lines, encouraging the men. In their rich uniforms, flag and standard-bearers, Centurions, Prefects, and Legates ran or rode to their stations and arranged the Cohorts and Centuries. The only type of units Spartacus had not seen were siege equipment—there was no plan to scale the Roman walls.

"Fuck the general's mother! I was having such a good dream!" somebody quipped from behind, and many chortled.

"Fucking his old mother? Oh, how desperate are you?" someone else said to laughter.

They were close to being out of breath when they reached the farthest end to the left flank and had to take some time to recover. They eagerly gulped from the water jugs from water bearers who ran around. With the expected efficiency of an experienced and disciplined army, the lines came to order rapidly, and a silence descended on the battlefield. The whistles and trumpets had died, the trotting horses were stationary, the officers stood straight waiting for the general to gallop across the front line.

And as it customary for Sulla to do so, the general appeared on his beautiful white horse, his purple cloak flying, his right arm held high as he received their salutes. He came to the left flank, followed by his commanders, and then, he turned and went back to his position somewhere near the center. It was now past the fourth hour of the afternoon, and the sun cast the long, ominous shadow of the wall of Rome behind them. The wind was picking up, getting colder, and they heard some clamor behind them. Many men turned, including Spartacus, to see armed men appear on the rampart. This caused some murmur and anxiety–for if they were to be pushed to have their backs against the wall, then not only would they be fighting the enemy at the front, but also the tormentors from above. This was an unexpected situation.

Spartacus hoped that the general was as good at this critical hour as he always was in the past, against all odds.

The waiting did not last long.

*Pfffommmmmmm! Pom! Pomm! Pommm!*

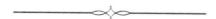

It was now over three hours since the battle began, and what started as the traditional lines clashing with push-and-shove had broken into various clusters swinging at each other in exhaustion and running away to find a quiet place to rest before returning. The left wing had completely disintegrated from any semblance of order. He could hear senior officers on horses charge through the lines encouraging men, but the situation was worsening by the hour.

Spartacus warily circled a Samnite fighter who had managed to match him step for step, for so long now that he had forgotten the passage of time. The man's eyes were bloodshot and wide; his saliva dripped from the side as he crouched behind his thick, blue-painted shield and kept the dangerous gladius low and ready to thrust.

The gladius in the hands of a skilled fighter was like a lethal snake. It struck with blinding speed and left pain and death in its wake.

They had clashed their shields and crossed their blades more times than he could count–but the shorter, stocky man was not cowed by Spartacus' height, for he had much confidence in his admirable skills. And now, with the fading light, the aching muscles, and an impending sense of doom, Spartacus' energy was finally giving away. His lip had been smashed, he had a bleeding gash near his knee, his ribs were sore, and his palm was slippery and sweaty from exertion. He stole a glance to see if any of his men were nearby and could come to his aid and then narrowly escaped the lightning thrust by the bastard Samnite who sensed an opportunity.

Finally, Spartacus had enough.

He dropped his scutum and lunged at the surprised opponent. He ignored the hard *smack* of the Samnite's shield on his body and then grappled with the edge of the shield. The panicking Samnite realized the danger quickly and let go of the shield, at which time Spartacus swung the gladius and hit the man's face with the broadside. The Samnite staggered back but began to regain posture. Knowing that he might not equal the Samnite in an unprotected contest, Spartacus launched himself and tackled the man to the ground. And when the Samnite lost the grip on his blade, perhaps due to exhaustion, Spartacus pummeled his face with his ringed fist, smashing his nose.

He then gripped his head and beat it so hard that the sound of the cracking skull was audible–and then he kept going until the head was a bloody, broken pulp.

He rolled and fell to his back to recover after grabbing his gladius again, afraid that another man may come upon him.

But the scene unfolding around him was disheartening. The left wing was in tatters, and it was impossible to see what was happening in the center or the right with the darkness. The wall rampart had many flaming torches illuminating the fighters below, and the gentle glow of the dying sun only left silhouettes desperately fighting for their lives. There were no retreat whistles or trumpets and no victory sounds, making everything even more confusing.

Had the general finally lost when it mattered most?

Had Zibelthiurdos abandoned the Maedi auxiliaries?

Someone galloped into the scene on his white horse, yelling, shouting. "Come on, men! Fight! Do not give up now!"

*Sulla? The general himself?*

But it was all noisy, and he could not be sure with the dust and darkness. He stood and ran toward another fighting pair. A legionary was losing his foot to a Marian soldier, and Spartacus ran his gladius through the Marian, saving the legionary, who was too exhausted to thank him, only collapsed to the ground and stayed there breathing hard.

"Erducos?" Spartacus called, but he knew it was futile, but to have his name on his mouth was a cry for some semblance of normalcy. But there was no response. He looked around for Florus, but the centurion was nowhere to be found, not fighting but nowhere on the ground nearby.

The battle took a strange turn, with many soldiers simply giving up and vanishing into the fields. In some places, it was evident that their men and the enemy were only separated by a few feet but were unwilling to engage, preferring instead to distance and walk away. The ground was littered with the dead, and for the first time, Spartacus realized that Sulla's army had taken significant losses, just as the enemy's, and yet it was unclear who was winning. A few dispirited whistles conveyed nothing, and men continued to do whatever they could.

And then, just as suddenly, there were some loud retreat whistles nearby. *Ours? Theirs?*

The situation left little for clarity.

Many groups of men, most that he recognized as his side, had begun to group, and run away into the darkness. Confused and not finding any of his Century in this dying light, Spartacus ran toward a wounded Legionary who was limping his way across the field toward the slope that descended near the end of the left flank.

He put an arm beneath the man's shoulder to help him. He was bleeding profusely, as evident by the slick blood on his arms, but it was unclear where he was wounded. He grunted in acknowledgment as Spartacus helped him stand straight and walk with him.

"Are we retreating?" he asked.

"I suppose so," the man gasped. "Who knows?"

"Aren't we supposed to stand and fight?"

The man looked at him, though his eyes and expression were hidden in the night. "Are you stupid? Fight with what? The entire left flank has collapsed, and the Legate commanding our section is dead."

"So, what happens now?"

Never having been defeated before, Spartacus had no idea of the rules of disengagement. He had only seen when the enemy surrendered or had been slaughtered. But the outcome was almost entirely left to the winning commanders.

"We run, and we hide. And when morning arrives, and the situation clears, we go to the victor. If it's Sulla, then we join him. If it's Marius, we surrender, and usually, they just make us part of their army," he said, wheezing.

He was weakening.

More shouts.

Whistles.

Running sounds.

Stones by the feet. Stumbling. Falling. Picking up.

Nothing made sense—what a strange battle.

*So many dead and no outcome.*

"I'm going to die," the man said bleakly. "So close."

"We'll see, Legionary," Spartacus said, his Latin now more than passable.

They stumbled along a narrow path, slowly, until they came upon a thicket next to a few boulders, slightly visible under the partial moon. He could still hear the distant sounds of the clash, though it was no longer clear who was clashing with whom, where, and to what purpose.

"I can't walk anymore. Do not go too far, or they'll think you're deserting and running away. Auxiliaries are suspected quickly," he said, and Spartacus realized how easy it was to identify him as different.

He helped the man sit with his back to the boulder, and Spartacus put aside his gladius and removed the corset that felt heavy and onerous. Without food and water and after hours of toil, he too could no longer function in any meaningful manner. It would be death if the enemy were to chance upon them now.

They said a few stars twinkled in the sky, sprinkled there by Sabazios. His eyelids felt heavy, and the struggle to keep them open got harder. He changed his position a few times to no avail as the exhaustion seeped into his bones, and his body was unwilling to reason with him. The Legionary had been stabbed in his belly, a terrible and painfully slow way to die, and also slashed at his knee. He was beginning to groan and whimper, and it was only a matter of time before his life came to an end.

*Stay awake.*

Someone ran in front of them.

Then a stampede, but none noticing them on the side, in the darkness.

*Stay awake. Help, Zibelthiurdos!*

*Stay.*

*St…*

*Slap!*

*A sharp pain.*

"What?"

"Wake up! Wake up! We have a deserter!"

Spartacus was woken up with slaps and blows by some soldiers. They gave him no chance to explain himself as he was roughed up, pulled to his feet. Still confused and groggy, he tried to answer questions.

"Did you kill him? Killed a legionary, you bastard?"

"No! I helped him. He was badly injured!"

The soldier he had helped was dead, his eyes open and staring at the unknown.

They tied his hands behind his back, ignoring all protests of innocence, and began to march him. It was now morning— he had slept all through the late evening and night. His throat was parched, and his stomach burned with hunger.

"Water," he croaked, only to receive a smack on his head.

They were back on the battlefield where gangs were now busy with the grim task of stripping bodies, heaping the dead, and by the looks of the men engaged, it seemed like those that prevailed were Sulla's men. Many beggars and scavengers had come to the field once the Colline gate of Rome was open, and they jostled with each other and army men on task. Dogs roamed around sniffing and biting corpses. Even though it had only been hours, the stench of the dead, urine, feces, blood, and mud was strong in the air. This time, it was a massacre, for the field was littered with corpses as far as he could see.

What had happened?

But no answers were forthcoming as the men dragged him to a holding area where hundreds of injured and defeated men, mostly the Samnites and Marians, along with some who looked like they were Sulla's army, were being guarded by Sulla's legionaries. They pushed him to a corner and leave him be, refusing to listen to his entreaties.

Frantic, Spartacus looked around to see if he recognized any of the men in the holding area or one of the guards—but none were familiar. He walked toward a man with a centurion's corset and sat beside him. "Centurion, are you from Sulla's army?"

The man looked at Spartacus with disdain. "Why do you ask?"

"Why are they holding us here, sir. I am an auxiliary who fought for the general. What happened?"

The man wiped his elbow and sighed. "They think we ran. No one ran. It was just confusion—some thought there was an order to retreat."

"I thought the same too! Will they hear us?"

"Depends on the General or the Legate. Only to have come so far and executed for a misunderstanding," he said, without emotion, nonchalantly. "You speak passable Latin for a barbarian."

"I have learned, sir. The left flank disintegrated. What happened afterward?"

"It did. But I learned more in the last few hours. It seems the general left the field to return to his camp. But the right-wing, under Marcus Crassus, crushed the Marians and routed them. When Sulla heard of this, he returned to the field in the night, re-engaged the scattering enemy, and destroyed them. He won!"

Spartacus marveled at this turn of events. This Marcus Crassus may have been an effective commander who helped turn this battle. But what would happen now? Soon, he finally saw Cleitus and a few others walk nearby, and Spartacus called out. "Cleitus! Cleitus! Where are the others?"

Cleitus stared at Spartacus, smiled, and then kept walking. *That son of a whore!*

The Colline gate was open, and men were going in and out, and a large contingent of Sulla's troops were at its entrance. Spartacus had to wait hours until finally someone came and herded all the men who belonged to Sulla's legions, including him.

A military tribune sat at the head of a table as men were dragged one by one. He could hear the pleading explanations, and men were sometimes ordered to bring someone else as an endorsement. Many were being let go, going by their gratefulness, kissing the tribune's hand, or the big smiles as they went toward a makeshift canteen and physicians' camp. But a small number were unlucky, as the tribune condemned them to death with a flick of his finger. They were led away somewhere behind the camps, protesting, weeping, or quiet. The end would be swift with a strike to the neck. Some may have been issued other punishments, but it was unclear.

Most were legionaries and their officers, but there were a few auxiliaries. A German in the front made much noise, but he did not know Latin, and the men either did not know or refused to engage, and he was taken away, still protesting and shouting. Another lunged at the tribune and was quickly cut down.

The pattern was clear–every barbarian auxiliary came under doubt without much consideration to their service, for it was customary for the Romans to see them as less and prone to corruption. And often, they were condemned.

His heart sank.

*Was this it?*

When his turn came, the tribune barely looked up when he asked. "Why should you not be punished?"

Spartacus stood straight and mustered his dignity. "I have fought with honor for General Sulla, sir. There was confusion."

The tribune looked surprised by the diction. He squinted his eyes and studied Spartacus.

*Was this it?*

He finally grunted. "Which unit? Endorsement?"

"Legion Six, First Auxiliary Infantry, led by centurion Florus, commanded by Legate Scribonius Curio."

"Does Florus know you?"

"Centurion Florus and honorable Curio both know my name and service, sir," he said.

The tribune raised his eyebrows, perhaps by the confidence of the words that even Legate knew a barbarian's name. He turned to a man by his side and ordered him to find Florus. "You wait," he said and then gestured for the next prisoner.

Spartacus waited nervously as only a few more men met unkind fates, but most were allowed to go back. It was not surprising, for the men of their station posed no danger and were happy to live and fight for whoever won. It was a waste of the workforce to execute them all.

It took some time, but eventually, Spartacus caught sight of Florus making his way to the camp. Even though he hated the man, he sighed with relief. Hopefully, soon he would no longer have to serve for this rat. Florus barely looked at him as he walked to the tribune and saluted him.

The tribune pointed at Spartacus and gestured for him to come near.

He looked at Florus, who looked well-rested, cleansed, and impeccably dressed in his uniform.

"Is he your unit?"

"Yes, sir."

"And you are in Curio's legions?"

"Yes, sir."

"Says he left in confusion."

"The left flank completely–" Spartacus began, addressing Florus and the tribune.

The tribune raised his palm as if to say *be quiet,* and Spartacus stopped mid-sentence.

"Centurion?" The tribune turned to Florus again.

Florus averted Spartacus' eyes and spoke to the tribune in a low but audible tone.

"He ran. He's a deserter."

# 20

## LUCANIA

───────◇◇───────

It was early in the morning when Mellius' henchmen accosted Felix, seized him, and dragged him into a large room in the estate house of the master, Publius. Not a sound came from his terrified mouth, and they would not say why.

They finally arrived at a large room on the east side, a familiar place, for this was a grain and cattle feed hold. Even before he entered, the room's quietness was only punctuated by the sobs of the women and the groans. His legs almost gave way, frightened of what this was about and what would happen to him, but the men had no difficulty in dragging him.

He suppressed a scream when he entered. There, tied to a wooden overhang bar, was a naked Nigrumus, his back and buttocks bleeding from angry red bruises due to the stripped-leather belt. Nigrumus was whimpering, barely coherent. And he did not acknowledge Felix as he came in. Standing near Nigrumus was Mellius, with the leather strip, and sitting behind him was the *dominus* himself, Publius. Beside Publius was his wife, the *domina*, and behind her, a sobbing Lucia, and her stone-faced mother.

*What had gone wrong?*

"Tie him up," Mellius said, and the men roughly dragged Felix to a wooden pillar and tied his hands behind. His legs began to shake.

When the sobs quietened and the room was covered with a thick blanket of fear, the *dominus* looked at Felix. "Is it true?"

Felix could guess, but his tongue was dry and stuck to his mouth.

Mellius walked across the room and slapped him so hard that the world spun. "The master asked you something!"

His ears ringing and head hurting, he finally mustered the words. "I beg your pardon, master, know what?"

Mellius lifted his hand to strike him again when the master ordered him to stop. Publius was a tall, gaunt man. His eyes were sunken in their sockets, and his loose tunic hung like a burden on his frame. He rose from his chair and walked to Felix.

"See, why would I bother gathering all these people?" he said, with his low voice that sounded like the hissing of a snake. "I'm a Senator of Rome. Owner of one of the largest estates in Lucania. And here I am, on the case of a stupid little slave boy and his father-like fool."

No one said anything. Felix was too frightened to utter a word out of his dry lips by then. Blood rushing in and out of his burning ears made it hard for him to hear.

"But the problem, boy, is that I have a reputation to maintain. No one needs to believe that the master cannot control the boys in his estate. Imagine if the news spread that Publius' boy conspired and had an estate overseer murdered," he said theatrically as he walked toward the sobbing Lucia. He stood next to the girl, who had not once raised her eyes.

He caressed her shoulder and continued, "And then, that he ran away with another pretty slave girl, one who is prized in the household, and for whose mother the master paid a significant sum which hasn't been recouped yet."

He looked around, and everyone's head hung low. Several other slaves were standing in the background.

"I am a merciful man. I have always been kind to you, unlike some other estate owners. But sometimes, messages must be sent. Slaves need to learn that when you are fed, clothed, and given security, you must earn a good living through obedience. Our soldiers do it, but it seems you have the impunity that they do not have."

Felix shook his head weakly. *What message?*

"Look at Mellius here. He's a good slave. That is who the others must be like," he said.

Mellius beamed. "Always at your service, *dominus*. I have never forgotten my station and boundaries!"

"I spoke with my wife, and we realized how well our household is managed," he continued. "In all the years in this estate, we have only had three slaves run. Two were caught and received just punishment, and only one vanished. That was years ago–and I have no doubt that he's dead in a ditch somewhere or living a worse life under the yoke of an opportunistic master. And no one has eloped with a slave girl; why do it, when robust slaves are afforded chances to keep companions and breed children? I even take care of their children! So why do it? What did you hope to gain from this senseless adventure?"

He looked around slowly at all the slaves and his men.

Mellius, ever eager to please, like a wretched dog, nodded vigorously. "Only those who think like sheep, *dominus*. To leave all the comforts of your beautiful estate and try something so depraved!"

The master scoffed and made a show of regret as he paced around the room. "Anyway, I ascribe this to the madness of youth, hatched by a young idiot and an old fool. Neither dangerous, but certainly embarrassing," he chuckled, causing Mellius and a few others to laugh like hyenas, trying to impress him.

"I would have swatted him like a fly, *dominus*," Mellius said, puffing up. "He's only alive due to your generosity and kindness!"

So far, Nigrumus had said nothing, and nothing had been asked of him while Felix was there. He was weak and whimpering.

A man with a rough-grain leather whip walked behind Nigrumus. The *dominus* nodded to him.

*Shwack!*

The sickening sound of the whip flying and lashing Nigrumus' back made Felix gasp out loud.

"Dominus!" Nigrumus screamed, his legs lifting off the ground and every vein in his thick neck bulging out.

*Shwack!*

*Shwack!*

*Shwack!*

Nigrumus was kicking and screaming, even as tears streamed on his gentle face.

*God, no! Please no!* Felix implored all gods on earth.

Nigrumus was shouting *Sorry! Sorry, Dominus! Never again!*

Felix could not bear the violence against his fatherly mentor. Nigrumus was almost jumping in the air, unable to bear the lashes on his already beaten backside.

It took a few more lashes, and then suddenly, his muscles slackened, and he seemed to lose consciousness.

Felix's heart was trying to explode out of his chest. How long would this cruelty go on? Why? Would they kill

Nigrumus, and then him? The terror in his being was preventing even tears.

Then, a man walked into the room holding a bucket. Steam rose from it.

*No, no, no, no, no, please master!*

Felix began to weep. *Forgive me, Nigrumus. Forgive me! May the gods forgive me and protect you!*

Sometimes punishments included scalding a slave with boiling water mixed with salt thrown on the wounds after whipping. It induced horrific pain but did not kill.

Without any warning, the man splashed the water on Nigrumus' severely bruised and bleeding buttocks, and the slave first gasped, jerking up from his barely conscious state, and then began to kick and thrash screaming. It felt like a molten rock being poured into Felix's ears.

*What have I done? What have I done?*

Nigrumus kicked and howled for some time, a sound so terrible that most of the slaves began to cry in terror, and Felix could barely breathe.

*What have I wrought upon you, father?*

In the months since they hatched their plot, Felix's relationship with Lucia had grown somewhat, infusing a certain gumption and bravery in him. And one day, in the excitement of their grand ideas, he had relayed to Lucia his bold plan and how Nigrumus would help them. Lucia was horrified but still excited, and by then, she too was tiring of Mellius and the prospect of becoming the old master's bed companion. A few days later, Lucia had told a worried Felix that she had relayed the details of the plot during a fight and argument with her mother regarding her future, hoping that her mother would support her. But Lucia's mother had only asked her to be quiet and do nothing.

There was no question that her mother had finally decided that it was safer to let the master know, rather than risk all their lives, should the truth ever come out.

*What a fool I am!*

The *dominus* walked back to Felix and roughly yanked his chin up. "Look at me, boy. You are a good runner, and you know this land well. He has served me well for many years. And so, I will let you both live."

Felix nodded in relief, his legs trembling and a puddle forming beneath his feet. The *dominus* recoiled and stepped back, wrinkling his nose.

The master's mirthless grey eyes bore into his. "But if you ever even speak a word to that slave girl, you will find out what nails driven through wrists and ankles feels like, and that's just the beginning. Do you understand?"

He nodded vigorously, feeling weak and almost faint. Nigrumus' screaming reduced to a whimper, and he again lost consciousness. His limp body dangled uselessly.

Lucia began to cry loudly.

"Tell her to shut up!" Publius screamed. Lucia's frightened mother chastised her and put a hand over her mouth. "You keep your daughter under control, or I'll sell her to someone far worse!"

The ordeal was not over.

A man came in with a slave collar and a small bronze plaque with some letters.

Publius held it in front of Felix. "Do you know what it says? It says—"

I AM FELIX, PUBLIUS' BOY. I HAVE RUN AWAY. HOLD ME. BRING ME TO MY MASTER BY METAP HORNS. BE REWARDED.

They forced it around his neck and secured the ends with a lock. It would remain permanently, forever reminding him of his shame and making it impossible even to attempt an escape without being apprehended–not unless a metal worker found a way to saw through the iron collar. It was rough and already scratched him. They placed another one on Nigrumus.

Slave collars were not unusual. He had seen it among some other slaves and been thankful that he did not suffer the ignominy of wearing one like a dog. But that slight sense of superiority was now over.

He then turned to Mellius. "Give him a thrashing but keep it short. I need him because he's our best grazer and shepherd. And take Nigrumus down, have the estate physician tend to him, and put him to work at the stables once he recovers. Let him live and die there."

Mellius' whip barely registered to a defeated Felix, who was resigned to the nature of the world and the will of the gods that a man condemned to be a slave deserved his fate and life to be so.

# 21

## ROME

"He ran. He's a deserter."

Spartacus froze. *That motherfucking bastard!* "He's lying! The centurion was nowhere to be found!"

The tribune was surprised by the outburst.

Florus shouted back. "You are a cowardly dog who abandoned your post! I saw you run away!"

Spartacus knew he was lying. His muscles contracted with stress, but one mistake now, and he would be cut to pieces. There was a reason why many expressed surprise that for a man so big, powerfully built, and with all the looks of a wild barbarian, Spartacus was thoughtful and quiet and rarely made hasty decisions. He would not go the German's way, yelling and then having his head cut off.

*I wish I had you in my grip, you slimy lying bastard!*

Instead, Spartacus made another gamble before the tribune made his decision, which rarely went against a centurion's recommendation. "The centurion may have been confused like everyone else, sir, and you know how it was. I beg you to find Legate Curio who can attest to my service! I did not run!"

Three legionaries slowly circled Spartacus, waiting for the tribune's order. Florus had the slightest smile on his face. *What a dirty, dirty coward!*

"Your officer seems to think you have, barbarian."

"I have served General Sulla every day since Dyrrhachium, tribune. My scars show my effort. I only beg you to seek the Legate's opinion before you cast judgment on me."

*How low I feel, Zibelthiurdos, to beg these scum for my life! Should I die valiantly? But what good does it do to lunge at a tribune who knows nothing about me, and then die without even making a case! Why do you make me pause before every decision, Zibelthiurdos?*

The tribune turned to Florus. "Well, I have rarely heard an Auxiliary speak this way. If his service is as he says, then our laws dictate we give him the benefit."

Florus was about to object, but the tribune cut him off. "I will have someone look for the Legate. You will remain in holding."

Spartacus glared at Florus, who looked back defiantly. The man could not find fault with him by way of conduct, so he had found another devious means to take petty revenge with no blood on his hands or mutiny of the auxiliaries. He could claim victory, ascribe any failures to Spartacus, and curry favor.

But not so soon.

And thus, the wait began again. It seems in the morning, General Sulla had gone with some legions to a nearby town named Antemnae to secure their surrender. He hoped that Curio had not gone with them or died the previous night. The holding area was only loosely guarded, and he could get a few swigs of water from an auxiliary sentry. Except for one aggressive guard shouting at him for speaking, most seemed disinterested in keeping the chattering, loud men under any rigid discipline.

Most were just tired and wanted to go home or sleep wherever they were.

His stomach rumbled.

*I hope they give me the lentil soup with the hard bread. It tastes good. But not that terrible one with barley. What mother conjured that hideous potion?*

And it was near noon when finally he was called before the yawning Tribune. "The Legate is on the way. Well, Spartacus, it seems he does remember your name."

"May Apollo bless you for your consideration, sir."

*Thank you, Zibelthiurdos. Thank you, Sabazios. Thank you, Kotys. For no Roman god alone would save my life.*

He nodded and leaned back on his chair. Florus was nowhere to be found.

When Curio arrived, the two men saluted each other. It was unclear how the two ranks fared or what relation the two men had, but there seemed to be mutual respect.

"We would rarely call a Legate to pass judgment after a battle, sir, but this man seemed credible. He is not like the other barbarians."

Curio walked below the tent for shade and stared at Spartacus. "It seems you are in trouble again."

Spartacus saluted the Legate. "I mistook the whistles for retreat, sir. I even asked a legionary and helped him as we left."

"And he is conveniently dead," the tribune said without emotion.

*Not conveniently, you ignorant fool. At least make a serious attempt to seek the truth.*

"He was injured, sir. I cared for him as much as I could, but he had been stabbed in the stomach."

Curio seemed to think as he chewed on his lip. His face had lost weight, his hair was prematurely greying, and the Legate looked older than his days in Thracia.

"Well. I know he has served his unit well, and the auxiliaries under his command are amongst the best. Where is Florus?"

"He left, sir. We do not know where he is. Should I send a scout?

Curio waved dismissively. "Never mind. I give you the benefit of the doubt. The general is back, and you will join a group to corral Samnite and Marian prisoners and take them inside the gates of Rome. Today you may enter the city without your weapons and wander. But be back by nightfall tomorrow, and camp at the gate for your orders."

A massive wave of relief washed over him.

*Is this what Erducos meant about Curio? That he would take the time to come to the rescue of an auxiliary and remember his service, even if he may see it as well beneath him. If Curio cared about a barbarian, how much more did he display to his legionaries?*

"I thank you, sir! And you too, tribune, sir," he said, on one knee. He hated this supplication, but he had become accustomed to military command.

Curio only nodded and turned to return to his horse. The tribune, for whom this was simply a regular occurrence, flicked at Spartacus to leave and curved his finger for the next prisoner.

He walked briskly toward one of the makeshift kitchens for some grain and soup.

*Oh for the wicked witches' sake, not barley! Not the bitter olives again!*

But he was too hungry to care, and once nourished and satiated, began to look for what was left of the unit. The previous night's deep sleep had given him sufficient rest; he roused the men around to find Erducos.

"Let us walk the length and breadth. I pray to Zibelthiurdos that he is found," Spartacus said, anxiously.

"He is likely dead, sir," one of his men said. "None of us have seen him."

"Miracles happen, and he has done much for us. I ask you," he said, looking at them, "to help me find him. If he is alive, we drink together, and if he is dead, let us consecrate him to his gods. Come. I will walk alone but not begrudge you, for you must all be tired," he said, keeping his tone low, his face gentle, and avoiding his battle-order posture. *Be with them. Among them. Understand them.*

Without waiting for a response, he turned and began to walk.

"Spartacus. Sir," one of them called. A Bessi man, at that. "Let us find our old mentor."

His chest swelled with pride. He had made many adjustments since Erducos' words, and he could see it working.

"It seems the pig-laugh hill has grown soft," someone said good-naturedly to sniggers. His laugh was an ongoing joke, and he often exaggerated it intentionally. They called him *the hill* for his size. Taller than all of them, wider, and with a great curly beard on an imposing and charmingly ugly (they said) face.

He smiled but said nothing.

Where was Erducos?

But two hours later, a discouraged Spartacus waited for the men to regroup. Erducos was nowhere, not among the resting troops, not on the ground, not in the piles of the dead, and not in the half-burned pyres.

Had he run away? Abandoned the field in confusion and never returned? Or had been arrested by mistake and already executed?

But there was one more section at the far left of the field. A still fresh pile that had not been cremated. *What was the point?*

But there was a point, for one of his men finally found his mentor.

Erducos was almost unrecognizable. His face was already bloating, his eyes glassy, and a part of his bloodied body peeping from the men heaped above him. Spartacus leaned to grab the corpse beneath the armpits, crusted with blood, and others joined to pull Erducos out.

They lay him on the ground. All metal on him had already been stripped away, and someone had cut off a few fingers as well. As the leader of his unit, Spartacus had a small cape, which he removed and placed on his friend. Erducos' chest showed a deep gash, and it was obvious that the enemy had driven his gladius through the admired Odomantean.

*I know you fought valiantly until the very end, my friend. And I hope you are now walking through the gardens of the afterlife.*

They prayed for him, asking Zibelthiurdos and Sabazios to bless him and to bring freedom to his family. Spartacus felt his throat constrict as he briefly spoke of his friend. "Like a hound that would grab me by the buttocks and not let go until he made his point," he said to emotional guffaws. Then they lifted Erducos and placed him on top of the pile.

"It is time to return," he told them. "We have sent him away, and now it is my duty to ensure you care for yourself."

"Yes, mother!"

"I will break your teeth," he said as he led them back to the camp.

But first, they made their way to the pay tents and baggage carts, still safe, and withdrew some of their salary with coin for their sightseeing.

"Men, time to see Rome!" he shouted, to the hurrahs and excitement of seeing the greatest city in the world.

# 22

## LUCANIA

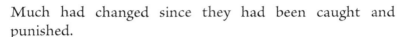

Much had changed since they had been caught and punished.

It took weeks for Nigrumus to recover from the savage treatment, and he was no longer the same. The light from his eyes had been extinguished, and Nigrumus now stayed at the stables, cleaning and feeding horses and keeping the areas clean. He had not spoken a word to Felix, who twice found the opportunity to talk to the man during his errands and tried to apologize, only to be ignored.

And now, Felix was alone.

His duties had changed too.

Felix was no longer overseeing the olive grows. He was almost always out in the fields, taking the cattle out to graze or tending the sheep. He had two boys and an older man, a guard of sorts, accompanying him. Since the beating, he had seen Lucia from a distance, and her guilt was palpable, but she had consciously stayed away from even meeting his eye, for the dangers were all too obvious. He was also frequently asked to join ditch diggers to route water around the field—back-breaking work with little rest.

Mellius was pleased with the outcome, and he redoubled his effort to have the master give Lucia to him in companionship, though nothing had happened yet. The overseer had become even more powerful now, taking his rage on any with little repercussion except an occasion chastisement from the master who did nothing else. The men and women in the barracks were terrified of him, and he relished their fear. No one even raised a voice when Mellius raped two girls in the full view of the barracks or when he almost beat an older slave to death for talking back.

But knowing his value in the fields, Felix was being fed better by the master's orders, had received better protective clothing, footwear, and a sturdier, brass-handled pole for protection. Felix had killed his desire to run given his somewhat improved conditions, for the more he thought of it, the more hopeless it all seemed. Now that the household knew of his intentions, there was no telling who was watching him and how soon he might be apprehended if he were to attempt.

And if he were caught again, the punishment would be horrible, and they would certainly kill him at the end of it. Why even run when he was eating and sleeping better, even if he had squashed all his other dreams. As much as he hated Lucia for opening her mouth, he knew it was not intentional, and there was no malice in her foolishness. He could not banish her from his thoughts, no matter how futile his desire.

Felix resigned to his new life, even though the ember of his desire to be free glowed deep within.

# 23

## ROME

What madness!

Even though a battle had raged outside a day ago, inside the walls of Rome, it was as if nothing had happened. The city's bustling narrow roads and shops hid the feverish plotting and politics within its lofty buildings and street corners. The impending arrival of Sulla had created a dense fog of nervous energy among the people. Rome was noisy, dusty, and dirty, with cobblestone paths busy with carts and people, sellers in shops on either side, multi-level mud-and-brick tenements jostling for space, and columned temples of all sizes nestling amongst the homes.

They had to walk carefully, for families living in cramped upper quarters filled buckets with excrement, and simply threw them out the windows. On the sides of these dense quarters were rivers of shit, and no one paid heed, for they were some amongst the millions here, making a living and caring little for where one came from or went. The city itself was rather dull, mostly grey, and yellow brick, with some buildings having red tile roofing, but the temples were opulent with marble and granite.

*Watch out, do you not see people walking below. I've had my fill with rotting corpses, I do not need your excrement to add to the joy.*

*It seems Hermos lied to Father. Not every building is made of marble, and not every man walks about dressed like a noble. What else did Hermos lie about?*

*So much for all the talk of discipline. This place is worse than any I have ever seen.*

Spartacus marveled at not just the bustle of a city, the likes he had never seen, but also the varied nature of the multitude–much different from what he had imagined. Romans, Italians, Egyptians, Numidians, Libyans, Gauls, Germans, Syrians, Greeks, Judaeans, and even some people of various colors he had never seen were all here, going about their lives. Some fully clothed, some partially, and some barely, whom he imagined being slaves. Who were nobles, who were free, and who were slaves was all entirely unclear. The men with him too were awed at the sights, and he had to warn them from becoming rowdy lest they be arrested or lynched.

*Surely men with torn fabric showing their many scars are slaves? But who knew?*

"Where are the brothels?" one of his men enquired. For those who had not felt the touch of a woman for a long time, there were few matters more pressing than quenching their desires.

Spartacus was no different.

*Valor, dignity, gravitas, self-respect can all wait for raging cock, my apologies Zibelthiurdos.*

Their minds free and loins desperate, they found their way to a brothel in a seedy corner off the main paths that eventually led to the aristocratic center of Rome. The madam who managed the dingy but three-storied structure would not let them in without extra payment. *You barbarians just from battle tend to be rough and hurt my girls, so leave a deposit first!*

His mind cleared after releasing his pent-up desperation, and with no one hurt or crying, Spartacus walked out and waited for the others to come out. The last one was followed by a cursing and angry madam who accused him of trying to run away with the girl. Another one complained that he could not get it up, and maybe he would need to look for a boy instead. It was then time for a drunken revelry, which led to a scuffle involving Spartacus and a Numidian, and both had to be separated after landing blows on each other. They then went to a garden adjoining a small temple of Apollo and lay there as the sun set in the sky. No one disturbed them in the park. They eventually fell asleep, with men rotating watch duties as if they had never left camp.

The Roman obsession with baths had grown on him. The next day the men made use of a good bath and lavatory, cleansing themselves even as some Romans glared at their loud behavior.

He groaned in pleasure, stretching himself under the hot water. "This is what a king must feel like, bathing every day."

"You don't need to be a king to take a bath every day," a Roman relaxing nearby said. "Does your type not have bathhouses?"

*An insult, or an innocent question?*

"No. We have beautiful running streams which we enjoy once every few days."

The man nodded. "The only streams we have is that of shit, as you've seen. Did you come with Sulla's army?"

"Yes."

"I hope he is good to the city. I am tired of all this fighting," the man said, and then closed his eyes.

*So am I, sir. So am I. Though some of my men live for conflict.*

They sat in the hot bath for an hour until their time was up and they were chased out.

The next stop was a roadside bakery that proudly advertised itself:

## FINEST BREAD ALEXANDRIAN WHEAT

They gorged on an expensive but delicious meal of flat, circularly shaped bread with small amounts of salt, some olive, pieces of purple carrot, slices of peach, grapes, and wine. Butcher's meat, they learned, was almost impossible to get unless they were wealthy.

*Available back home, and so simple to procure,* Spartacus thought. *The greatest city on earth, they say, and you cannot even get meat!*

"I really do not like barley," he said as he chewed the bread. "This bread is Zibelthiurdos' gift to earth."

Often the coarsest bread, *panis sordidus,* was made with bran and barley and given as ration during the marches. He *hated* it.

"You've told that to us a hundred times, sir. We know. You don't like barley. Cockroaches are the most disgusting of all creatures. Nothing tastes better than a fat strip of meat. Our *sicas* are more dangerous than gladiuses. Think before you act. What use is valor without a plan to victory. We've heard it all many times."

"Hu, hu, hu," he laughed, with his mouth full and little pieces falling off his thick beard. It had taken multiple washings to clean the blood from the thick hair, and he was thankful that Sulla had allowed the auxiliaries to keep their beards and long hair after arriving in Capua. *Gives them a fierce and backward look,* someone had apparently counseled the general.

"Let us see the city!"

He ordered that no one would be allowed to drink or run into another brothel, causing some to groan and complain.

"Why do you pain us so, Mother, sir?"

They took one of the main paths and walked further south, where the more impressive temples, theaters, and government structures lay. But their stroll came to a halt when roads leading to the most spectacular sites and the seats of the Senate had been blocked by armed guards who warned people to stay away. This was unsurprising given the happenings and impending change of power. Irritated but with plenty more to see, Spartacus and the men turned to other avenues.

They also had to watch out for pesky street urchins, naked or barely so, running around in gangs and harassing walkers. He had to twice swat away hands prying at his belt, trying to dislodge the money bags. *Little runts!* "I will break your hand and nail you to the wall," he bellowed at one frightened boy. He *would* break a hand if someone tried again. While there were regulations against carts in the narrow streets, some clearly ignored it and created traffic jams, causing everyone to curse the driver and his mother.

"Watch out, you fucking oaf!" he yelled at a cart whose wheels almost ran over his legs.

"Language, mother!" one of his men ribbed.

Spartacus enjoyed the sights and smells of the chaotic city, ignoring the assault on his senses. In one area, they came upon an open market with hawkers, vegetable stalls, an exclusive butcher's shop selling pork, a Syrian cloth merchant, several crowded food stalls with bakeries inside and hungry eaters sitting on stone benches, a seller's center where loud men sold sheep and cows to buyers, and next to it, a slave auction. Spartacus was fascinated about how this worked, and he stood and watched as a seller announced prices for a young man who looked Italian, perhaps a criminal at some point, and a woman of middle age. The man was naked, the woman barely clothed, and buyers inspected their condition before offers were shouted and one accepted.

More slaves waited behind, standing in a line, and most were shackled. Spartacus wondered if he would buy a slave if he were to live in Rome, for it seemed like the city had *so many* of them, though he may have mistaken many citizens for slaves. A family with two children, a man and his wife, came next. There was great sadness in their eyes, and bruises on the man's back were evident on inspection. The buyers seemed interested in only buying the children, and on realizing this, the woman began to plead with the seller in her foreign language that he could not recognize. The man stood with his face like a stone while the seller shouted at her. Eventually, another buyer offered to buy the entire family, much to her relief, and they were carted away. Spartacus thought that purchasing a family had its advantages–the children could be put to delicate work until they grew, and all of them together meant less trouble and violence. Perhaps that is what he would do if he raised a household in this land.

His companions had vanished to do whatever they wanted, but they knew the orders–return to the Colline gate by dusk and prepare for the next day. His legs were aching from all the walk, and he hoped for another night's sound sleep before re-entering Rome the next day. What after that? Would they all be paid out and asked to haul their loot and find their own lives? No one knew what General Sulla intended for them. Eventually, before it got too dark and he was berated for tardiness or some other indiscipline, Spartacus made his way back to the Colline gate and reported to the officer for the next day's duties, stating that Legate Curio had asked him to be a prisoner procession guard. Sulla had disbanded the army but had asked the men to remain in their station and within a few miles of Rome, should there be recall orders.

The officer entered him into the duty records. "Fine. The general speaks to the Senate at the temple of Bellona by noon. You will be part of the guard that takes about three thousand Samnites and Marians to an open area near the temple. Be here when called."

After another restful night under the stars and open air, away from the stench of now rotting bodies, Spartacus prayed to his gods for his impending peaceful and bright future. His mind drifted toward a life in Italy for a few years to gain sufficient wealth, and then a return to Thracia. Out of caution, he withdrew his entire salary's arrears from the camp treasury along with two gold rings and a brooch. He left the heavier prized weapons in the baggage train to retrieve them after the completion of the day's mission, except for the one exquisite, serrated dagger he had pilfered from a dead centurion. He secured that on his belt, along with the leather bag with his coins.

Spartacus offered a prayer to Zibelthiurdos and Kotys to offer his friend a satisfying afterlife. Erducos had been his mentor, friend, advisor, and he will feel the loss on lonely days and when he needed wise counsel. If he ever returned to Thracia, he would make a trip to Erducos' town and try to find his family.

Most of his unit had vanished–either dead or simply dispersed into other units.

Florus was nowhere either.

He joined a large contingent of armed men under the order of a Legate to enter the city and march the prisoners. The Samnite and Marian captives were in a sorry state with their torn clothes, bloodied bodies, and bleary, red eyes. They had fought valiantly but lost, and it seems the general had not yet pardoned them. The rumors were that Sulla wanted to parade them by the temple of Bellona so that the

Senate could see the final remnants of a resounding Sullan victory. They could then be released or inducted into some legion outside as was customary.

People lined up the street to see this procession and shouted all manner of abuses at the captured. Some threw rotten fruit and torn slippers, and others spat. A few threw their shit-buckets at the men. This time Spartacus got to gawk at some magnificent temples, baths, theaters, forums, and luxurious villas on a hill on the way. *Perhaps Hermos was truthful about a few things.*

Eventually, the crowds thinned, and the space opened. Ahead, he could see the semi-circular structure of a theater and a few temples to his right.

Many toga-wearing men, Senators, stood on the steps of the temple of Bellona, watching the procession warily. A narrow passage in front of the temple turned right, and after a short distance, opened into a quadrangle surrounded by several buildings.

"Hurry up! Go inside! Sit! Sit!" Senior officers forced the prisoners to the center and ordered Spartacus and other soldiers to hem the captives. The area was not large enough for the contingent, and men jostled for space. Prisoners who pushed into the surrounding guard lines were beaten and stabbed to keep control.

He was told that General Sulla would enter the temple of Bellona at noon and address the Senate. Sulla had already sent the severed heads of several defeated enemy commanders, an unusual display of ruthlessness, and cowed the Senate. This speech would conclude the transfer of powers and appoint Sulla as dictator.

Spartacus admired Sulla. The man was a genius on the battlefield, clever and ingenuous in his methods to entice the enemy to defect to his side, and ruthless when he needed to be. *The way I should mold myself.*

Noon was near, and Spartacus hoped that this business would be completed so he could resume his everyday life.

Suddenly, loud whistles filled the air.

Spartacus was surprised to see many legionaries running through the narrow passage and taking position behind the guards, along all axis of the quadrangle. They held no swords or pilums, but on their belt were several darts. Why the excessive security for beaten, unarmed men, standing fearfully and already surrounded by armed guards? Was anyone in the crowd making mischief? He saw nothing of the kind.

*Why all this clamor when all we have is these miserable, beaten men complying with every order?*

Murmurs filled the narrow, stifling space. Many of the squatting prisoners stood, looking around. Some began to shout, asking to be let go.

Officers sounded whistles for the guards to bring their shields up. Spartacus took a defensive stance and readied to push prisoners back, should they try to break the lines.

*What is happening?*

It was a bright, cool day, and finally, the sun was almost at its zenith. He felt the breath and adjustments of a legionary right behind him, heard men removing a dart from their belt and position to launch them.

*What are they doing?*

With a hair-raising _whoosh, a dart, almost invisible due to its proximity and speed, slammed into a man nearby, ripping through his chest and punching another behind.

Whoosh, whoosh, whoosh, whoosh, whoosh!

The entire quadrangle erupted with screams as darts whizzed past the crouching guards and pierced the panicking and running men.

*Why were they doing this to unarmed, surrendered prisoners? Did the general order this? What foolishness is this!*

Spartacus could not believe the vicious massacre launched from behind his shield. Some of the hapless prisoners tried to jump on top, only to be pushed back, stabbed with pilums, or targeted by the unerring accuracy of the dart throwers. Others tried futilely to play dead, only to be trampled by panicked fellow prisoners. Many got on their knees to beg their killers, but no mercy was forthcoming as legionaries advanced into the crowd and systematically began to stab them.

*Stop, stop it! What are you doing?*

He held his shield and pushed back men who were frantically trying to jump over the human barricades and cursed himself as the desperate men died right in front, unarmed, unable to defend themselves, and murdered through sheer brutality. Who gave this despicable order? What kind of *leadership* was this?

Three thousand men! The massacre continued for a long time until the howls and cries reduced to a whisper leaving tortured breaths of men bleeding from their eyes, nose, and mouths. And then officers ordered the guards, including Spartacus, to step into the quadrant to stab the still-living men, most of whom were in a state of shock, or were whimpering and seeking relief. Drenched in blood, Spartacus himself was in a state of disbelief at this pointless savagery, but who knew what these men had wrought? Perhaps this was unfinished retribution. The grim scene was further compounded by rivers of blood that gave the ground a grizzly red color.

*Disproportional revenge on unarmed people. Just like how the Bessi came to my village and wiped it out. How different was Sulla from Durnadisso then?*

All the screaming and shouting had attracted hundreds of onlookers. More guards moved into the already crowded space. People were tripping over dead bodies, shoving each other. The indiscipline hindered an orderly exit from the one passageway. He was being jostled around in the crowded disorder. *Can't lose my money!* he thought, as he placed his palms on his belt to check that his money bag and dagger were still secure.

"Move, move, idiots!" he whispered under his breath while shoving other guards and some citizens. *What fools would come here to look like this was theater!*

*Agh!*

The sharp pain of a slicing blade just below his right ribs caused him to yell and turn. Did some idiot run around with an exposed blade?

It took a moment to recognize the swaying figure that stared at him, gaunt, unsmiling, and in civilian clothes.

Florus!

A very drunk, red-eyed, death-stared Florus.

The centurion had misjudged Spartacus' stance and missed the chance to deliver a fatal stab from behind.

And right by him, Cleitus!

They gave no time for Spartacus to think, for Florus swung his knife low again, trying to stab Spartacus, taking advantage of the cacophony and struggle all around.

Cleitus tried to maneuver into a position but was pushed back by some guards trying to make their way to the exit. Spartacus could not make out if others were aiding Florus.

*This is the way he wishes to finally end me!*

Spartacus dropped his shield to ease his movements.

He did not have the time to pull out his prized serrated dagger.

In lightning speed, much to the surprise of those who wondered how a big man like him could move so quickly, he slammed his elbow to Cleitus' torso, throwing him back. Then the drunk Florus lunged forward, thrusting his knife, at which instant Spartacus grabbed his wrist and twisted it. Florus was no match for Spartacus when it came to raw physical strength. He yelped when his wrist broke.

Spartacus kicked him with as much force as he could muster, causing Florus to crash into the men behind him. But no one was paying heed as every man was forcing themselves to exit the scene, fearing worse could happen. An instant rage enveloped Spartacus. He had had enough of this bastard and his attempts at his life.

*Enough! You grim-faced sisterfucker!*

Spartacus jumped on Florus' chest, pulled the serrated dagger out, and stabbed him in the chest.

Florus' eyes opened wide at the realization.

*Bastard! Motherfucking pimp bastard! Bastard! Bastard!*

A fountain sprang from the centurion's ruptured heart.

Spartacus stabbed him repeatedly until Florus coughed up copious blood and fell dead.

But even in that noise, Spartacus heard Cleitus shout. "This barbarian stabbed an officer! Stabbed a centurion!"

Spartacus knew instantly the incredible danger he was in.

"He stabbed an officer! Catch Spartacus!"

There was no time to seek Cleitus.

Someone grabbed his collar.

"Hey!"

More men crowded around, pushing, shoving.

"Stop, you!"

Spartacus rammed into a group, ignoring their shouting. Before soldiers turned attention to him, he hunched amongst an exiting crowd and ran out of the passage into the main thoroughfare that was now a mad scene.

And then he ran.

And he kept running until he was out of another gate on the eastern side.

# 24

## ROME

———◇———

Cleitus was brought in fetters before Curio. As was customary, the investigators had tortured him even before questioning. They broke a finger, pulled a nail, and beat the back of his thighs, severely bruising it.

He hobbled on one foot.

What travesty was this? He had helped Florus, but now Florus was dead by the bastard Spartacus' hands, and somehow Cleitus was now answerable to this mess.

The Legate was in a toga, having shorn his uniform within city gates. The men had hauled Cleitus before him after Cleitus loudly protested his innocence and knowledge of the whole affair and why he must be brought before the Legate Gaius Scribonius Curio.

The Legate looked irritated at having to preside over another dispute. "Tell me your story, Cleitus. What shame has the auxiliary brought to me this time? And how is Spartacus involved again?"

Cleitus struggled to speak through his swollen lips. "No, Legate, sir. These men would not listen, but I speak the truth, sir!"

"Well, tell me then," Curio said coolly. "And if you lie, I'll have you tied to a horse cart and dragged out of Rome."

"May the fires of my gods rain down upon me if I lied, Legate," Cleitus said, displaying the best of his Greek, a language he was reasonably good in, and used it to his advantage when needed.

"How many times have I heard these phrases," Curio said, sardonically. "Well, go on."

Cleitus then spoke about the friction between Florus and Spartacus, which became worse after the pay incident. Curio was surprised to hear of the accusation of wage theft but did not comment. Then, Cleitus said, Florus felt slighted by the Legate letting Spartacus go unpunished for thievery. The animosity has worsened during the campaign, but Florus knew that Spartacus' prowess and his hold on the Century made it difficult for him to get rid of the man. Finally, after the Colline gate battle, the Legate sparing Spartacus greatly humiliated the centurion, adding fuel to the fire, leading Florus to enlist Cleitus to bring Spartacus to justice.

"So Spartacus had been up to mischief, by your assessment?" Curio asked.

Cleitus nodded vigorously. "Always, sir! He murdered Durnadisso and made others lie about it. I was there when he killed my chief unprovoked!"

Curio looked surprised but said nothing.

Cleitus winced in pain and caught his breath before continuing. "Then, he spread rumors that the centurion was skimming wages. As if that was not enough, he often insinuated that the brave officer would not fight as hard as the rest of the men. He even extorted men of his unit and took part of their spoils! Finally, he ran from the battlefield and took advantage of your mercy to escape justice."

Curio looked unconvinced. "From what I've seen, he fought hard for Rome. Most of his men seemed to respect him. I put Florus where he was for a reason. And it is known to us that you," he said, pointing to Cleitus, "a man of the Bessi, would have natural hostility to the Maedi."

Cleitus caught his breath. *How did Spartacus have such a senior officer remember and side with him?* "Spartacus is a clever man, sir. he sought to take advantage of the tribal divisions and the centurion's appointment to the auxiliaries and tried to exploit it."

"What do you have against Spartacus, personally?"

He was caught by surprise. "Me? He murdered my chief, sir! And he has been unfair toward the Bessi, he–"

Curio raised his hand to stop him. "What were you both doing at the field?"

"The centurion wanted me to accompany him and accost Spartacus, sir. He wanted to arrest him–"

"For what?"

Cleitus put on a pathetic voice. "How can I, a barbarian, ask questions of my commander, sir? He asks, I obey."

Curio shook his head. He was tiring. "And Spartacus attacked Florus without reason and killed him?"

"He was mad after the massacre, sir. Florus only wanted to speak to him when he attacked, like a crazy dog, like he always does, sir!"

Curio sighed. "It all seems odd that a centurion would ask a barbarian like you on a personal mission to arrest a member of his unit. But as you say, perhaps there is history between those men I am unaware of."

Cleitus bowed several times. Of course, he would not tell the Prefect the truth.

Florus had approached Cleitus after Curio had recommended the tribune to let Spartacus go. Florus had been deeply humiliated, and worse, if Spartacus had a chance to speak to the Legate, then the wage theft and the lies about Spartacus having run would make Florus' situation precarious. Knowing Cleitus' animosity toward Spartacus, the centurion had enlisted him on the scheme of using the pandemonium at the massacre, of which he had advanced knowledge, as a front to murder Spartacus. But the drunk Florus had misjudged the situation and gotten himself killed; the pathetic centurion had indeed lost his once greatness and become a scheming coward.

A coward now dead.

Curio rose from his chair and got ready to leave. *Does he have any order to issue?* Cleitus thought, for this whole affair would be worthless if all he got out of it was a beating and broken bones!

The Legate looked at him with cold eyes. "In any case, no barbarian has the authority to kill a citizen and officer of Rome. We have laws to deal with disputes, and it seems this man prefers to take it into his own hands as if he were still in his backward tribes. He must be punished. You will go find where he is, and if you get him arrested, then I will reward you with two years' pay and recommend you for citizenship."

*Yes!*

"Yes, sir! I thank you, Legate, sir! That will be my mission, sir!"

"And there is no time limit on this. Justice must be done, even if it takes years. Rome never forgets."

Curio refused to put Spartacus' name on watch circulation, for he thought that the garrisons and road blockades were already busy with Sulla's proscription lists. Adding a runaway auxiliary would only look poorly on him. Cleitus was to find Spartacus as a personal mission, one favored by the Legate himself.

Cleitus was giddy with happiness even with various throbbing pains coursing through his body. Not only could he finally take revenge on the Maedi bastard, but he could also get rich and raise his stature, all at the same time! He banished any thoughts of guilt–after all, Spartacus was innocent of all the charges leveled, but such was life. And now, instead of reaping the rewards of victory and valor, the Maedi pig was running to save himself. Spartacus had once slapped Cleitus, and now life was about to hit the arrogant cocksucker harder than anything else.

Curio gave Cleitus an order of free passage throughout Rome's dominions, approved physician care to mend his injuries, and told him not to come back unless the mission was completed. Cleitus marveled at the awesome power these men wielded.

Finally, before leaving, Curio said to Cleitus, "Spartacus is an interesting man. I must know what happened. Bring him alive."

# 25

## ITALY

———◇———

Spartacus exited Rome through an eastern gate toward the Campus Esquilinus, unhindered and taking advantage of the general tumult in the city. He had lost some of his pursuers soon after the attack, and then with his knowledge of Latin, which was the predominant language on the streets, found his way out through a different gate. Soon, he had to make a difficult determination: to walk the trodden paths and find his way to Brundisium and sail out, or to vanish into the wilderness of Italy for some time, live as a bandit, and then find his way home.

He contemplated the advantages and risks of either approach. The north was an unknown–he had heard of larger Roman garrisons, remnants of Marius' army, more roadblocks, and challenging geography. Still, most importantly, he had never been to northern Italy and knew nothing of it. This posed a significant risk.

He was more familiar with the middle, having marched with Sulla's army from Brundisium to Rome through Capua. The merchant traffic and people traveling between these larger cities were higher, giving him the chance to meld with the crowd and access food and shelter. He was confident that given the utter chaos in Rome and the preoccupation of transfer of power, a stabbing of some officer in civilian clothes would get no attention. Thousands had died in the last few days, and he was just a low barbarian of an auxiliary. He was sure they had forgotten about him entirely.

If he were stopped at any checkpoints, he would show his release paper, the absence of slave markings, and his knowledge of Latin and Greek. He would be another traveler looking to go someplace. The people in some of these Southern cities spoke other languages like Oscan, but he was confident of overcoming language barriers.

With these determinations, he made his way to a cobble-stone path that originated in Rome and went to Capua, known as the Appian Way, and joined the throngs. His salary would last him a few months, and he would find odd jobs to sustain himself for a trip to Macedonia. But his gait, stature, and undeniable warrior looks would always be a risk for various nefarious recruiters, and he would have to be careful not to provoke violence or find himself in the middle of it.

He took off-beaten paths where there appeared to be military activity and always returned to the main road. Capua was a large city, and it took him not too long to find employment and a place of rest. There were always things to be constructed, protected, cleaned, patched, dug, delivered, recovered, extorted, maintained, broken, built, or managed. Spartacus' build made it easy to join the crews.

He kept to himself, said little of his past, even to slaves and freedmen from Macedonia and Thracia. Being careful was of utmost importance, for he knew that the murder of a Roman centurion was *never* worth bragging about, no matter how friendly someone seemed. Men were always looking for awards. Living amongst civilians also gave Spartacus a first-hand glimpse into the lives of slaves, and he realized the dreadful existence, which was all too important to note, for he did not want to be caught and sold to this life. Having slaves was good for the masters who had complete ownership, but being one was utterly terrible. The conditions of their servitude were far worse than those back home.

Life in a city, while glamorous at first, was stifling. There was little privacy; the ugly mud and brick homes fighting for space with bathhouses, brothels, temples, theaters, granaries, shops, and storehouses were a world apart from the comfortable huts and greenery all around where he came from. He wanted to shore up his reserves and make way to Brundisium as soon as possible.

Cleitus took a few days to recover from his injuries and enjoyed his freedom. The Senate nominated Lucius Cornelius Sulla as dictator.

Rome was a tense place, for the general, no, dictator, had instituted proscriptions causing many rich and famous to lose their lives and properties. But Cleitus ached to start his new mission in life—hunting down Spartacus and earning his awards.

With the army disbanded, Cleitus had nowhere to go and nothing to do, and he had no desire to join some faraway garrison or take up farming. Why go through the toil when a much simpler task would yield much greater riches? Legate Scribonius Curio was now an established man within Rome. Cleitus wondered if he could return with Spartacus and find employment in Curio's household. *Maybe lofty dreams, but why not?* he said to himself.

He hired two mischief-makers with the promise of riches within a year and set off on the trail of Spartacus. It was not difficult to get on his track—Cleitus surmised that Spartacus would leave Rome for his safety and then plan to head home. And how would he do that? Take the route back to Brundisium. He got lucky as he began to trace steps away from the temple of Bellona. Two shopkeepers remembered the blood-drenched burly man with a slight limp headed toward the eastern Esquiline gate.

Cleitus was no fool.

He had served Durnadisso for years.

He had been a scout.

He hunted down errant tribe members and stalked enemies on numerous missions.

He *knew* how men on the run thought. Where they might go, what they might find comforting, and how they might act.

And thus, slowly, and methodically, Cleitus began his pursuit. And within weeks, it became clear that Spartacus was probably headed to some city in the south along the Appian Way, with Capua being a prime candidate.

# 26

## CAPUA

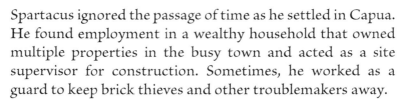

Spartacus ignored the passage of time as he settled in Capua. He found employment in a wealthy household that owned multiple properties in the busy town and acted as a site supervisor for construction. Sometimes, he worked as a guard to keep brick thieves and other troublemakers away.

He lived in paranoia for the first few months, fearful of someone pursuing him, orders for his arrest, betrayal by men who toiled alongside, and so on. But nothing materialized. Everyone here intended to make their coin, fill their bellies, get drunk at every opportune moment, and fulfill whatever desires they had–family, house, whores, wealth.

In this period, he made a few friends. None were from Thracia, for few had yet made way into Capua. Some were local, having never seen anything outside, a few were Greek settlers, some were Samnites, and some were from the north. Latin was not favored, for they disliked Romans, but Greek was acceptable. He had his little group now, men who accompanied him for long sessions of drinking and discussing matters of much and little. He had also attracted the attention of a few women, though none so close as to build a relationship, and in one case having to protect himself from an angry husband. And when there was no woman to be by his side, there were always brothels, and there was no shortage of them in the town.

Spartacus had kept his history closely guarded. His name had become a generic Marcus, giving him the anonymity of a common name. He was a Macedonian of a made-up tribe and even more made-up stories about why he had no impeccable command of Greek.

He cut his hair short, dyed it with streaks of orange, tried to mask some of his tattoos, and attempted as best as he could to erase his reality. *Too many lies make it impossible to keep the lie,* he told himself, and often limited any conversation on his history before his life in Capua. He had come to Italy with Sulla, he told everyone. He had been to Capua during the siege and liked it. When Sulla disbanded the army, he had returned to Capua, which he preferred to the dirty, dingy, crowded Rome.

He told only that he was an auxiliary in Sulla's army to keep a semblance of reality and not be caught in a lie. Given that the military had many auxiliaries from all lands, nothing was unusual about his case.

The peaceful life dulled his intense desire to run back home. Go back for what? His village was gone. Knowing how much distrust there was even amongst the villages within the same tribe, even if he made it back, there were no guarantees that he would be welcome amongst the Maedi. There was also the perennial risk of encountering Roman garrisons and dealing with the uncertainty of not knowing whether he was on a wanted list or not.

He would wait maybe another year or two before deciding. For now, he would eat well, sleep well, make money, and maybe find a fine woman.

Spartacus, no, Marcus, was content for now.

Even as he settled into his life, there were aspects of local life that he was curious about. One was the increasingly popular gladiatorial shows and the other the terrible Roman practice of crucifixion.

On a rare occasion of a free day, he decided to visit a gladiatorial event along with one of his friends, Opiter, a man who had never been outside Capua and an expert on all things local. Opiter had more than once pestered Spartacus to accompany him for this "entertainment," which Spartacus initially considered distasteful. For him, having grown with the norms of the tribe, men fought for valor and not for cheering audiences. It dishonored a warrior's prestige. But with Opiter's insistence and his growing interest, he had managed to save sufficient coin to go and witness one at the arena in a Capua. This large amphitheater was used for many purposes, including circuses, plays, and now these combats.

The event was advertised thus:

COMPANY OF GLADIATORS OWNED BY LUCIUS ASINA AND GNAEUS TULLIUS WILL FIGHT IN THE CIRCUS. THERE WILL ALSO BE MUSIC AND COMEDY. FLAVOR WATER PROVIDED. AWNINGS PROVIDED. SPONSORSHIP COURTESY OF LUCIUS AEMILIUS LENTULUS.

*Exciting! Events back home had none of this pomp.*

The gladiators were amongst the lowest of the society. While he thought he could excel in the sport of fighting another man and making coin, he had no desire to associate himself with these degenerates who had committed various crimes to find themselves in the arena for the entertainment of others, as if they were circus animals.

Some gladiators made good names, but they were so few and so short-lived that there was not much worth in it. There was Gnaeus Lentulus Vatia, a local crook who was establishing a gladiatorial school, for which Spartacus had acted as a construction gang supervisor for an expansion of his villa and training facilities. Lucius Asina owned the largest gladiatorial training school in Capua. People knew that sometimes even free citizens entered the gladiatorial arena to make some money, but they were seen as without dignity and shorn of self-respect.

Spartacus considered perhaps offering himself for a reasonable price but then decided not to sully his name or put himself in the path of accidental death.

*What free men stooped so low to make a mockery of their dignity, fighting before howling crowds as if they were warrior monkeys?* On further thought, even the idea repulsed Spartacus.

He was surprised by the celebratory nature of the event. The narrow street leading up to the arena was packed with makeshift shops with yelling sellers–trinkets, clothes, snacks, perfumes of questionable origin, olives and grapes, bakery, annoying conches, whistles, all available for the festive entertainment. Prostitutes in their garish makeup enticed single men for a "quick rendezvous" before the event, and there was even an enterprising "guide" who would tell people all about the history of fights for a fee. Spartacus was taken in by the atmosphere, forgetting the rather steep price he had to pay to get in.

The amphitheater had several entrances, and there was a strict hierarchy in who sat where. Opiter and Spartacus, as the working class, would be in the more distant upper levels with stone benches, from where the arena may not afford the thrill of a close-up. They made their way to their location, aided by shouting organizers, and sat on the warm stone platform waiting for the event to begin. There was a Senator from Rome in attendance, an ex-consul, two wealthy patrons of the city, and some other dignitaries from Roman client states.

Some small talk, and finally, the organizers announced the evening's affair.

*Songs by the enchanting Verginia!* (Many cheers)

*A play by the master of Capua, Lucius Gellius Fado!* (Some cheers)

*Two spectacular gladiator fights between the Capua's Lucius Asina's ludus and Gnaeus Tullius of Herculaneum!* (The loudest cheers and jeers)

*A closing ceremony of song and dance!*

"Watch Verginia," Opiter opined, "Amazing voice, and even more amazing breasts!"

"Is that why you're here, for a sweet voice and sweeter tits?"

"Ah, Marcus, making jokes for a change!" Opiter said, laughing. "Who knew that such words would come out of a serious man's mouth."

*Was he really that serious? Did he take his leadership behavior too far, even amongst his friends? How I miss your counsel and wise words, Erducos.*

Verginia was indeed enchanting, with a full voice that met every corner of the amphitheater. Her song bounced around the arena, filling their ears.

She was also beautiful with her flowing hair and a sensuous *stola* that left just enough for the imagination.

He imagined her bouncing breasts beneath him. Wonderful. But so out of reach.

Spartacus found the play by Lucius Gellius insipid–a play about the greatness of characters he cared little about and philosophy he barely understood, and with no comics, Lucius Gellius' play was beginning to bore the audience who soon began to jeer the actors and started yelling for the gladiators. Spartacus, curious and now immersed in this unique experience, looked forward to what was coming next.

Finally, the first set of gladiators was introduced with a clamor, with cymbals clanging and trumpets blowing. Great cheers rose when they ran into the arena, their hands held high and as they took laps. One man was well built, wearing a large, bronzed helmet and a metallic ankle pad, holding a full-sized scutum and a standard legionary gladius in his hand.

"Murmillo," Opiter yelled into his ear. "That one is a Murmillo!"

"What's a Murmillo?"

"Heavily armed gladiators with that costume, that's a Murmillo. They were originally named after the Samnites, but it made people angry, so they changed the name."

"And the other one?"

Opiter pointed to the second man who was now taking his position before the Murmillo and waiting for instructions to begin. "Thraex! Supposed to be Thracians!"

Spartacus almost chastised Opiter but bit his tongue. No one knew he was a Thracian. The Thraex was a stocky man with a pointed helmet, a small circular shield, and a curved blade, mimicking the *sica* of some of the tribes back home. It was a reasonably faithful representation of *some* fighters. Spartacus hoped that this Thraex brought glory to his namesake.

There was one referee to the match, and he issued elaborate instructions to the combatants, part of which Spartacus could not understand. But once that was done, the fighters stepped back and took their stances, hunching, drawing back their weapons, and preparing to launch their attack.

*Pheeeeee!*

The shrill whistle and the crowd's roar signaled the gladiators to put on the show. The Murmillo was quick on his feet for his size, thrusting his gladius expertly at the Thraex, who, it became pretty apparent to all quickly, was not quite as skilled. At every chance, the Murmillo slapped the Thraex's shoulders or the side of his torso with the broadside of the gladius, causing the Thraex to lose his footwork or grunt in pain. Only once did the Thraex manage to inflict a minor wound on the Murmillo's thigh, but it was clear that neither was fighting to injure or kill the other grievously.

No matter the intent, Spartacus had to admit that the fight, with its rounds, the clashing of metal, the often exciting footwork and rules, the baying of the crowd, trumpets, and drums, screaming of the betters, all made for a thrilling spectacle.

There were women, *women*, among the spectators, shouting for their players and yelling. It was such an unusual sight. *What self-respecting woman would scream a lowly fighter's name in full view of other men?*

Back home, women were wild and allowed to be themselves during select ceremonies. But outside that their role, as the gods wanted, was to care for their fathers and husbands, and not bray like wild donkeys. They were fierce but dignified. This display was embarrassing and inappropriate. These Roman women, and men, had strange ways.

The Thraex was tiring and was now mainly on the back foot, parrying the opponent's thrusts and twice falling on his behind. The crowd was losing interest, with many shouting for the Murmillo to stab or kill the Thraex, though nothing suggested that either would kill the other.

Finally, the Murmillo drew blood by slicing the Thraex on his chest, causing his torso to become wet. Unable to control himself, Spartacus too rose from his seat, cursed him loudly in Maedi, and then realizing what he had done at Opiter's confused look. *I swear in many tongues when angry,* he joked.

The Thraex gave up. He turned away, knelt, and raised his hand. Betters screamed aloud, the audience rose to its feet bellowing, and the referee brought the match to a halt. The Thraex limped away to many boos and shouts, and Spartacus wondered how he would be received by his owner and what might happen to him. Some threw rotten fruit, sandals, and clumps of mud at the departing fighter.

Spartacus sat back, satisfied, looking around at the excited audience. This was a sport, and the people loved a good fight.

The next one was from the up-and-coming *ludus* owned by Lentulus Vatia, the local owner, and it was positioned as light entertainment.

Both from Vatia's school, the two fighters could not be more different. One man was big and powerful, wearing heavy armor, holding a long sword, and thick ankle padding. The other was scrawny, holding a wide wooden paddle and wearing only the briefest loin cloth.

Spartacus was intrigued by the development.

The scrawny man had a voice worthy of great adulation, for the speech carried to the arena. "I will beat this fat arse to the ground and spank him like a whore who paddles a kinky barbarian!" he said, to much laughter, "and his red buttocks shall become like a monkey's!"

The big man waved his sword with anger and shook his bottom. Spartacus had to laugh out loud when he noticed that the big man's kilt was ripped at his buttocks, exposing the hairy abomination to the world.

Their fight was immensely entertaining as well, with expertly choreographed steps, evasions, attacks, mid-fight little dances, and abuses, causing the audience to hoot and laugh at their antics. The act ended with the scrawny man slapping the big one's bare bottom loudly with his paddle, causing the big one to collapse on the ground and roll around comically with his palms on his buttocks. The referee decided that the scrawny man won and declared him victorious, causing the big one to shake his head with great sorrow and heave as if crying loudly. The audience stood up and hollered its approval.

Spartacus was greatly amused. *This* was the type that he could sit and enjoy.

The final combat was with a different costume and fighting style. It was the most exciting, perhaps intentional, so the evening ended on a high note. Spartacus felt that both the gladiators were former soldiers, seeing their legwork, the calculated thrusts of the weapons, and the long period for which they were involved in the ritual of combat. The conflict ended when a sharp thrust pierced the thigh, and the loser collapsed, bleeding profusely, and had to be hauled away by his team. But the audience roared its approval, for the losing man had demonstrated admirable skill.

The day ended with a surprise dance performance of Aphrodite's birth.

Spartacus' stomach growled in hunger. He joined the exiting crowds and purchased bread and olive oil, along with the luxury of a lick of salt. He sat on a bench and ate, cursing how the sellers were swindling him dry. Opiter laughed, saying that these events were becoming popular and eating before the event was what wise men did.

Returning home, his thoughts on gladiators or the sport had not changed. As exciting as it was, watching the lowest of the society, the criminals, and slaves, fight each other for entertainment simply felt beneath his dignity.

He would never do it.

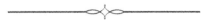

"Marcus, hey, big fat Marcus, you are late for the second time. Sleep less!" Pollio, the supervisor of a large construction site, yelled at him. This villa at the edge of the town was for a Roman senator.

"There's no urgency. We haven't been paid for the last seven days, so why should I come early?"

"Do not be a greedy bastard. Keep the men moving–you will be paid this evening."

Spartacus waved at Pollio and walked to the site. It was a mess, but expectedly so in this earlier building phase. Bricks lay in large stacks, mud piles in different corners, various implements–shovels, picks, hammers, all scattered on the ground as the workers lazed around.

"Get up, up, move!" he yelled as he chased them around, holding a stick. Violence was rare on sites, but men were not usually motivated without shouting and screaming. It had almost become a comical occurrence, much like the haggling in the markets. Shopping was never complete without some energetic negotiations, mutual accusations of stealing and extortion and niggardliness. Construction was never without threats of breaking bones and causing welts. Since none of these men were slaves who could be grievously mistreated, Spartacus had to tread carefully, lest he lose some, and then he'd have to deal with recruiting.

With the workers now going about their day, Spartacus met up with a few of his "site friends," including Pollio, to talk about the usual daily business, plan for the end of the day, and new opportunities.

"Vatia is building a new barrack, large, near his school. He is expanding the arena. May want some good men," Pollio said. "He will want to employ a hefty angry-face like you, Marcus."

"Many want my angry face compared to your mousy donkey-face, Pollio. But somehow, it's always you who gets the lucrative contracts and makes more money by swindling us."

"That's because of my intelligence, barbarian," Pollio said. The staunch Roman was a great believer in their ways. He was all business and cared little for anyone's bloodline or station, so long as they served his needs. He had been good to Spartacus, and in turn, Spartacus had benefited Pollio well by running his projects without trouble.

"I thought Vatia was a crook who doesn't pay the men," Spartacus said. "So why do more work for him?"

"He used to be. But his business is growing, and I've heard he has borrowed heavily to expand. He knows that not paying for the work leads to bad luck and worse outcomes. I think he will pay this time."

The work on Lentulus Vatia's gladiatorial school began two months later, and it had now been over a year since Spartacus' escape from Rome. He had settled well in the town, made a name for himself in his narrow circles, but stayed out of trouble. Vatia's school and his home were connected, and the site had an impressive plan. Upon completion, a twelve-foot wall would surround the area. The villa would have tall, ornate arches and multiple open porticos. A long corridor would connect it to the slave quarters and gladiatorial section. The slave barracks were as expected; small, congested tiny rooms for some families, stone benches with nooks for shackles for everyone else. The gladiatorial quarters were slightly better, with a dedicated kitchen, a bath, and several rooms presumably for the more accomplished gladiators. None had windows. The quarters opened to a larger arena where men could practice. However, various precautions had been built into the blueprint to prevent men from breaking out or attacking visitors. The arena pit would have walls with smooth stone and nearly thirteen feet high with a single entrance and exit. And guard sections on the parapet should anyone get too adventurous.

Spartacus spent the better part of the beginning of the year until summer on Vatia's construction site. He never saw the owner, but having been paid well, this was just another job until it was over, and he moved on to something else. Having seen the plan and the construction, Spartacus told himself again never to even consider being part of gladiatorial combats–it was entirely distasteful and a terrible way to live and die, no matter what the glamor some portrayed.

He decided to take a hiatus from construction work in the middle of the year and simply indulge himself in various pleasures–baths strolls, brothels, playing games, visiting some local scholars to listen to lectures–the last of which his friends found most amusing.

"Marcus, are you ready to work? There's a new job."

"Maybe next month, Pollio."

"Look at you. You've put on weight like a pig. Your fellow barbarians would be ashamed by your decadent living."

"Why do you care what my fellow barbarians think? I thought Romans cared for nothing except their greed."

"Do you not see that I am shaming you so you can get back to work and make me some money?"

"How could I forget that Pollio would look out for himself and no one else."

Spartacus offered Pollio some beer, a cheap concoction made by a seller nearby. It tasted bitter, was more affordable than wine, and Pollio deserved nothing better. But to the man's credit, Pollio made sure to enquire about Spartacus regularly and tried to entice him to his many legitimate and nefarious schemes, including trying to swindle a local garrison commander Spartacus would have none of it. The biggest reason for Pollio's fondness of Spartacus was that he had once saved the Roman from an angry lynch mob that accused him of stealing their wage.

"By the way, Vatia managed to raise money to finish his work, so we're back at that site finishing the arena."

"I'm glad I got paid."

"He hopes to attract the rich and famous from Rome and Pompeii, and also rent his men to other arenas."

"I think it's ugly Romans want to watch men fighting in cages for causes, not of their own."

Pollio scoffed. "You know who they are. Rapists. Murderers. Delinquents. Some are there by choice. Do you want us to feed them meat and shower flowers?"

Spartacus had no answer to that. After all, one might argue that this scum of the society may earn their redemption rather than be simply executed somewhere. The people seemed to enjoy the shows; it kept merchants happy, and if there was commerce to be made, then why not?

"But what if some are innocent and condemned to be gladiators?"

Pollio looked at him like he was mad. "Innocent? You sympathize too much with them, Marcus. Were you an abhorrent in your past?"

"I was only speculating. Do not forget that I am not of this land, and these customs are unfamiliar to me."

"The Republic brings us slaves, and slave labor helps us get rich. It is simply our right over the conquered and the wretched."

"That may be so, but our gods would not condone the mockery of justice by putting condemned men in an arena to fight to the death for someone's entertainment."

"Who is fighting to the death? Those occurrences are rare, and just stories. And why is that any different from torturing them to death? Surely your tribes do that."

Which was true. But there was a difference. The torture and execution was *not* for entertainment. There was a sanctity to the process blessed by Zibelthiurdos. People did not gawk at the dying. The execution after sentencing was always a solemn affair at the Maedi. Compare that to the Roman crucifixion–a terrible, degrading practice. While it was not widespread in Capua, for the *summa supplicium*, ultimate punishment, was mainly reserved for slaves. Since slaves were not cheap to buy, it was administered only in egregious circumstances. The condemned were left hanging on posts by major crossroads, and people gathered around to stare. Some were nailed, some just tied and left for nature to take its course. People mocked the hanging. Some threw stones. Dogs bit into their legs.

Once, out of curiosity, having never seen a crucifixion during his marches, he had walked to a crossroad where a man had been crucified. He was nailed through his wrists and ankles and tied to the T cross. They had flogged him, for his chest and shoulders were bloody with bruising and had gruesome patterns of ripped skin and muscle. His face and neck were swollen. His hands were becoming purple. The man was barely alive, wheezing torturously and trying to haul himself to a standing position. It was an ugly sight, and Spartacus took no pleasure in this display. Torture was meant to elicit information or for proportional justice, and not for wanton display of cruelty. What was this man's crime? A young boy who was gawking at the man poked his ribs with a stick for the amusement of his friends. Spartacus yanked his bony hands so hard that he yelped in fear, and then he chased them all away. He hoped that the man would die soon and escape the torment.

It was a terrible, unfair way to die. But what if the Roman gods sanctioned it?

Spartacus had no good answer to Pollio's question. "We do not have gladiators, and we do not have as many slaves."

Pollio waved his hand to the bustling surrounding. "When you become powerful, like an empire, you too can enjoy these benefits."

"My empire would treat its slaves better, and there would be no fighting to the death for entertainment. Justice will be swift and certain."

"You have strange notions of justice and right," Pollio said, chewing on his lips. He stood and strutted around, mocking Spartacus' light limp and pushing his hands out. "I am Marcus, king of the barbarians. In my kingdom, the slaves shall rule the masters, and any citizen may fuck my wife, huhuhu!"

Spartacus laughed. "Is your mother available to marry, Pollio?"

"Look, the gentle giant made a joke! Are you well? This beer is terrible. Are you trying to poison me? Anyway, what fine Roman woman would want you? Or maybe they would; one never knows."

"Those that have been with me swear by my prowess."

Pollio raised the beer cup. "You are a dreamer. Anyway, let's talk about work. I will pay you a third more. Is anyone else tempting you with better pay?

"I told you I have not been looking."

"Well, someone else has been looking for you, it seems."

# 27

## LUCANIA

———◇———

Senator Publius Vedius Porcina breathed a sigh of relief. The worst was behind him. For months he had stayed in his villa, too scared to venture out, too worried to go to Rome, too frightened that some Samnite or Sulla's commander would pay a visit.

Sulla had no affection for Lucania, for he saw it as the den of his enemies. Porcina had managed to stay neutral during the conflict between Sulla and the Marians, deftly navigating the politics and supplying both armies while convincing each that he was on their side. When Sulla's men visited him after the man became the dictator, Porcina had almost fainted from fear, but he had escaped death by paying heavy penalties. A significant portion of his assets–gold, silver, grain, cattle, and even some slaves, had been levied as a penalty, but his life was spared. And now, much of that ugliness had become history, there was peace, and he was back in the good graces of the dictator after favoring him in the Senate.

But he had to rebuild his estate to keep his favorable position. Money brought power and influence, it helped finance influential men and curry favors, but the money came from production and sales. He needed to sell more milk, more cheese, more slaves, more olives, more olive oil, more barley, more fruit. But to produce more, he needed more slaves, more workers–freedmen or citizens, more guards, more materiel.

More of everything.

At the height of his fear and subsequent penalty payment, he had lost more than half his slaves, farmworkers, guards, and enforcers. He had to sell much of his cattle, and a part of his olive grove had wilted without care. Now he had to nurse it all back to health, so he had borrowed from a more prosperous, previously Sulla-aligned owner of multiple estates, *latifundia*, and repayment would start in a year.

So Porcina was desperate. It also frustrated him that his existing slaves had somewhat noticed his predicament, and the chatter in the barracks had grown louder about their treatment. Mellius was an excellent overseer, but he was vicious, which sometimes created unnecessary disturbance and conflict. Felix, the grazer boy, was one of his best, and he trained others, but Publius worried if the boy would run away anytime. The six other herders were good but not the same caliber. Porcina had tried futilely to purchase robust young herders. And now he worried that Felix might be training the newcomers poorly to sabotage Porcina. He wasn't sure. The Aethiopian, Nigrumus, once a respected slave who imparted much wisdom to new inductees, was no longer himself after the punishment a year ago. He could not be put back among the majority, given his history. Many other slaves outside the household had become weak and lazy, and it all had to change.

Lucia had become sullen but even more beautiful. Porcina, even with his failing health and weakened loins, had enjoyed her. But now, he needed to find a sturdy slave, one right for her, to produce children. Mellius was too eager, and she hated him, and he did not want her to hurt herself. Besides, her mother had rendered good service and begged him to find her daughter another man. The rest of the selection was slim, but he would decide one way or the other soon.

Porcina decided he needed more farmhands and herders, slaves or otherwise, and began fresh recruitment. Once he had thirty or forty additions, he could have them trained, stop worrying about boys like Felix, and get rid of many old-timers who might indulge in mischief sooner or later.

Work them to death; problem solved, he thought, relishing the idea.

# 28

## CAPUA

———◇———

"Well, someone else has been looking for you, it seems," Pollio said nonchalantly. "Your fame is spreading far and wide!"

Spartacus was alarmed. The tingling sensation in his neck told him that no good came of men enquiring about him. He tried to control his emotion and surprise and took a swig at his beer. "Well, I am a diligent worker, Pollio. Why else are you here every other week to harass me?"

"It is hard to find loyal, hardworking people these days."

"But it feels good to know I'm wanted, and my work ethic is appreciated. Who was asking? What was the job?"

Pollio narrowed his eyes. "Now you're interested. I do not know. He was not a Roman either—might be one of your old barbarian acquaintances. He did describe you quite accurately."

Spartacus' heart quickened. *Erducos? One of his other Maedi auxiliaries? Cleitus?*

"I did have others fight with me. We were all disbanded long ago. Did he say his name? Erducos?"

Pollio poured the beer on the floor. "Nasty. I should get you better wine. No, not Erducos. I had no patience for their inquiries. Just told him that yes, you were working for me but were no longer."

"When was this?"

"A few days ago. Maybe I should have told him where you live. But you never know with these fraudsters. Mousy looking man–long hair, thin nose, and teeth missing. Do you know him?"

Cleitus.

That bastard!

Spartacus knew that to pretend otherwise would not escape Pollio's sharp eyes and a keen sense for human behavior. "I had a dispute with him years ago. He stole my loot after a battle, so I beat him, and now he has a grudge."

Pollio laughed. "He looked too eager, and the way he mentioned your name had a tinge of distaste. Which is why I did not give him your location."

Spartacus was thankful. In his strange ways, Pollio was kind to Spartacus. "Was he alone?"

Pollio shook his head. "No. The main reason why I suspected something was off was that he came to the site with two men, but he left behind two legionaries. Why were soldiers with him? He also referred to you by another name, but I forgot what it was."

Now Spartacus was alarmed. Was his name on a list? What was Pollio revealing and hiding? The Roman could keep him at ease until Cleitus arrived with his men. But then Pollio could have easily trapped him without all this banter. Perhaps he was looking after Spartacus.

"You have been a diligent and honest worker," Pollio said as if reading his mind, "And I have not forgotten that you saved my life. I have no desire to put you in harm's way for something from your past. But know that you may be at risk. I can find you a place to hide."

"I, uh," he stammered. *Hide or run?*

"Think carefully. You do not have much time. They *will* find you sooner or later. I have always thought your name was not what you said, and you are not from where you said you are, but those are not my concerns."

Spartacus rubbed his chin. "You have my gratitude, Pollio. Perhaps my past is best buried. But know that I am innocent of charges, whatever you imagine them to be."

Pollio nodded. "It seems you are safer if you leave Capua. There are a few military garrisons and roadblocks from the radiating roads. Stay away from them. Do not go north toward Rome. Find your way to Tarentum or Brundisium and get out."

Spartacus acknowledged Pollio's astute observation. He was a good man, after all.

"Should I take the road from Capua to Tarentum going east?" This was the path that he had marched on nearly two years ago, from Brundisium to Capua. It was where he had fought in Sulla's army almost two years ago, and the rain, the muck, the heaps of rotting dead all reminded him of the terrible days in which he sought glory. And now it all seemed pointless.

Pollio slapped his shoulder and cursed. "You are stupider than you look! If you are in trouble with authorities in Rome, the worst thing you could do is take the main merchant route along the Appian! Soldiers and roadblocks and inspectors everywhere. Your path to Brundisium or Tarentum will not be easy, but there is a way. But first, you must go to Lucania."

Spartacus listened intently as Pollio explained. The man had traveled the length and breadth of the Italian land and knew much about the geography and the politics. They both walked to a dusty area, and the Roman squatted with a stick in his hand to draw on the sand.

"You should go south. The further you go, the more distance you put between you and Roman military presence."

"Avoid big cities like Pompeii and Herculaneum. Keep going south where the towns get smaller, and the mountains get larger. Lucania hates Rome, and you will find people favorable to your travails."

He scribbled a map on the sand to give a sense of the country. "And then, somewhere here, a few days south of Pompeii, you should cross the mountains to get to the east side near the sea. Get to Metapontum. And from there, make your way north along the coast until you reach Tarentum. It will be easy to get lost in Tarentum or Brundisium; the people are far more interested in trade and large criminal enterprises. Find someone to take you to where you want."

Spartacus asked some more questions to get a better sense of what he would need to do—and there was no question that a part of his journey would put him in Lucanian wilderness where he would have to fend for himself and live as a bandit. But he was almost heartened by it—for it was his way since childhood. The mountains, forests, and lakes were no cause for concern. If you respected them, they gave you life, and they gave you much joy.

He thanked Pollio profusely. It had been very long since someone had lent such a helping hand.

"I have repaid my debt of life," Pollio grinned. "Now leave before my greed takes over. Surely there is some money to be made by handing you over! Get out of the south wall. It is almost always unguarded."

Spartacus knew that his time of peace was over. It might take months to get to Metapontum, and winter would arrive soon, which was good for most garrisons retreated to winter quarters, and the roads were often empty.

He leaned forward and tapped Pollio's chest with affection.

"For a Roman, you are an honorable man," he said. "May the gods keep you well."

"And you too," Pollio said. "Make me your treasurer once you build an empire! I love those barbarian women—so feisty. Get me, wives! Now take your valuables and get out!"

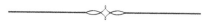

The hasty exit from Capua was reminiscent of his run from Rome. How long could he keep doing this?

Spartacus yearned to be back in Thracia. Those beautiful mountains, lakes, forests, and a more straightforward way of life and code of conduct amongst his people. He recognized that he sometimes created a glamorized version of his home, shorn of its pettiness, constant tribal warfare, lack of advanced engineering to support agriculture and defense, ill-treatment of women and children compared to Roman and Italian households. The people here did not sacrifice their own for god's blessings. But even with all that, the Maedi land was *his home*, and he could go back and rebuild his village, perhaps unite the tribes. He would bring a particular ambition and aspiration which no other Maedi had ever brought to the tribe.

The southern gate was unguarded, and Spartacus made his way to leave the main road, crossing fields and rejoining the south road toward Pompeii. Having disguised himself as a merchant and concealing his weapons, he avoided the checkpoints near the city and then paid for a cart space on a merchant caravan going past Pompeii. He kept curious chatters away with his gruff demeanor and caught some sleep as the cart trundled along. It would take weeks or even months to get to Brundisium, and then he would have to figure out how to sail across to Dyrrhachium or some other port.

He had a terrible scare when the carriage stopped at a military checkpoint. But the soldiers had no interest in the individuals but were instead concerned with what was being transported. He chastised himself for the carelessness and having already learned the questionable nature of some of his co-passengers, made a pact with a man by his side to rotate sleeping duties. This served them well on the highway toward Pompeii.

As they neared Pompeii, Spartacus marveled at the spectacular looming hulk of the mountain Vesuvius. It soared into the sky, its dense forests at the top melting into the wispy whiteness of the clouds above, as if the gods themselves had decided to bond the earth with the heavens above. It was said that many bandits roamed near its top, untouchable. Its massive bulk was bigger than the great mountains back home. The carriage bypassed Pompeii as it traveled south.

The population dropped sharply as they went further south, and the farmlands fell away. It was greener here, the mountains more numerous, the path narrower and in bad shape.

"Welcome to Lucania," the cart driver said, laughing. "I hope your bones aren't brittle, or they will all break and become powder."

Spartacus disembarked from the cart to indulge in purchases at a small town Pollio had mentioned. He replenished himself with hard durum bread, barley cake, corn, and cheese.

He found a small rest stop where he idled for two nights. The owner spoke no Latin or Greek, and Spartacus knew only some sentences in Oscan, so they conversed through sighs. He was helpful. He showed the best route to Metapontum through a mountain pass, drawing on the ground and gesticulating wildly.

But as he lay there quietly in the night, contemplating his next leg of the journey, familiar dread came upon him. If Cleitus was hot on his trail and had resources to aid him in that, there was a limit to how successfully Spartacus could evade him so long as he was in familiar territory. Cleitus had proven to be a wise man. He was cunning, had profound experience as a scout, and it would not take him much to realize Spartacus would soon make his way to the east, either to Tarentum or Brundisium, and then try to escape Italy. And if he were to make that determination, he would no doubt rush to one of those locations and find others to scout the other. There was another option—and that was to travel further south to the end of the Italian land where a narrow strait separated it from Sicilia. And from there, he could take a boat to cross into Sicilia and then wait to take a ship that could take him to Libya or back to Greece or Macedonia. But that was a much longer, harder, uncertain route.

He would take cover in Lucania, go to Metapontum, and then escape via Brundisium.

But what to do about Cleitus?

The only weapon against him was time.

Wait him out.

Tire him.

Make him expend his resources.

Cleitus had always fantasized about a grand living in Italy. He had no desire to return to his homeland, and once he gave up on finding Spartacus, he would probably vanish in the throngs of Rome.

Spartacus would have to hide in the wilderness as a bandit or as a worker in some estate inside Lucania.

When Cleitus and his men found Spartacus' modest little rental room, it was too late. He had vanished, and no one knew where he went. But Cleitus continued patiently, and soon, outside Capua, he got his only hint–Spartacus might make his way to Metapontum.

Cleitus would wait for him there, so he took the speediest route from Capua to Metapontum.

# 29

## LUCANIA

———◇———

"What Thracian tribe are you?"

"Oganti, sir."

"I have never heard of the Oganti."

"We are few, sir. We are a small sliver on the south of the Odrysian kingdom."

"Can someone vouch for you?"

"They are all dead, sir."

"So you say you were in Sulla's army and disbanded after Colline gate?"

"Yes, sir."

"You speak Latin and Greek rather well for an auxiliary."

"I was taught Greek at home, sir. As you know, the Macedonians have much influence there. I have an ear for languages and learned Latin during the campaigns."

Porcina eyed this fascinating man. A hulk by size but almost scholarly in his demeanor. A barbarian scholar, of course, with none of the finesse of a true Roman or Greek.

"I will tolerate no lies. How did you find this estate and what were you doing before? It has been a while since Sulla disbanded."

"I foraged in the wilderness, stole sometimes, and lived for some time as a bandit, sir."

Porcina was taken aback by the honesty. He had suspected strongly that this oversized man could be engaged in violence, for such was the nature of these beasts who needed it when the war ended. But it was as if Alexandros read his mind.

"I have caused no death, sir. What I received, I did for survival and through intimidation. And when I saw the board that you were looking for strong, sturdy men, I decided to embark on an honest path."

He nodded. Surprising, though one never knew the truth.

"So, Alexandros, what are you good at, besides fighting. I do not need soldiers. Guards, maybe, and I need someone who is not lazy to work."

"I am a quick learner, sir. As you can see, I have learned passable Latin already, which is not my language and not introduced in the Odrysian lands."

"That is true. We have had one or two from your lands, though I hear the dialects are all different and there are many tribes."

"Yes, sir. And we all also hate each other."

Publius laughed.

The tall and hefty man before him, with his thick hair and golden-brown curled beard, was also well-spoken. There was a deliberate air about him—in the way he paused his words, his thoughtful manner, and in the clarity of his speech.

He had several tattoos on his shoulder, the most prominent being a lion's. It seemed strange that he was here, so far away from Rome, seeking employment. For now, Publius desperately needed capable hands, and Alexandros, as he called himself, seemed perfectly up to any task.

"As you can see, my estate is growing and needs good people. Remember that while you may be a free man, you are still governed by the laws of this estate, and you are not a Roman citizen. Mellius," he said, pointing to his overseer, who had brought Alexandros to him, "is the supervisor of the slave barracks and manages most of the estates' work. He decides who should do what, and while he is a slave, he is earning his freedom, and you will report to him."

"Yes, sir."

"Mellius will tell you what to do, and you will do it. You will be paid every thirty days at the same rate as you were paid as an auxiliary, which is very generous for barbarians. And you will have three meals and space in the freedmen's quarters."

"Yes, sir."

"I do not get many of your stock. Hardy workers, but often unruly and undisciplined. I hope your time in the Roman army has taught you well."

"It has, sir."

"Who was your Legate?"

The man seemed to hesitate. Porcina had not become a successful politician without identifying and exploiting human nature. Why the hesitation? Why not speak the name proudly?

"Quintus Metellus, sir."

Publius frowned. "Hmm. I do not recollect that name. Too many officers these days. Who else have you worked for?"

The man hesitated again. "Gnaeus Scribonius Curio, sir."

"Ah, I know him. A rising star in Sulla's constellation."

"I was honored to have fought for him, sir."

He studied the man quietly for some more time. And then he asked, "Are you sure no one is seeking you for desertion or some other mischief, Alexandros?"

The man's eyes narrowed, and he shook his head emphatically. "None, sir. I worked various jobs as a construction supervisor, farmhand, loan receiver, trench digger, and wall builder in other towns. I got tired of the noise and dust. I came to Lucania for mountains and forests and wished to serve in the estates I had heard much about."

That seemed like a reasonable explanation. Perhaps the barbarian missed his homeland. "Anyway, Alexandros, I must attend to other work. Mellius, put him to use. My biggest worry is the training and security of herders. The cattle need to be healthy for us to increase production."

"Yes, *dominus*," Mellius said. "I have the activities in mind."

"Very well, then. Mellius will explain the rules, and I expect you to adhere to them. I will require status in a few weeks."

Both saluted the Senator. With that, Porcina left. He would put out some discrete inquiries, later, to ensure no mischief was afoot, for this unusual man was quite certainly not whom he said he was.

# 30

## LUCANIA

———◇———

Mellius was an arrogant bastard, but he had an astute knowledge of the estate's working. He had never served in the army, but he pontificated about how armies should run and what tactics they should use. He knew nothing about the lands east but had many comments about the tribes and their backward bearing as if his German tribes were vastly better.

But most importantly, Mellius relished his power over all the estate workers, slaves, and freedmen alike. The only ones he did not command were Roman citizens in the employ of Publius, the *dominus*. And when he spoke of slaves, it was as if he was removed entirely from the wretched lot and saw himself as a freedman and vastly superior.

"You are a sturdy man with military experience," Mellius said, looking him up and down. "I have a few jobs in mind for you. Train some of our new guards. The old ones have gotten too comfortable with the workers. I also need you to oversee work at the olive grove and then maybe spend some time with the shepherds and cattle herders, as the *dominus* suggested."

"I know nothing about shepherding."

"What you do not know, you will learn," Mellius said imperiously. Like many Romans, he had shaved his head and had a smooth face. But Mellius was not wanting for muscle, even if his mid showed signs of aging. "My tasks for you are more to manage the activities than doing them yourself.

When you're out shepherding or cattle grazing, I want you to see how they do their job, keep an eye, and get them in line. We have had many difficulties in all these areas I told you about."

"Yes, Mellius."

"The *dominus* has cut staff significantly, and there are too few enforcers and too many slaves."

"Do you fear riots?"

Mellius laughed. "No. There has *never* been a riot. No one is so bold as to try something so foolish. They know what will happen to them. I make sure we're always in control."

"So why the need for enforcers?"

"Because they can slow work. They can steal. They can cause unnecessary conflict and fights. They can fail to train others. They can feign illness. Many things keep them from doing what they should for the master: work. He did not buy them to do as they wished. Our job is always to keep watch and discipline them."

It was strange listening to speak of "them" when he was one himself. Mellius was every bit a politician and an opportunist, not unlike Porcina.

"And what does discipline entail?"

Mellius' eyes lit up. No doubt he thrived on control.

"For one, do not beat them so hard that they cannot work. The *dominus* does not like it, but it's necessary sometimes. I'm sure you are well versed in torture–there are ways to break them without breaking bones. Drown their faces in water; deliver a little whipping and add some salt; threaten the men with castration; pretend to drag them to a crucifixion–that really gets them going," he said, laughing. "And women? The pretty ones get special treatment."

Spartacus thought that perhaps most deserved their fate. He would know more as he began to supervise.

Mellius took him on a tour of the olive grove. A part of it looked healthy while the rest looked unkempt. Women, primarily slaves, worked mostly unclothed in the hot sun, digging, pruning, watering, collecting.

"Do not get tempted to fuck one of them. They are unclean. Besides, you need the *dominus'* permission. Anyway, the current supervisor of the northern section is quite useless. He's usually drunk or making attempts to screw one of them, and I'm sick of him. You will keep discipline here for part of the day."

"What can these women possibly do that they need an overseer?" he asked. None of them looked very healthy, and they had their heads down and were busy working.

Mellius scoffed. "You have never seen to the affairs of an estate, have you, Alexandros? A Century may be easier to manage than a group of quarreling women. Have you seen them? Gossiping about each other's looks, who has the master's eyes, about men, about comforts, about food. They fight like dogs on the street if one does not keep them in line with a whip."

Spartacus had never had to manage any group of women, and that too slave women whose conditions here were far more wretched than those back in Thracia. Women back home had to follow strict codes of conduct, as they should by the words of a man, but they were not treated as property without a voice. In any case, he saw it beneath his station, as once a son of a chief, and then an auxiliary leader, to watch over lowly women.

"Surely there are other activities I am better suited for," he said.

Mellius became serious. "You must do some for which you are not well suited and do some for which you are. And for the morning, this is what you will do. And then, in the afternoon, you will accompany the shepherds and herders. We have some troublemakers there."

"What kind of trouble?"

"A couple of ring leaders who think they know it all and are intentionally bringing some cattle home without their bellies full, or losing a sheep here and there, lying that they were stolen. Watch them. Put some fear into them."

"What happened to the current guards who accompany them?"

"We have never had to have guards until an incident with one of the boys a while ago. Since then, we have had a couple of guards, but they find the activity too strenuous—lazy bastards. The *dominus* thinks they're involved with the boys in some conspiracy. I want to pull them off duty and put you instead, and you will lead a couple of them."

"It seems odd that you would put all this effort to watch and manage a bunch of cattle grazers."

Mellius laughed. "You will understand when you start, Alexandros. All is not what it appears to be. Healthy cattle means more money."

"So, what do you expect me to do?"

"First, you will watch the two head boys in how they direct the new men who are learning how to cattle graze–"

"Are there not enough grazers?" Spartacus was surprised. "Why is the *dominus* talking about herders?"

"They are in demand. You can get plenty who say they do it, but few do it well, know when and how to manage the beasts, and have the fortitude to do it. Many think herding cattle is like lazing in the grass fields, but this is not grassland.

You will find that it is not an easy task. These boys are good, but as I said, we think they are deliberately sabotaging work. The *dominus* wants you to fix them—meanwhile, he is looking to buy reliable ones from neighboring estates if we do not make progress."

"So I watch for deliberate mischief, laziness, and take action."

"Yes. You must speak no words with them, for they lie effortlessly. Keep your distance but let them know you will deliver pain if they misbehave. Do you as wish, but do not yet break bones and beat them to the point of incapacitation. At least not until we have replacements."

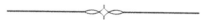

Watching the women was not as difficult as Mellius projected. Apart from breaking up a few quarrels, he needed to do little. Some were taken by him, but he made sure they understood not to approach him. Their gods ordained their life, and he was not the one to remove them from their situation. Mellius also had him inspect the barracks in the night–the smelly miserable dungeon where the slaves lived and slept. He had to check the ankle chains, and a few who were being punished also had restraints on their necks or wrists. They were a pitiful bunch, and Spartacus had no desire to spend more time with them than he had to. They had no fight in them, but he could sense their resentment during inspections and cared none for it. There was a corner in that room that Mellius derisively called the *happy corner*. In that corner was a shredded but visible woven mat, and on it were several bones, with one which looked that of an arm, still attached to a shackle bolted to the wall. A particularly troublesome slave had been whipped, shackled there, and left to die, Mellius said. It was an example for the rest, listening to the man cry and moan and go delirious, seeing his eyes protruding and tongue rolling, listening to his gasps and pathetic lamentations until he died. The corner served as an example of what might happen to the troublemakers.

But three days later, he was put to work on the pasture–accompanying two boys, twelve and maybe sixteen or seventeen, three other men of weak disposition but candidates for training, and then two men assigned to him as guards.

The job was to watch the grazers do their duty, herding the cattle to the richest grass, ensuring they were content, warding away any danger, and then corralling them, so all the animals reached home. Mellius introduced him to the lot, threatening all manner of violence if their sabotage persisted. They protested meekly, but Spartacus felt that their displeasure was just a show, and their constantly shifting eyes suggested they were measuring him. Would they test his patience?

But the activity, which he thought was relaxing and mundane, was extraordinarily exhausting. Keeping the splintered animals in check across the grass, rock, knolls, hills, ravines, and gravel-filled landscape while watching for wolves, foxes, competition, bandits, wild cats, all under an increasingly warmer sun and swarms of insects was far more challenging than he imagined. Besides, none of these slaves were allowed to carry weapons as required by regulations, for Rome's long arm reached here too. The older boy, Felix—they often called all these boys *Publipor*, Publius' boys—was the one fingered by Mellius as the chief troublemaker. And the slave collar around him was evidence of his troublesome past. The younger one, whose name he could not remember, was a Celtic boy who seemed mute, for he spoke no words at all.

Felix was a gangly teen, his limbs lithe and lean. He had the carefree gait of a boy with little concern for the world, and yet his ravaged back, with its numerous scars borne of whips, told a different story. His eyes were intense. There was a rebellious streak in this boy, a dangerous hunger, and while he spoke too little to anyone around him, his command over them was evident. Felix knew his role, and thus he knew how to game it best. He looked like he might be of Lucanian stock, perhaps with some Greek heritage, but his face had similarities with the Northern Macedonians and even Thracians. Had this boy been condemned on account of a crime in his younger years, or was he born into this by way of his mother's or father's miscreance, Spartacus wondered? These grazers were not given any food for the day, which meant they were forced to dig up roots, find fruit, kill the occasional bird, rat, or rabbit to eat. What was the purpose of slowly starving them? Some of Mellius' and Publius' directives made little sense.

He noticed no mischief in the first many days. They were clever, knowing that their new overseer would be vigilant. The boys were gifted. They knew all the calls for the cattle and sheep; they learned to anticipate the beasts' paths and moves; they knew how to ward danger, keep predators away, and direct the animals to the proper pasture in the often-rugged landscape. They knew many paths and had an intimate understanding of the land.

Spartacus had never been a farmhand, for much of his youth was spent defending his village, acting as a guard for merchant convoys, and helping his father administer his domains as a messenger, enforcer, and judge. He had spent time on pastoral activities but found little love for it.

The boys seemed to show off their ability, zigzagging, sprinting, hooting, calling the various cows, bulls, sheep by names, scolding them like they were children. One hefty bull was called *Felixpor*, Felix's boy, and it received a more affectionate treatment than others–quite unlike how Felix was himself being treated by his master.

But all through this, he exchanged no words with the boys except very occasional mundane questions like where they would go next or when they would return. He had to ward off intruders twice, and his physical presence was a deterrence to shepherds of a neighboring competing estate. He could sense the boys' relief by his presence. Neither of them had the physical stature to fight.

But on the ninth day, Spartacus got a glimpse of what Mellius had warned. The boys herded the cattle to a dry area with insufficient grass and kept them there for hours, wasting time as they idled sitting on rocks or pretending to check the perimeter. Only as the evening began did they take them to another familiar area, richer in grass, when they could have very well gone there before.

Spartacus decided to investigate.

"Why did you not go there?"

Felix looked at him defiantly. "Dangerous to go to good grass before evening. Wolves."

"Wolves do not hunt at noon."

Felix looked surprised. But his gray eyes never flickered. "In Lucania they do. And bandits."

"Why do you think I'm here?"

Felix did not answer. Instead, he wandered away toward an errant cow.

Spartacus let it be. He would ignore the contemptuous behavior. How dare the *slave boy* treat him that way? He would give him the benefit of the doubt.

For now.

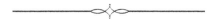

But the behavior continued sporadically, and each time they gave one excuse or another. In one instance, Spartacus delivered a stinging slap in response to an arrogant answer, but the defiance in Felix's eyes had not reduced.

The mischief continued.

Spartacus' patience was thinning.

A few days later, the boys sat on a boulder, and the men in training ran around frantically, trying to bring back some of the sheep. It was evident to anyone with any shepherding experience that men running without a herding maneuver would do little to control the sheep, and the boys, knowing this entirely well, sat laughing.

He had had enough.

Spartacus walked up to Felix.

"Why are you not teaching them how to do it?"

"They will learn," he said, with defiance in his voice.

"It is your job to teach them, boy, or have you decided you are above them?"

Felix shifted on his feet. He refused to look at Spartacus. The boy was perched squatting on the boulder; he jumped off it with ease, leaned against the stone, and then sat down, ignoring Spartacus.

The utter defiance!

Spartacus rushed around and grabbed him by his lanky arm and yanked him to his feet.

Felix yelped.

And now, there was fear in his face.

"Listen, *Felix*, I may not be a Roman, but test my patience again, and I will rip your ear off. You will not die, and you can continue your work," he said as he grabbed an ear lobe and twisted it hard enough to make Felix scream.

Spartacus' rage flared as the boy would not apologize. Like a father whose anger grows like a fire when disciplining an arrogant yet errant child, he let the ear go and slapped the boy hard enough for Felix to turn and fall. He then looked at the terrified younger boy. "Go and help those men, get the sheep back, now, before I skin you!"

The younger boy jumped down and ran, and Felix staggered to his feet.

He wobbled.

But the eyes showed no remorse, and the lips said no words of regret.

*The arrogant slave motherfucker!*

He whipped Felix around and held him in a choke hold. And then he gripped the boy's right arm and began to twist it in a way that he knew caused immense pain but would not pop the socket or break a bone.

Felix finally screamed. *Mother!*

Spartacus let him go in shock. Tears were streaming down Felix's face as he nursed his shoulder. As Spartacus watched, Felix staggered back, put his back to a boulder, and began to sob, his face away from Spartacus. The boy's lean, scar-ridden back shuddered. And he began to rock, singing in a language unknown to most.

*Do not cry, my little one, my sweet flower, my lap is soft and full of love my strong little one, my bolinthos. Do not–*

"Say that again. Again!" Spartacus said, even as a rising heat engulfed his face.

Felix turned toward him, looking confused. His defiance was gone. He nodded and said between his weeping hiccups. "Mother. My mother. Please do not. I was just calling her. It was something she would sing to me, and I never forgot."

"Sing it again."

Felix understood. And this time, he choked his emotions and said the phrases in a dry tone. But there was unending sadness in those defiant eyes.

Spartacus felt something deep within him. A shame that bubbled up in a way he did not expect. A terrible realization grabbed his belly, squeezing it, saying *what kind of man are you?* He gripped Felix by his shoulder and dragged him away from the lingering guards.

"Please do not–"

"Quiet!" With his voice low, he asked, "Are you Maedi?"

# 31

## METAPONTUM

—————◇—————

Cleitus was getting frustrated. It had been months with him encamped in this tiny, decrepit town that had little love for an outsider—a barbarian who was once a Roman auxiliary. His money was dwindling. The two rogues who were with him had fought for more money, accused him of scamming him, threatened to kill him if he did not part with some of his loot. So Cleitus had paid one man and then murdered the other.

He sat in the dwindling light of an oil lamp in his cramped little quarters for which he paid an exorbitant price. He had resorted to working for the room owner to preserve his savings, doing odd jobs like dragging carts, digging ditches in his farm, milking cows, things he had little interest in. The town was conservative too, for no brothel was within its borders, its women too haughty to fuck him, and Cleitus was getting sick of waiting for Spartacus to come this way.

What if the wily Maedi had changed his mind?

What if he had simply bypassed Metapontum and gone off to Thracia via Brundisium or Tarentum?

Had he been fooled?

Cleitus spent much time by the road coming into Metapontum, watching out for Spartacus in any form on disguise. But as days passed, his hopes began to dwindle. He had offered rewards to many shopkeepers and innkeepers that should a big man with a slight limp and a foreign accent come by, they should let him know.

He was busy cutting grass for one of his inn owner's properties when a portly shopkeeper, one of his informers, came huffing and puffing. "Cleitus. Hey, Thracian!"

Cleitus looked at him, irritated. This man often came with many proposals to swindle Cleitus of his money. "What now?"

He rubbed his palms. "You will like this, Cleitus. And this time, you will want to open your money bag and give me all the coins you have."

Cleitus groaned as he straightened his hurting back. "I have heard that many times."

"Two men have arrived from Senator Publius' estate by the mountains, about a day's journey from here. They are asking interesting questions."

Now Cleitus' interest was piqued. "What questions?"

"About a man named Alexandros. A big man with a little limp."

# 32

## LUCANIA

"Are you a Maedi?" he asked again. "Boy?"

Felix recovered somewhat, now knowing that his voice was gentler and there was no indication of more violence.

"I do not know what a Maedi is," he finally said haltingly.

"How did you know those words?"

"She used to sing for me as a child. It was one of the familiar songs. I do not even remember what it means–I just know how to speak the words."

Felix's song was entirely in the Maedi dialect. Bolinthos meant bull, and her song was even known in his village, for it was a song sung by all Maedi mothers to calm their crying babies.

Spartacus inhaled sharply. "Was she brought here as a slave?"

Felix nodded.

"And since when have you lived as one?"

The boy smiled, but it was one with no happiness behind it. "Since she brought me into this world."

Spartacus was angry with himself. What crime has a child committed, being born into slavery? Even among the Maedi, a child born to a slave mother was granted rights as a free born, leaving the sin and station of its mother behind.

Spartacus' accompanying guards walked nearby, curious about the exchange. He lowered his voice. "Now, Felix, listen to me. Do as I say, and do not resist. But we shall speak in a few days."

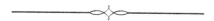

Mellius was pleased that Spartacus had so quickly brought the herders to heel. *You are effective,* he said, *but keep an eye out for some more time.*

This gave Spartacus the chance to converse with Felix in a quiet, relaxed atmosphere, away from the eyes of some other guards. In the last several days, his performance had made a glad Mellius pull the other guards off "herder watch" duty and put them someplace else. The estate was still short of finances. Publius had not yet managed to buy enough slaves or guards and other freedmen, so the directive was to do more with less. And this meant many things–guards working overtime without being paid, slaves working longer hours without rest, replaced clothing, or even sufficient food. The emaciated creatures suffered with no one to care a whit for them.

With the warm wind upon their sweaty necks, Spartacus bade Felix walk with him. The boy was reluctant, having already received an earful from Mellius about an injured cow the previous day. Spartacus knew that Felix was blameless, for the errant cow had lifted her tail and ran off to a creek, driven there by a curious dog, all before the boys or the men could act on them. The intentionally tightened shackle had left red bruises on Felix's leg.

Mellius was a tyrant. He was a lowly, power-drunk, vicious man who saw himself as the king of his slave empire. The whole setup was distasteful, for there was no justice in the actions, no code of conduct, and even the blood-thirsty and perennially quarreling tribes back home never treated their help or the conquered this way. There may be an odd savage or two, but they learned their lesson if their miscreants came to light, but no man, including the chief, could get away with what Porcina did under the guise of law. There were a few Egyptians in the army, and they too said that slaves lived a far better life in their land, a very ancient land, than what was known in Rome and nearby.

The boy walked aside Spartacus, perhaps now realizing that the big man had no intention to inflict pain. He hummed a Latin song as both his raised hands pushed a pole held on his shoulders behind the neck. With no other guards to watch, Spartacus now had the free time to converse with this strange boy.

Felix had already lost weight since he had first met him because Mellius was withholding evening meals, a deliberate act of starvation. There was only so much these herders could get for food without butchering their animals. This was a cruel death sentence.

"Felix, put the cattle to pasture in a place where the others can control them well. And then you walk with me. I want to talk to you."

Felix looked at him curiously but did not question. "Yes, sir."

When they came to the right location, Spartacus ordered Felix to sit by the stump of a tree. And then he lay on the grass, raising his head and torso, with his hands supporting his body.

"What do you know about Thracia?"

Felix did not answer the question, but instead, he asked his own. "Are you a man of the Maedi, sir?"

"I am. And that is how I recognized your cry."

"I did not cry," he said somewhat indignantly.

Spartacus laughed. "They have not broken your spirit yet, boy."

Felix finally smiled. "The gods have kept Mellius from killing me."

Spartacus marveled at the boy's belief that the gods had still not forsaken him. "Why does he have such contempt for you, even though they all seem to acknowledge that you are exceptional in your ability to find pasture, keep the animals safe, and do the hard work well?"

He pulled a clump of grass and threw it. "I do not know," he said haltingly. "He is a cruel man."

*He is lying.*

"Felix, I was the son of a chief. You are protected by me and have nothing to hear. I am not Mellius' spy."

"Sir."

"It is my word that you shall not be harmed. Last night a lion came into my dreams, but it protected a bull from a snarling wild dog. And then Zibelthiurdos raced across the sky, smiling. My god commands that I, Spartacus, take you under my protection."

He felt strange as he said that. He did know this boy. Nor his mother. Felix's life had nothing in common with him. The boy did not even have a birth name–for the title a master gave was the only one the slaves had. And outside those who know him well, he was just *Publipor*, Publius' boy, just a property, like a cow, or a table. Someone among the slaves had once called him Felix, and that name has stuck. Perhaps it was Spartacus' yearning for home, for his people, for his land, that created this strange protective desire to look over this hapless slave boy. A *nobility* required by his station among *his people*. And Felix was one, with his mother betrayed by the turbulent rivers of fate, finding herself far away from home as a slave in a cruel master's hold and bringing into the world a son who knew nothing at all about the goodness of life. But surely Zibelthiurdos had a message for him.

Felix seemed unconvinced. His head was low, and he idly carved patterns on the muddy ground.

"If you fear Mellius, perhaps I can help."

Felix turned to him. "No one helps me. Nigrumus almost died."

Trust would be hard to earn, and words meant little to the boy mistreated since he learned to walk.

"Who is Nigrumus?"

Felix shook his head. "Check the stables. Aethiopian."

Spartacus had seen an older man tending to the horses but had never spoken to him.

"You have nothing to fear from me. But for now, Felix, for your safety, make no mischief with your training and your duties," he said, smiling knowingly.

Felix finally grinned, the mischievous smile of a boy who had been caught after doing no good. He nodded.

A mutual understanding, one small step at a time.

"You are Nigrumus?"

The gentle-looking man, Aethiopian per Felix, stood slowly. His hair was short strands of curled white, and deep wrinkles lined the eyes. "And you are, sir?"

"Alexandros. I am a new guard supervisor, and I work with Mellius."

His eyes flickered with fear. "I have been obedient–"

"I am not here to hurt you. You have done no wrong in my eyes, and Mellius does not know I am speaking to you."

He seemed relieved. "How may I be of service, master?"

"Felix."

Nigrumus' lips quivered, and that dread returned to his face. There was undoubtedly a history that Felix had not revealed but had pointed Spartacus to Nigrumus with intent.

"You have nothing to fear. I only seek some information, and Mellius will never learn of it."

And with a little more coaxing and a few more days of friendly visits, Spartacus learned more about Felix. The boy had been born to a young Thracian woman sold to Publius. Nigrumus did not know who the father was—perhaps he was an overseer, a slave trader, or a real husband who had long since vanished. Felix had started doing small jobs that required delicate hands by the time he was four, and when he was five, his mother was set free, for she had produced enough children who would remain behind in the household. She left, leaving them behind, and without coin to free any of her children but one. Felix showed an uncanny connection to animals, causing the overseer to put him to herding work with Nigrumus. The Aethiopian saw himself as a father figure. Nigrumus was a master on the grazing fields and had trained the boy well, and a great bond developed between them.

And then Lucia gained Felix's attention and became a target of his youthful desire, causing him to enter dangerous territory.

Nigrumus and Felix had barely spoken since Publius and Mellius uncovered the murder and escape plot. Spartacus was incredulous at the utter stupidity of the plan. But then what better could two slaves do, lacking any training or education?

"He is a good boy," Nigrumus said. "But his days are numbered. Felix will be discarded once they find a good replacement or the Gaelic mute grows. Mellius will probably work him to death first as he did to others."

"Does the *dominus* know about Mellius' behavior to the slaves under his oversight? He must care for their well-being so that they are effective workers."

Nigrumus scoffed. "They enjoy the cruelty. Only now that the master is pressed for money that the more productive slaves are being treated slightly better, lest they die or stop working. But when the harvest is bountiful, and milk is plenty, the master's ill-treatment grows."

It was perverse. Mellius had scuffled with Spartacus over trivial things and the perceived threat to his position. And Spartacus worried that perhaps the estate questioned his story.

"He is a good boy," Spartacus finally said. "And I wish to keep him safe for the benefit of the *dominus*. Your words stay with me, old man. I am a man of my word."

Nigrumus nodded slowly. Those eyes had lost their fight long ago, and the savage punishment had extinguished any spirit in the man. He returned to cleaning the horse.

"Why are you taking the slave boy's side? You should warm his hide when I tell you," Mellius commanded. "He may have improved, but I have sent observers who say the boys are too comfortable. The mute is not yet as good, and the three male slaves haven't learned enough."

"It takes time, Mellius. Good shepherds and cattle grazers must do it for long periods to gain skill, no different from soldiers."

Mellius poked a finger at him. "Well, they should be faster, or he is playing truant. The question, Alexandros, is *why* you have been kinder to him. My men say they have seen you in a comfortable conversation. Is he from your tribe?"

Spartacus was alarmed at Mellius' astute observation. This could be dangerous. "He is a slave boy. My tribe does not accept low outcasts, and his station means I have nothing in connection."

"So, he *is* your tribe? He is a Thracian. I thought you said–"

"I did not say he is my tribe, Mellius. Stop imagining. The gods have made him, and *you*," he said, pointedly, "slaves. And it is not my desire to create a favorable relationship with boys chained in a barrack."

Mellius took slight at his words. "I will be a freedman soon, so do not hold yourself so high. You are a barbarian, and the reality will be around your neck sooner or later."

*What did he mean?*

He continued. "It will be your duty tonight to shackle him, and this time, a hand as well."

"How can he take the cattle out if he spends the night contorted, in pain, and unable to sleep?"

"He can and he will, unless he wants another night that way."

"But why, Mellius? What has he done? Doesn't the dominus want healthy slaves, so he does not have to purchase new ones? That was his instruction."

Mellius was visibly angry now. "I decide how to protect the master best! He thinks Felix has learned his lessons from the mischief he committed long ago, but the boy has not. It is only his reputation that has kept him alive, but I will squeeze that life out of him."

And there it was. This man would slowly torture Felix to death, and there was no reasoning with him.

"And I will not let you do that. The master expects me to keep the slaves productive."

He stared at Spartacus, his face now red with anger, eyes alight at this defiance. "And who are you to decide that?"

"I am another protector of the master's interests, a free man, *unlike you*, and wish to earn my keep. And this boy has done nothing so egregious."

Mellius' face turned to granite, and his eyes cold with fury. "You speak too much, Alexandros. Or are you Alexandros? I guess we'll find out soon."

Mellius had slipped up. The overseer knew something he did not—had they sent out people to find out who Spartacus was? Whom would they ask? Where? Rome? Brundisium? He kept his expressions controlled and pretended as if he did not care. "Wasting more of the master's money and time, I see. I wonder what he might feel when he realizes that the days his men spent on verifying my identity and spending his money was pointless."

Mellius laughed, but there was dreadful malice in that sound. "It shouldn't be hard to track a Sulla's auxiliary. The Romans are good at keeping records, and surely a big long-haired barbarian with the slightest limp is not too difficult to track."

Spartacus felt his skin go cold. He was under the delusion that somehow his employment would get no scrutiny—but he was too different from being accepted without questions.

"Well, it will make no difference," he said, with an edge in his voice.

But Mellius moved forward menacingly. "It seems the authority has gone too much into your head, Alexandros. I tolerated you all this time, but the good news is the master didn't buy you paying a handful."

Mellius implied that an untimely disappearance of Spartacus would only save the master the wage, and no one would miss him. The situation had gone dangerous quickly. Mellius was an unhinged idiot whose solutions to problems were mistreatment or murder.

"Watch your words. You are not my master, Mellius. Do not forget who you are."

That stopped Mellius and his goons. But he warned Spartacus before turning. "Sleep well, Alexandros. Sleep very well."

That night Spartacus had one of the guards he had befriended keep watch in turns as he slept. Spartacus knew Mellius would not let the slight go. It was a restless night. Now both he and Felix were in grave danger.

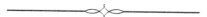

"Here, eat well," Spartacus said, offering Felix a thick loaf of bread, a piece of fine salted meat, and a ripe fig. "I want you to get better. Do not ask how I got all this."

Felix devoured it all, not speaking a word, relishing every bite and morsel, for the boy had never been fed well, and any delicacy he ate was a stolen leftover or a rare offer of mercy by someone.

"Mellius might try something sooner or later, and you must be prepared."

Felix looked alarmed. "What do you mean?"

"The *dominus* is away in Rome. You know what that means."

The boy looked crestfallen. "And you. Will you be here in the estate?"

"I do not know," he said. "I am now in danger as well, for Mellius suspects me. It is only a matter of time."

"If you go, I am dead. If I run away, I am dead," he said, smiling ruefully.

"I told you that Zibelthiurdos has commanded that I protect you, and I shall do that. Not everyone is supportive of that tyrant."

"What do you mean?"

"What I mean is sometimes you find the right time."

Felix's face showed an understanding. "You know what happened to Nigrumus."

Spartacus smiled. "I am not Nigrumus. And besides, I trust you know how to keep your mouth shut. I hope you are not talking to Lucia now."

Felix pretended to be nonchalant. "She is the master's property. I have no interest in her."

His expression and the melancholy in his voice betrayed his desire for her. But helping his romantic interest was not Spartacus' priority. "Good. Keep her out of mind for now and listen carefully."

He outlined a few possibilities as Felix listened intently.

# 33

## LUCANIA

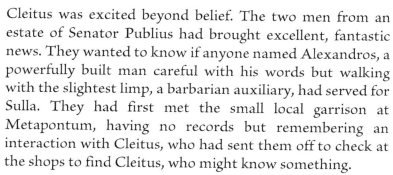

Cleitus was excited beyond belief. The two men from an estate of Senator Publius had brought excellent, fantastic news. They wanted to know if anyone named Alexandros, a powerfully built man careful with his words but walking with the slightest limp, a barbarian auxiliary, had served for Sulla. They had first met the small local garrison at Metapontum, having no records but remembering an interaction with Cleitus, who had sent them off to check at the shops to find Cleitus, who might know something.

*Oh, I know something. I know a lot more than something,* Cleitus had told them. *But you would have to take me there to show him to me and pay me for my service.*

He had convinced them by simply describing Spartacus' mannerisms and style. *Tall, thick black-brown hair and narrow black eyes. The slightest limp, yes, the right leg. Big nose. Speaks slowly and deliberately. Sounds wise, like he is a philosopher. Thick neck. He is not a Macedonian. I assure you that.*

And now Cleitus was on the way with them. In only a day, he would confront Spartacus and take him back to Rome. How easy it had all been! He had spent a few pleasant months at Metapontum, even if annoyed and a bit anxious, but how superb his intelligence and action had been to come here and wait!

Metapontum was in a reasonably flat area close to the sea. Still, the journey inwards became increasingly uneven, with low hills and large mounds making way to larger mountains, river streams, patterns of farmland, pasture, estates, forested hills, little lakes, and barren patches. Accompanied by two armed citizens and armed with a travel note, he felt safe and comfortable, even if annoyed by their air of superiority and disdain that they had to take this barbarian to the Senate. He had thrown around the name of Legate Curio, *a confidant of General Sulla,* and how Cleitus was known and sent by the Legate himself to awe them into quiet submission.

"How much further?" he asked the men. "We have been walking for more than a day. You said one day."

"A day. Two days. It depends on the route. We're taking a slightly longer one for safety, so about another day."

"You are citizens with swords with a letter of authority by a Senator of Rome! What are you afraid of?"

The man was vain and proud. He puffed up his chest. "All that is true. Farms and estates respect that, not bandits. And add to that hot-headed Lucanites who detest Rome."

"Will the Senator be back by the time we have reached?"

"We do not know. If he has not, you will lodge within the estate and wait. The overseer, a slave in fact," he said, distaste evident, "will decide what you should do next."

"The Senator has a slave as an estate overseer?"

"Mellius will be a freedman soon. He has served our Senator well."

*Interesting.*

Cleitus wondered if he could become Curio's overseer in one of his several estates. That must be a luxurious and comfortable job. If a slave could be one, surely, he could be too. It was said that Curio owned more than one lovely property but further north and closer to Rome, which was all the better, for Cleitus loved Rome and all that it offered.

And so, they trudged on, up and down little hills, across streams in the ankle and knee-deep water, and only once were they accosted by estate guards who let them proceed unharmed after the men presented their note. *We hope Rome burns and your fucking Senator dies like a dog* one of them politely said before letting them proceed.

But the journey itself was no longer that terrible. They struck a guarded camaraderie, cracking jokes and exchanging stories. The men found his broken Latin and torturous accent amusing and hollered as he sang bawdy Latin songs learned from the marches. They, too, had served in legions long ago but had returned after discharges. Cleitus told them more about himself–an orphan whose life was spared by an omen and the grace of a Bessi priestess. He had grown in his tiny village, working for various households, until he found favor in Durnadisso's home. The son of the chief then, Durnadisso was a mercurial man who, for some reason, took favor to Cleitus, whose ideas and cunning he appreciated. Cleitus helped Durnadisso's rise, helping him wrestle control of the chieftain's position from his four brothers. He became the Bessi chief's eyes and ears and his master scout and messenger. *I am a bloodhound*, he said proudly to his fellow travelers. *I find anyone, anywhere, once I set my mind to it. If you have a task to capture a runaway, I am your man.*

Cleitus had a family too—two wives and three children, though he had no idea how they were. If his wives had difficulties managing their household, they had permission to sell one of the children. He could always produce more on his return. This his fellow travelers found distasteful, which was preposterous considering how they treated their slaves. The Bessi had slaves, too, as did most Thracian tribes, but the slaves were unpaid servants, no less, and were treated relatively well and had many rights. The powerful Bessi priestesses and priests had always said that Sabazios did not look kindly upon those who mistreated the servants in service of their households, which the Bessi took seriously.

His heart quickened when finally the borders of the estate neared.

"The Senator owns a large estate, and in fact, it was one of the largest until General Sulla caused him to sell parts of it to pay penalties," one of them said, not sounding too bitter about it. "The estate has an olive grove, a stable, a large cattle ranch and sheep farm, and some other minor produce."

"A wealthy man," Cleitus said with envy.

"Used to be. Not so much now with the politics, but he's a resourceful man and will recover."

"I hope he pays me!" Cleitus exclaimed, causing some chuckles.

When the gates of the estate loomed, he became anxious. What if he was walking into trap? But he dismissed the thought—what trap would he be walking to, for he was of no consequence. "Whom am I meeting?" he asked, having forgotten.

"Mellius. The overseer. But be careful of him," one of them said.

"Why?"

"He sees himself as greater than he is, and the Senator has confidence in him. But he loses his temper quickly, so pray that you are right. I hope you can fend for yourself, for the man is known to use his fists liberally."

Cleitus grunted. He hoped that this Mellius would favor him for his knowledge and mission. If Spartacus had annoyed this hot-headed overseer, all the better, and quite likely, knowing the big murderous bastard.

The long road from the gates to the estate was lined with trees and flowering plants. This was Cleitus' first visit to a real luxurious villa with its red brick top, white limestone walls, soaring arches, and ornate doors and windows how these men lived! The overseer, Mellius, German by his looks, was quite pleasant. His two guards first spoke to him quietly as he appraised Cleitus, who waited anxiously.

Finally, Mellius walked forward smiling. "Welcome, Cleitus the Thracian. I hope you had a comfortable walk with these two oafs!" he said good-naturedly. The "oafs" chuckled and then bade goodbye and sauntered off.

"They have been great company, Mellius," he said, struggling to find the right tone for this man was an overseer, important for his mission, but then was also a slave and thus beneath his station.

"I will be a freedman very soon," Mellius said as if reading his mind, "So you may speak and be comfortable."

"Ah, yes, of course."

"Your Latin is passable, it seems."

"Yes, learned during the marches."

"Very good. I must keep you hidden for now," Mellius said. "I am told you also have a mission, a most important one for a powerful Legate. We are very curious. Come with me."

They entered the old but beautiful villa and walked through a long, ochre-floored corridor rich with various blue and white flower patterns.

"Indeed. You will find my visit worthwhile. Very much so!" he said enthusiastically, looking at the silk-draped cushions, Syrian wood tables, little mermaid-statue fountains as they moved to his quarter.

Mellius maintained his pleasant demeanor. "If you want to be safe, stay inside. I wish to know all the details. I will be back."

"Is the Senator back?"

"No. It may be several days, but he has given me his instructions. I decide what is right."

Did he? Did this slave-to-be-freedman understand politics like how Cleitus did?

"Do you know Roman politics, Mellius? Because this goes beyond my identification of this man and who he is."

He looked curious. "Yes, the men told me. That if he is the man whom you say he is, whoever it is, then a politician in Rome wants him."

"Not any politician. And if your master wishes to ingratiate himself further with the dictator in Rome, then this man could be the key. The man whom I helped take off your hands."

Now, it was more than an Italy-sized stretch that a Roman Senator could benefit by Cleitus taking an errant centurion-murderer back to a Legate who might not even remember him anymore. But in the absence of any verification and this slave overseer's minimum knowledge, he could boast and exaggerate any detail. Finally, making good money from this Senator and getting his handsome reward by the Legate would make him a rich Thracian, far more prosperous than he ever imagined. And with Roman citizenship, his power would only grow. Everything was going much better than he ever imagined.

Mellius only knotted his eyebrows. "So you say he's that important to Rome. What makes him special?"

"And I will tell you more. I am hungry. Will there be service?"

# 34

## LUCANIA

———◇———

*Felixpor,* Felix's boy, the bull, was quite the beast. Beautiful with his majestic horns, a glistening black skin like coarse velvet, a bold hump, muscular limbs, he was quite the cows' bull and did whatever he wanted. Felix's stick did little to dissuade him from his pursuits, and it took much coaxing to get him to stay in the herd. He had fathered many calves and was a prized animal in the cattle barn. Herders had very clear expectations to keep him full and happy.

Athena was the queen and Felixpor the king.

"Come back, my boy, you fat ugly arrogant bastard," Felix yelled, clinging to the bull's neck as it tried to swat him with its enormous tail. Felixpor had no desire to comply, and Spartacus laughed at the antics. When he moved to nudge the bull, it swung its horns in anger, causing him to jump back and be mocked by Felix.

Spartacus had defied Mellius more than once to accompany Felix, and he knew that the day to decide whether to run alone or take Felix with him was near. The problem was that Felix's slave collar would make it impossible to take the boy uncontested, unless he found a metalworker willing to risk his life and free a slave— extremely unlikely in this country. But to leave him behind would be certain death for Felix, and thus Spartacus was vexed by the situation, for he had developed a genuine affection toward Felix.

The mute boy and the other herders were far away on this grazing field, but it was a pleasant day, with clouds blanketing the sun and dulling its power. Birds chirped, and it was as if peace had descended on this beautiful earth. Spartacus wondered how wonderful it would be if it could be this way forever. It reminded him of the many days, months, years even, of bliss back home.

But the reality lurked like a monster beneath the water, ready to rise, ready to grab him by the ankles and drag him deep into the dark embrace of evil.

But when?

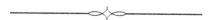

"It's getting late, boy, let us return!"

"Fine. Mellius will have something else to be cross with me about. I'll call the others."

They began to corral the animals. The other herders got ahead, and it was always custom for Felix to be the last, ensuring the herd was accounted for and that every beast returned home satiated. Felix had a spring in his step, for Spartacus was feeding him, and the food had done wonders for the boy's trust in him. He had put on a little more weight, which only caused Mellius to suspect something afoot and frustrated that he could do nothing. Not so close to being a freedman, so he did not want to do anything risky—and this alone was Spartacus' comfort. But all that could change once the Senator returned from his trip to Rome.

The walk would be about an hour, taking them through a flat field, then an upward slope on a broad-based low-lying hill, finally descending into the estate. They would enter through a rusted iron rear gate.

When they came near the base of the hill, he thought he saw some heads peep from beyond the hilltop. This was not unusual as there were often people simply walking by, or mischief-makers from neighboring estates kept a watch, or it could even be Mellius' idiots.

But this late?

And then, as they took more steps, the figures became more apparent.

Two guards.

Mellius.

Cleitus.

# 35

## LUCANIA

Cleitus almost laughed. Spartacus, a farmhand. A cowherd! It was comical and ripe for much loud derision if the situation wasn't that serious. Mellius had become very excited once Cleitus divulged why Spartacus was a wanted man. They could not afford to wait and lose him, and Senator Publius would be thrilled at the mileage he could get from the capture of this murderous thug. Cleitus would get rich, and Mellius, by his association, would benefit as well. The consensus was they would do this discreetly–corner Spartacus far away from the estate where he would have no one to support him and capture or kill him if it came to that. Mellius had an issue with some herders and why Cleitus did not know nor care, but the overseer preferred that the boys be spared unless they posed a significant risk.

Two of their guards had gone around the hill and appeared behind Spartacus. The herder boy named Felix walked with a large bull. The others had separated and had already passed them on the way to the estate, creating the perfect conditions for an attack. The gods were surely with him, Mellius thought, for the time was right, the men were motivated, and there would be no witnesses.

Spartacus had a keen eye–he recognized Cleitus right away, and his body went rigid. He was a big man, but he was fast. The question was whether he would flee or fight. Mellius was supremely confident that there was nowhere Spartacus could run without being caught, for a cavalry rider was at hand nearby. The rider was a poor fighter, and for that reason, his job would only be to take someone on pursuit if need be. Unfortunately, no man with Mellius was a warrior on a horse, which was a disadvantage, but they would have to do what they could with what they had.

They drew their swords and began to trot down the hill. Cleitus had warned Mellius not to underestimate the slow-drawl philosopher-tongued big man. Warned him repeatedly. He hoped Mellius knew how to make the best of four men around one man. Now, Cleitus was no champion himself, but he had fought many battles and survived. He knew his way with a gladius, and if these men followed his instructions, they would all live and become rich. The only problem? Spartacus had a gladius with him. Unfortunately, the bastard was not unarmed.

"Walk closely with me," Cleitus told Mellius, who nodded and followed meekly. The understanding was that the overseer would shut up and follow orders on this occasion. "Do not rush at him. Do not swing your sword like a maniac. Are your two guards trustworthy? Will they follow instructions?"

"Yes," Mellius said, his voice somewhat high-pitched with excitement or fear, Mellius could not say.

They cautiously advanced as Spartacus stood where he was, scanning around him. The two other guards were so far following the orders–they were crouched with their swords out but moving slowly. The *Cleitus noose* was closing in. He hoped to have Spartacus drop his gladius and surrender to face judgment. Cleitus did not care what happened to the man so long as he got paid, and then Spartacus would not be able to touch him. If he were killed, it would be a little harder to wrestle his rewards–surely the Legate would not be very interested in seeing a rotting corpse and deciding its fate.

So Cleitus hoped to do his best.

Spartacus did not advance or attack as they neared earshot. It was as if he was expecting a parley.

"I have no intention to kill you, Spartacus," Cleitus shouted. "We just want to talk!"

"And you, Felix, stay where you are!" Mellius screamed at the frightened lanky boy who stood frozen, restraining the bull.

"What's there to talk about?" Spartacus said, switching to the Maedi tongue.

"Let me speak to him in his tongue," Cleitus said to Mellius, who agreed. They had spoken of this possibility before due to Cleitus' weak command of Latin and inability to enter into a nuanced negotiation.

Mellius was getting impatient.

He saw himself as the hero who could show himself as a glorious keeper of his master's interests.

"There is much to discuss. You should know why I am here. No one will hurt you."

Spartacus scoffed.

The *arrogance* of the bastard.

"I say this by pledging to Sabazios and the omens of the great eagles. I wish to speak and wish no harm upon you. And you two," he said, gesturing to the guards, "stay where you are."

The men stopped.

Spartacus took a deep breath and stood straight. He had gained some weight—must have been the good living since the escape from Rome.

"You lived well in Capua," Cleitus said, attempting a conversation. "And look well."

Spartacus did not smile. "What do you want, Cleitus?"

"The Legate wishes to see you. He asked me to seek you."

He looked surprised. Curious. He shifted his stance, but he did not relax.

"He pardoned you for running–"

"I did not run."

"Well, it seems he believed you. And he wishes to have you in his presence."

Spartacus had his palm clasped firmly on his gladius. "And why?"

"The Legate is about to begin a new mission in Gaul. He wants a capable commander for his Auxiliaries."

His eyes flickered. The words of recognition and promise of glory were enough to stroke any man's ego.

"Is there no one else?"

"What the Legate thinks or wants is far above my station, Spartacus. We do not ask; we only obey."

"When is this new campaign?"

"I do not know. I did not ask. He only said to bring you."

Spartacus looked thoughtful. This was almost too easy.

"When did he ask you?"

When Cleitus told him, Spartacus was surprised. "You have been seeking me since then?"

"Yes!"

"How did you find me?"

Mellius opened his mouth. "Cleitus got lucky. It would've taken time if we hadn't cleverly sent men to Metapontum, trying to find who you are!" he yelled, jeering, swinging the sword low. "Alexandros, indeed!"

This stupid idiot! He shot an angry glance at the overseer and desperately tried to shut him.

Spartacus was quiet. And then he looked at Cleitus. "So you waited in Metapontum until fortune favored you when the men from the estate came looking. Not quite the urgency for a Legate's order. Why are no Roman legionaries with you?"

Cleitus' frustration came through his voice. "Enough questions, Spartacus. Obey the order for once and let us go! Do you want to discard your supreme commander's order?"

He smiled. A knowing curl of the lips. "You want to take me back for Florus' death and reap a reward, do not you?"

Cleitus' heart sank. Mellius looked confused. "You said–"

"Be quiet," he snarled. "Just be quiet."

He turned to Spartacus. "You have nowhere to go. If you run, the severity of your transgression will multiply. Come with me, and there may well be hope for you."

Spartacus' back hunched slightly. He was preparing to fight. Like a big cat ready to spring.

*Mellius, you stupid goatfucker!*

"You have been lying to me while taking the word of Sabazios, so why should I believe what a godless man has to say?"

Mellius was swaying restlessly, and the two men behind Spartacus had tired to crouching. They held their swords upright, adjusted their flimsy bronze helmets, and shifted on their feet.

"It is in your best interests to surrender, Spartacus. Roman law will never forget that you killed a centurion."

"Roman law should know that it was in self-defense after the coward tried to stab me in the back," he said. "And if the Legate had no ill poured down his ear by the likes of you, he would simply ignore the act and recognize it for its intent."

"What is he saying? What is he saying in that annoying slow drawl?" Mellius asked, impatiently, irritated by not being to understand the language.

"Be quiet, you *idiot!*"

Mellius chafed at the insult. "Watch what you say, rat-faced son of a harlot!"

Cleitus ignored the sleight. This was not the time for stupid quarrels. The sun was beginning to set, and this was no place to engage in deadly conflict under fading light.

"This is your last chance, Spartacus. Would you rather take your chances before the Legate or die here, far away from home, without the chance to see glory or laying between the thighs of a beautiful woman?"

Spartacus threw his head back and laughed. "You sound like a terrible playwright, Cleitus; even dogs will shun your speech."

Cleitus was tiring. "Fine. As you wish," he said and turned to Mellius. "Do not kill him if you can help it."

And thus, they began to close the gap with Spartacus. The two men behind him advanced as well, hunching again, careful, heeding the many repeated instructions Cleitus had given them. *Do not rush him like monkeys after a banana*, he had said, *you will die like dogs before you know it.*

Cleitus felt vulnerable without a shield, but four were against a skilled fighter. Spartacus was alone.

But still.

This was nothing like fighting as part of an army, surrounded by those that might protect him and with the support of javelins and cuirass and ankle shields.

All Spartacus had was his gladius.

No armor.

No helmet.

All they had to do was get their blades to slice any exposed part to weaken him. Do it a few times, and he would give up. The body could only handle so much blood loss.

If Spartacus died, Cleitus would cut off his head and hasten to Rome—taking the whole body was impractical. There were methods to preserve the head for a few days.

He stood scanning the sides, looking back and ahead. The herder boy had moved away a little, with the bull looking around anxiously. The bell around its neck tinkled softly as it grunted and shook its head.

They'd need to take care of the boy next, no matter what Mellius thought.

Then Spartacus crouched, and Cleitus knew the beast in the big man had awakened. His muscles, glistening due to the sweat, rippled under the dying sun. The gladius glinted from the golden light upon it.

He spoke no more words, and his eyes darted rapidly.

Suddenly Cleitus felt vulnerable. He should have told the men to fashion some crude shields with wood and leather! He had let his hubris get the better of him. But it was too late now, so he kept advancing.

Mellius moved away slightly, and Cleitus put some distance between them, as planned.

*Converge on him from the corners so that he cannot attack more than one man at a time,* he had counseled them. *Do not cut each other in panic.*

He could hear Mellius breathing harder now. The overseer had never been in combat—all his bravery was in beating, scalding, and whipping tied, unarmed slaves. The fool had already broken his stance by standing straight and slowly swinging his sword as if it were his cock.

*Idiot. Idiot!*

But Cleitus had no time to counsel anyone anymore. Four against one. *Sabazios* would make him victorious. Surely the god still seethed from the transgression Spartacus perpetrated years ago.

Five steps closer.

Spartacus was crouched and tensed, and he looked behind. The two guards were still a little too far away, *fools!* taking steps too slowly, afraid, tentative.

Wish they could–

The Maedi bastard pivoted with lightning speed and rushed toward the two guards, charging them like a bull.

Shocked by his incredible pace they instinctively fell back and lost their composure. And in a fraction, he thrust his gladius with such force that it sliced clean through the first man's chest and exploded his heart. Spartacus kicked the man to free his gladius and turned on the other man whose hand had finally gone up to swing the sword.

Cleitus ran toward him, but it was too late. Spartacus ducked the guard's swing, and then rising to his full height, a head taller than the guard, swung the gladius upward like a bolt of god's anger, and severed the man's head with such force that it flew off, leaving behind a springing fountain of blood. The headless body fell to the ground.

Cleitus closed the gap and thrust his sword, but Spartacus parried the attack and jumped back, forcing Cleitus to lunge. *Where was Mellius?*

From his peripheral vision, he noticed that Mellius was frozen. Pretending to fight, but far away, holding his sword, and shouting something illegible.

*Help me, Sabazios!*

Spartacus' face was contorted with rage. His eyes narrowed, jaws clenched tight, but he retreated a few steps avoiding Cleitus' push. He repeatedly thrust, missing the big man. The dance continued as Mellius stood there, dithering, the coward.

*Move, Mellius, you sister-fucking rat!*

There was no way Cleitus could defeat Spartacus in an individual match, which was why he had four men. Four!

*No! By the grace of Kotys, Mellius, move!*

"Mellius!" Cleitus screamed. "Mellius! Come forward!"

Spartacus glanced at Mellius, who had broken from his trance. He took a brave stance and began to advance. That idiot would be *no match* for Spartacus.

Cleitus felt the cold icy fingers of fear grabbing his neck. Flee?

Give up on this nonsensical mission? He could save himself.

But the promise of a glorious life was like a vice that grabbed Cleitus, and it would not let him go.

Spartacus lunged at Mellius, and his gladius made hard contact with the terrified overseer's sword, causing him to flounder. Then Spartacus swung, severing the man's hand at his elbow. Mellius screamed in fright and pain, his useless hand hanging by a tendon.

Cleitus was frozen; his legs felt like heavy iron at the brutality and power of Spartacus' attacks.

Spartacus did not kill Mellius, but instead, he brought down his lethal blade on the other hand and cut that one off below the shoulder, and the limb fell like a branch of the tree. Mellius' breath caught in his throat, and then he let out a loud howl–a guttural scream of a man who knows his stupidity is about to cause his death. Mellius swayed, disoriented, when Cleitus, unable to move, saw the herder boy push the bull toward Mellius.

Cleitus' ears were ringing so loudly, blood rushing into his head, that he could barely hear a word or scream.

The massive bull charged Mellius and smashed him to the ground.

Then the slave boy, holding a large rock, ran toward Mellius.

*Impossible. He is so thin!*

The boy smashed the rock on the screaming face of the writhing overseer, turning it into a bloody pulp, breaking his teeth, and smashing his tongue.

The blood-stained rock rolled off the broken face. The boy ran to it and picked it up again.

And then he smashed Mellius' face again and again.

Mellius had gone from misguided bravery to spouting blood from his severed hands to having no face at all. Pieces of his skull, fragments of his brain, and smashed eyeballs all splattered on the gray-green earth.

He was now a free man, just not in the way he imagined it to be.

Spartacus calmly walked toward Cleitus, who finally broke out of his terror-induced inaction. He tried to stay low and fight like a–

Spartacus' gladius struck Cleitus' sword, sending shock waves through his elbow and shoulder.

Cleitus yelped.

Spartacus hit his shoulder this time with the broad side of his weapon. Cleitus staggered but tried to fight. But the Maedi slapped Cleitus so hard that his world went deaf.

The sword slipped from his hand.

He turned and tried to run, and then he felt the sharp pain of a blade's prick behind his right thigh and the sensation of warm blood down the skin. He hobbled on, senselessly, not looking back, as if he would get away.

*Help me, Sabazios! Help your disciple!*

Then it was Spartacus' iron grip on his neck.

*Where was the cavalryman?*

But there was no one else to rescue, and in this desolate spot and at this time, no one would be coming either.

*Save me, Kotys, and I shall forever sing your praise!*

With his hand on Cleitus' neck, squeezing the life out of him, Spartacus kicked him in the back, almost breaking it, and let him go. Cleitus collapsed and could scarcely breathe.

"Stop, stop," he gasped. "Stop!"

Spartacus knelt before him. His face was a cold slab of granite devoid of any emotion. "Why are you here?"

"I told you–"

He gripped Cleitus' knee and drove the tip of the gladius into his thigh and kept it there.

An incandescent white-hot pain seared up his leg and torso.

"Stop! We are both Thracians!" he screamed, tears of pain springing from his eyes.

"Tell me why, or I will slice your thigh open and leave you to bleed to death. You still have hope."

*As if he would let me live.* Cleitus knew the code of his warriors. Mercy was not reserved for those who hunted others and then were defeated by them. It was only a question of a painful or a quick death.

"Why?"

Cleitus clutched his bleeding leg and rested his back on a mud mound. "I was offered a bounty and Roman citizenship if I brought you to Curio."

"And why would Curio care?"

Cleitus grimaced. "Are you a fool? You killed a centurion in his legion. Romans do not forget that!"

"You know why I killed him," Spartacus said. "But how did Curio learn of Florus' death?"

Cleitus's head felt light from the stress and injury. "I told him. Listen, Spartacus, you will hear nothing more of me. Just let me go."

Spartacus stared at him, not saying a word.

"I fought bravely in the auxiliaries, like everyone else. We may have not seen eye-to-eye, but would you fault me for trying to make money?" he said, clenching his jaws in pain, aware of how pathetic he sounded, all his bravery seeping into the grass like his blood.

"You hunted me, Cleitus. You wished to make money on my death."

Cleitus' head was swimming. The world felt like it was on a swing. The rays of the setting sun stung his eyes.

"You do not know if Curio would have you killed! What if he let you go and even rewarded you? You would be a free, rich man, and so would I!"

It all made perfect sense.

"But you came with Florus to murder me. How would that make me rich? You failed in your mission, and that is why I am still alive."

The herder boy was now standing beside Spartacus. The sun was now a distant orb, setting behind the hills of Lucania.

What a stupid way to die. So far from home, and with nothing accomplished.

He sighed and put his head down in defeat.

"Cleitus the hound, now just a pathetic dog," Spartacus snarled. "But desperation and greed make men to terrible things, and yours was not the worst. You did indeed give me a chance to parley."

Cleitus nodded weakly.

"Here is what I will do," Spartacus said, and he grabbed Cleitus' right hand and pushed it down to the ground. Cleitus was too tired to protest.

Spartacus pressed Cleitus' palm firmly to the ground, and in one swift motion, sliced off his thumb and two fingers, like a woman cutting vegetables on her cutting board. Cleitus howled and tried to retract his hand, but the Maedi jackal would not let go. Instead, he tore a piece of Cleitus' tunic and bound the injured stumps tightly as he doubled up in pain and vomited.

Then he fell back, exhausted. All his limbs felt like they were on fire.

"Perhaps *Zibelthiurdos* disapproves of me giving you a chance to live, but may you never raise your hand against a fellow man again. Now run to the estate and save yourself if you can," he said. "Felix will help you. Be kind to him, for he is the most innocent in this all. I hope *Sabazios* sees my mercy to you."

Saliva dripped from his lips, but Cleitus murmured a word of gratitude.

Spartacus pulled up his chin and stared into his closing eyes. "If you come after me again, I will gut you like a pig, very slowly, and hang you by your entrails."

Cleitus nodded weakly. The relief of being allowed to live coursed through his veins.

He would think–

Spartacus rose and said something to the herder boy, who nodded fervently. Cleitus' ears were ringing, and he was too disoriented to make much of their conversation. Then Spartacus turned and sprinted and soon vanished into the darkening evening.

A great relief coursed through Cleitus, knowing that the danger to his life had passed. He slumped where he was. The boy squatted near him and said something, and Cleitus barely made out what he said. *Stay here?*

The boy got up and began to run. *Wait! Don't abandon me!*

Cleitus tried to shout, but nothing came out of his mouth. With great difficulty, he rose to his feet and winced. His body was on fire, but he knew he had to get to the estate if he wanted to live!

He stumbled forward, his head swimming terribly.

And then he noticed that there was a ditch in the front. It was too late, as he stumbled and fell into it. The breaking of his ankle was the last sound he heard before his world went dark.

# 36

## LUCANIA

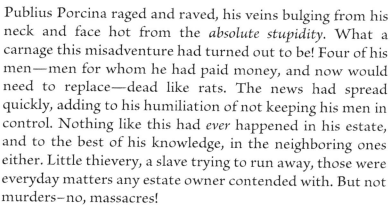

Publius Porcina raged and raved, his veins bulging from his neck and face hot from the *absolute stupidity*. What a carnage this misadventure had turned out to be! Four of his men—men for whom he had paid money, and now would need to replace—dead like rats. The news had spread quickly, adding to his humiliation of not keeping his men in control. Nothing like this had *ever* happened in his estate, and to the best of his knowledge, in the neighboring ones either. Little thievery, a slave trying to run away, those were everyday matters any estate owner contended with. But not murders–no, massacres!

He was nowhere as wealthy or influential as Rome's famous senators and consuls, but he had come a long way before being pushed to desperation by Sulla. And now he was clawing his way back, one bribe, one enticement, one indebtedness at a time, and these *motherfuckers* had to bring peril to his feet. He was *this close* to becoming destitute! His debt was growing, and even losing a man or buying a slave only added to his burden. He had to ramp up his olive and cheese production with what he had, without incurring new costs, even to have the hope of repaying his loans and rebuilding his finances.

He had very briefly met Curio in Rome and mentioned Alexandros the auxiliary by chance. The influential legate did not remember Alexandros, but when Publius described him, Curio remembered Spartacus. He was wanted for the murder of a centurion and asked why Publius was harboring a fugitive.

Publius extracted himself from the dreadful situation and hastened back, but it had been a day too late. Cleitus, the man on the mission to find Spartacus, had arrived at the estate in his absence, and then the idiot Mellius had gone off on a trip to secure the man, only to be murdered. This Spartacus had severely injured Cleitus who had fallen into a ditch, broken his leg, and was saved by the slaver herder boy. But he was alive and under care, and it would take weeks, if not months, to recover fully, thus costing him *more money. Stupid sons of whores!* Cleitus was necessary to curry favor with Curio, though he did not yet understand the relationship between these men.

And now Felix, the slave herder, and several estate guards accompanied Porcina to the field.

"How much further?" he asked, irritated, as they climbed the low hill.

"Almost here, *dominus*," Felix said, urging them on. The ten guards were all heavily armed just in case this murdering Spartacus was nearby. Felix said he had run away when the attack began and saw Spartacus vanish in the darkness as he observed the fight from the hill. *How much of that was true?* Publius wondered. He could have Felix tortured, but what good would that do anyway except to lose his best grazer.

He was shocked when he went to the field. Felix described the surprise attack and Spartacus' savage response. The odious smell hit his nostrils even as he descended the gentle slope. The hot sun had ripened the maggot-ridden corpses that were already discolored and had flies swarming over them, thrilled by the delicious meal.

Mellius was nearest. His face was unrecognizable–smashed into a pulp and its remnants gracing the ground.

But what was worse was both his hands had been severed, and the bones jutted out as he lay dead in a tortured, grotesque pose. *The fool.* Now Porcina had to waste time finding a new overseer.

The two guards were further out. One lay on his back, his chest showing a clean gash. But the other one was headless– with a vulture picking on the rotting neck nearby. Publius stepped away from the stink.

Where was this man, Cleitus, who came with Curio's orders? After all, he was the one who instigated these idiots into an unprepared attack.

Something was nagging Porcina–how did Spartacus smash Mellius' face with what was a rock when he would be fighting with a sword? But he brushed away the thought–it no longer mattered, and strange things happened in battle anyway.

"What do we do about Mellius, sir?" a guard asked.

He looked distastefully at the rotting corpse of his overseer. Citizens who died in the estate, rare but often due to natural causes, received a funeral. But Mellius was a slave, he had served well, but he had never built a bond with the man. "Leave him there."

He would find this Spartacus, one way or the other. He would not let go of this misdeed unpunished; not by the hands of a *barbarian* who *dared* to deceive him and then commit such crimes on *his land!*

He would pay!

Rome's long arm could reach the end of the world.

# 37

## LUCANIA - A FEW DAYS BEFORE

Spartacus knew that his days in Publius' estate were numbered. Felix had to understand the situation, but there had to be a way to help him. The idyllic scene in front would not last forever.

"They will come for me. It is only a matter of time."

Felix was fearful. "And I cannot run. I cannot stay. Who is coming after you?"

"A man named Cleitus. He found me in Capua, and he will find me here. Look at me," Spartacus said, smiling, "I am not difficult to find."

"But in this large country, with so many people?"

Spartacus nodded. "What makes you special, *Felix*? Do you not have a talent with the animals, as if *Zibelthiurdos* himself has blessed you?"

"I suppose it is that god who has kept me alive," Felix said thoughtfully, for if he were any less of a herder, he would be long dead.

"Then Cleitus has that special skill too. I have seen men like that in Thracia. They are like human hounds–they know how to think like the men they seek, they know to ask the right questions, they know how to lay in wait like hunters."

"What will you do if he comes here?"

"He will be here with the desire to kill or capture me."

"So, will you run?"

Spartacus rubbed his chin. "No. I know how Cleitus thinks. He prides himself in his skill, but he is a coward. He will have to convince Mellius and the Senator that I must be captured. But he will not fight me in the night."

"You trust the men keeping a watch?"

"I do. I have saved them from Mellius more than once."

"As you have done for me."

"And I will be always armed. The omens tell me that it is on these grounds where they will meet me. If they come at me, I suspect it will be a small team with Mellius. I will kill all of them. You must run away and pretend it was a surprise."

Felix contemplated the situation.

"And Felix, I will kill Mellius. With him gone, you might get some respite."

"And perhaps freedom someday," he said ruefully.

"Surely Zibelthiurdos wishes that. You must be patient. Do your job well and earn the master's trust. With Mellius gone, perhaps the next overseer will be kinder and be focused on the work."

Felix did not look convinced, but there was little either of them could do. Trying to run with the boy was out of the question—especially with the collar around his neck and his lack of experience in fighting.

"Will we ever meet again, Spartacus?" he said. For everything Felix suffered, his curiosity and spirit had not diminished. "I am the lord of these mountains. I know them so well. I can tell you where to hide and where to go."

Spartacus laughed and slapped the boy's arm hard enough for him to flinch and rub the skin. "We will meet again if the gods will us to," he said.

# PART II

# ITALY 73 – 71 B.C.

MUTINA

ROME

CAPUA

VESUVIUS

POMPEII

IMAGE: UNITED STATES GEOLOGICAL SURVEY TOPOGRAPHIC MAPS

# 38

## THRACIA

─────────◇─────────

Once Spartacus made it to thriving and busy Brundisium, it became easier to hide in the crowd. He had sensibly kept sufficient coin with him during the trips with Felix, expecting trouble and the need to run, and it had helped him make his way unhindered. The garrison in Brundisium had no interest in him, and he paid to be taken to Dyrrhachium from where he joined a merchant's wagon as a guard to make his way north toward the Maedi lands. And finally, after nearly two months, he was home, among the familiar hills and valleys.

The nightmares had not died, but they were losing their power. Happiness had returned, and the thought of being reunited among his people filled him with hope for everyday life. He had returned without the riches, being on the run, but he had learned to fight, to organize, to strategize, and he would put that to use among the tribes. The Maedi had a capital, one with a King even–but he was useless, preferring to take his quarrel with neighboring Thracian tribes and staying ensconced behind the twelve-foot walls of his little city. They sometimes ransacked provinces in Macedonia, but those days had long passed. Spartacus had been to the city only once and resented the pomp of the palace as the people lived in squalor. The affairs of the capital and its king had no effect among the villages that dotted the mountains and valleys far away.

Spartacus would build a new kingdom, powerful, *independent*, purposeful, able to face the Romans in the west and Mithridates in the east, giving no quarter to those that tried to make Thracia their vassal states. Could the runaway son of a village chief become king of all Thracian tribes? The ambition was audacious, but he had seen in Sulla's campaign how men with purpose conquered what seemed like insurmountable odds—so with Zibelthiurdos' grace and Kotys' blessing, why could he not?

His village no longer existed, for it had been erased from the earth during the Bessi attack, every hut burned to the ground, stone structures razed, and fields gutted. A melancholy passed over him as he surveyed the now dry and empty land with grass covering what was once his family's plot. No one had tried to rebuild here—and whoever survived would have sought a new life in a different, better-secured village. He and his father had failed to protect them.

His first call then was to the chief of a neighboring village several miles north of his own, with cordial relations between his father and their leader. But Spartacus knew that his visit was not without peril—for their ways were unmerciful to those that ran from the battle and abandoned their people. And surely Spartacus' conduct was always under suspicion, and news would have traveled about the raid. Did they know he had run away?

There was only one way to find out.

And as surely as he thought, he was seized once his identity became apparent as he sought an appointment with the chief. Customary to their laws, he was placed in chains, beaten into submission, and made to wait for a trial before the chief and the elders. And when the day came, Spartacus stood before Kintoi the Wise, the grumpy leader of his people, a man who had earned his nickname by his decisions and his fifty-year rule as the chief. He had come to this position at only sixteen years of age at his father's death and had since seen to the safety of his people.

Spartacus had great respect for him and knelt with some effort, grimacing in pain from the blows inflicted on his back and shoulders.

Kintoi sat on a stone throne, wearing what looked like a diadem, a practice drawn from Macedonian influence symbolizing royalty. The old man saw himself as a king in his little corner. A delicate threaded golden necklace hung from the wrinkly neck, and a gold brooch, worn on the chest, adorned his crisp white tunic. His three sons sat to his side, and several elders and senior guards sat in a semi-circle, watching him.

"Spartacus, the son of Spartacus of the Maedi, what brings you to me?"

"I have returned from my quest of revenge, glorious Kintoi the Wise, and I seek a place in your family."

Seeking a place in the family did not have to be a betrothal. It could simply be a chance to be among the close circle of the chief.

Kintoi's eyes flashed anger. "It is only your father's reputation and the fondness in my heart for his great name that you still stand tall, son of Spartacus. It is said that you ran, like a coward, when faced with the Bessi attack!"

Spartacus took a deep breath. It would all come to this—how he responded and how the dialog would unfold.

"What no one has said to you, glorious Kintoi the Wise is that I avenged their deaths instead of dying in vain."

Kintoi looked surprised. "Speak."

"It was I who led men to defeat the Bessi. It was I who killed Durnadisso and his henchmen! I did what no one would do, no one!" he exploded, now pointing at the men sitting around. "Who among here raised an army to attack the Bessi after my village was slaughtered? Who raided the Bessi and brought Durnadisso to justice? No one! And yet you think I should have fought a party fifty times larger and died without doing justice to the death of my family? This is why the Maedi is weak!"

They were taken aback by his accusation, and it took a moment for Kintoi to compose himself, having learned new details.

"Speak louder, and I will have your tongue cut off!" he yelled, like a chiding father tired of his child's insolence. "You say things that no one can prove!"

"No one can prove because no one is brave enough to go to the Bessi village by the Lake and find out. If anyone did that," he scanned the room, "they would know the news of Durnadisso's death, for it has surely traveled by now. And ask about the famed Cleitus. Ask if he has returned!"

When no one answered, he continued.

"It is with these arms," he said, pointing to his bruised shoulders, "that I have fought bravely, put to rest the sad souls of my family as I plunged a dagger into Durnadisso and sliced off his man's fingers. And it is with these hands and head that I have learned much about warfare and bring to you a way to become a stronger tribe!"

"You speak big words, Spartacus, son of Spartacus. Just because you fought with the Romans does not make you a general," said one of the sons. The others sniggered. But the dangerous moment of them questioning his bravery had passed. They knew about his involvement with the Romans for he had told his captors at arrival.

He bowed to the man whose name Spartacus did not recollect. "Your words do not pierce my heart, son of Kintoi. But which Maedi has ever returned from a Roman army to share his skills? Which Maedi has led a Roman Century?"

Now they were surprised. Fighting as any soldier in the Roman army was nothing special–many of the tribe had done it, seeking glory or fortune as a mercenary.

"You were a centurion?" another man asked, and Spartacus was surprised by the knowledge.

"Not a centurion, but an auxiliary leader who was next only to a centurion. And if anyone knew my centurion, you would learn that it was I who did the role."

He did not elaborate, but the others understood.

"It has now been more than three years since you left," Kintoi finally spoke. "Why did you return?"

Now it was time to embellish.

"The irresistible pull of my people," he said slowly and deliberately. "And the promise of what we can achieve, and the power we can rise to."

"And what promise is that?"

Spartacus raised his hands and shook the shackles. "If I must speak of what we can do together, perhaps I deserve to stand before the Wise unshackled."

Kintoi smiled, and deep wrinkles lined his sparkling eyes that hid below his bushy, silvery eyebrows. The old man had not yet lost his hair, for it cascaded down on both sides like a white waterfall. "You are a foolish but bold man, Spartacus, and you remind me of your father. Unshackle him!"

"But, Father…" a son began and then shrunk under the glare of the chief. No one was allowed to question Kintoi when he made his decision.

Free of his shackles, Spartacus rubbed his sore wrists and took a few steps to energize himself.

"Look at us. We have a *king* that no one hears from and does nothing but enrich himself. We quarrel amongst our villages, and we raid others. We, including me, fought with the Romans, never seeing how they used us to drive wedges amongst our own, even as they build mighty–"

"They are not mighty! They–" began one of the elders.

"Have you seen their entire legions? Have you seen the armies they muster? Have you seen how they fight? Have you fought with them?" Spartacus said sharply, discarding the pretend protocols of politeness when addressing the chief's council.

The man stammered, and his only retort was to rebuke Spartacus for his rudeness. But the Kintoi ignored it all, sending a signal to Spartacus that he could continue.

"It is only a matter of time before all of Thracia becomes part of the Roman dominion. And the only way to stop it is by uniting and fighting them."

Kintoi leaned back and smoothed his beard. "These are very bold ambitions, Spartacus. What makes you think the other tribes even care about uniting and fighting the Romans? Some are entirely happy to side with them, trade with them, and enjoy the peace."

And now it was Spartacus' turn to stammer. He had led his life as the son of a chief, running errands and never really thinking deep into the politics and policies of the various tribes. His father too paid little attention to the concept of tribal unity, and Spartacus himself had only rarely questioned their methods in his earlier days.

"And if they have not thought so, it is now time!"

Kintoi laughed, but it was hollow and without humor. "You know nothing of our past and how the leaders think, son of Spartacus. The Odrysians see themselves as separate from the rest of us. The Bessi have no desire to work with anyone. The Odomanteans are perfectly content sending their men to fight with the eastern despots or the greedy Romans so long as they're paid–they'll kill their own if they must. We hate each other more than we hate outsiders. Do not forget, Spartacus, that you joined the Romans to fight the Bessi."

"And I did, Kintoi the Wise. And that is what we must leave behind. I hang my head in shame for having joined the Romans, yet I have learned much from their organization and way of life. And I can be your messenger, wise Kintoi, and I shall walk the path to every tribe to say this message!"

Kintoi closed his eyes and leaned back. When he opened his eyes, there was a gentle reproach in them. "Your idea is noble, Spartacus, son of Spartacus. And yet they are of a mind with a shallow understanding of our world. You say you wish to take a message of unity, and the purpose behind that message is to unite us all?"

Spartacus nodded.

"Then tell me, son of Spartacus, who will be the king under whose scepter we will rise and unite and fight our enemies?"

Spartacus expected this question. It troubled him the most. "It should be one with the strength and skill to organize our men with one purpose, Kintoi the Wise. Every tribe can keep its chiefs and kings, but they must fall under a King of Kings."

"Well, how many current chiefs do you think will sit back and let someone else be the King of Kings?"

Spartacus had no words to offer, but he knew the answer. *No one.*

Kintoi raised his bony hand and wagged it around. The loose skin jiggled on the ancient bones, and the bronze bangle slid down to his elbow. "You need a match to set fire to a haystack. A floating branch does not set it on fire, just as words will do nothing to force the tribes to act. There must be an immediate threat of annihilation of *all* our tribes, and no such threat exists—"

"Rome—"

"Quiet, Spartacus, son of Spartacus!" his cracking voice thundered.

He bowed in deference.

"No such threat exists. There must be a tyrant that rules us all and sparks the fire of rebellion, and no such man exists. What is it that will force our men to rise in a mass by setting side all their centuries-old differences?" Kintoi said, looking around the room. No one answered, for it was evident to all, including Spartacus.

The old man was in the mood to impart his deep wisdom. "What do you know of the politics of the tribes, Spartacus? That the Dardani hate the Scordisi for how they ravaged their lands in their forefather's times? That the Odrysians see the tribes to their south as inferiors worthy of being only slaves? That the Bessi have killed so many around them that no tribe wishes to align with them? Or that the Caeni raped and murdered the daughter of the Satrae? So, tell me, Spartacus, son of Spartacus, how will you unite us all under a common banner when we are enemies of ourselves?"

And then Kintoi spoke the truth that perhaps played in everyone's mind and had settled in Spartacus' thoughts long ago—it was just that no one dared speak it loudly. "There is only one way for all our tribes to unite, dear boy. And that is for one Thracian tribe to conquer the other, bring them to an agreement, and then subdue tribe after tribe until there is only one standing and supreme. Only then will there be unity behind a great cause. But until then, so long as is there is peace, the bellies full and minds busy with petty quarrels and satisfied cocks, no great idea will come to fruition. But I praise your lofty thought, son of Spartacus, your father would scoff, but he would admire it."

Spartacus felt deflated. He had averted danger to his being and roused a few sentiments, but his grand ideas of tribal unity and creating some sort of a Thracian empire had elicited little excitement. At best, he would get some more nodding heads and unsolicited advice, and at worst, he would get himself killed.

Kintoi continued. "But I see merit in your skills. You say you trained with the Romans and even led a century. Tell us your tales, Spartacus, and I may induct you to our council, and you can teach our boys to fight!"

The elder son, tattooed and hefty, his hair tied up in a bun and his brownish-red beard curled and braided, seemed displeased. "Father. He has just arrived out of nowhere, telling us big stories. The man ran, leaving a dead wife and father, and you trust him without question?"

"I am judge foremost, son," Kintoi said, "and this man I judge to be of good character. How many times have I been wrong?"

And to that, no one objected, and a few praised the chief that they believed his sound sense of character. The sons were displeased by Spartacus' arrival and demeanor, but they did not question their father, as the code of conduct expected.

Kintoi was readying to leave. "Then, Spartacus, son of Spartacus, I will welcome you to my house. But you cannot be within the council without proving some of your words—so you shall begin by training our boys. Let us see if you have the skills you do. There is one more thing—an aging bull like you must spread his mighty seed before it is too late!"

Spartacus shook his head theatrically as the men hollered.

Kintoi grabbed his crotch and yelled. "A man of your station cannot remain unmarried, so we shall find you a wife. I have someone in mind!"

# 39

## ROME

Publius Porcina had finally managed to find the opportunity to meet the fast-rising Gnaeus Scribonius Curio, now in Sulla's inner circle and a much-wanted man. Porcina was sure that someday this man would be Consul. The main reason for his visit was to raise money, and curry favors in Sulla's inner circle, but he also had other business, one with a more personal nature–but that was minor and secondary. But it was the little issue that had helped him receive an audience in the first place. As a Senator, he had many chances to speak to Curio, but it was never in an intimate setting where he could have the man's ears all to himself. Besides, under Sulla, the Senate rarely met, making it even harder for a man such as himself who only came to Rome infrequently.

Curio was a theatrical man; he moved around like an actor as he spoke, modulating his voice and gesticulating. He had a fine residence in Rome near the Tiber and a large estate further north.

"Publius, my secretary says you have been hounding him to get my time. What is so urgent?" he asked, the gloating evident in his face.

"Ah, yes, Gnaeus, I have more than one matter to discuss, but with my schedule and yours, it has been impossible to find an opportune time."

*You are not the only busy one, mouse-face.*

"True. We are busy men. Have you smoothed relations with the dictator?"

What did Curio know that he did not? Publius worried. In politics and the military, the man with information on others around him was always the most powerful.

"I have paid my price, Gnaeus. And it has been a steep price."

Curio smiled. He paced around in his impeccable courtyard, which had a mermaid fountain in the center and a garden of flowers surrounding the water pool. "Sulla is not a very forgiving man these days, a departure from his earlier years," Curio agreed. "But you are fortunate to have escaped with partial levies and still keeping your head."

Publius subconsciously ran a palm over his head. "That is true. But he has weakened my private affairs so much that I am about to become destitute."

"You own a sizeable estate in Lucania, do you not? I was surprised to learn that a Roman Senator had an estate in that part of the country–the men are not quite favorably disposed toward Romans."

"Not large by any means. A modest one, but one that still requires care. The hate for Rome vanishes when the coin appears. But running an estate there has its challenges."

"I understand. What is it that you seek from me, Publius? Surely this is not a courtesy call."

Of course, it was not. He took a deep breath. Politics in Rome was all about give-and-take. Scratching a man's back so that he may scratch yours.

"I need your help. And I can offer you something that might favor you as well."

Curio raised his eyebrows and held his arms out like an actor, as if asking *what is it?*

Publius stood from his wooden bench, adjusted his new white toga, and walked next to Curio as they paced around the ample space.

"A luminary such as yourself, with military accomplishments under the general, surely does not seek to remain in your current position forever."

Curio understood, but he said nothing.

"Every vote for a Consul is hard fought for and hard-earned. You know that. I know that. And the courtship begins early and earnestly before a campaign, and it is a costly affair."

They both knew where the conversation was headed. Curio nodded slightly and grunted. "It is a miserable time for any aspirant, I am told, and a real drain on their coffers," he said, and Publius recognized Curio's willingness to pursue this conversation.

He had warmed up.

Excellent.

Porcina lowered his voice and clasped his hands behind him. "Would it not benefit you if you were to receive my vote without having to spend any denarii?"

Curio stared at him briefly and then continued to pace. "That is a welcome proposition. And what is it that you seek from me?"

Publius gripped the Legate's shoulder as they walked. "I need a loan to tide me over my misfortunes. Lucania is fertile ground, but I need capital to hire slaves and workers and buy more cattle and sheep. I am barely breaking even in my current state after paying off my current obligations."

"I thought you said you were saving me the costly affair of courting you," Curio said, smiling.

"Of course, I am, Gnaeus. I am asking for a loan, not a bribe. Not only do you get your money back, but you also get a vote. If I prosper, which I will, a strong financier for your future military campaigns, perhaps as a proconsul."

"That is a compelling argument. You will now ask me to give the loan on very favorable terms," he said, grinning.

Porcina smiled. "If I wanted to raise money from a high-interest lender, why would I find time with you? Pompey and Crassus think they are too high and mighty to speak to me."

They discussed the terms–low interest, longer return terms, and conditions for loan waiver. It took a few goblets of wine and some good-natured ribbing, accusations, and counteraccusations. Eventually, a secretary worded the term on parchment, and both men placed their seals on it.

Porcina was thrilled–this gave a new lease of life for his estate and a chance to prosper far beyond his current state and return to his glory days.

"There is one more thing, Gnaeus," he said, "A curious matter that I must bring to your attention again."

"I am listening."

"Do you remember a man named Spartacus, someone from your Auxiliary?"

Curio frowned. It took him a little time, but he finally remembered. "Yes, now I do. Brave man. And now that I remember, he was on the run after killing one of my men, and I recollect another barbarian going after him in return for a promise of some reward, I think. I must ask my secretary."

"You remember well. Now this man's tale did not end there, Gnaeus, for this will surely make your blood boil."

Now Curio was curious. And then Publius shared all the details of Spartacus' attack on his men in Lucania, embellishing the story making Spartacus the perpetrator of many heinous crimes, and how Rome's long arm must reach this man.

# 40

## THRACIA

———◇———

Three months after his presence by Chief Kintoi, Spartacus was married in a ceremony at the sacred temple, a stone edifice dedicated to Zibelthiurdos. Kintoi and his council, elders of neighboring villages, two ambassadors from the Bisaltai and Dardani tribes, priests and priestesses, and some dignitaries from the village attended the occasion.

After offerings of blood and fruit to the god, they sat before a blazing fire as priests chanted verses in their ancient tongue, conferring blessings on the bride and groom. Spartacus placed a beautiful gold chain, gifted by Kintoi, for he had no money to buy something so valuable around Antara's neck. The diminutive woman, a priestess herself, smiled shyly as he locked his eyes onto her.

"Do you hold the hands of the woman as your wife, yours for all life, for you to protect with your blood and strength, and whose obedience you shall receive, and who is blessed by the gods to bear you the most beautiful and strong children, and who shall be by your side to your last breath?"

"By the blessings of Zibelthiurdos, I do."

"And do you hold hands of the man as your husband, whom you will serve as his wife, to whom you will bequeath your attention and affection, bear and rear his children, and care for his strength and be devoted forever?"

"By the blessings of Zibelthiurdos, I do."

Celebrations went late into the cloudless night, with much wine and dancing and singing. As was customary before sending the couple to their hut, bawdy songs and lewd gestures brought much mirth to the gregarious crowd. The red-faced Antara and a half-drunk and giddy Spartacus entered their home. And then, in a perfunctory ceremony, he had to beat many "bride kidnappers" with a sword-shaped wooden ladle and "protect" his wife as she exhorted him to "fight" them and protect her honor.

With that completed and the crowd hoarse and exhausted, the ritual ended with the couple kneeling before the chief, who blessed them with long life, a bountiful harvest, and many brave sons.

When the noise quietened, and silence descended like a gentle veil, he turned to look at his wife. He had barely seen her before marriage, for it was forbidden for the man to pursue his bride, especially as she was a priestess, before the wedding. And having taken hospitality and patronage of this village, Spartacus had no desire to fall afoul of their customs.

But Kintoi had chosen well.

Antara was petite, but she was a radiant beauty. Dark hair speckled with strands of gold and red cascaded down below her shoulders, complementing her large and beautiful black eyes. She had an oval face, a delicate nose, and thin, red lips. Her hips were broad, a great symbol of fertility that she could bear many children for him, and her full breasts thrust through the diaphanous fabric draped over her nude body.

Spartacus was aroused as she neared him with a mischievous smile–the priestess knew the way to increase a man's heartbeat. Antara was from a neighboring village and had been another man's wife years ago, married when she was fourteen years of age. Her husband had died of illness when she was seventeen. And now, childless at twenty, she had accepted when Chief Kintoi had offered her to Spartacus.

She gasped when he grabbed her by the slim waist and pulled her toward him, almost lifting her light body off the ground. The rose perfume smelled heady as he gently kissed her neck. It had been years since he had slept with a beautiful woman who not only aroused his passion, but with one, he could have a future.

Antara looked at the giant of a man against whose hairy and enormous chest she was pressed. Heat radiated from him, and his thick beard tickled her. She was full of pride, for *her husband* was one of the most impressive specimens in a tribe that had many impressive ones, blessed by their gods. But *her husband* was something else. She knew it the first time she laid his eyes on him when he formally introduced for the hand in marriage. But she was behind a veil, for she was a priestess, and her customs forbade revealing herself during introductions. But now when looked at him, she saw gentle eyes, a charmingly ugly face with his thick eyebrows, broad nose, and lip-hiding moustache that merged like an unruly river into the golden-brown of his cascading beard.

She gently ran a finger on his shoulder. Even in his evident urgency, he was considerate, for no violence was forthcoming even if his profound erection rubbed against her inner thigh.

"Your beard pokes me from above, and something else from below," she said, teasingly.

He was surprised by her bold words and his bushy eyebrows narrowed. *Did she offend him?*

Then Spartacus threw his head back and laughed. A mirthful open-mouthed laugh, truly... *peculiar*, for his shoulders shook, shaking her alongside, and a guttural *hu, hu, hu* filled the space.

When he calmed down, he looked at her. "There will be a lot more poking," he said, and laughed again, very pleased with himself.

How could this man be the fearsome beast that Kintoi said he was? But his oiled body screamed with many scars of battle–long lines on his thigh, two crisscrossing on his chest, a deep one on his cheek, one on the temple, a puncture on his shoulder–she might lose count. He was also missing a tooth on the side. The more she *soaked* in his heat, looked at him, even while still enveloped in his powerful arms, the more she was filled with affection.

She closed her eyes for a moment and thanked her glorious gods for finding him for her. Her connection to the divine was powerful, and she was sure that the gods had found him only for her.

"You are more beautiful than any woman in Rome," he finally said, in his deep, cracking voice and in that slow deliberate manner.

"Not on all this earth?" she said, twisting her lips.

"And as full of spirit like those who rip their underwear in gladiatorial matches," he said, and cackled with his lips closed.

But she was so pleased with his words. "My gods have gifted me to you, Spartacus, my husband, and for that I am thankful."

"And Zibelthiurdos has looked down upon me and blessed me with you," he said seriously. "For this union I shall protect forever, and with everything I have."

Antara knew his past, but she was wise enough not to bring it up. Kintoi had told her that it was a source of deep pain and shame, and never to reveal that she knew he had run from his village. But he had sought and received revenge, and he had fought to wash that shame. And she knew then that his words had a deep meaning, and for that she was grateful. Her husband would wreak violence and burn the earth if needed, she was sure. And as she should, imbued by the spirit of their gods and for the pride of the tribe.

She grabbed his thick neck and after failing to pull his heavy face forward, pushed her mouth onto his, surprising him again. He behaved like a wolf that is afraid of hurting a cub even playing by accident. But she would show the side that had the grace of Dionysus.

When he pulled his face back, he said, "You are not wanting for a powerful spirit in you!"

*Our women that are adherents of Dionysus are known for their feisty, wild nature. Have you not learned that?*

And when he grabbed her and rolled on the bed, she came on top of him. She bent low to his ear and whispered. "They say you are a bull, so let me ride you."

# 41

Spartacus settled into a life of domestic bliss with his new wife. His duties included being the chief's guard, trainer of the Maedi men, accompanying the chief or his sons on various neighboring missions, and sometimes as a farmhand, shepherd, or cowherd. The comfort of living had dulled the edge of ambition and great desires. The daily squabbles among the tribes highlighted challenges with forging unity, and Spartacus left those worries behind.

What if the Romans came this way? They were known to institute their governors, encourage trade and order, and usually beat down errant populations—indeed, all that could not be bad. He had seen the discipline and order they brought, even if some of their customs were abhorrent. Still, tribes that cooperated would be allowed to live as they always did so long as they paid taxes, supplied grain and manpower to military campaigns.

But the Romans seemed to be busy–there was no news of any army headed their way, and Mithridates too was preoccupied in regions further away, leaving their lands alone. Some tribesmen searched for fame or money, some died in skirmishes and raids, but nothing much happened in the two years since his marriage.

He had two children by Antara, a boy and a girl. And as was their custom, the children would grow under the mother's care until the boy could be put to work under his father's aegis, and the girl under the mother's.

"Look at him, already strong," he beamed at his toddler, who was larger than children of his age.

In time, Spartacus' fame grew as the "Maedi centurion."

He sometimes traveled to other villages to teach them how to fight—though it was almost always a useless attempt, for without time and rigor, men fell back to their habits—but it made him coin or gave him goods to use.

His wife had resumed her duties as a priestess, and she was a devout adherent of both Zibelthiurdos and Dionysus, the Greek god who had found a home even in the Thracian lands. Spartacus had found a passion for her as he had never done before. He grew to love her deeply and feared her power of communicating with the gods, for as priestess, she knew of things beyond his realm. And yet, as a wife, she was the ideal Maedi woman, dutiful, well versed in all matters of the house, and a good mother. She had a sharp tongue and a temper, and her futile attempts at unleashing fury with her fists on his chest only made him love her more–for he saw nothing but beauty in her blazing eyes, flushed-red face, and flaring nostrils.

The only irritation was the eldest son of the chief. Kintoi was weakening quickly, and by law, his first son would wear the mantle. But he was a petty man, resentful of Spartacus' physical prowess, illustrious background, and adulation from the people. He had pushed more than once to banish Spartacus, saying his service did not absolve him of his past sins but seethed as his father overruled the desire. His brothers, too, saw no threat from Spartacus, whom they saw as a valuable ally for their defense. But no one knew how things would change if Kintoi died.

But then days became nights and a season rolled into the next, Spartacus remained loyal to his new home, chief, children and enjoyed his life as his wife gave him the bliss he had always yearned for.

"Eat less fattened meat, look at your stomach! Have you no shame that you try to teach men to fight with that gut?"

"I don't want to eat the same thing every other day! Learn something new to cook! Talk to your sisters!"

"Come here, don't be angry. Don't call your gods upon me! Hu, hu, hu!"

"Other wives wash their husbands' feet when he gets home. What makes you so special? It can't be that the children get all the attention!"

"If Chief Kintoi's elder son annoys me one more time, I swear I will break his neck like it's a little bird's. My patience is wearing thin. I know, I know you want me to calm down."

And with squabbles, affection, arguments, fights, laughter, and all the usual domestic nature of life, three years passed that way.

Then Chief Kintoi stumbled from his high throne, broke his hip, and died two days later.

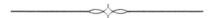

Meanwhile, the annual election for a new Consul in Rome was not without its usual drama, politicking, and bribing. And from all that maneuvering, two men emerged victorious: Gnaeus Octavius, a man with many ailments and terrible oratory, and Gnaeus Scribonius Curio, a fine orator, and an accomplished commander.

Porcina, now thriving again from the capital infusion through Curio's loans, played a role in Curio's victory. His estate had grown, adding new slaves and freedmen to the force, buying adjacent land, expanding the olive grove and the cattle pen. His new overseer was a freedman named Quintus, not quite the brute like Mellius but intelligent enough to know how to keep the growing size of the slaves in the household. The days of savage beatings, torture, and occasional murder of slaves were over. Instead, Quintus had created competing groups of slaves, punished or rewarded for their behavior, work ethic, or loyalty. This ensured peace, and any plots or even hints of mischief were promptly reported. The management of barracks had become more burdensome, the shackles tighter at night as needed, and rations carefully distributed based on good behavior. This created a pliant workforce—and some said Porcina was still too harsh in his treatment and not compliant with the magistrates' orders on matters governing the treatment of slaves—but it was his household, and he was free to do as it suited him. What could they do? Arrest the Senator whom a Consul favored?

Felix the herdsman, Felix, *Publius' boy*, no longer feared for his life. Spartacus was a distant memory, and he was lucky not to be investigated further in the unfortunate events surrounding the attack on the man who called himself Alexandros. Cleitus, the instigator of the attack, had been retrieved grievously injured. Once he recovered, he barely remembered the specifics of Felix's role in the events, thus sparing him from any punishment. He accepted his fate, and that shameful chain around his neck, as if he were a dog, remained where it was, reminding his overseers and supervisors constantly to treat him with suspicion. Besides, many rumors circulated after Spartacus' escape and the death of the guards that Felix may have had a hand in it all and that he may have been the Thracian's lover, all of which he vociferously protested at every chance he got. He remained gaunt and lean, and yet his knowledge of the region was most profound, his skill in herding and gathering unparalleled, and his love for Lucia undiminished, even as she remained out of reach and mothered Porcina's' child. This child only lived forty days before it died of disease. The *dominus* had lost interest in her, much to her relief, but had not given her to another man. She glanced at Felix again, and there was no one to reprimand him for glances, for there were other pretty girls in the household.

Felix hoped Spartacus would return to free him, for of all the men he had known since his childhood, only Nigrumus and Spartacus had cared about him at all. And of them, Spartacus had the skill to do what was needed, and Nigrumus had failed terribly. Nigrumus had grown sicker, and his spirit never returned to him, but he toiled in the stables as he always did, just a little slower. Felix had managed to speak to Nigrumus again, but the relationship never recovered from what Mellius inflicted upon them.

The estate had grown larger, busier, and more herders were inducted to the ranks, and Felix wondered if it were only time before he lost his mantle and his life, should the past rear its ugly head.

And when the year ended, and the Consulship of Gnaeus Scribonius Curio ended, he received the proconsulship of regions east. He set forth with his legions to fight the Dardani, who lived North of the lands of the Maedi and other Thracian tribes.

# 42

## MEIDI LANDS

"Spartacus, Kintoi wishes to see you at the council," a messenger screamed from outside the tent, waking him up from a deep slumber. Since his father's death, the son had taken his name and was thus called Kintoi, the son of Kintoi. This was a clever way for him to remain in the minds and favor of his people, who still looked fondly on the leadership of his father. While the son had some commendable qualities of the father, like an astute sense of the politics and balance of the region, he was less in other ways–with a temper, cunning, and a desire for greater power.

*What now?*

Spartacus' children slept peacefully, and his wife was in the corner, lighting an animal-fat lamp to begin the morning prayers. She leaned down and swayed, chanting in her mystical tongue, summoning the graces of gods to be upon her and the family.

"What does he want?" he yelled back. "I have prayers to make."

"It's urgent, Spartacus. It concerns a threat!"

Spartacus jumped out of his weaved cot and wrapped a garment around his waist. He then wore a long tunic to protect his body from the fierce cold winds and wrapped himself in a thick sheepskin coat. He stretched and walked out into the chilly morning. Mist hung low on their heads, shrouding the green mountains in a cloud of milky fabric. He walked briskly toward the chief's hut along with the other man.

"Do you know what this is about?" he asked.

The other man shrugged beneath his blanket. "Rumors, but who knows?"

"What rumors?"

"Just ask the chief. My teeth are chattering."

The chief's hut was humming with activity. Kintoi sat on his father's throne, surrounded by his brothers, village elders, high priestess, senior guards, a shaman, and a few others he did not recognize–possibly from nearby villages. He had attained some stature in the council that gave him a seat–Kintoi had not yet stripped him of his privileges. A fire was lit in a corner, attended by two servants. It was barely enough to infuse warmth into the hut.

Some more men streamed in, and Kintoi finally ordered the door shut. "Everyone, quiet! It is time we speak."

The room fell silent quickly; a quiet unease was evident on the faces. *What was happening?* They were all hunched in the cold, trying to keep warm inside their coats and sitting close to each other. Some rubbed their hands, and others jostled for a space near the fire.

"I had to order you all to the council on an urgent matter," Kintoi said in his guttural voice. "The situation is changing quickly."

Everyone looked on expectantly. Spartacus' pulse quickened.

"The Romans are back. And this time, they are passing north toward the Dardani. But unlike the last time, several years ago when they bypassed us, it seems to they plan to give us a visit."

People shuffled where they sat or stood. A village elder asked what was in all their minds. "What is this *visit* Kintoi?"

Kintoi stood. "A Century–they tell me it's about a hundred soldiers–"

"Eighty," Spartacus interjected, irritating Kintoi.

"Eighty. Hundred. It doesn't matter because we are not about to fight them. The Century is heading here, backed by a much larger force about two days away. They say two legions are in our lands. Spartacus, how much is a legion?"

"About four to five thousand. So about eight to ten thousand," he said, surprised at the size of the Roman contingent. "What do they want?"

"They are seeking tribute from every major village, and they want hostages."

Suddenly a big murmur rose in the air. *Hostages?*

Spartacus was intimately aware of this practice. He was sure many in the village knew that as well, knowing Roman operations in the past and how the Bessi was subdued during his time in the Auxiliaries.

"Why hostages? We have posed no threat to them!" Kintoi's brother growled and spat on the ground.

Another man stood excitedly, waving his hands. "This is preposterous! They seek out people and our valuables for no good reason! We shall defend our dignity!"

Indignant protests filled the air, and Spartacus watched quietly, without speaking a word, realizing the foolishness of many of the uttered words.

Surprisingly, Kintoi, the son of Kintoi, said nothing either, and finally, he stood and signaled people to quieten down. "I know nothing more. What we must decide, once our tempers are cooler than our balls, as my father used to say," he said, grinning, causing howls of laughter, "is how we must respond. It is mystifying to me why they seek our hostages and make enemies of us, and what stops them from asking for more and more?"

That caused many people to slap their thighs and shout in agreement. *Where would it stop?*

"This is just greed. That is all it is! They are greedy, and they believe they can add to their loot by extorting us on the way to their real target, the Dardani!" he said, echoing the sentiments of many in the room.

The man knew his politics well but having lived only here and only dealt with tribes all his life, he understood Romans little.

Spartacus rose and walked to the center of the semi-circle purposefully. "It has nothing to do with greed," he said, loud enough to catch everyone's attention. Suddenly the room was quiet–regardless of each man's admiration or disdain for him, he was the *only* man who had served in the Roman army in a senior capacity and returned. Even if he knew little, he still knew more than them.

Now that he had their attention, he took a deep breath and spoke slowly. "Our frustrations and anger are borne of the injustice we perceive, and that is entirely valid," he said, standing straight as if he were addressing his Century. He knew that his growl and his imposing stature brought him their attention.

"But the Romans do little without sound purpose when under the command of their illustrious commanders. And this time, the purpose is defense and not greed."

"Defend themselves against what? No one amongst us threatened their march!" Kintoi said, too many nodding heads.

"You know the fickle minds of our tribes, Kintoi. We hug one day and stab the other," he said, raising some chuckles. "But look at the Roman destination."

He pointed his finger to the ground, creating an imaginary map for them to follow.

"The Dardani are to our north. As the Romans go further, they are vulnerable on their rear by many other tribes. They know that no common purpose unites the tribes, but they are also unpredictable. There is no guarantee that a force might not form that marches to their rear and catches them by surprise. The Dardani are no weak hearts. They are more numerous, their cavalry is known for its power, and they have instigated Romans enough that they are now a target," he said, as they listened in rapt attention.

"And so, if Chief Kintoi was a Roman commander, what would he do?" he said, looking at Kintoi, placating the irritated chief and giving him a chance.

Kintoi reluctantly answered. "I would seek hostages and tribute from all lands I pass to ensure they make no attempts to threaten my army's rear."

Spartacus did not gloat at his success in making them see the strategy behind these actions. "It is not greed, but a method they use for their safety. But let there be no doubt— if we refuse, you should expect the full force to be upon us and that no one around us will lift a finger to help."

*And this is why I pleaded with your father upon my arrival.*

But the Maedi were warriors with hearts of lions, and there was no question that the thought of fighting the Romans would go unannounced.

Kintoi's brother took the stage. He had always been favorably disposed toward Spartacus, who respected him. "Can we fight them, Spartacus? Even if we manage to put all our men on defense and bring other Maedi and friendly tribes to our side?"

Spartacus had become their advisor now. Kintoi bristled but kept quiet, knowing the seriousness of the situation.

"We can fight them, but only if we have a powerful alliance. We could warn the Dardani and tell them we are on their side, ask others—"

Kintoi raised his hand and interrupted. "We will raise no hand to help the Dardani. A feud of generations runs amongst us, and our gods have told us through many priests that there shall be no truce with the Dardani. We will not fight them, but we will not *help* them."

Many others echoed the sentiment.

Spartacus continued. "If our purpose is to die a valiant death and kill our families by our own hands so that they do not fall into Roman hands, then yes," he said, preferring to be stark in his assessment. "But we have neither the training nor the men to fight one Roman legion, let alone two. If we fight, lose, and then surrender, then prepare to have many of our men hauled away to fight for them and the rest, including our families, sold as slaves. And the lives of slaves in their world is wretched and may none of us have the shame of condemning our wives and children to Roman slavery!"

Most of the council nodded gravely.

He continued. "And even then, if we win, there will be more marching toward us within the year. And unless all our tribes are united by then and ready to fight them with a large force, we will be extinguished. And now," he looked pointedly at Kintoi, "with the disunity among tribes, we have no time to do much, especially if their envoy is here within a day."

The murmurs were low, and no one yet had an answer. They all looked at him as if he would conjure magic. He had a thought in his mind, but before he presented him, he wanted them to assess the bleakness of the situation.

"There is one other thing," he said as he moved around slowly, ensuring their eyes were upon him. This was a technique he had learned from Florus, who, ignoring his failings, could be highly effective in the rare occasions when he addressed the men. And some said that Florus had learned it from Curio, an expert orator.

A quiet descended upon the room like the morning fog.

"I thought you had trained them well, Spartacus," Kintoi said, but Spartacus ignored the slight, and no one joined the chief in his barb.

"What other things," an elder inquired, now curious.

"This may greatly offend you all, for this is not the heart of the Maedi, and this, I was accused of, even though I have since avenged my wrong."

The eyes narrowed. They knew what he was about to say, and how that would create great cries of *coward!*

"We evacuate. Not because we are weak or fearful. Not because our hearts are not that of lions and wolves. Not because the power of Kotys and Zibelthiurdos does not flow in our fiery veins. But because we are unprepared for battle, unlike the trained and prepared Romans. And in that, we are unequal, and we shall bide our time to fight them. But for that, we must live another day, and for that, we must evacuate."

No one spoke a word. It was unheard of that a man of the Maedi would say in the full council and advise them to *evade battle!*

Finally, Kintoi decided he would assert himself. "Run, he says!" he scoffed. "Well, running may be your trait,

Spartacus. It is not ours. *This* village did not breed cowards, and no one will run anywhere. And even if we did, where would we run? To the Odrysians who might themselves massacre us? To the Bessi who salivate at the thought of putting our heads on pikes and raping our wives? Or live like animals in the forests, fearful of every footstep?"

Spartacus chose to ignore the insults, for he knew he would evoke this reaction. But Kintoi was true in that there was nowhere to go. But he pressed on. "If we take the message of an imminent threat to our neighbors, this is our last chance to push for a greater coalition. Perhaps not all tribes will accept, but we might be able to threaten the Roman rear in just a few weeks and then take the time to fortify before they come again. A bigger coalition, Chief Kintoi, will give us the power to negotiate and forge even greater alliances! If we grow in strength, Mithridates will no longer see us as a source for his soldiers but instead as worthy allies!"

*Why did they not see it, even after generations of quarrel?*

"You say the same things you always did, Spartacus, for you desire greater powers. We all see it. Zibelthiurdos sees it. The brave men of this village will not run. We will stay where we are, we will negotiate favorable terms, and then we will grow our strength."

Spartacus realized the futility of his mission, for he knew by the demeanor of other men that no one would speak up against the chief and support the cause of vacating. The concept of strategic withdrawal and regrouping with greater strength was simply not understood or appreciated by men who valued individual valor and bravery above all else. Battles were meant to be waged head-on, death glorious even if futile, and ruses, cunning, or strategies to gain advantage were seen as weak.

He argued some more until his idea of vacating was firmly rejected by the council's vote, with only the Kintoi's brother voting for his side and everyone else meekly submitting to the chief's intent to negotiate. And if the negotiations failed, they would fight. And in this, they were willing to listen to Spartacus and decided to send envoys to nearby Maedi villages to ask if they would ready their men and prepare to march at a day's notice. He had little hope that this would do much. And if it came to fight the Romans, Spartacus would lead them, in glory or death.

And then, as was customary, the shaman slew a goat in the middle of the room, letting its blood saturate the mud floor and inspecting the patterns for signs. He chanted various hymns as they watched in the now smoky space, warm by the fire on the side and inside their fox and sheep fur coats. He slit the goat's stomach and reached inside to pull the entrails out for more signs, and then, satisfied, he stood and made his proclamation.

"The patterns speak of peace, for there was no frothiness in the blood, and the entrails show no damage, and thus speaks to the continued health of the tribe."

Spartacus bowed to these words even though his instinct told him otherwise, but these were the words of godly men, and one had to bow before their interpretations.

Kintoi would not speak further about what he wished to negotiate and how much to the displeasure of those around him. But as chief, he was entrusted with the village's well-being, and thus all had to believe that he would do what was right. The anxious council was relieved for the day, and Spartacus was responsible for calling all the men to order and prepare them for battle. But there would be no overt display of armed power, no ditches or ramparts until Kintoi spoke to the Romans. A display of aggression even before discussions could result in unpleasant outcomes.

When he returned home that night, weary and tired from a hectic day of preparations, his wife washed his hands and feet and fed him. But there was fear in her eyes, and it worried him.

"The winds blow cold, my dear husband," Antara said fearfully, "I saw an eagle swoop down snowy mountains and kill a resting wolf!"

He held her close and spoke to her of the day's events.

"Who will they want as a hostage?"

"Usually, the chief's children or a wife, and sometimes the children of other influential men."

"Ours?" her eyes glistened in the lamplight.

"It depends on how many the commander has ordered per village. They do not want a large baggage train with children, so it will likely be only a few."

"When will they let them go?"

"It depends on what is being negotiated. Often the hostages are free to leave at the end of the campaign, and the Roman commanders are usually true to their word in these matters."

"Are they treated well?"

"As well as a marching army treats the baggage train. But they are fed, clothed, and will have a roof over their head. They will be spared of other hardship."

She sighed and rubbed his shoulder. "Do you think we will fight?"

"It depends on the negotiation," he said gently. "And if we must fight, we will."

"And I will cheer you on, husband," she said. "And we will not fall into Roman hands."

"You infuse me with the strength of gods, my love. But if I must fall, I ask that you run and find another day to avenge my death."

She looked surprised. "Run? It is not our women's–"

"I know. But not all our ways are the right ones. If our son grows, then you have the chance to find retribution. What justice is there in all of us dying, fighting ill-prepared?"

She searched his face and then caressed his beard. "I will do as my gods compel me to. And if you fall, I know that you will speak to me from the afterlife."

He nodded. Perhaps that would be how he would tell her what to do.

They both sat by the fire and prayed, and she did many rituals to ward off the evil that would visit them the next day.

# 43

## MEIDI LANDS

———◇———

Spartacus watched the scene unfold.

Kintoi stood in the front at the gate, and behind him, his brothers, the elders of the village, two envoys from neighboring towns, and several guards. Spartacus lay hidden from plain view, off to the side with a hundred men crouched behind a dense cluster of bushes and trees, and he would act only if there were an unprovoked attack by the Romans. He had a clear view of the waiting contingent and the narrow path in front.

It did not take too long, for a messenger had arrived in advance, telling them that the Roman force was not far behind and would be there within an hour.

Finally, as if appearing like ghosts in the cold mist, the unmistakable visage of the Roman Century appeared. In front, on a horse, was the centurion, clear by his transverse red plumed helmet, and beside him walked the *Aquilifer* with the Roman eagle, which was surprising for this standard of the Legion was rarely sent out without the Legion behind it. Sending the standard for the mission was a serious message–a hint that the Roman Legion was *behind* it, and the recipients of the notice must take it with utmost seriousness.

Behind them walked the Century, in this case a five-man per row column, the soldiers walking cautiously with their shields up, their javelins visible like thorns rising from a bronze field, and their gladiuses swaying gently from their belts. They stopped some distance from the wooden-spike wall that surrounded the village, and the centurion dismounted his horse and waited.

Kintoi sent one of his men. It was unclear if the man knew Latin or Greek, or whether the centurion knew a Maedi language or Greek. They would know soon.

No one moved as the unarmed man, intentionally clothed only in a ceremonial strip of cloth around his waist, neared the Roman. And then another man, covered in a thick fur coat, his face, and body hidden in the layers, limping slowly, appeared behind the centurion–possibly an interpreter–and they all conversed. Nothing could be heard from where he was, but the gesticulations suggested an amicable conversation. Eventually, the centurion began to walk with the Maedi tribesman, and his men advanced until near the gates and stopped. He, the interpreter, and his Aquilifer entered through the open gate and approached Kintoi.

The anxiety melted once the men exchanged formal courtesies and the chief pointed the way for the Roman officer and the two accompanying him to his hut. A few of Kintoi's senior men and his brothers followed the head, and they all entered the house.

The negotiations would begin now. Spartacus turned to his men and told them to disperse quietly but be fully ready for any engagement. He had a bugle and a whistle and had conveyed them a protocol that signaled a battle order. He hoped that it would not come to that. The Maedi forces were positioned to massacre just by the advantage of sheer numbers and familiarity with the terrain, but that would only be the pretext for a Roman retaliation.

Who was the Roman general in charge of the Dardani operation?

Had Sulla returned?

Eventually, he returned to his hut and to his anxious wife, who was relieved to find that nothing had happened. He knew nothing about the discussions in the chief's hut, but there were no sounds of panic so far. She was upset that he had been excluded from the council, *the son of the chief is an idiot, and I do not need gods to tell me that!* she pouted, and he laughed at her protective indignation.

He was hungry, and her meal of boiled meat, cornbread, grapes, and olives was delicious. His stomach full and with no sounds of conflict outside, he lay on his cot for a nap, and soon his world dissolved into gentle, satisfying darkness.

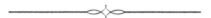

*He is on a boat on calm, beautiful waters. No land is visible in any direction, and no one else is on the vessel either. Seagulls make a ruckus, sitting on the sides, and the boat is moving smoothly all on its own, without a mast or rower. There is no sun in the sky, and yet it is bright. Suddenly, the waves transform and swell all around him, become more prominent, more powerful, and begin to rock the boat. The shaking is powerful and frightening–*

"Wake up, husband, wake up," his wife was shaking him vigorously, bringing him out of his snore.

"What happened? What?" he said with worry as he jumped up to a seating position. One of the village elders was peeking through the door.

"You are wanted, Spartacus."

"Have the Romans left?"

"No, they are still with the chief. But they seek your opinion on some matters."

Antara looked at him anxiously. "Why you?' she said aloud and then turned to the elder."Be truthful, elder grandfather, is he wanted as a hostage?"

The man's wrinkly face revealed little. But he said gently, "No. There has been no talk of taking anyone as a hostage, but they are arguing about security to the Roman army and other things I do not understand well."

Spartacus searched the old man's eyes but found no deception. There was always the lingering worry in Spartacus' mind for his role in Florus' death and the killings in the Roman Senators' estate. When he had been in the army, there were numerous stories of how the Romans never forgot attacks on their men and pursued retribution years after.

But would they pursue a lowly barbarian auxiliary?

After all these years?

Would anyone even remember him?

He knew nothing of what was happening in Rome or its politicians, for no such news ever traveled. And only now, after years, had there been any contact. Besides, a long chain of information and decisions would have to have taken place for them to even think of looking for him, here, in some Maedi village. Spartacus smiled inwardly–he knew he sometimes overestimated his importance or ability to convince. *You are the king in your head*; his wife would sometimes tease him.

Perhaps he *was* worrying too much, thinking that a Roman legion was here looking for someone who killed a Roman officer many years ago. People fought and died all the time, often in thousands. He shook off his doubts and prepared to leave.

"Kintoi wants your wife as well," the old man said, "They need all the priestess to bless the negotiations. The two others have completed their prayers."

That was puzzling but not entirely surprising. Vital occasions needed all the prayer the tribe could muster. Antara donned a crisp white tunic, tied her hair with a band, wore her golden bracelets, and prepared to leave with him. The two children were sleeping, and they left them there.

Two Roman legionaries stood guard outside the chief's residence with two Maedi guardsmen. Spartacus was not allowed to take his sword, a condition imposed by the Romans. When he and Antara entered, the scene inside had none of the calm projected outside.

Kintoi sat on his throne, and the serious centurion stood nearby, flanked by his interpreter and Aquilifer. The room was smoky again due to the fire trying desperately to warm the large enclosure in the corner. Spartacus was surprised by the number of Roman soldiers inside. How could Kintoi allow them here? Wasn't this a negotiation? Did something go wrong?

Someone closed the doors behind.

Every man in that room looked grim. Kintoi was looking at the floor and rubbing his chin nervously. A few murmured as Spartacus took a few steps toward an empty chair, but a Roman soldier shook his head.

*What was happening?*

It was time to ask the chief. "For what have I been summoned, Chief Kintoi?"

Kintoi did not answer. Instead, his eyes went to the centurion staring at Spartacus.

"Is this him?" the centurion asked, turning to the heavily attired interpreter.

The man turned toward Spartacus, his face still hidden under the hood and the wisps of smoke. Then he pulled the coat hood off his head, revealing a pock-marked face, now older, gaunt, and his lips curled up in a wicked grin, revealing a mouth with three missing teeth.

Cleitus.

# 44

## CAPUA

————◇————

Gnaeus Cornelius Lentulus Vatia's enterprises were many, but few thrived. The brothels brought steady customers, but the regular fights, diseases, girls escaping with men, truant customers all added to the strain. They impacted the margins, making it a not-very-attractive business. The bawdy plays and theater were clean, but entertainers were hard to book, and it was tricky to predict crowds and how to price events. It was too seasonal, not very profitable, and he was tired of dealing with the more famous entertainers who thought too much of themselves. Nearing fifty years of age, Vatia had no desire to become destitute, see his argumentative wife divorce him, and die drunk on one of the filthy streets of the crowded city.

But one business was beginning to thrive–gladiatorial combats. His school was small, only twenty-seven fight-ready men, most of them Celts and Germans, a miserable and rowdy bunch. But the gladiatorial performances were the best earners of all his endeavors. People clamored for a good show, and the city's newly expanded theater and arena had the capacity for large crowds, and large crowds meant more money. He had already staged several shows to packed houses, making a handsome margin. However, he resented being only the third largest gladiatorial school after Asina and Bibulus, rich, whoremongering bastards who had patronage from the pigs in Rome.

But there was only so much money to be made with a small group of gladiators.

They got hurt, they got sick, some were simply not good enough in the arena to captivate the crowd's interest. While profitable, it was the most complex of his endeavors. Procuring gladiators was expensive—well-built men condemned to slavery through magisterial orders, crime, or conquest was the first lot. A few citizens willing to fight for money and fame were the second, even if fleeting and shorn of any dignity. Either way, buying them was costly. Then came housing, keeping them in reasonable barracks, having them train and exercise, all that bled more coin. Feeding them, especially meat, even if occasionally, was very, very expensive, but it was essential to keep their strength and bulk. Investing in gladiators was like investing in a business–some made attractive profits to make up for the loss in the rest. The most vexing issue was the increasingly bloodthirsty demands of the crowd. The days of a good spectacle where both fighters walked away to the crowd's adulation was fading–now the mongrels demanded someone *dies*. Not enough for blood to soak the husk-sodden floor and leave an injured man. If he didn't allow for death here and there, the crowds would start dwindling, and his coffers would fill less. If he allowed for more death, his costs of replacing the dead and keeping a deep bench of fighters would increase. So far, none of his fighters had died on the arena–that was simply not the arrangement in the events. But he was sure that the sentiment would be in Capua soon, for fights to the death were already gaining popularity in Rome and Pompeii. He had to balance the price and the cost and make more money. And now, the only way to do that was to more than double his *ludus*, gladiatorial school.

He had planned shows in Capua and Pompeii, and if circumstances permitted, he might even go to Rome or Brundisium. The following month he would go to the private slave auctions in Rome to procure the best gladiators and do that every three to four months.

But for now, his thoughts were busy with how to divest his unprofitable ventures and become one of the leading gladiatorial owners in all of Capua. And maybe eventually, in all of the country. It would be his way to money, fame, and perhaps even a seat in the Senate or a respectable position in Capua.

He shook away his thoughts and rose from his wooden chair. Vatia had lost much of his hair to his chagrin and wife's derision, and his short stature did not help. But what he lacked in physical prowess, he made up in cunning and acumen, and it was those flashy golden brooches and silver rings that got him a younger, fine woman as a wife, courtesy of her greedy father.

It all just came down to money.

# 45

## MEIDI LANDS

---◇---

"You bastard!" Spartacus screamed, knowing now what was happening, and lunged at Cleitus. And before the Roman soldiers made contact to stop him, his fist smashed into Cleitus' face.

*Crunch!*

Cleitus clutched his face and fell to his knees, his nose broken, and a tooth knocked to the ground. He was bleeding copiously onto the floor and rolling in pain, grunting and cursing. But before Spartacus could do anything more to the sniveling, treasonous coward, the soldiers were upon him, beating him with the backend of their *gladius* and punching his stomach. He could barely hear his wife screaming, and no one was coming to his rescue.

*Cowards. Cowards!*

Someone had a thick noose and placed it over his head, tightening it, even as other men restrained him. He fought, and he fought hard, twice throwing off a man grappling him, causing more to punch, hit, and push him down. Finally, like a bull tired of the swarming hunters, he fell, and they pulled his hand back and tied it.

He was pulled up to his feet even as his stomach and shoulders were on fire, and he gasped to take his breath. Cleitus was up–his blood having soaked his neck and the front of his fur coat, his nose grotesquely twisted to a side, and his mouth and chin wet with velvet. He shook as he grinned again, an evil, vengeful grin, and he said something no one could make out, and his attempt only caused him to spit more blood.

Spartacus shouted at Kintoi, who refused to look at his face. "Son of whore, what respect do you have to sell me out? You traded me for other hostages, didn't you?"

Kintoi would not take the slight. "Yes, great Spartacus. Why should you be spared? The Romans are happy to take you and leave the rest of us alone! I have spared my village, and it seems you are a wanted bastard!"

Spartacus spit to the side. "A little dog you are, that you had to bring me here by deception!"

"Would you have come willingly?" Kintoi mocked him. "I have done what my father would have, saved the village and rid myself of a fool!"

"I will go with him," Spartacus' wife shouted. "May the fire of gods descend upon you, Kintoi, and may you drown in the sorrow you brought upon us!"

Kintoi made signs of warding off evil. "Take the witch!" he said to the centurion, "perhaps she will fetch a good price as well."

"No, leave her. She has nothing to do with this," Spartacus shouted as he continued to struggle. He would not beg, he would not beseech them, but he would find time to take revenge, as he always did.

"No, husband," Antara said resolutely, "I will go with him. If not, I shall consecrate myself to the gods!"

The centurion, who just watched quietly, finally stepped in. He was a powerful man, his face set in hard lines. "Enough! You two will come with us," he said and turned to Kintoi, "And you will keep your promise of holding our rear."

Kintoi said nothing.

Spartacus cursed them as he was bound in chains and led out, followed by his wife, who was now crying in despair about her children. But then two women on the crowd outside promised to care for them, for they wished no ill on the mother for her husband's sins.

The soldiers tied his hands to another rope held by a horse rider, and she was bound to him. Someone hit him from behind, "move!"

As the village watched in silence, Spartacus was led out of the gates of the village he had called home for years, betrayed by a man who thought little to what this would mean for him or his village. The Romans would return for them soon, he was sure.

Cleitus, his face bandaged with a cloth, was put on a horse. It seems he had some value to the man who sent him here.

Spartacus controlled his rage and trudged along the rough path, his body shooting bolts of pain all over, but it was his heart that hurt the most, hearing the sniffles of his innocent wife. For years he had hoped Roman influence would not appear at his doorstep, and now it finally had.

Where were they taking him? To whom?

# 46

## MEIDI LANDS

———◇———

Spartacus and Antara were exhausted and hungry when they reached the vast and familiar Roman camp a day west of the village. They had been forced to match and barely fed, with some sip of water and some grain soup to keep them moving. Killing them was not the centurion's intent, for their heads would be rolling in the forest long before if their execution was to be the outcome.

They were left tied to a pole for a few hours before the same centurion came with two legionaries to take them to the Legate's camp.

Spartacus knew by then that Curio was the commander of the camp. Why had he returned? To conquer all of Thracia and Macedonia before going further east? And why did the Legate, leader of Legions, want to drag a lowly man like himself and not just order whatever it was?

Curio was dressed in a Senator's toga rather than in a general's cuirass and cape when Spartacus was dragged into his presence. Antara collapsed on the floor when she was let go, and Spartacus could barely stand, his stomach empty and with no energy in his being.

The Legate turned to them and first looked confused, and then it registered to him at whom he was seeing. Curio had grown older, wiser looking, his hair now sprinkled with silver, and his long fingers adorned with politician's rings. The casual friendliness as a commander was missing in his now Consul-like demeanor.

"Spartacus the auxiliary?" he said to no one as his eyes darted between Spartacus and the centurion.

The officer saluted. "Yes, sir. We found him through the help of Cleitus, your scout, and brought him here with his wife."

"Where is Cleitus?"

"I will bring him here soon, sir. He was injured during the capture."

Curio nodded and turned toward Spartacus. "I do not want you dying here of hunger," he said in Latin and instructed the centurion to bring them both some bread and water. He then had the soldiers untie the ropes.

Spartacus could barely mutter a *thank you* as his hands shook and legs trembled. He chewed the bread greedily while helping his wife, who could barely sit. Curio was quiet as they ate and gulped the cups of water. The centurion looked puzzled at this rare and strange display of kindness shown to a low erstwhile-auxiliary barbarian, but then many accomplished Roman commanders were known to display such acts to all ranks of their army.

Satiated, strength returned to Spartacus' limbs. Antara remained seated on the tent's floor, and Curio let her be.

"Greek? Latin? Do you speak any of our languages?"

Heartened by the chance for a dialog, Spartacus decided to endear himself to the Legate. "I learned Latin while in your service, sir."

Curio's eyebrows rose. "I am surprised, barbarian. Your kind rarely attempts to learn our language. Now I remember you better."

"I have served you honorably in Thracia and during Sulla's march, sir."

Curio nodded. "I freed you after Colline gate, did I not?"

"Yes, sir."

"And why did I free you? What had you done then?"

Spartacus did not know if Curio was simply testing him while knowing answers. It was always dangerous to be caught in a lie.

"I was accused of running away from the battle in the night."

Curio took a sip from his wine cup. His gray eyes were penetrative. "And did you? Runaway from the battle?"

"No, sir. There was much confusion, and I, like some others, believed there was a retreat horn. I helped a legionary, and we sought safety."

"And where is this legionary?"

"He did of his wounds the same night, sir."

"I recollect your service, Spartacus. I only remember you because you are of unusual size, especially when compared to my men," he said, laughing. "And your gait. I now remember you fighting and encouraging your men. You have gained weight like a man of the family."

"Sir."

He kept the cup to the side and crossed his hands. "Do you know why you are here?"

There was little left to hide.

"The death of centurion Florus, sir."

"He was your commanding officer, was he not?"

"Yes, sir."

"Why did you kill him? What dispute did you have with the man?"

Spartacus had seen Roman officers argue before their commanders. It was not frowned upon, so long as they did not dispute their officer once a decision was made. Some travelers said that this was different from eastern courts and military norms.

"May I present my side, sir?"

Curio looked offended. "Do you think I would have bothered to have you brought here otherwise?" he said, his voice sharp. "I could have had you executed on discovery and moved on. You are a curious case. Go on."

Spartacus bowed in response. "Florus first took grave offense to my objection on his skimming of our wages—"

Curio's eyes flickered. Perhaps he knew something of this matter. Did he remember that he had stepped in to prevent Florus from punishing them for taking after-battle loot?

"And since then, he slackened on his duties to train us. He exposed me in battle and often shirked from leading from the front."

Curio walked back to his chair and sat down. But he made no remarks.

"At Colline gate, he falsely accused me of running away and gave false testimony. He wished to have me dead, but you intervened."

"I remember that. But one must wonder, Spartacus, that if you found yourself in trouble often, then who is it that causes it? You also killed the Bessi auxiliary leader; I forget his name."

"The gods have tested me, Legate. I sought no conflict until it was brought to me."

Curio did not look convinced. "Continue. Take me to when you killed Florus. Cleitus has given me his account. Let me hear yours."

"Sir. I was assigned as a guard to take General Sulla's prisoners to the open area near the temple of Bellona."

Curio's face darkened. Spartacus knew that the Legate was aware of the grave injustice of that hour, where surrendered men had been slaughtered by deception. But not knowing Curio's role, he decided to keep his tone neutral.

Spartacus continued. "During the confusion and terror of the operation, even as I was defending my line to prevent the condemned men from breaking out, Florus appeared with Cleitus and tried to stab me from behind."

Curio leaned back on his chair and rubbed his palm on the hand rest. His eyes narrowed at Spartacus' remarks. "And you say that an experienced centurion *missed* stabbing you from behind. Why must I believe that?"

Spartacus had only a hunch. "The centurion was heavily drunk, for his eyes were bloodshot, and he wobbled unsteadily when I turned on them. I had no time to reflect on the future, sir, and I am surely afforded the chance to kill my attacker. Why was Florus there, right behind me, when he was not assigned to any duty?"

"Cleitus says Florus was there to oversee operations clandestinely and report it back when you saw him and attacked them, taking advantage of the disorder."

*Cleitus is a lying son of a whore.*

"If that were the case, then it was he who tried to take advantage of the situation and try to kill me out of slight or fear that I would report his methods, sir," he said, more forcefully this time.

Curio rubbed his chin. "Both stories seem plausible, Spartacus. But you do realize that you were in Rome, and you killed a Roman citizen, an officer, and your commander. Whether by mistake, or some other personal reason, it matters little. Our army is powerful because the men know that their unfair deaths, outside battle, will be avenged, no matter how long it takes."

That was an exaggeration, but Spartacus did not respond.

"Normally, you would be executed. Some might even seek to crucify you, for that is what is done for criminals, slaves, foreign murderers," he said, staring at him unblinkingly. Antara was sullen and silent, not knowing the languages but sensing the darkness in the mood.

But Curio's preface made it sound like the Legate had something else on his mind. If his fate were crucifixion, he would do anything possible to die fighting the punishment rather than being hoisted upon the cross.

"But this has become a little more complicated and interesting than just putting an unruly barbarian to the cross," he continued. "It seems you took employ at a Senator's house, one that is my benefactor, and made some mischief there as well."

# 47

## CAPUA

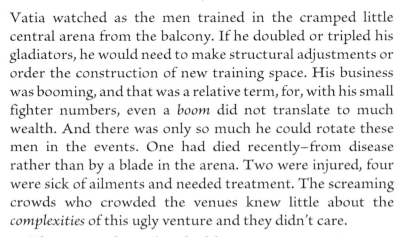

Vatia watched as the men trained in the cramped little central arena from the balcony. If he doubled or tripled his gladiators, he would need to make structural adjustments or order the construction of new training space. His business was booming, and that was a relative term, for, with his small fighter numbers, even a *boom* did not translate to much wealth. And there was only so much he could rotate these men in the events. One had died recently–from disease rather than by a blade in the arena. Two were injured, four were sick of ailments and needed treatment. The screaming crowds who crowded the venues knew little about the *complexities* of this ugly venture and they didn't care.

The events themselves had become more ornate, more celebratory, more elaborate. Gone were the days of a *good fight*. Now they wanted horses, they wanted men dressed in various gear, they wanted fighters of different sizes, skills, colors, they wanted beasts in the arena, and most of all, they wanted visceral violence on the field. Many of these came from the larger shows in Pompeii and Rome, and the pretentiousness had seeped into Capua. And to satisfy these needs, the schools, like his, had to adapt their training methods and equip their gladiators with many implements. But did the complexity end there? No! He had to compete with other schools in the region to ensure *his* men got the chance to fight. The event's organizers who drew the most crowds were picky in whom they admitted to the contests, which meant paying bribes, coddling them, and most importantly, sending skilled and exciting gladiators. It was a virtuous cycle–better fighters, more events, more money, more fame, more fighters, more events... one that had to be sustained through hard and dirty work. Eventually, he would make his school big enough to host his events and rid himself of his dependence on the "sponsors."

There was a bright side to gladiators dying in the arena. It was becoming more common for training schools like his to charge the sponsors of the events forty to fifty times the rent cost of the gladiator if one lost his life. Now, that might seem lucrative, but when one considered the overall cost of training, boarding, feeding them, he would barely break even for all that effort. With increasing demand, he hoped that he would have a larger stable of fine gladiators and that the loss would be compensated at eighty to a hundred times, at which this business would become truly attractive. But for now, he had to hustle, beg, borrow, and do everything to make his school the preferred source for events, *significant* events.

The significant events attracted the rich and the famous. Occasionally, a big name, a Senator, Consul, Proconsul, general from Rome, made their way to Capua or Pompeii, taking a break from their politics or a detour from one of their seaside villas. Such situations afforded him a chance to increase his influence.

His thoughts were interrupted when one of the fighters yelled in pain and anger. He was a new inductee, inducted recently after a purchase. He had been condemned for repeated thievery and banditry and come from somewhere north. He was not quite a fighter for all his bravery as a bandit, and Vatia was annoyed at having spent so much on these lowly men.

"Do not beat him to death even before he learns, Crixus!" he scolded the hefty Gaul. Crixus was one of his better gladiators. Vatia had purchased him a year ago for a not a low sum, for he was sought by more than one school upon his sale by the owner.

Crixus had been a slave in an estate after being brought there through capture in some troublesome outpost in regions far north and then sold through traders. Crixus was a hothead; his thick gold and brown hair hid a terrible temper and lack of discipline. But that also made him an enjoyable watch and a good trainer because he was rough and relentless. He was crude and garrulous and often had to be told to shut up, and Vatia knew that he had deep-seated hate for Romans for whatever they had put him through. But in Vatia's school, Crixus had been fed well, he had the luxury of a small room for himself, an incentive for his performance, and good fights were rewarded with the chance to fuck a fine prostitute. There was a curious phenomenon of even citizen women getting excited by these condemned men fighting like caged animals. Still, Vatia would not allow such contact to avoid the evil attentions of scrupulous magistrates or jealous husbands.

Crixus spoke Latin with a heavy accent, whether intentional or not, and it was often a challenge to communicate with the man. But Vatia mainly dealt with the primary trainer, *lanista*, Canicus, also a man of similar stock as Crixus, but more refined in his manners and with a better grasp of the language of his master.

"Better he dies now than embarrass me later!" Crixus yelled to chuckles. He also saw himself as a comedian. His terrible Latin was a source of derision and humor, especially in the Pompeiian arenas where people spoke Oscan and enjoyed watching a loud, wordy Gladiator abusing them in the horrifying accent of people they disliked. But Canicus was sick today, so Crixus was training some newcomers and was no inspiration.

Vatia sighed and turned away. He needed more trainers, money, and gladiators.

But the future shined bright. He was about to entertain a new guest this evening, a potential investor in his enterprise, with promises of rich returns for his coin. Publius Vedius Porcina, an estate owner in Lucania and a Roman Senator, was the fourth influential name making rounds in the gladiatorial business. With Publius' investment, among others, Vatia would soon be a formidable force in local affairs.

"You have an impressive training school for a newcomer in the venture, Vatia. Making good money, are you?" Porcina said, admiring the arches and paintings and the structure of the building. He had shown the Senator the underground barracks, holding cells, kitchen, training arena, visitors' balcony, security towers, and his private quarters.

Publius Porcina was a slimy-looking, gaunt, silver-haired, beady-eyed vulture, and Vatia had dealt with many like him. Spending time in Roman politics for so long made these men bigger crooks than all the crooks they punished. If crossed, they were also dangerous, so Vatia had to play this game with finesse. Give some, get some, and always make sure both are indebted to each other.

"I am not quite a newcomer, Senator. I have been in this for a few years already, and I have learned my ropes and am looking for a significant expansion," Vatia said, feigning humility. "And my villa is nothing like your beautiful estates, I am sure."

They did some small talk, tired of it, and got down to what Porcina was here for. "What kind of returns can I expect?" he asked, his eyes scanning the surrounding.

"If all goes well, twenty to thirtieth of a hundred, audited by your accountant, of course."

Porcina looked unimpressed. "I can make more loaning to slave traders or silk importers."

"This is only the beginning, Senator. Expect to make a fiftieth in two years and double the year after. We know the slave trade and import vagaries, all held hostage to external factors. But this is assured, attractive business, all driven only internally within Italy."

"What will you use my money for?"

"The most urgent need is for buying new gladiators before their price goes up due to the demand. It takes months to find the right ones, but I hope to double the number in six to eight months. And that doubling will mean retaining services of physicians, expanding the kitchen, making–"

"How many do you have now?" Porcina asked, cutting him off.

"Twenty-five," he said, and then he shook his open palm. "The numbers can fluctuate if someone dies or becomes grievously injured."

Porcina waved his cup, and a slave girl hastened to fill it with fine wine. He eyed her bottom as she walked away and vanished behind the curtains. "You have a pretty slave," he said, grinning. "German?"

"I have twenty-five gladiators now, and in a year, I wish to have fifty."

Porcina returned to the topic. "Fifty?" he raised his eyebrows. "And you think there is enough demand for that large a number?"

Vatia scoffed. "Fifty is *nothing*, Senator. Many smaller venues make do with men pretending to be gladiators because the sponsors can't rent good ones from schools like mine. And these games are becoming much more popular now—it is no longer entertainment for just rich Romans or Pompeiians."

"Well, the more you make, the better for me," he said. "What terms have you offered others?"

*Why do you need that?*

Vatia shook his head most seriously. "You have the best ones, Senator."

Porcina laughed. "You know that to be a lie. I know that you know that to be a lie. But so long as I get my returns, you will have no quarrel with me."

Vatia smiled and bowed as he raised a cup. "And if you would entice some of your esteemed colleagues to grace my *ludus* and demand my gladiators in their shows, it will help both of us."

The Senator grinned. "The most subtle of all kickbacks, Vatia; I like your acumen."

# 48

## THRACIA

—◇—

"It seems you took employ at a Senator's house, one that is my benefactor, and made some mischief there as well."

Spartacus knew that the wheels of fate would finally arrive at his doorstep. How foolish was he to think that after killing a Roman officer and then butchering a few at a Senator's estate, the long arm of Roman influence would not grip his throat?

But he was innocent of all his doings. Would Curio see that?

But he had nothing to lose now, for death was hovering over his shoulder.

"Mischief made not of my hands, Legate—"

"It seems it is always someone else," Curio said testily. "The only reason I have you here, auxiliary, is because your story was intriguing."

"Sir."

"So, what happened at the estate?"

Spartacus recollected the events. He had served the estate to stay low from the eyes of authorities, and then Cleitus had tried to capture him. And in the absence of trust and unsure of the purpose, Spartacus had fought his way out and escaped. Could he be blamed for Cleitus' intentions? Would anyone in his place willingly lay down and be captured?

Curio asked a few probing questions but seemed satisfied with Spartacus' version of events.

"It seems the gods wish to leave you with no peace," he finally said.

*I have offended Sabazios so profoundly that he has not forgiven me yet.*

"Their ways are mysterious, Legate, and I am but only a man."

"You speak with gravitas, Spartacus. Who was your father?"

He talked fondly of his father, how Spartacus' upbringing involved reading and learning Greek, and how those around him often teased him as a philosopher, 'deliberately slow speaker,' 'fat-nosed-big-arsed-politician.'

This brought a few smiles to Curio's face, which was a good thing, he thought. The levity might dull the sharpness of his fate in the Legate's hands. But the Romans thought of them all as less, and whether this conversation would make any difference was yet to be seen.

Finally, Curio came to the crux of the matter. What to do with him.

"You present a vexing problem. I could simply have you executed, perhaps in a compassionate manner, recognizing your service and station among your people. But that does not solve other considerations."

*What other considerations?*

Curio was up again, now moving slowly in the tent, speaking like a politician, with his eyes turned to the faraway and his limbs in animation.

"For someone like me, a Consul, and now proconsul, keeping their word to their powerful supporters is one of the most, no, *the* most important thing. And in the strangest twist of your life, Spartacus, you have somehow become a part of such decisions."

Spartacus had no idea what the Legate was attempting to say. He kept his head low. His wife had stopped sobbing, but she sat quietly staring into the floor.

"Now, if the only charge was your hand in the death of Florus, I might have simply let you free, perhaps after a few lashes. But it is your conduct in the estate–"

"Legate–"

"Be quiet as I speak unless you wish to be flogged," Curio said testily, with his palm up.

"Sir."

"The man in whose estate you worked in is one of my benefactors, and he has a personal favor, or a grudge perhaps, that I must satisfy. Besides, some of my detractors have gotten wind of how I *casually* let the murderer of one of my officers get away unpunished. It means little in the grand scheme of things, but it means much in our politics. They will blow it out of proportion and scream it in the forum."

Spartacus' skin began to get hot. This saga would not end that quickly with a few welts on his back.

Curio continued, not looking at Spartacus. He walked up to a small metal plate hanging from a wooden crossbar and tapped it absent-mindedly. "You were no slave when you worked for him, but as a barbarian outsider, you had an obligation to serve him in return for the wages he paid you. And that you did not fulfill, and you do not have the same representative rights as a Roman citizen."

"Sir–"

Curio's cold and hard eyes stopped him mid-sentence. "You might re-consider your argument when fortune benefits you, soldier. Be quiet."

"Yes, sir."

"Ordinarily, as required by our norms, I would have you flogged and sold to the many traders who swarm my camps or send you back in chains to Porcina with instructions to mete out the appropriate punishment and exact his revenge for your conduct. You could have surrendered peacefully, and yet you did not."

*How could I?*

"But it seems Porcina is more forgiving. He told me, twice, that you were an exceptional worker and could be a good hand for the estate's security–so it appears inflicting abuse is not what is on his mind."

Spartacus' heart began to fight his ribs. He knew what fate awaited him next–returning home was now only a memory.

"I have no option but to condemn you to slavery, for you are not a man who abides by the rules set for freedmen in employment."

Spartacus controlled a rush of emotions—anger and despair, for he could show no impetuousness at this order. *Slave?* Those wretched creatures who toiled in Rome and the rest of their dominion, like animals, and were looked down upon as the lowest of the low. He would be one of *them.*

Curio continued as if this was all casual. "I will send you back to Porcina, who is well within his rights to punish you, but I will caution him from needless execution on account of your service and for the time I have invested in getting you back to him."

A deep, hot shame enveloped him like a thick, warm rag on a humid and blistering day, miserable and terrible. To even think that he, a chief's son, would now be a slave, through *no fault of his!*

What would his tribe think?

How could the gods let Cleitus get away with this heaping of injustice on him?

*Zibelthiurdos, why have you forsaken me? I have been nothing but a faithful servant, and my conduct justified!*

He suppressed the tears of rage, for like always, there would be a time when he could break out of his shackles, and the next time he would go far away from any Romans. The first time, he had run and then exacted his vengeance on Durnadisso. And then he had kept his actions controlled and saved himself from Florus. He had carefully prepared for potential capture and killed his pursuers. *Zibelthiurdos* had taught him that patience was a virtue that kept him alive.

Curio was watching him quietly, and then he continued. "And instead of fighting with your neighbors here," he said, sweeping his hand in an arc, "You will live a comfortable life in a rich estate, so long as you serve and obey orders. But that is Porcina's problem–and with this arrangement, you live, he gets his due, and I keep my word. Not that I need to justify it to you."

Blood roared in his ears like a cascade. No matter how he rationalized his state of being–*Slave?* How could it be that a man who has lived free, fought with honor, has had a station in life, suddenly becomes *lesser* simply by the word of another man? Now that he was about to be that lesser being, it all seemed absurd even if it was the way of life, in his land, in Roman lands, and all the lands he had heard of.

Spartacus knew better than to argue and make the situation worse. Valor without support to victory was just foolishness, and besides, he could not let them abuse his wife for his transgressions.

"May I translate this to my wife, Legate?"

Curio flicked a finger as if to say *yes*.

Antara cried again, and he admonished her to regain composure and not break into her chants, for that may enrage the Romans and put them in even worse situations, fearing that they may be attracting evil to their camps.

*You should return, my dear wife, to our children and people.*

*I will not! They will be taken care of, as it is in our custom for children whose parents are lost to conflict or disease.*

*As their mother—*

*As your wife! My place is beside my husband, and my gods tell me so in my dreams, in the patterns of the clouds.*

*You—*

*No, husband, and you will listen to me this time. I will walk by your side, or I shall take my life to the gods and watch upon you from the skies.*

Her eyes flashed in anger, and her face was resolute in her action. As a woman of god, she only listened to him on matters of the house and his authority as her husband—but when she made up her mind on *her* duties, she was stubborn as a mountain mule.

He tried some more, knowing Curio's patience was waning, but she was firm and unwilling even to consider the thought of being sent back to her village. And there was always the terrible danger that once out of his watch, she might be raped on the way back and murdered, and no one would ever know.

He realized he could not let her out of his sight.

Even as his heart ached and hurt, knowing he would now be taken away, like a slave, he decided to seek one last permission.

"If I were to go back to Lucania, I ask that you allow my wife to accompany me, for this is our way of life. And with her by my side, I may have a calmer mind and be of better service to my…" he paused, unwilling for his tongue to say *master.* "Supervisor."

Curio looked at his wife, her head disheveled and held low. She was swaying and made her incantations silently. He turned to his secretary nearby. "Amend the order to include his wife, and specifically instruct Porcina not to separate them."

Spartacus knelt before the Legate in gratitude, and his wife, who now learned of the order, did the same. It was the gods' will that they would bow to the man who had condemned them, and yet the man who condemned them had saved him more than once before and had now chosen the route that inflicted the least pain of available options.

He felt a mix of respect and anger at Curio for having decided the path of hunting him down, but he only superficially understood the Roman mind, especially one of a high rank.

Curio nodded to the centurion before him. "Have them transported, but make sure they are not treated like the rest," he said, the distaste evident in his voice. "And send an advance message to Publius Vedius Porcina that Gnaeus Scribonius Curio has kept his word."

And when he was about to be led out, he saw Cleitus, standing aside, his face covered in bandages and crusted blood still on his chin. But his baleful eyes tracked Spartacus and the mangled lips twisted into his signature vicious grin.

# 49

## ROME

Spartacus learned very quickly that those enslaved from this region back to Rome were not small in number. The long caravan of captured men and women, a result of any resistance to the advancing legions, snaked through the valleys going South to one of the departure ports from Macedonia. The sorry lot, made of everyone except the very old, infirm, or the very young, had little idea of their future. Spartacus knew that for some who had already lived lives of immense hardship, the prospect of a stable and peaceful house or estate, a kind master or mistress, and the chance of three meals and a roof was a welcome one. But for most others, it would be a life of hardship and humiliation, and one that they would need to adapt to until they died. It seemed like the line was comprised of those from not only Thracian tribes but also Macedonians and some Dacians–that land far to the east. But here, none were superior to the other, and it was just a wretched mass of humanity.

The traders were a rough and cruel bunch, for profit was maximized when they spent the least they could on those transported and extracted the best price they could in the auctions. And that meant keeping the caravans moving quickly with the assistance of whips and sticks, feeding the people as little as possible, and simply abandoning or executing those that could not move fast enough. He and Antara were only marginally treated better, grudgingly, with some extra bread or soup and with the chance for his wife to stay on a carriage for a few hours each day.

Cleitus had accompanied the march, often walking by the shackled Spartacus, not speaking but mocking him. He had not regained his ability to speak easily, but that did not stop the man from finding every opportunity to needle them. He sometimes showed his hand with a few fingers short to remind Spartacus what he had done. But Cleitus soon tired of his antics and was no longer seen as the march progressed.

The travel lasted for just over thirty brutal days and ended in a small departure port on the west, where they were all crammed onto boats headed to Brundisium. This was the now-familiar path to Spartacus, who had first disembarked in that bustling port town in his campaign and then escaped the country. And now, for the third time, he would be back, and this time, not as a soldier, not as a bandit, but as a slave. Antara, not accustomed to such hardship, had lost much weight because she was a priestess who lived in relative comfort in her village. The mirth of life had left her eyes, but her devotion to the greatness of her gods had never wavered. Spartacus had to protect her from intrusive slave traders, and other people who suspected her of being a witch or some sorceress, for her chants and swaying caused many to fear her.

*I foresee a terrible life,* she had said, *but like a stormy night that leads to bright dawn, you too shall walk into one, my husband.*

He had more than once reminded the mishandling slave traders that he had been sent as a *gift* from the proconsul of Rome to a Senator of Rome, and they could only imagine the wrath if the goods were damaged in transit. Eventually, the traders provided protection from other angry or fearful captives.

Brundisium had grown and was busier than ever before, and many of the transports were auctioned off in the city. Those held as special shipments would next head to Rome, but near Tarentum, Spartacus and Antara were finally separated from the rest to make a different journey, to Lucania, via Metapontum.

The gift to senator Publius Porcina.

His pulse quickened when the walls of the estate appeared.

What did Porcina want?

Would he try to exact revenge over something that happened with his guards years ago?

But then, Spartacus knew little how the Senator's mind worked.

The memories of years ago came flooding as they were taken through the corridors that he had frequented many times during his stay here, and destiny had brought him back. Was *Publipor*, Felix, still around? Nigrumus? The estate seemed to have grown, its walls glistening with fresh paint, the gardens colorful with blooming flowers, and several new structures on the ground.

The guards shackled them in a damp room but fed them regularly. He had no tears to shed, but his wife repeatedly remembered their children and wept for their lives. But there was a comfort that they had not been pressed to slavery, and he hoped that they lived well under the care of the village elders.

It was two days before they were roused from their slumber.

"Get up, the Senator will see you now!" someone barked, and the iron chains jingled as they were both led out. Spartacus had considered breaking out and fighting but had put a pause to those thoughts due to the presence of his wife. If Porcina had a hideous punishment planned for them, he would kill Antara first and die fighting. But it was always his thoughtfulness that gave him a second chance, so he would wait to see what transpired.

Publius Porcina waited in a large courtyard. The Senator's hair was entirely silver and his face gaunt and severe. His improved condition had not lightened his grim facade. He watched as the guards dragged Spartacus to his presence. Cleitus was by his side, now somewhat healed from Spartacus' attack. His nose was permanently disfigured, broken in, flat as bread, and his lips were a pulpy mess. But the glee in his eyes shined brighter than ever before.

The Senator pulled out the parchment that Curio had dispatched and waved it around. "Every barbarian should know that they cannot escape the long arm of Rome," he said, his voice raspy like a nail on the wall.

"I have committed no crime, Senator, and I stand before you even though innocent."

"Lying," Cleitus squeaked.

Porcina seemed taken aback by the response. His eyebrows rose. He studied Spartacus. "That is what they always say. Always. Every criminal is innocent, yet the world is full of crime. How do you explain that?"

"It does not mean every man is a criminal, Senator."

"Watch your mouth, barbarian," a guard growled at him as he yanked the chain, causing Spartacus to wobble.

Porcina rubbed his thin, dry lips. "I remember that your manner was unlike the many unwashed belligerent barbarians. But the qualities of a wild beast are the same among your people–you butchered four of my men, on *my estate grounds!*" he said, his voice rising, breaking, as he pointed a bony finger at Spartacus' face.

"They attacked me first, Senator."

"He is lying!" Cleitus said again, with some effort. "Every word is a lie."

Porcina ignored Cleitus and addressed Spartacus. "Now, why would I care to have you hunted and brought before me? It is because you are a strangely interesting creature, *Spartacus*. I always knew you were not Alexandros. And yet the more I learned of you, the more I was filled with curiosity and anger. The audacity of killing a centurion and then deceiving a Roman Senator in his house. What do I call you? A bandit? A criminal? A thief? A murderer? You are all of those at once and yet none."

"You may call me innocent, Senator. Does Roman law not respect innocence and fidelity of conduct?"

Porcina scoffed. "You use big words, Spartacus, but that does not make you a Roman or be worthy of our laws. You see yourself as innocent, a man of noble deeds, but I see you for what you are—an opportunistic brute with a boat full of excuses. Bringing you here was just a challenge, that is all, for I do not need another guard or a fighter. It was just a small demonstration of my power and reach and a lesson for you and your kind."

*What did he want?* Spartacus hid his worry. If Porcina had no desire to employ him as a slave, then what?

Porcina continued. He reached his hand to a secretary who handed him another parchment. "See this? This is a magisterial order confirming your status as a slave. This means you," he waved his hand toward Antara, "and your wife have officially been entered into our records. There is nowhere to run and no one else to murder without the most serious repercussions. And you know precisely what that means."

*Crucifixion.*

The Senator glanced at Cleitus and turned back to him. "This man, Cleitus, barbarian of your stock he may be, has served Rome. He becomes rich with the rewards from Curio and me. He will even get to own slaves and live a comfortable, safe life. All it took was obedience to our laws and loyalty to the end. But you? What should I do with you?"

Spartacus did not answer the rhetorical question.

"Oh, I have employed Cleitus. He will stay in these beautiful grounds as a free man and serve me. Such a wonderful difference compared to your future."

Spartacus did not remark. Cleitus was a donkey-fucking coward who would lick Porcina's boots every day. It meant nothing.

Porcina seemed annoyed by the lack of response. "Cleitus did ask me to release your pretty wife as his slave. What should I do?"

Cleitus grinned hideously and intentionally placed a palm on his crotch, rubbing it deliberately.

*No!*

"Senator, what punishment you sought for me I shall accept. But I beg you to be honorable to the proconsul's words–that we will remain together," he said, keeping his voice low, respectful, without challenge to Porcina's authority.

The Senator looked somewhat mollified, and a little piqued that his *honor* was questioned. "We keep our words, and I intend to keep mine," he said. Cleitus did not look pleased.

But Porcina was not done yet. He ran his fingers on his long thin neck, scratching it.

"Should I have you digging ditches? Pick olives? Water the gardens? Man the gates? Graze the cows? Shear the sheep? Clean horses? Fuck the women slaves so you can produce strong little barbarians for me? All while feeding you, giving you a roof, and wondering if you will lose your mind and kill some more of my men or maybe even me?"

Cleitus nodded fervently.

Porcina shook his head and snapped his fingers. He turned his piercing stare on Spartacus. "No. Instead, I have a brilliant plan for you, Spartacus of the Maedi," he said, his face betraying his gleeful cruelty.

Saliva dripped from the corner of Cleitus' lips.

This time there was no excitement as the carriage trundled into Rome. It felt like the world moved in slow motion, dull and lifeless. The buildings looked ugly, the people miserable, and the noise unbearable. Antara sat beside him, gripping his shoulder, and it was her untiring counsel and effort that had kept him from lashing out and ending it all. *The gods speak to me in my dreams, my husband,* she said, often, *and they say greatness will emerge from the darkness.* His faith in her words and trust in Zibelthiurdos' plans was what kept him subdued. And yet, as a test to his control, a hissing rage often bloomed in his belly and rose to the throat, choking, squeezing, *hurting.* It was late in the morning, and the bustling city screamed with the cacophony and incessant energy of its millions. Spartacus and Antara were tightly packed with eight others–six men and two women, presumably wives. Spartacus had inferred that all of them were foreigners. But they were not allowed to speak, and thus he knew nothing of their circumstance or their origin.

But one thing characterized all the men–they were built better than normal men. Either by height or by the thickness of their limbs.

They came to a halt in a cramped yard surrounded by storehouses. Armed guards led the rope-tied caravan into a large, foul-smelling room with many already sitting inside, shackled to the walls.

"There, there!" they shouted as they led them to a different corner. "Sit, sit."

Antara heaved twice at the odor emanating from one wall, which was used as an open toilet.

One of the men yelled at a supervisor who walked in. "Special shipment, sir."

The man nodded and eyed the new group. "For tomorrow's event. Feed them in the morning and have them washed and oiled."

The restless night inched forward as hunger gnawed at his insides. His shoulders and back hurt from the uncomfortable position of being forced to sit with one hand raised and locked into place. His wife woke, moaning in pain twice in the darkness. At some point, she woke him up, saying a snake had curled around his head, and that is signified that he was destined for greatness. He had to comfort her.

He could hear similar sounds of distress, quiet weeping, and loud sighs until dawn arrived.

They were all taken to an adjacent bathhouse and allowed to clean and wash, and throughout, Spartacus worried about being separated from his wife. But the guards allowed the women back to their men, and they were all fed a filling meal of bread, olives, water, grapes, and even thin strips of goat. Once they finished the meal, others were taken to another area where slave-servants oiled their bodies. The men received strips of a garment to tie around their waist, and the women received fabric that barely covered their upper bodies.

Then the guards brought wooden placards, *tituli,* for each slave and hung them around their necks. The placard had their name and a brief description.

### SPARTACUS THRACIAN OF THE MAEDI BARB. THIRTY-FIVE. AUXILIARY EXP. NO DEFECTS LATIN. GREEK. SP. ORD.

### WIFE OF SPART. SP. ORD. NO DEFECTS

Spartacus inferred those special orders were in his name, though he knew not what they were.

He managed to read one of another man nearby.

### OENOMAUS GAUL OF THE AQUITANI BARB. THIRTY-FOUR. FIGHTING EXP. NO LATIN. NO GREEK.

That completed, the guards had everyone extend their left leg and placed thick white chalk marks on each. "This will let everyone know that you are barbarians not of this land," one of them said, smirking.

Once again, they secured the group, each person tied to the one behind them through ropes around the waist and made to walk about a quarter mile through bustling streets.

"Faster! Walk faster!" the guards screamed, threatening them with whips. Some people watched them curiously, a few yelled at them, calling them criminals and thieves, some men boldly reached out to grope the women and the guards had to push them away. But most simply ignored the sorry lot, for roped men or women on their way to something was a common sight, and it seemed like every other wealthy household had slaves procured through similar means. The best-treated slaves were the Greeks, who were often taken into homes to serve as tutors, artists, or singers. Beautiful girls found good homes and fetched good prices—and they would act as hairdressers, maids, cooks, greeters, and serve their masters' sexual desires.

But he was neither Greek nor beautiful, and barbarians usually had a much harsher outcome. His biggest concern was keeping his wife, who *was* beautiful, with him—Curio had promised that, but would the sellers honor the proconsul's word?

The group arrived at a busy square and was led into a drab gray building that housed a large internal courtyard. They were all corralled behind the wooden podium in the courtyard's center. Spartacus still found it difficult to accept the fate the gods had decided for him–that he would one day stand on a platform and be sold like cattle. He had long looked down upon slaves, for his own station in Thracia and even in Italy afforded him the luxury of doing so. And now, fate had turned on him.

Finally, near noon, they were directed aside and the first man from their group was made to go up on the podium. Unlike other auctions that Spartacus had witnessed, this was a more orderly affair with distinguished-looking men sitting on chairs in the front. Near the walls on three sides were heavily armed guards, including an archer who stood discretely on the far end. *So much fear.* The audience was affluent buyers seeking specific slaves, for this auction was private rather than in the full view of gawking crowds.

The event began with a declaration of the process and reading the rules. Three bids per slave, and the seller guaranteed the worthiness of the goods through a contract. A magistrate sat on the side before a table to ensure fair proceedings.

The auctioneer, a portly man in a loose and crumpled toga, gesticulated flamboyantly. "We begin! First, this man, a Celt with plenty of fighting experience. Captured during our campaigns in Gallia Cisalpina, he is a beast that must be tamed. Perfect for the arena!"

He elicited a mixed response, for he was not the biggest of the lot nor the fiercest looking. He was eventually sold to a businessman from Pompeii. At the end of the transaction, the auctioneer handed what seemed like a contract for the buyer and his accountant to study. Slaves often came with guarantees if there were "defects" not mentioned prior to sales.

Three others too found buyers, with Oenomaus eliciting an enthusiastic reception. Distracted and his mind full of anger and sadness, Spartacus stopped paying attention to who was being auctioned and who was buying them.

One of the couples was separated, the woman dragged away crying, and the man pleading fruitlessly. The auctioneer was entertaining–he kept the audience's interest with tales about the one auctioned. His descriptions were flowery and painted that every man for sale was superhuman in *something*. Everyone there understood the game; the auctioneer wanted the best price for the goods, and the buyers wanted the best bargain and see through his deception. The buyers came with their physicians, who inspected the men on the podium and whispered into the buyer's ear.

Spartacus held his wife's hand and squeezed it, not speaking, fearing a similar outcome if he broke the rules now. It was also an eye-opening dichotomy of how the Thracians were hailed as warriors and the bravest lot, and yet their station was one with animals. It became apparent that he was being kept for last. A relief coursed over him when his name was finally called. This ordeal would soon be over, and he could settle to his fate as Zibelthiurdos desired.

A guard slapped his shoulder and gestured him to advance to the steps of the podium. As he ambled to it, the auctioneer announced loudly. "The best for the last! Spartacus the Thracian!"

Waves of humiliation went over him as he stood before the gawking multitude. The auctioneer pointed to him and began.

"Look at him! A lion from the darkest, deepest valleys of Thracia! A man known by his tribesmen as the *Maedi devil!*"

*Does he not see from my tituli that I understand Latin?* No one had ever called him the Maedi devil.

Spartacus had a clear view of his audience from here. Fourteen men were remaining, all unmistakably of the higher class. Their secretaries, accountants, and physicians sat nearby.

"Now, this Spartacus is *exactly* what any ambitious *ludus* needs. A rare jewel, this man, with a very colorful past. I bet you wish to know what brought him to this wretched state," the auctioneer said theatrically, rubbing his cheek with one hand and scratching his head.

"Well, don't tease us, Lucullus, you whore!" someone from the audience said to laughter.

Lucullus was mighty pleased with the response. "Patience! Patience is a virtue! For starters, this man," he said, walking closer to Spartacus and slapping his thigh, "is not any other type of barbarian. He served as a distinguished soldier in Sulla's victorious army as it rampaged from Brundisium to Colline gate."

Now *that* brought much interest to the audience. Many of whom leaned forward.

"See? I told you that this is a tale with much juice. Keep that coin ready because there is more, much more!"

"Hurry up, Lucullus, you've kept us here all morning already!"

"All right. All right. But I know that beneath your impatience is curiosity. You *want* to know more so that your purchase is justified. Well, how many here know that after the victorious battles, he was awarded the legate's honor, an infrequent occurrence for the auxiliaries, especially one in the infantry."

He had never won such a medal, but his bravery had been lauded and even saved his life.

"But wait, you distinguished gentlemen are wondering, how did he end here on the auction block?"

Lucullus had their attention. "As you know, the barbarian stock can maintain order only so long. Peace is an alien concept for Thracians who thirst for mischief and blood at every opportunity. This man is no different. There are many stories about what happened after the Colline gate. Some say it was a military dispute; some say it was passion, some say it was greed, some say it was just the violence of the heart, but he killed a centurion, no less," he said, his voice dropping low, conspiratorial.

Spartacus stood quietly, saying nothing, pretending not to care.

"Did the saga end here, my distinguished guests?" he said as he walked in front of the podium, slowly, looking at every man and meeting his eye. "No, you guessed it right. It did not!"

No one complained about rushing Lucullus this time, for the story was riveting enough that even Spartacus wanted to know what happened next.

"He escaped authorities and ran to Capua where he was involved in the unsavory yet popular business of running brothels, and they say he ended the lives of two men who crossed his path and snapped the neck of a woman who would not fulfill his carnal desires."

Spartacus fidgeted. The lies!

"Well, the last one, that is unconfirmed, but who knows! Did the story end there? Did he get caught? NO!"

Lucullus was clearly enjoying this. The more the men were invested in the story, the greater the bid.

"He escaped again and got himself a fine job at a Senator's estate. Now, I will not name the kind and trusting Senator taken by this man's deception. But did this man-beast end his trail of destruction? Not at all. He then kills four of the Senator's men on his land to escape our law and evades his pursuers!"

At this point, one of the buyers spoke up. "Why is he still alive? He might be too dangerous to employ."

Some heads nodded.

Suddenly Lucullus had to control the damage. There was a thin line between alluringly dangerous and just dangerous. "Well, let me finish the story, Gaius. What he did does not mean what he will be. Anyway, the long arm of Roman law finally caught up with him. The troublemaker he is, his people gave him up to our proconsul Curio, who promptly sent him back to Italy—but with a magisterial order that will put him and his wife to the cross if they do anything dangerous. In addition, with the calming influence of his woman, he is now a tamed beast. But imagine him in the arena!"

Spartacus' hopes that he might somehow escape the wretched living of a gladiator were dimming quickly.

"Is he not quite old? He is thirty-five!"

Lucullus looked very offended. "Old? How old are your formidable Centurions that have brought Rome all her victories? What about your best generals? With age comes experience and expertise–how many others like him have you procured?"

No one responded.

Lucullus turned to Spartacus. "Walk, move around."

Now unshackled, Spartacus awkwardly walked around the platform.

"I notice a slight limp. Was this recent?" someone said.

Lucullus was ready with the answer. "By birth. Not by injury. And that is what adds to the allure of this man. Imagine this: a large, powerful *Thraex* walks in with a slight limp. Imagine the anticipation of the viewers!"

"Does he move quickly?"

"Of course, he will! You heard all I said about him. Who else have you purchased recently with such a past?" Lucullus said with as much indignation in his voice. "May honesty reign in this room. Most of our gladiators are criminals, tribal fighters, and societal degenerates—few like this man. And oh," he said theatrically. He pivoted on the balls of his feet like a dancer and pointed to the *tituli* around Spartacus' neck.

"Has anyone noticed? This man speaks Latin *and* Greek. A learned man with Hellenic influences! It seems he was once the son of a mighty chief. How much more colorful can this tale get?"

Now he had the full attention of the audience. No one else objected.

"Who wants to inspect him?"

Six men converged on Spartacus–squeezing his shoulder, punching his chest, rubbing his back, pressing his ankles, inspecting his teeth, rubbing his hands in the hair, and inspecting every area. He shuddered at their ugly touch and ignored his wife's silent tears. At some point, someone even removed the brief cloth around his waist, rendering him naked. It was such indignity, for nudity on behalf of inspecting men was a profoundly humiliating thing.

Lucullus waited for the inspection to be over. Spartacus was thankful that his wife had been left alone, still standing with her head low. They had not disrobed her as they did to one of the women before. Was the *special order* protecting her? Or were they aware that she was a priestess?

"With good training and reminding him of the consequence, you will have one of the finest gladiators in your *ludus*. I guarantee that! And I know that the most ambitious and enterprising buyers will take the risk without hesitation," Lucullus roared, standing straight, pushing out his dropping man-breasts and ample belly. "For without risk, is there a reward?"

No one from the audience left. Someone said drily, "Start the bidding."

Lucullus cleared his throat. "Yes, yes, sir. As the last word, I mean it! Look at his height, the thickness of those thighs, that chest, and even that brutish face. Is he the youngest of the lot? Not at all! But take that physical stature and add his experience and wisdom of the years, distinguished buyers, and you have a real winner. It's a package deal; it comes with the wife, who can be a helping hand in the kitchen. Special orders approved by the magistrate and certainly in your best interests–the wife must come with him and remain as his wife. Well, for this spectacular specimen, the starting bid is eight-thousand denarii!"

It felt like a great weight was lifted off his shoulders, knowing that for now, his wife would be safe and accompany him. His thoughts shifted to other matters–like the opening price. *Eight thousand?* A typical household slave was purchased at a thousand to two-thousand denarii. A beautiful girl might fetch as much as six thousand. Two Thracians and a Celt had fetched between seven to nine thousand denarii. But the floor price for his bid was already eight thousand.

But the responses were quick, to his surprise.

"Nine."

"Nine thousand five hundred."

"Ten."

"Eleven."

Lucullus was thrilled. He exhorted the buyers with exuberant gestures and exclamations. "Eleven? Well, we finally have someone who knows the worth of this man. I say eleven is *nothing! Nothing!*"

"Twelve!"

"Thirteen!"

At that point, four men rose and left. Lucullus waited for them to be out of earshot and remarked. "It seems only the most discerning and the wealthiest remain!"

That attracted a few sniggers and puffed-up chests. And now the bids rose, but at a slower pace.

"Thirteen-five."

"It seems the great Asina is determined to win!"

Asina had bid from the beginning. It dawned upon Spartacus that this was the owner of the biggest *ludus* in Capua, and he was a competitor of another owner from the region whose name he could not remember.

"Fourteen!" said another man.

"Gaius Quintus! So much ambition!"

The fourteen put a stop to other bids, and after some failed attempts to elicit more, Lucius, the auctioneer, finally readied to call closure. "Anyone else?"

A short, balding man with sharp features raised his hand. The same man who had purchased Oenomaus. His voice was high-pitched. "Fifteen."

Many turned to him. Lucius, pleased at this, asked the audience again. "Anyone for more than fifteen? This man is worth thirty!"

No one took the bait. And then it was over with a sign. "Done! Spartacus the Thracian and his wife sold for fifteen-thousand denarii to Gnaeus Cornelius Lentulus Vatia of Capua!"

*Vatia!* Spartacus remembered that name. He had never seen the man but had worked on the construction and subsequent expansion for his *ludus*. What was Zibelthiurdos telling him? What signs might be seen in all this? His wife would help him interpret these coincidences. All he knew from wagging tongues was that Vatia was an ambitious, crooked man who would do anything it took for success and fame.

Vatia's men read the contract and ordered another round of inspection. Once satisfied, Vatia finally signed the purchase. They secured Spartacus and his wife and directed them to a carriage where two men waited. Forbidden from interacting, they all sat in suffocating silence as the horse-drawn carriage shook and swayed on its way out of Rome.

As the great city's walls receded, Spartacus reflected on his life and wondered about the uncertain future. And amidst the anger, despair, and his wife's tears, his mind would not let go of his persistent thoughts.

He would bide his time and fight this injustice.

No one had dominion over him.

He would turn the tables and wreak revenge on those that had wronged him.

On Porcina. On Cleitus. On Curio. On Kintoi. On Rome itself. And anyone that abused him or his wife.

It might take days, months, or years, but Zibelthiurdos surely had some design for a man who was once a soldier.

But now a slave.

## END OF BOOK I

# THANK YOU FOR READING

Thank you for reading the first book of the series! You should grab "Slave," the next book in this trilogy. We will see in Spartacus in the arena and experience life as a gladiator.

Your reviews and ratings make a huge difference! I would be immensely grateful if you took a few seconds or minutes to either rate the book or leave a review if you enjoyed it.

You can also go to https://jaypenner.com/reviews for easy links.

A detailed notes section will be available at the end of the trilogy and cover various aspects of the book–fact, dramatization, and the rationale for certain decisions.

Did you know? You can go to https://jaypenner.com/the-spartacus-rebellion-maps to do a Google flyby of all locations mentioned in the book.

Join my newsletter https://jaypenner.com/join to know when the next book releases, or follow me as an author on Amazon and you will be notified.

Until next time!

-Jay https://jaypenner.com

# REFERENCES

The following works provided helpful historical references and commentary on the Third Servile War (the Spartacus War).

1. Spartacus and the Slave Wars - A brief history with documents (Plutarch, Appian, Sallust, Livy, and other), by Brent D. Shaw

2. The Complete Roman Army by Adrian Goldsworthy

3. The Spartacus War by Barry Strauss

4. Spartacus by Aldo Schiavone

And numerous papers and articles on the time, the man, and his circumstances.

Printed in Great Britain
by Amazon

87827126R00214